Red D

The Fiv

Wendy Mewes lives in western Brittany on
the fault-line between legend and history.
She writes as full-time as is possible in such an
alluring place, and when not working on books or
articles, walks or reads tarot (but she is not 39 and
has never been separated from the love of her life).

www.wendymewes.net

Other books by Wendy Mewes

FICTION:

Moon Garden

NON-FICTION:

Finistere:Things to see and do at the End of the World
Walking and other activities in Finistere
Discovering the History of Brittany

THE FIVE OF CUPS

by

Wendy Mewes

RED DOG books

THE FIVE OF CUPS
published by Red Dog Books
ISBN 0 9536001 7 3

© Wendy Mewes, 2006

The right of Wendy Mewes to be identified as the author
of this work is asserted in accordance with sections 77
and 78 of the Copyright Designs and Patents Act 1988

British Library Cataloguing-in-Publication Data
A catalogue record for this book is available from the British Library

All rights reserved. The publisher's prior written consent is
required for any reproduction of this work in any form
whatsoever.

This is a work of fiction. Any similarity to any person living or
not is purely coincidental.

Red Dog Books is based in Axbridge, Somerset and in Brittany.
Enquiries should be addressed to the editorial office at
Red Dog Books, Le Guillec, 29410 Plounéour-Menez, France.
Tel. 00 33 (0)298 24 15 19
email: reddogbooks@tiscali.fr

www.reddogbooks.com

Cover illustration: 'The Five of Cups' by Jane Brayne
© Jane Brayne

Printed and bound in Great Britain
by Cox & Wyman

This book is dedicated
to the memory of

ELAINE BARRY

great singer and friend
much loved
much missed

ACKNOWLEDGEMENTS

Special thanks to:

Jane Brayne for the quality and sensitivity of the cover painting (and responding to my urgent appeal like a true friend)

Zoe Hart who has contributed much to this book and for whose friendship I am always grateful

Penny Allen, understanding friend and astute critic

My friends and colleagues at Morlaix market who have followed the book's Saturday morning progress (and lack of it) with characteristic humour and goodwill

Caroline Wood, a fine tarot reader herself, for her support and help

Sharon Walker, Marie, Samara and all the other readers at TABI for their wisdom, insight and hard work

(see p270 for a note on tarot)

PEOPLE & PLACES

La Folle is a place of my own invention, an amalgam of various small towns in Finistere. All the other places and megaliths are based on reality, although sometimes geographically squeezed. The Monts d'Arrée are only ever themselves. With one small exception, all the people in the story are entirely fictitious.

I would also like to point out that the fine balance of spirit and stupidity displayed by a certain four-footed character in this book bears no resemblance whatsoever to my dogs Rufus and Brian.

Prologue

Zena drove off the ferry apprehensively. It was barely light and beyond the harsh glare of the terminal, the world looked black and uninviting. She took the first road into the town centre and within five minutes was sitting in a bakery café with hot black coffee and a croissant in front of her. This was better, this felt like the familiar, manageable France of school trips and family holidays. She wished she could stay here eating patisserie for the next six months instead of making her way out into the darkness, where there lay a land of the unknown.

The landscape on the drive to Morlaix was only faintly visible. She negotiated a series of roundabouts the right way round by a determined exercise of concentration and a close adherence to the English number-plate in front. She didn't dare look at the boats along the estuary as the convoy of cars crossed the long bridge and the others shot away on the dual carriageway at giddy speeds, leaving her chugging along in the inside lane.

When the lights of the city were only just up ahead, Zena gripped the wheel tightly and leaned forward, ready to follow the sequence of directions she had memorized to bypass the centre. At each junction she went slowly, looking for the red cross of the hospital sign that would point the way, and then finally, after a long steep descent to yet another of the interminable roundabouts, she turned away from the houses to find herself in semi-darkness again.

There were no other cars on this road. She seemed to

have left the known world and entered a place of mystery and wonder. At a bridge over a little river, the sign read 'Queffleuth'. A name of fable, a word both exotic and rather scary, Zena felt.

She drove on grimly, as a series of bends coiled out in front of the car. Just as she was beginning to suspect that she was the only living thing for miles, a deer leapt out into the road, its horns a dark silhouette in the headlights. The animal came to a momentary halt of surprise and through the windscreen exchanged a split-second glance with Zena who had been flung forwards by the jolt of an emergency stop. Then the deer tossed back its head and bounded into the dark strip of trees on the other side of the road. She drove on with her heart thumping and hands trembling on the wheel, still scared by her first encounter with the wildness she sensed all around, beyond the metal margins of the civilised invention that protected her.

As grey fingers of light began to push away the gloom, the outlines of the trees became clearer, russet leaves still clinging to many of the beeches even at the very start of the year. The road rose up over a barren shoulder of hill. Bands of mist clung lovingly to the contours of the land in the early morning light, but above it she could see a pointed peak, sharp-edged and stark, a sombre watch-tower over the tracts of heath slowly unravelling on each side. This untamed moorland landscape roused in Zena much the same feeling as the name Queffleuth, an attraction tempered by fear. It coloured her arrival with the hue of adventure, a journey into uncharted lands. A quest even. And in a perverse sort of way, it was.

Chapter One

The fizzy promise of arrival was soon over. Zena had felt a moment's excitement on nosing the car down the zigzag bends of the hill to arrive in front of the house. It was only when she got out and studied it properly that disappointment began to set in. She could hardly complain, having rented the house on the strength of a few photographs, but, if the outside was unpromising, it felt as grim as a lost struggle within. The furniture was adequate, shelves, table, four chairs and a wooden-framed sofa, but beyond that stared dirty walls, paint that might once have been green now grey and scarred with the graffiti of children – a heart, stick men and the name Maude in ragged letters. She could well imagine that there was little else on offer in the way of entertainment if the weather kept the occupants indoors. 'Not suitable for young children' the details said, referring to the unfenced river racing past behind the house, but she could just imagine the damage to spontaneous young spirits in this dead-end space. There was no television or video, no radio. The garden was little more than a yard plastered with tarmac, a grand reward for the road after its tortuous course down the steep-sided valley.

And for this, she'd left England. No, that was stupid. It wasn't the breeze-blocks and mortar of the house, but the idea of this place that had drawn her. Space and tranquillity was what she needed. A chance to look at her life from a new angle. And she had to get away after a year of moping, waiting for phone-calls and letters that never came, her life drying up like old skin as she hoped for unlikely signs of renewal. She had to move on, to go forward. But had she? Had she really done that, when five minutes' drive away from here was the town where Lucas' mother was buried.

'Anyone at home?'
Not in this place, was her first thought as she went to greet the visitor.

Monique was dark, with a tiny sparrow's skeleton, which made Zena feel like a lumbering prehistoric animal as they brushed shoulders in the entrance. She lived at the top of the hill, the nearest house, the only neighbour for some distance. It was too far from the shops and the school, she spent all her time driving from one errand to the next. Her husband liked the country, or the idea of it. He left the plants to her, of course.

She talked quickly and with animation. Zena struggled to follow the French, her mind whirling forward to when she would be expected to respond. Keep it simple. It was only 20 odd years since her A level, there must be something left, or lingering traces of all the efforts she had made when Lucas appeared, although he'd insisted on speaking English as if his maternal tongue would leave a bad taste in his mouth. If only Zena had kept things simple with him, would that have prevented loving turning so swiftly to leaving?

Monique continued, swift and voluble. She was full of information and instruction, where to buy bread, where not to buy meat, who could be trusted not to cheat you, who would take your money on any false pretext. Zena was exhausted, spattered by all these facts and suppositions. She barely had a chance to draw breath before the questions started.

'How long are you here for?'

That was not so difficult to understand and answer. The arrangement was quite specific.

'For six months.'

Foreign words struggled out, stilted and unfamiliar.

'You have family?'

This was not too bad either. Zena managed to say she had a mother in London and a brother in Glastonbury. She decided not to attempt the explanation that Stephen lived with a mad woman who believed she was the goddess Isis and her mother was, by any calculation, eccentric.

'Do you have children?'

The hard one, that cruel question slipped in amongst a pile of harmless enquiries. Did she look too old to say 'not yet' with any conviction? Zena could hardly go into details now about Lucas, putative father of her unconceived child, nor could she face that particular lift-shaft of fear and desolation today.

She said no, without qualification, lowering her eyes as if it was a guilty admission.

Still the inquisition continued.

How was she going to occupy herself?

Learn something new, Zena replied with a sudden smile, remembering that there was a positive side to this strange exile she had undertaken.

Just one thing? Monique also smiled, but Zena felt a hint of criticism.

No, many things, Zena hoped politely, but a potential

new career was the most important. She was going to design cards. Up in the attic with the large velux window and clear north light, she would paint flowers and cats and boats, all the failsafe subjects the agent had recommended.

They did not seem particularly interesting to Monique, who said only that it was much too cold to be up under the roof at this time of year, before departing breezily with instructions about the rubbish and the local market drifting back down the hill as she disappeared from view.

Zena waited until the last waft of perfumed confidence and command had evaporated before she went back inside. There she sat down wearily at the table, feeling the after-trauma of a quick-fire quiz show contestant, and then suddenly began to cry as she had not done for many months.

It was the same old theme, not yet quite worn through, still serving to undermine her fragile equilibrium. It seemed so hard to stop dwelling on the past, which was packed with event, and put mental energy in the alarmingly empty space of the future. She tried to avoid the cliché of bewailing the fact she'd given the best years of her life to Lucas, feeling they both deserved a fairer assessment, but the fact remained that she had met him at 35 and lost him at 39, so, as far as motherhood went, maybe it had been the last shot. But this was in retrospect, this prevalent issue of children. At the time he left she'd had more immediate concerns.

Not knowing where Lucas was had been the hardest aspect of their break-up. It was ironic, considering he had been away so much during their years together, but suddenly, in a true state of separation, it became unbearable not to know the setting in which he was moving, talking, eating and waking. She preferred not to think about the sleeping.

After he came to live with her in Bath he had given up his London studio flat, never more than a base for coming and going, and their shared space had become the starting and finishing points for all his journeys. And Lucas was quite a traveller, mainly in eastern Europe, writing his impressions in a succession of serious, well-received books and capturing changing societies in stark black and white photographs that were the subject of exhibitions in their own right.

But when he left Zena's basement flat for good, after years of leaving with the exciting promise of return, he had effectively disappeared from her life. No telephone call, not even a brusque postcard. A chance meeting with one of Lucas' acquaintances told her that he'd passed through Paris soon after, but there was no other word, not even to confirm his continued existence.

And now, nearly a year later, here she was in a corner of north-western France, filling in that blank sheet of tomorrow with new enterprise, giving herself the challenge of a different environment and finding out if she could stop being Zena-who-loved-Lucas and become simply herself again without any hyphens. The attempt might have been more convincing had she chosen another area.

The first time she had been here was with Lucas himself, more than four years earlier. They had been together for only a few months then, still urgently happy and greedy for sharing, at that significant stage of a relationship when the new partner was woven into the fabric of a pre-existing life. Arriving in the little town at the edge of Brittany where his mother was buried in the granite churchyard, and visiting scenes of his boyhood games and ramblings had brought them closer, given roots to the grafting of their branches. She was proud of this new knowledge, although she would like to have known his mother, to pin down the elusive foreign touch of his character. He had seemed equally at home here as in London or Glastonbury where they'd first met, speaking the language easily, in tune with the rhythms of French rural life, which struck so strange a note to her. They had held hands as they strolled through La Folle to the restaurant by the lake to celebrate her thirty-sixth birthday, drinking toasts to their future and, in Zena's heart at least, to the family of their own they would have. On that magical evening, she had never dreamed of actually living here, cut off from her own background, still childless at thirty-nine, and very much alone.

Zena jumped to her feet, and forced herself to start unloading the car. She was impatient with her own feebleness, her inability to shake off what had happened and rise from the ashes of lost Lucas. She had conned herself that living in the surrounding countryside rather than in La Folle itself meant she was not engaged in an emotional quest, just returning to an area not entirely unfamiliar to her. If she dwelt on the subject much longer she would have to admit her motives, face up to still clinging instead of breaking free.

This was ridiculous – she'd only arrived an hour ago and already the whole bold scheme was exposed for a sham. She must go upstairs at once and unpack her materials or even make a start on some painting, but at least show an understanding of the seriousness of her decision to make a new life. She put one foot on the staircase and then stopped. She suddenly remembered the arrival present she had bought herself in Roscoff. That was one reliable and familiar thing about France, the unfailing quality of its patisserie. Perhaps that wasn't such a bad reason for coming in itself. She went back out to the car to fetch the chocolate cake.

'What's she like?'

Monique's husband asked about the new neighbour as he opened a bottle of wine in the surprisingly small kitchen of their large modern house. Since coming home from the noise and clamour of the printing works he owned, he had greeted his two children briefly but fondly, listened without responding to a catalogue of their latest misdemeanours from his wife, and spent a quiet half-hour of routine recuperation under a hot shower.

He was a large man, generous and expansive in behaviour, full of bonhomie for the world in general, but passionately committed to a long war of attrition and astringency with his wife. After meeting on his native soil in the hot south of France, she had insisted on making their home near her parents in this miserable northerly clime, where an overcoat could be necessary in May and it took several years to establish cordial relations with just about anybody. He had vowed to repay the favour and derived a great deal of pleasure from their skirmishing, but had he not loved his little girls and felt a strong sense of responsibility for the jobs of his workforce, there were times when Jean-Yves would happily have driven back to Marseilles without a backward glance.

Now, as he lent on the work-top with a glass of wine in his hand, he was ready for talk. He noticed the disapproving twist of Monique's mouth and determined to bait her, whatever he discovered about the foreign resident at the bottom of the hill.

Monique pushed past him to open the fridge.

'I don't know when she last visited the hairdresser.'

'Phh!' Jean-Yves brushed aside this trivial detail with a flick of one large hand. 'But is she really here alone? No husband?'

'There is no-one else there.'

'What? No-one to guard and protect her?' The dramatic sweep of his arm almost knocked a bowl of fruit to the floor, but he just caught it before Monique could vent her fury. He waited until she had finished manhandling the vegetables on her chopping board before trying again.

'And her name?'

'Something strange...Zee... Z... Zelda?'

'Zelda, Zelda, all alone in the world, no friends or family!'

Monique shook a tea-towel violently in his direction as if she'd like to swat him, but he was too quick for her.

'She mentioned a mother and a brother, but I think there is something else, something not said.'

'So she has secrets,' Jean-Yves said, with satisfaction. 'A woman of mystery.'

'She is an Englishwoman with a bad haircut. That is all,' said Monique crossly.

'But why is she here? Out in the country in the middle of winter?'

'She is going to paint little pictures up in the attic.'

'But how charming! The lonely artist in her garret! I must call on her and admire her work, give her encouragement.'

Monique banged the lid onto a saucepan in annoyance.

'My God, you are such a fool! Why would she want to see a great gushing bear with no sense?'

Jean-Yves unfolded his napkin.

'Perhaps a more welcome visitor than a sour bitch like you, my love. Now what delicacy is in store for us tonight?'

Getting out of the dreary house was a relief, and crossing the bridge felt even better. On the other side of the river, a path ran along the bank and Zena followed it slowly, watching the thin sun glinting on the water. Pine trees pressed down the rocky hillside here. To the left she found a narrow path leading up into the wood. The weeds, plentiful even in winter, were unbroken at first as if it was a virgin track, but beyond she could see a smooth way where nothing grew, deprived of light by the canopy of branches. Stepping over the sparse brambles, she followed this route as the trees grew denser, and then stopped when the path petered out, her feet sinking into layers of needles, nostrils full of the smell of resin from the bark. She closed her eyes, savouring the fragrance of the forest, waiting, without knowing why or for what. A faint rustling in the air fanned her ears like the whispering of spirits. After a moment she seemed to lose her awareness of the present, falling into a dream of possibility, lulled by the seductive scents of pine and damp earth. She had an agonising glimpse of Lucas' face, felt the touch of his skin...

A movement among the trees caught her attention and she opened her eyes quickly. There was a child in a glade nearby, a little girl, about eight years old, turning slowly in a circle, holding out her arms, head tilted back to gaze up at the trees. Round and round, completely unselfconscious under Zena's gaze, her pinafore dress swinging in a circle with the movement. Long fair hair gleamed almost silver in the sun as it caught a shaft of light and then plunged into grey as she spun back into shade. She moved like part of the forest. Zena wondered where the girl had come from. Could this be one of Monique's two daughters, playing alone so far from home? Somehow, she didn't think so. It was hard to connect this natural sprite, so completely at ease, with the brittle Monique.

Zena took a step towards her and tripped over a loop of bramble. Flinging her hands out, she managed to protect herself from a heavy fall, but when she hoisted herself up again, the child had vanished. Bewildered she peered all around through the trees. Could she possibly have imagined it? That seemed surprising. She thought of her mind as being rather prosaic, despite artistic abilities, with her painting firmly rooted in reality, in observation rather than imagination, and she sometimes suspected her natural skills were more mechanical than instinctive. Certainly she was not prone to conjuring up visions on an everyday basis. Still, it was not impossible that a child actually was out playing in the woods. This was rural France after all, and Lucas had always said it was like England thirty years ago.

She wondered whether to go in search or continue her own walk. Higher up the slope, the rock-face was just visible, a glimmer of grey through the trees. She began to move in that direction, but it was further than she'd thought. Fallen branches made the way hazardous, forcing her to scramble and shimmy up the hill. The rock seemed to retreat through the sentry-like trunks of the firs as she advanced. At one point, amidst the silence of the forest, she thought she heard a little voice singing, fading away below her, and dithered once more about following the child. But then there was only silence and she went on, forcing the whippy branches of undergrowth aside, her leg muscles aching with the unaccustomed effort of plunging up and down from a base of thick wet leaves.

Just as she was beginning to ask herself what on earth this was all for, the trees finished and a wall of rock rose almost sheer above, blocking all progress. Zena caught her breath. She was sensing a change in the atmosphere, a feeling of anticipation in the air as she rounded an outcrop of rock and saw the mouth of a huge cave just before her. This was not welcome news for Zena, who was claustrophobic enough even in a shopping precinct, but she wanted to go on now, to explore what had apparently been her destination all along. She took a tentative step forward and then stopped in the mouth of the cave.

Mist rose up out of the damp earth floor in puffs, like the breath of a ghost. Beyond was darkness and stillness so profound that it oscillated in her inner ear like the heartbeat of a baby in the womb. She tried to move a foot, but it remained rooted to the ground, holding her in a trap, a prisoner of the past, her bones old with its scent.

She dipped her head forward towards the darkness and saw something move in the shadows. There was no-one there, rationally she knew it, but something had moved inside the cave, turning over layers of time like the pages of a book. And the movement was reflected inside Zena herself, softly, viscerally, as if she might strip off her skin and slip inside another. She was alone and yet a trick of the insistent rhythm inside her head brought her voices, rough patterns of speech, dancing on the walls of the cave like beads of light. She put a hand on the rock to steady herself. She staggered back at once at the shock that travelled up her arm with the contact of skin and granite, wrenching her fingers back, breaking the thread that had bound her so tightly. Split rays of sunshine streaked suddenly over her shoulder so momentarily she could barely distinguish what was light and what was darkness, and then the moment was lost. Her feet regained their movement and it was all over, finished.

Zena was not normally superstitious nor given to flights of fancy. It was quite a momentous occasion, her first day of living in a foreign country, her first day of a new life – would that explain the tricks her mind had played? The little girl and the talking cave?

She shrugged it off, made her way surprisingly easily back to the path, and resumed her walk and her thoughts of Lucas as if nothing had happened. But something had.

Chapter 2

La Folle had changed little over the years. It stood on a slight rise below the main range of western Brittany's high hills, the church spire visible for miles around. The ancient garbled legend of a local healer, either saint or witch, had given the place its unusual name. Zena rather liked the idea of living somewhere called 'the mad woman.' A straggle of houses lined the road leading past the cemetery to the centre, where a row of medieval houses remained around the market place, their jutting wooden facades now covered by slates mined from the Monts d'Arrée. Traditional stone-built dwellings were matched in number by modern white-rendered houses with their raised ground floors and roomy basements. The mairie, flanked by flags and a little garden, and the post office were tucked away in a square behind the market place. There were a couple of bars and a hotel, the essential bakery and pharmacy and a few other shops. Every Thursday a lively weekly market drew shoppers from all over this sparsely populated rural area, as Zena discovered when she tried to find a parking space.

It was a bright, chill day. The stall-holders were wearing hats and scarves, stamping their feet against the cold. She strolled around, taking in the unfamiliar rhythms of conversations around her and the all-pervading smell of fresh shellfish. To a bout of laughter, a man was walking a crab on a lead in front of a line of stalls laden with pink and white mounds of filleted flesh.

Zena's first purchase was a woven shopping basket with leather handles, which she soon filled with locally produced bread, vegetables and cheese. She took all that back to the car and then returned to examine the rest of the market: clothes and shoes, jewellery and watches, lace and books. It was the colourful energy that attracted her, the good-humour and passion generated by simple commercial transactions on a winter's day. She felt surrounded by life; ironically, in this foreign setting, in touch with a reality that had eluded her over the last year. She listened to a surprising number of Welsh voices from small groups of old men gathered here and there chatting with unusual animation and interest. A coach trip from Cardiff? She smiled to herself as she examined some silver earrings with twisting serpents dangling from the hoops.

'They're not supposed to be funny. Work of art that is.'

The words of English in an unmistakably Welsh voice came out of the bushy black beard of the stall-holder who loomed towards her. He was very large altogether, with huge shoulders and bulky body.

She smiled.

'Sorry. I was just thinking how odd it was to find so many Welsh people in a spot like this.'

He drew himself up even taller and exaggerated a look of menace.

'I'll have you know I'm the only Welshman in La Folle. Descendant of Llewellyn Ap Gruffyd, I am, Prince of Wales in the 13th century. There'd hardly be room for another here, now would there?'

Zena laughed again.

'That's very impressive. But what about them then?'

She pointed out the nearest group.

Llewellyn looked at her with tender concern.

'You haven't been here very long, have you?'

'About twenty-four hours.'

'Ah. And what's your name, my lady?'

'Zena.'

'Zena!'

It sounded like the name of an exotic goddess on his full lips. He came round the side of the stall and stood very near to her, leaning down to speak close to her ear, as if they were sharing a secret. One huge hand lightly took hold of her arm.

'Those gentlemen are locals, my pretty Zena.'

'Why are they speaking Welsh then? Is La Folle twinned with Llanelli or something?'

He gave a great loud laugh.

'That's Breton, sweetheart. And it's more like Cornish than Welsh as it happens.'

She stepped away, feeling stupid, and tried by effort of concentration to stop a blush from spreading across her face. 'How much are these?' She held up the snake earrings, desperate to put an end to the sudden intimacy with this large Welshman.

He took the hint and her money with equal equanimity.

'Funny time of year to be on holiday,' he said as he handed her the little package.

Zena could not resist a chance for conversation in a language she could manage, so she told him her situation, up to a point, fudging the issue of why she was there in the first place. He was interested by her artistic intentions.

'You must meet my sister. She's an artist too.' He

gestured at the jewellery and fabric bags on the stall. 'Erin made all this.'

'She must be very talented,' Zena said sincerely. She could happily have spent a fortune here. 'I'm just starting out really, and it seemed a good idea to get away to somewhere where I could concentrate.'

She thought she'd made it sound reasonable and convincing, but he was looking at her as if he knew better.

'You might like to consult her too,' he said, 'she can read the cards, you know.'

Zena didn't want to know, but conventions of politeness held her fast.

'That's interesting.'

'She's very good, they all come round here to ask her things. Even some of the old farming boyos. She'll tell you what's going to happen. Who's going to come into your life, that sort of thing.' He gave her a distinct leer. 'What to watch out for, if you like.'

Zena gave an involuntary shiver and tried to disguise it by pretending to be cold, from lingering too long in one place.

'It sounds rather alarming. I think I'd rather not know about the future.'

As soon as she said it, Zena realised she was lying. She wanted more than anything else, and would have paid a fortune, to know one thing about her future. Was Lucas in it?

Llewellyn must have read her look. He regarded her with renewed interest.

'You'll find us just round that corner. There's a sign by the door. Call in any time.'

'Thanks.' She finally broke away from the intrusive light eyes and walked quickly back to the car, her heart thumping for no obvious reason. She thought about Llewellyn's sister and her cards. It's a pity things like that are just a con, Zena said to herself. Otherwise I'd be round there like a shot.'

In fact it was two days before she found herself on the doorstep, admiring a painted wooden sign of sun, moon, stars, rainbow and river.

In the interval she had made a start on the business of drawing sketches for her card designs. Shivering slightly up in the cold attic, a pencil clasped in her mitten-covered hands, she had begun with the market scene while it was fresh in her mind, inspired by the first personal contacts of her new life. She did not include the encounters with Monique, who had appeared again in a smart silver car to say that she was having wood delivered the following week and Zena would be wise to order a load at the same time. Although it was a helpful gesture, her imperious tone made Zena silently determine to make her own arrangements. Asking Llewellyn about it would provide a pretext for calling at the house and getting a sight of his sister, with or without her tarot cards.

Did she dare to ask about Lucas? To bring it all out into the open again, after carefully shutting him in her inner world for so long? And how would it all sound to a stranger? Probably just sad and spineless, she thought wearily. Even to herself it was hard to pretend any more that Lucas could have any real surviving feeling for her in this vast spell of silence. He had gone forward into another phase of his life while she still floundered and wallowed in the muddy aftermath of their relationship. The nugget of hope she had carried everywhere was insecurely based on their very last exchange.

'I have to go,' was all he'd said on that last morning before kissing her lightly and loading his books into the car. They'd never quarrelled or fully discussed the end of their long relationship. Lucas had tried, surprisingly inarticulately, to explain his need to move on, to expand his persona into a wider sphere than – although he did not actually say this - Zena could offer with her settled occupation and fondness for stability.

'It's not the right time for this,' – he waved an expressive arm at the neat, comfortable living room – 'that's all. In a few years maybe, but not now. And it's better for you to be free to move on yourself, not to keep waiting for me.'

'I could come with you. Give up the flat.'

He shook his head with a mixture of affection and exasperation at her brave words.

'That's not the answer. I'm sorry.'

He pulled her to him, not intending to be cruel, she knew, but only emphasising the chill of physical loneliness in store. She felt herself trembling, clinging to him, numb with the shock of his decision and powerless to prevent the catastrophe of his departure.

He whispered into her hair. She struggled to make out the words, too choked to ask him to repeat them. 'We'll love again in another time and place.' Had he really said that? Was it fuelled by his relief at her passive acceptance, a sop to the well-behaved? Or had she heard the message of hope she longed for where there was none?

But it was certainly those words, real or romanticised, that had planted the seed that led her eventually to leave England. Lucas had always said that when he was tired of travelling he would like to settle in the Brittany of his boyhood and write a book about his family and the hardships of rural life they had endured for generations.

In a moment of emotional honesty, Zena would have had to admit that her supposed refuge here near La Folle was no more than a new way of keeping Lucas close. In a flash of searing truth, scraped painfully across her heart, she acknowledged the cherished scenario of Lucas' face – a mixture of surprise and delight - when he came across her, by chance, at his mother's graveside...

The door was opened by a pixie. At least, that was Zena's first impression of the elfin figure before her. Large green eyes dominated the pale face, and three long curly tendrils hung down from what was otherwise very short black hair, the colour of coal from Erin's native valleys. Her direct gaze stopped Zena in her tracks. She knows why I've come, was her first thought. I won't be able to hide, to wrap it all up in some acceptable form. She'll see through me, I'll be exposed...

'You'd better come in, Zena,' Erin said, taking her sleeve in a tiny hand and tugging her gently inside. The same soft, sinuous touch of her brother, despite the ridiculous contrast in their sizes. God, she really is psychic, she knows my name, Zena thought wildly, forgetting that she'd told it to Llewellyn.

A large lumpy young woman with a mass of frizzy, red-fringed yellow hair and her arms full of vegetables galumphed down the stairs and almost cannoned into them in the narrow hall.

'Can't stop, I'm late, forgotten the sweet potatoes,' she muttered, manoeuvring past with difficulty and a breathless giggle, scattering largesse as she went out kicking the door shut behind her.

Erin retrieved a fallen carrot and smiled.

'That's Poppy, our lodger. She works at the restaurant by the lake.'

Zena nodded nervously but said nothing. She was phased by Llewellyn's noisy absence and beginning to regret her impulse to come.

The small living room was certainly colourful despite the dim light. Against a luminous orange background on the walls great swathes of vegetation were painted – trailing boughs of hops and ivy, interspersed by sprays of oak and olive. Here and there among the foliage, fairies and hairy-faced leering men peered out.

No sooner had she taken in the surrounding scenery than Zena found herself seated at a little round table covered by a purple cloth, with Erin opposite, a pack of cards in her hands.

'I'm not sure... I mean, this is a bit... Well, how much does it cost?'

She was struggling.

Erin shrugged, fixing her eyes on Zena again.

'It's up to you. There's a bowl over there for donations. Pay me something or nothing, whatever feels right to you when we've finished.'

Zena was having trouble swallowing. That was exactly the sort of arrangement she hated, where the onus for decisions affecting someone else was put on her. She could already feel the tears welling up in the back of her eyes, waiting for the barrier to fall so they could flood out into the open. She feared there'd be enough to fill the room and drown both her and the young sprite opposite.

'Would you like some tea?' Erin was saying, casually although she had clearly noticed Zena's discomfort.

'Yes, I would. Thank you.'

Anything to put off the moment of truth, or deception, if she could only muster the strength to pretend. But why else was she here, in a strangely comforting stranger's house, if not to unburden herself and seek encouragement of all her fondest hopes?

They sipped in silence. The tea tasted oddly of aniseed.

After a minute, Erin put down her rainbow decorated mug, rested her pointed chin on her hands and re-engaged Zena with the full power of her green eyes.

'Despite what my oaf of a brother may have told you, I don't do 'fortune telling'. The tarot can shed light on the future, but you have to remember that it's your choices that decide what happens to you. I can read for problems that are concerning you now and get a new perspective to help you deal with stuff. You can choose – either ask the cards a question or for a general look at your situation.'

Is he coming back? Zena screamed inside.

'Just a general look will be fine,' she said politely, brushing away the first tear as Erin closed her eyes for a moment of connection with the cards before shuffling and presenting them to Zena.

'I'm going to use just one card. Would you like to choose it yourself?'

Zena hesitated, both attracted and repelled by the idea. It seemed extraordinary that she was to commit herself to one card out of such a large pack, to make such a decisive choice out of so many possibilities. Surely her plight deserved more than a solitary card?

She did as she was told. A shiver of alarm ran through her as she saw the single card, face down on the table between them. It was like the axe falling, the Rubicon crossed, the sort of decisive act she feared more and more these days.

Erin turned it over.

A woman wrapped in a grey cloak seemed to be leaving the scene of dark mountains and wintry skies. Her eyes glanced furtively over her shoulder to where three golden goblets lay emptied on the ground. Unnoticed to the other side of her, stood two more cups.

Zena did not like the look of the card one little bit. It was brooding, heavy and desolate. Good choice then, she thought bitterly. Erin seemed to be lost in thought, her eyes distant and unfocused. The silence made Zena nervous. She had to resist a sudden urge to tear the card up into little pieces and stuff them into her mouth to conceal the evidence of her feelings that might be revealed.

'The Five of Cups.' Erin spoke at last.

'Weather looks about right,' Zena joked.

Erin ignored her. She was still looking at the card, twirling one of her long strands of hair round a thin finger with purple-painted nail. When she finally raised her eyes, Zena knew her secret was out.

'How long ago did it end?' Erin asked as naturally as if they'd spent the last few hours discussing Zena's failed relationship.

'About a year.' 376 days, she thought.

'It can take a long time to get over things.' There was

an easy sympathy in Erin's manner, the sort of responsiveness which had long since run dry in Zena's own friends.

Dear God, I've come here looking for new audiences, Zena thought. I've pretty much exhausted the sympathy vote in England, so now there's Europe to conquer. I shall probably end up in the Himalayas in a few years time telling some Tibetan monk how I'd do it differently this time if only Lucas would come back.

'What does the card mean?' she rallied.

Erin smiled gently.

'The Five of Cups is usually a card of loss and disappointment.'

I got that right, Zena thought. Perhaps I'll turn out to be a natural card-picker.

She forced herself to listen to Erin's quiet voice.

'You're still overwhelmed by those feelings, trapped if you like. You can't move on as long as hopes of being reunited take up all your energy.' (Ouch! Zena winced.) 'Like the figure on the card, you are drawn to what is spilled and gone, not the cups that remain upright. Perhaps you don't want to acknowledge that there's something else going for you. It's often easier to stay stuck.'

She smiled at the scowling face opposite.

'I can see I've touched a chord.'

Zena shook her head resignedly.

'I came over here to try to move on, get a new life, but it doesn't seem to make any difference inside my head. The loop just goes round and round.'

'And the 'if onlys'?'

Zena nodded sadly.

'We've all been there, you know. And we all get out of it eventually.'

Erin looked as if she really did understand.

'But some take longer than others.' Zena stood up abruptly. 'Thanks for the reading...'

'Wait. We haven't finished.'

Erin's expression was so full of concern that it made Zena even more anxious to go.

'Sorry. I really need to get back.'

Eyes full of tears, she blundered out of the room, dropping a ten euro note into the blue bowl as she passed. Erin made no move to follow her, and Zena found herself alone, choking back sobs, in an empty street.

Poppy was glad to get out of the house before Llewellyn was up. She knew she looked even more of a mess than usual, her hair wilder than ever and safety pins holding up her long skirt because the seam had split when she tried to do it up. She couldn't be putting on yet more weight, surely? It was so hard to be working in a restaurant and at the same time trying not to eat so much. But she always ate when she was unhappy, or nervous or especially low in confidence, and really Llewellyn was enough to sap anyone's confidence with his endless jokes and jibes. She tried to laugh, but it was wounding to have attention drawn to your failings all the time. She'd followed him and Erin to La Folle after they met at a celtic music festival the previous year, although she'd never let on and always pretended it was a coincidence that they wanted a lodger when she needed a room.

So Poppy had stayed on in France, despite her parents'

misgivings and incredulity that she preferred a foreign country to their cosy house in Ilfracombe. Poppy was genuinely sorry to disappoint them because she was tender-hearted and loved her parents very much, but now another stronger passion had entered her life for the first time. It wasn't always easy being in the same house as someone you really loved, and Llewellyn's teasing made it all the harder, although she tried to keep her feelings to herself and not spoil everything by any kind of declaration, just a bit of mute staring when she thought she was unobserved.

Poppy was red in the face and ten minutes late by the time she reached the restaurant, but no-one seemed to mind. Despite her clumsiness and the mess she often created in the kitchen, she was well liked for her interest in food and her willingness to lend a hand at anything else. So sometimes she cleaned the guest-rooms on the upper floor and sometimes she took a turn at serving, where she was popular with the customers, although a little inclined to bump and jog them as she tried to squeeze between the tables. With most of her meals free at work, she managed the rent and her meagre personal expenses out of what she earned at the restaurant and making the occasional cake for English people who missed their fix of sponges and rich fruit. And despite the odd disaster, it was a labour of love, because cooking made Poppy as happy as anything could, but it was not food that occupied her dreams each night, as she slept wistfully under the same roof as her beloved.

Llewellyn appeared in the kitchen as Erin was making another cup of tea.

'Is it safe?'

'If you mean Poppy, she went to work a while ago.'

'Thank god for that. I can't stomach those cow eyes at this time of the morning.'

'You're an unfeeling bastard sometimes. And you make it so much worse by taunting her the whole time so the poor girl doesn't know where to turn.'

'It's poor Llewellyn you should be thinking! I can't help being such a magnet for women and driving them wild with longing, now can I? I don't see how you can hold me responsible for something I was born with?'

Erin frowned at him.

'I shall certainly hold you responsible if she looks for more restful accommodation. We need her rent, so don't go driving her away. It'll be you making up the difference if we lose her.'

'Fat chance of that. She's working all hours and not earning enough to pay a commercial rate.'

'All the more reason to be more sympathetic and understanding.'

Erin had seen enough of her brother playing with his victims to make it less palatable as time went on. He was thirty, hardly a kid anymore and she was beginning to wonder if, despite their blood-tie, he really wasn't a very nice person at all. He'd sworn that the baby born to Paula Williams back in Swansea was nothing to do with him, but her five brothers thought differently and Llewellyn had not shown any desire to go back to Wales in the last year. She herself liked it well enough in La Folle for the time being. She was inclined to take things as they came, resistant to long-term plans, but she had no idea of remaining in exile for ever.

'She's not a child, Erina,' Llewellyn was complaining. 'Even Poppy must be thought of as a woman at twenty-two, although I agree her mental age may be nearer twelve.'

'Just go easy on her, will you? Make life a bit more pleasant for us all.'

She went out of the room without waiting for a response.

If I ever do get on Poppy, I shall give her a very hard time indeed, Llewellyn thought to himself with some satisfaction. She might do, after all, what with the local supply of women running rather short in these winter months.

Zena walked quickly away, turning into the market-square and then downhill. She knew where her footsteps were heading and couldn't help herself. It had been hard not to give in to the urge on her first visit to the market when she'd met Llewellyn, but now she just needed something, some connection with Lucas to remind her of what all this emotional morass was really about.

She pushed open the tall wrought-iron gate of the cemetery. It was an early 19th century development, established when the meagre grounds of the old church on the hill were full. A small chapel stood on a raised mound in the centre with a weathered calvaire outside. The granite and marble graves lay all around in regimented rows, packed close as soldiers. In more recent times, some enlargement had been required and the surrounding wall knocked down and then rebuilt to enclose a new sector around a small stand of yew trees.

The family of Lucas' mother had been fortunate, Zena

had thought ruefully when she came here with Lucas all those years ago, to get the best spot in the whole place. Here the graves were better spaced, the ancient trees forming a sombre natural backdrop to their setting. There was a rough wooden bench beneath them for those who chose to linger in this quiet spot.

Approaching the grave, Zena felt the odd contrast of her heartbeat quickening and her limbs growing heavy. She stood facing the headstone and bobbed her head in a little bow of respect, as if Lucas' mother could see her or would know who she was if she did. It was a family grave, with Rolland-Bellec, the joint names of Lucas' grand-parents, emblazoned on the simple black marble background. A separate plaque recorded the death of Thérèse, 2 February 1996, aged 55.

I was thirty then, Zena thought. Still hopeful, still waiting for someone like Lucas to come along, still enjoying my work. No money worries, no family problems, except my mother's total dottiness, just tick, tick ticking along but alert for that vital moment that would snatch me up and whirl me off into the maelstrom of life where everyone else on the planet appeared to dwell. And Lucas was here in Finistere – the end of the world, as she'd recognised in the name from her schoolgirl Latin – seeing the end of his mother's life, gobbled up by the greed of cancer. She knew that he had stood here on this very spot and shed tears for the loving woman who had encouraged him selflessly throughout her life.

He had never known the English father who left Thérèse when he found out she was pregnant. She'd met him in London where she'd gone to work in the restaurant of some relatives, to improve her English. Her own parents' war-time experiences had taught them to look outwards, to count the English as friends and allies, so they had encouraged their daughter to broaden her experience of the world. They had not expected her to return, pregnant and strangely distant, the faintest shadow of the bright, laughing girl who had left them a year earlier.

But Thérèse had loved her son. She named him for the light he would bring her, the serious little boy, keen to investigate every corner of the wild scenery around La Folle, and the man who devoted his time and energies to travel much further afield. He had never entirely left her though. Hardly a week passed without a postcard or a letter, and he would always appear unannounced around the time of her name-day.

Lucas had told Zena this when they stood here together, hands clasped, four years before. She looked again at the headstone now. It was only a month until the anniversary of Thérèse's departure. Zena was ashamed of her fervent hope that he would come back as regularly to honour her death as he had her life.

Chapter 3

A large black-coated figure was peering in through the glass-panes of the front door when Zena returned to the house. He swung round as the car drew up, arms outstretched in an expansive gesture of welcome, strong white teeth exposed in a wide smile. She got out of the car hesitantly.

'You are Zelda,' he informed her in heavily accented English.

'Zena, actually.'

'I welcome you, Zelda, to my little corner of paradise.'

The arm-waving took in the concrete yard, the river and the hills beyond. She wondered for a second if this could be the landlord she had never met, but the agents had told her the owner grew cauliflowers near Brest. The sleek and prosperous appearance of this man didn't fit her image of this occupation, but she remembered the Welsh/Breton confusion and how little she knew about anything here.

'Thank you. I'm sorry, I'm not sure....'

'So charming, so delightful, so English!'

He had taken her hand and was now clutching it to his chest. She felt the glow of warmth emanating from his body and the discomfort of trying to keep the rest of her body arched away from him.

'And how do you like your little home? It is very ugly, no?'

Not the landlord, she decided, having translated his

elaborate 'ow into 'how' and 'ome into 'home'. She'd forgotten the French difficulty with aitches.

'And you are...?'

'Yes, I am very much, thank you.'

He was still grasping her hand. Zena tore it away, suddenly exasperated by the inequalities of the encounter.

'Who are you exactly?'

Jean-Yves waved his arms about forcefully to semaphore his understanding of her concern.

'But you poor lady! I am Jean-Yves, of course. The husband of Monique – yes, thank you, I see you understand how hard that must be - but I am strong, like a leon.'

'Lion.'

Jean-Yves looked hurt.

'No, it is true. I suffer very much. But perhaps you can comfort me and I can help you with your art...'

Zena stepped past him to unlock the door.

'It's very kind of you to offer your help, but I'm fine, really.'

He was so close behind her that she moved swiftly inside intending to keep him at bay on the step, but somehow they were suddenly both inside the main room, which seemed to shrink with his presence. The door closed behind him.

'I expect Monique told you about my cards.' She wanted to retain an image of his wife on the room with them. 'I had some designs accepted by an agency in England and I've decided to give up my day job and try to make a go of something different and a bit more inspiring than office work.' She had no idea whether Jean-Yves was following this, but she felt a compulsion to keep talking in English, to retain the initiative if only to avoid being swamped by any further aspect of his largesse. 'I've only just made a start on the drawings. They're not that good really. Just little sketches. I'm out of practice....'

Zena ran out of words under Jean-Yves' rapturous gaze.

'Would you like some coffee?' She turned in confusion to the kitchen area. 'I've only got instant.'

He gave a growl of distaste. 'I would prefer to see the pictures. They are upstairs, no?'

One large hand rested on the banister, and one large foot was firmly fixed on the bottom step. Zena couldn't see any way out of this without being rude, which was in some ridiculous way unthinkable in a foreign country.

'OK.' She hoped the bedroom door they must pass was shut, although the sight of her untidiness and disregard for appearance might be helpfully off-putting to a suave seducer like Jean-Yves.

He moved aside to let her go first. It felt oddly intimate leading him up the stairs, conscious of his eyes on her rear view. The landing was dark as all three doors to bedrooms and bathroom were closed. Another door led to the attic stairs and now light flooded into the stairwell from the large velux windows on both sides. It was a perfect studio space, despite the cold.

Jean-Yves went straight to the easel and looked at the market scene she had finished that morning, a bright colourwash illuminating the faint lines of her original sketch.

His silent appraisal was unnerving in contrast with the earlier ebullience. Zena wondered if by any chance he did actually know something about art and might genuinely be interested in her work. She bit her lip to stop herself asking if he liked it.

'I like it,' Jean-Yves said, looked from the painting to Zena and back again. 'It is good. You have the eye, yes? The sight of an artist. Look here' – he pointed to a minute detail of a child's hand clutching its father's trousers – as if it was his own private discovery and not something she herself had formed. As he continued to talk in broken English about the merits of her composition, Zena felt both pleased and marginalised at the same time, temporarily forgotten as a person in her own right in all this enthusiasm for the painting and his desire to instruct her in her own cleverness.

The exposition finally came to an end. Zena thanked him with some embarrassment and turned to lead the way downstairs when he made a sudden grab for her, one hand snaking round her waist, pushing her back against an old cupboard. Their faces were inches apart. Zena felt the raw shock of proximity to a man after so long an absence from the sexual arena. He must have seen the expression of horror on her face because his hold loosened a little and she was able to give him a good shove away with both hands.

'Stop it! Don't you dare come in here and think you can maul me about!'

She was breathing heavily, truly angry at this invasion of her space. Jean-Yves looked sheepishly contrite at the force of her objection.

'Zelda, I am sorry. I am stupid, but you are very beautiful and I am overcome by this...' - a large gesture towards the easel - 'and that you are alone in the world. But perhaps I do not appeal to you?'

He put on such a sad face that Zena laughed.

'It's not that. Of course, you're very attractive' (what was she saying?) 'but I'm just not interested, quite apart from the fact that your wife is looking after your children in your house just up the road.'

Jean-Yves gave a huge shrug.

'A man must have passion in his life.'

'Well, not with me. I've come here to get away, to be on my own for a while.'

A shimmer of comprehension came over his face.

'I know it, there is someone else. You have a heart broken. You want to forget!'

'Something like that.' She had no intention of going into details.

'But do not worry, my Zelda.' He advanced to a respectful proximity and took one hand tenderly between his huge bear-paws. 'Jean-Yves will look after you. I will be your friend and protector.'

'Thank you'. And she was grateful when he moved away to the top of the stairs. She went past, feeling that she handled an awkward situation rather well. There had been no offence at her rejection and certainly nothing that was likely to disturb Monique.

'But if you change your mind...' he said softly as she passed.

As she worked in the cold attic later, Zena wondered if she could ever stand another man physically close to her again. It was hard to remember life before Lucas now. She could only recall strained blind-dates organised by friends, and the odd disastrous liaison with colleagues from work. Most of the time she had just jogged along, neither happy nor unhappy, but always with that sense of waiting, marking time until something important happened. At thirty she was unworried, with time stretching ahead and plenty of others in the same state, still looking, still trying to make up their minds. At thirty-five, the perspective had changed. Time became finite, something precious, something to calculate – if I meet someone this year or next year at the outside, maybe marry within a year, get pregnant the year after... Still time, still hope. That was the trouble with maths, it had so little relation to real life and the vast emotional desert for a single woman between thirty and forty.

When she met Lucas she had almost given up hope of a relationship that made her heart sing and the future seem exciting. Work had become dreary by then too, the job so well-known, its scope shrunk to daily routine with all the usual irritations of office work. A full-time occupation organising the lives and adventures of others and having none oneself was an unpleasant irony not lost on her, but she was good at it: efficient in arranging itineraries and accommodation, and quick at problem-solving when things went wrong as they so often did with travel arrangements. Dealing with all the financial side of expense accounts and over-spent entertainment budgets was not much fun, but she could be tough when necessary and shame the worst offenders into cutting down on their most outrageous demands. She did not envy them the jetting about the world – as far as she could tell, few ventured further than hotel bars and the venues of appointments – but the sense of being on the move, somehow progressing was something that really did seem absent from her life. Stagnation was setting in and she couldn't see a way to rouse herself and make a break to study art or be a single mother with a test-tube baby or fulfil a single one of her other fantasies.

But it was through work that she had met Lucas. He had somehow talked GPE into giving him sponsorship for a trip he wanted to make to Latvia. She remembered being asked to arrange a hotel in the town for this little-known traveller when he came to discuss the project and the ways in which he would promote the company's new digital cameras in return for a fair sum of money.

She had not expected to meet him herself, but the MD had gone early for some domestic emergency and left Zena to greet Mr Rolland with apologies and escort him to his hotel in the town centre. Zena waited alone in the reception area after everyone else had gone, drumming her fingers impatiently as she looked forward to getting home and having a quiet evening painting.

Lucas came into the reception area just before seven o'clock, shaking rain from his long dark hair, smiling an apology for his lateness. He insisted on buying her dinner at the hotel, attended closely to her every word and talked with such intelligence and humour about his proposed trip that she went home with her heart pounding and head throbbing, as well as a date for a repeat performance after his crucial meeting the next day. She didn't dwell on whether his attention and interest were calculated to smooth his path at GPE, or if he always reacted to the company of women in this way. Such niceties were irrelevant. For Zena had fallen deeply in love at the very first sight.

By the end of what had turned into a typically drizzly

day, she was happy with what had been achieved up in her garret. Two market-scenes, full of colour and noise, were completed, a satisfactory warm-up exercise in preparation for the real work ahead. She planned to go out the next day in search of subject matter for the designs she had promised herself to send in by the end of the month before the agent's enthusiasm waned.

Not following up on successes had been a weakness in the past – she once won a competition and was asked to contribute some pictures to an exhibition on the strength of it, but the timing was bad, coinciding with a rare month of Lucas at home. She had chosen to devote what time she had outside work to looking after him instead. Had she told him about the chance, Lucas would certainly have urged her to make the most of it, which was perhaps why she'd not mentioned it at all. Another time a designer at work had seen some of her sketches and offered to recommend her to a friend looking for a book illustrator, but Zena had not taken him up on it, assuming her work was nowhere near good enough for a professional project.

Now she had another chance and she was determined not to let it slip through her fingers. Then at least if Lucas came back, she would have something to show him, something to make him proud of her.

The phone was ringing as she came downstairs.

It was her mother.

'I had a dream last night that Hermione was a White Russian soldier. It quite upset my digestion.'

'How are you, Mum?'

'I really don't know how your brother puts up with that woman.'

Zena was about to say Hermione wasn't that bad, but in fact, she was. A hippy primadonna who positively seethed with malice when faced with the human race.

'He seems to like her.'

'It's ridiculous. All that psychic posturing. She's about as mystical as a toothbrush. You must talk to him, Zena.'

'OK, will do,' she said cheerfully in the typical doublespeak of most conversations with her mother. Trying to reason Stephen out of a liaison with Hermione was something she had no intention of doing, satisfying though a successful result might be. Zena loved her long-suffering younger brother very much, but he always seemed to attract such awful women and Hermione was beginning to look alarmingly long-term. Presumably they had great sex of the strictly non-tantric kind every night. Zena couldn't think what else was keeping them together.

'Is that why you were phoning?' she asked her mother.

'Of course. I need my sleep, you know.'

The call ended abruptly as her mother's attention was taken by something closer to hand and the phone as so often went down without a goodbye.

'Yes, I'm fine,' Zena said into the silent mouthpiece. 'I've got an ill-assorted French couple for my only neighbours and the house is not exactly warm and cosy, but the scenery's great, thanks for asking....'

She looked around the room, comparing its appearance to that of a week ago when she arrived. It was certainly brighter. She had covered the sofa with a bright throw of African design, covered with wiggly snake-like patterns in warm caramel and cinnamon colours - an improvement on the taupe suedette. The walls now sported a couple of her own paintings and a framed photograph which Lucas had taken in Poland on his first working trip after their relationship began.

Just looking at it now reminded Zena of that homecoming. Based in different cities, the state of separation was no novelty, but there was an extra expectation in welcoming the traveller home from his first venture abroad during their own personal history. He had been in the Mazurian forest on Poland's eastern border with Russia, a wild land where bison still roamed free in the vast un-peopled landscape, and later in the capital Warsaw, now seething with western-style commercialism in stark contrast to his visits in the early 90s. He had shown her all his photographs: gypsies begging on crowded streets, gaggles of prostitutes round a fire under an enormous flyover, and from the forest, a hunter prowling through the trees, with only his profile visible against the strong straight line of a pine's trunk. She looked again at the familiar stark image – felt hat above a large nose and a moustache huge enough to create its own outline, gun poised ready. If Lucas had made a sudden movement, he might have been killed himself, but the hunter remained totally unaware of the camera and the fact that he was someone else's prey. The thought of Lucas being in some sort of danger made her muscles clench with fear. If only she knew where he was now, it would be something.

Zena resumed her assessment of the room, noting flashes of colour in her pottery cups, the tablecloth from her former flat and a white vase she had filled with un-seasonal flowers from a shop. It was odd to see her things here in a new environment, enlivening the sparse furniture and drab décor. She sank down on the sofa in a sudden burst of depression. Despite all her efforts, the original atmosphere of dinge and neglect persisted below the level of this superficial improvement. It didn't and never would feel like home, a place where she could be completely relaxed and centred in her own element. She felt more alone than ever, pitched up in this foreign place with only the amorous advances of Jean-Yves and possibly the death card from Erin to look forward to. God, she was miserable. The Five of Cups was about right.

She wondered what Lucas would make of this place. He never seemed particularly responsive to his surroundings indoors. The confinement of a room didn't really suit him, he was too limited and inhibited by the narrow confines of regular walls and solid furniture. Perhaps if she hadn't tried to create such a comfortable nest for him at the flat, he'd never have flown away.

Stop thinking about Lucas! She heard the words clearly inside her head as if her obsession had finally driven some alter ego to a spontaneous explosion. Acting on the impulse, she strode across the room and took the photograph down, leaving its face turned to the wall, and then moved about restlessly, thoughts churning.

What had Erin said that wretched card meant? She preferred being stuck to moving on? God, it was true. Zena banged her head experimentally against the wall a couple of times, as if she could dislodge or crush all thoughts of L.... No, not even the name again! Erin was right, she was trapped, or rather she was trapping herself. She had to break out of this cycle of remembrance and pain, familiarity and loss. Now. Or all the efforts she had made in leaving work and family and security would be wasted. She had to take control of her thoughts and refuse to allow the L person so much as a syllable inside her head. Every time she started to formulate that word she would substitute another – banana, for example – and every time her train of thought veered directly towards forbidden territory she would immediately go upstairs, whatever time of the day or night, and lose herself in painting.

This was a resolution. Tomorrow would be a new start. She finally admitted to herself that L – or banana, as she would now think of him - was not coming back and it really was over. But her life wasn't, and tomorrow she would go out, working, open to new experience, new people, whatever life had to offer her. She'd had her wake-up call from the universe and she'd respond.

Zena went to bed feeling calm and almost happy. She managed to keep her drowsy thoughts on scenes she would find the next day and the great success her designs would surely be and how everything was finally changing for the better. Goodbye, Five of Cups... was her last thought before she fell asleep.

Chapter 4

After puffing her way up the last few metres of hillside, Zena gave a genuine gasp of astonishment as she sank down thankfully on a huge slab of granite and saw the panoramic view spread before her. A jagged range of rocky peaks stretched away to east and west, rising like grey teeth out of the barren slopes of gorse-covered scrub. Far to the north she was sure she could glimpse the steely waters of the Channel off Roscoff, but it was the southern view that demanded her attention. A large expanse of water, almost Mediterranean blue under the clear light of the January sun filled most of a vast bowl inside the embracing hills. In the distance she could see a steep mound surmounted by a little chapel, a man-made interpretation of the other craggy summits littered with huge boulders like the remnants of primitive temples.

She sat transfixed for a long time. What might have repelled others in its starkness seemed to draw Zena close, gathering her to the wild spirit of these hills, to the hard rock and moist earth, the gorse and heather, the birds of prey performing their aerial acrobatics above her head. She closed her eyes and listened to their high-pitched mew, hearing it as if for the first time in the clearest acoustic air could provide. She could have been alone in the world, and, up here, it did not seem like such a bad thing. Even a few cars glinting on half-hidden roads below did not detract from the sense of lonely freedom that rose inside her at the sight. It was like the fulfilment of the promise made by her first journey on arriving in Brittany. The land itself was speaking to her, making a connection with some forgotten part inside her.

She felt fit and strong as her bodily tensions dissolved and the benefits of all her vigorous exercise made themselves apparent. As she sat on the rock gazing across what felt like an ancient landscape, Zena experienced a tiny flicker of hope that maybe she had done the right thing for the right reasons after all by coming to a foreign country to shed the stagnation of the past year. It wasn't easy being alone in a strange place, nor struggling to make oneself understood in a foreign language to achieve even the most basic transaction of buying bread in the village shop. But there was something restful about the lack of expectation from others. Her Breton neighbours and those she met casually on walks were polite and helpful but they did not pry or give her the sense that they were speculating about her singleness behind her back. The only people who had showed any curiosity were Erin and Llewellyn. Zena did not count Jean-Yves, who continued to dog her footsteps offering services of various kinds whenever Monique's attention was fully engaged elsewhere.

She really was free at last, free of entanglements and demands, free to choose her own path. All she had to do was concentrate on her painting and on exploring her new environment. Looked at from that perspective, it was an exhilarating prospect. She leapt up and began to dance an uncharacteristically light-hearted little jig on the granite ridge.

Tramping back along a track riven by deep puddles and

deceptively thick sludge, she carefully picked her way to avoid going up to the ankles in grey glutinous mud. At the foot of the hill, she stopped at a junction of paths, uncertain of the way she'd come. It had taken the best part of two hours to walk from the house to the top of the Monts d'Arrée and she was starting to wish she'd brought some chocolate or a bottle of water to keep her going on the journey back. Was it this way, into a thicket of spindly trees? She tried to judge from the position of the sun and decided to follow the path although it didn't look well-walked.

After a couple of minutes Zena found herself in a small clearing, facing what appeared to be a long low giant's table made of huge slabs of granite. She knew from her earlier visit to Brittany that this was a dolmen, the Breton word for 'stone table,' an ancient burial place. She approached it with a strange mixture of caution and respect, a funny sensation between laughing and crying starting to throb in her throat. The burial chamber was below ground level, with some of the supporting stones on each side missing, but the capstones still in place, preserving the dimness of the womblike cave beneath the stones. She crouched down to peer inside, one hand resting on the massive roof. At once she felt again the fainting sensation from the cave. Her eyes closed as her mind drifted in a dark space, where she could smell smoke and the heat of fire...

The sharp bark of a dog startled Zena out of this reverie. She scrambled up unsteadily to face a kind of beagle, black and tan splashes almost obscuring a dull grey coat. It was the sort of hunting dog she'd already often seen around here, usually lost and roaming the countryside wondering where their masters had gone. It stopped a few feet away, paws forward, body pulling back as it continued to bark a warning. Normally she liked dogs, but this one seemed deliberately unfriendly.

'Good boy,' she said nervously, keeping as still as possible.

To Zena's relief a man suddenly strode into the clearing. He was too smart-casually dressed to be a hunter, and more importantly he wasn't carrying a gun. At least, not obviously.

He bent to put the dog on a lead, but it neatly side-stepped his attempt and shot off into the undergrowth, despite his exasperated yells of 'Fido'. How unoriginal can you get, Zena thought, giving your dog a name like that. He looked pretty ordinary too, fair hair cut short and too neatly, conventional clothes. She thought of L... the banana's long dark hair...

'Sorry.' The man turned back to Zena. They were the same height and she found herself looking straight into his hazel eyes. 'I didn't expect anyone to be up here. There isn't usually.'

'You're English!' It had only just dawned on her, despite the Fido clue.

He looked round nervously as if he'd come across the local nutter and wanted to eye up quick escape routes.

'Sorry. Is that a problem? You appear to be too, if you don't mind me saying so.'

She couldn't help laughing.

'It's a relief! My French has been sorely tested and found wanting since I got here. I'm Zena, by the way.'

He offered his hand briefly.

'Ian. I think you'll find there are plenty of English

people about.' He didn't sound very thrilled by this.

'Do you live here?' she asked.

'Not exactly. I'm working on the cottage and trying to get some writing done at the same time.'

'You're a writer?'

Ian gave a quick smile that definitely improved his features, Zena thought.

'Not exactly.'

The conversation was harder work than she was prepared for and she found herself now longing to get way from him and back to the sense of un-restraint she'd been enjoying out here in the hills. He seemed to feel the same unease and turned away abruptly.

'I'd better go after the dog,' he murmured.

'Isn't it supposed to be the other way round?' she couldn't resist calling after him.

When he'd disappeared, Zena went back over to the dolmen and rested her head against the stone. To her surprise it was warm to the touch, not the sharp electric current effect she'd felt at the cave, but as if a deep internal source of heat was radiating out just as far as its outer edge. She remembered the banana telling her that these dolmens were said to be the homes of fairies and goblins in legend, and imagined them underground cooking bacon in a large frying-pan. This thought immediately translated to her own growing hunger and Zena set off again in what she hoped was the right direction, wondering if Fido had managed to elude his master completely.

Ian strode home with a temporarily chastened dog at his heels.

The cottage he had bought three years earlier stood alone on the edge of dark pine woods, on the lower slopes of the Monts d'Arrée. A basic one-room-plus-attic structure, built from local granite blocks with a roof of thick slate, it was still in a state of renovation and he was in no hurry to finish it. He stressed the very slow progress in its habitability every time his wife enquired, in case she pressed to come out again before the summer.

All this time the little house had been his bolthole, a refuge from a miserable marriage and a place where he could work without interruption on the research that absorbed all his waking thoughts and often his dream-world as well. Whilst Leah thought he was fitting new units into the corner kitchen of the main downstairs room, he had actually been making the adjoining stone wood-store into a little office for himself. A makeshift desk stood by the small window with its view down the valley, where heavy evergreens gave way to pasture land in which rich red herds of cattle grazed. The temptation was to spend all his time reading, writing or walking the bleak hills when weather permitted instead of the sawing, hammering, plastering and painting which he had promised to get on with during this spell in France.

He was on sabbatical from his college for six months, a welcome chance to carry on with his own research into celtic legends, to steep himself in the landscape and scenery that, in his imagination, was peopled with spirits at every turn. What was to be different and exciting in the book he finally produced was its close connection between the land and the stories it had given birth to.

Ian had learnt to keep this aspect of work to himself. His colleagues in the department, being practical men, were little interested in the world of the imagination. They joked about his evil spirits and asked how the fairies were coming along. His wife Leah didn't even take it seriously enough to comment. She wanted to tell people about their house in France, as if it was a palatial residence instead of a simple old cottage with basic facilities. No amount of DIY was going to make it more than that, but Ian was happy enough with it in its natural rustic state. A wood-burning stove in the big stone fireplace kept the living area warm and the bedroom in the attic above too at this time of year. He'd managed to fix a wall-heater in the little bathroom on this trip, so that was one improvement he could emphasise under the heavy fire of Leah's questions.

There was no doubt that things had reached rock-bottom between them in the last few months. It was clear that neither any longer derived pleasure or support from the relationship, much less the love that had long since vanished. They had no children to distract attention from the yawning gulf between their individual needs and desires. Leah had refused to consider either fertility treatment or adoption, and Ian felt he must respect her decision. His emotions were already too stunted by the course of their marriage to leave him the energy or passion necessary to break through her barricade of self-protection. It had all settled into silence. Their conversations were limited to the practicalities of everyday life, the endless lists of tasks she drew up for each of them, ticking off their lives in tiny segments. She redid the house from top to bottom with new décor and furniture, pouring her thwarted creativity out into the tills of John Lewis and Liberty.

She refused to consider Ian's suggestion of getting a dog, something he had always wanted, with fond memories of all his childhood pets. Perhaps finding Frodo at a rescue centre within a week of arriving out here in Finistere this time was an oblique way of making a decision he couldn't normally face thinking about. Nothing had been said about his return, and if he could only keep Leah away, it meant a few months of the sort of freedom only a long-term prisoner could appreciate.

This was the first time Ian had been out to Brittany in winter and he was revelling in the peace and quiet he'd found here. Meeting that English woman on the hill had come as a shock. In other circumstances he might have been more friendly. She was certainly pleasant looking, like a celtic hunting goddess with that long wavy brown hair and natural glowing skin. But social intercourse had little attraction for him at the best of times: here it simply spoilt things. He usually had this whole area to himself, especially in the woods or up on the quartz peaks. Occasionally a tractor with a load of wood or hay driven by the friendly farmer who was his nearest neighbour trundled along the lower tracks, but there was no-one to disturb him and he very much wanted to keep it that way.

'Who's going to look after the stall when we go off to Quimper next week then? Or shall we just let it go for once?'

Llewellyn had to repeat his question before Erin looked up from the workbench where she was twisting delicate strands of silver with a minute pair of pliers.

'No, we need someone to fill in.' She screwed up her

forehead as if it was an effort to think. 'What about Poppy? Is she free then?'

Llewellyn gave a great snort.

'Definitely not Poppy. She'll give half the stuff away and the rest will be nicked from under her nose. Might as well just make a large donation to charity than let Poppy loose on our livelihood.'

Erin laughed.

'OK. You're probably right. What about Christian, could he manage to keep an eye out?'

'He'll set up the stall for us, no problem, but we need someone to mind it. I'll ask around in the bar, get someone to do it for a few euros.'

Erin put down her tools and pushed the large magnifying mirror back. Her round green eyes blinked as they changed focus to look directly at her brother.

'Ask Zena.'

'Zena? Who the hell is Zena?'

'Your irresistible sales-patter lured her here for a reading last week, if you haven't had so many hangovers since then that you can't remember.'

'You mean Zena who can't tell Welsh from Breton and blushes when anyone tries to have a joke with her?'

'No, I was thinking of Zena who's sensible enough to recoil from your bullshit and who will be responsible about our stall.' As he pantomimed an expression of complete incomprehension, Erin went on. 'Zena, who's new to the area and might welcome the chance to meet a few people on the market.'

'Oh, that Zena. Now I get it. She's your latest project, is she? And what did the cards tell you about Zena that's made her so interesting and deserving? Go on, you can tell me in confidence, you know that.'

'I'd ring the front desk of The Sun before I'd choose you as a confidant. Now get out of my way and let at least one of us do some work today.'

It wasn't entirely in joking spirit that she said this. Llewellyn made a rude face and shambled out, not noticing Poppy hanging out a sheet on the line behind the shed.

Erin reflected that Llewellyn was getting lazier by the day. The weekly round of markets he had once followed had shrunk to two days, La Folle on Thursdays - not a great effort to move 100 metres from their front door - and a bigger one at Lesneven every Monday. The rest of the time he was to be found in the bar or chasing after local women and female tourists. Their original agreement that Erin would spend her time producing the merchandise and he would use his gift of the gab and monstrous ego to sell it on the stall five days a week had fallen into abeyance. They'd done well at the start, but less and less money came in now in the winter season, and her brother's personal expenditure seemed to increase in direct proportion to the decrease in their income. Even with Poppy's rent, they could certainly not afford to miss a single week of the market at La Folle.

Erin sighed. It was unusual for her to feel stressed and pressurised, but making enough jewellery for the big craft fair in addition to the commissioned pieces she was committed to complete as soon as possible was taking its toll. And Llewellyn certainly wasn't pulling his considerable weight. She would have to think what to do about it.

Zena roamed the market. This was her second week of life in Brittany and she was beginning to establish a sort of routine that suited her. She worked best in the afternoons, so the first part of the day was for walking or shopping, like today. She loved the atmosphere and sense of community in La Folle when it was packed with people stocking up with local produce before retiring to the shelter of their houses for another week. She had already been struck by the normally uninhabited aspect most villages presented to the casual observer. Between the flurry of early morning activity at the baker's and perhaps another foray in the late afternoon to get bread for dinner, the streets were virtually deserted. Family life in the winter was a self-contained affair, and she imagined that many houses were dark by ten o'clock at night, so it was a relief to find a scene of reliable midweek lively bustle.

As she went slowly past the biggest vegetable stall admiring the extraordinary artistry of colour and presentation, someone cannoned into her, knocking her off balance.

'Oh, no. Sorry. I didn't see you...'

It was Poppy, Erin's lodger, trying to manoeuvre a laden basket to a safer position. Zena noticed at once that her eyes were red from crying and asked her if she was alright.

Poppy laughed, although her eyes remained sad.

'It should be me asking you that as I nearly had you over. I'm so clumsy. I'm really sorry.'

'It's fine, there's no problem honestly. We met at Erin's, I don't know if you remember. Are you sure there's nothing wrong?'

Poppy's bottom lip was trembling as if more tears were not far off. She shook her head miserably.

'No. I must get to work now. We're always busy at lunch-times.'

'I must come in and try out your handiwork soon.'

'I don't do any of the meat cooking. Salads and veg, mostly. But desserts are my speciality. The chef is teaching me to make chocolate.'

Zena felt very ancient beside Poppy's youth.

'Look, if you do need to talk – I mean, I'm sure you've got plenty of friends, but I'm...'

'No, I haven't,' Poppy said, smearing her face with a handkerchief, 'I haven't any friends at all, but I can't talk about it. I'm sorry, I just can't. Thanks anyway.'

As she vanished into the crowd, bumping and bouncing off people like a pin-ball, Zena resumed her progress round the market. She was disturbed by the pain she'd seen in Poppy's face and resolved to try to see her again and give her another opportunity to talk. Perhaps the girl was homesick, or lovesick more likely at that age. Still, she was about the last person who should be giving advice about that.

As she moved from stall to stall, Zena was very aware of Llewellyn's large presence opposite the church, and felt both drawn and repelled by the thought of talking to him again. Jovial, cheeky types always made her profoundly uneasy. She seemed to get the worst of it when she rose to the challenge, but chickening out gave an impression of dullness and stupidity. She didn't feel any anxiety about brother and sister discussing her affairs; there was an air of containment about Erin that she trusted and anyway, what was there to tell? An unhappy ending to a love affair was hardly unusual. Being deserted by a banana didn't make her an emotional leper after all. No-one here knew, that was the beauty of being in a foreign country...

She spun round as someone tapped her on the shoulder and finding no-one spun back the other way to be confronted by Llewellyn's self-satisfied grinning face.

'Hello, my lovely. I was hoping to see you. Bit of a favour to ask you, actually.'

'Oh yes?' She heard the wariness in her own voice.

'I was hoping you might like to run away with me.'

'Now there's an offer I can refuse,' Zena said boldly, meeting his eye.

He laughed and gave her a congratulatory pat on the back as if she'd passed a test unexpectedly.

'OK. What about a bit of stall-minding next Thursday then? We're off to a fair elsewhere, but Erin wants to keep business as usual here.'

'But my French is still very rusty and I don't know anything about selling anyway...'

She was following him back to the stall as she spoke. He held up a beautiful silver necklace decorated with a row of arrow-pierced hearts.

'Read that,' he said, shoving the price ticket close to her face.

'25 euros.'

'Good girl. I can see you're going to be a natural at this.'

She couldn't help laughing.

'Don't tell me. I exchange this' – she took the necklace – 'for the customer's money. Stick it in a bag and hand it over.'

'Brilliant. You'll be a business mogul yet.'

'And what do I get out of it? This minding the stall lark? Money?'

She rubbed her thumb across her fingers in his face.

'Steady on, now. You may have grasped my basic training quickly, but that doesn't mean you're ready to enter the heady world of negotiation.'

Zena looked at the necklace again. It seemed a suitable enough symbol.

'I'll do it for this.'

Llewellyn looked uneasy for the first time in their acquaintance.

'That's a valuable piece of art, that is!'

'What are the hours of the market?'

Now he was flummoxed.

'8.30 to 4.30, but...'

'So that's 8 hours work for 25 euros of necklace, just over 3 euros an hour. What is the minimum wage over here anyway?'

'Now look, we don't want to get into any type of salary discussion here. It's a one-off favour, and I'll ask Erin about the necklace, but just put all that workers' rights stuff out of your pretty head, OK?'

'OK.' Zena smiled sweetly.

Llewellyn gestured at his neighbour, busily engaged in selling stripy Breton T-shirts to a group of middle-aged English couples, probably from the unseasonal tour bus Zena had noticed in the car-park.

'Christian will set the stall up and have the gear for you to set out, so all you have to do is turn up and make lots of money for us by chatting up the customers.'

It wasn't a prospect she was particularly looking forward to, but getting her hands on that necklace should make it all worth while, Zena decided as she drove back to the house.

She could not deny that she was well-pleased to be asked. It made her feel like someone in her own right again, a perception it was hard to maintain when she lived alone at the end of a road and often saw not a soul from day to day. She'd even hid behind the curtain the day before when Monique's car had streaked into the yard, reckoning she was not yet desperate enough for company to actively encourage her neighbour. But in general she felt she should make more effort to talk to people now she'd settled in, despite the conspicuous lack of success she'd met with the man on her walk. He'd looked almost as if he resented her presence there, although the hills were hardly private property, and he was clearly not bowled over by her conversational brilliance. But to hell with him, Zena thought. There were plenty of others to meet and the market would be a perfect opportunity to do so. Suddenly the world seemed full of possibilities.

Chapter 5

Zena concentrated hard on her work for the next few days. After studying a map of Finistere, she drove along the Crozon peninsula to the Atlantic coast, making for Pen-hir. Just on the edge of Camaret, she caught sight of rows of huge stones, arranged in a sort of square formation on the windy headland and stopped the car abruptly to get out and walk amongst them. Despite the surrounding ugly modern houses and tarmac roads, she again felt that strange pulsating beat of the past as she touched the megaliths one by one, tracing the pattern of five thousand years of history with her fingers. She felt small beside them and yet part of some greater whole they represented, connected by their silent presence to a human chain and a divine source. It was an odd thought for her, unused as she was to religious impulses and this strange sense of discovering a sort of identity in the monuments of this mystical landscape.

She drove on to the point, and walked out past the huge sober monument to those who gave their lives in the war. After taking a couple of photos of striking rock formations, she sat on a ledge and watched the waves pounding a series of rocky humps breaking through the surface of the grey waters. She had not been this far afield with Lucas on their brief trip to Brittany, which made her value her personal discovery all the more, proof that she was here on her own account and determined to expand her horizons.

There were few people about on this blustery January day; the wind whipped through her layers of clothing and screeched in her ears until they were sore. Reluctantly turning her back on the savagery of the sea, which seemed frighteningly alluring, Zena took the car down into the town of Camaret to seek the more peaceful images she needed for her work.

She had a sandwich on a covered veranda in front of one of the brightly painted cafés along the quay, whilst she watched the boats and odd moments of sunshine lighting up the ochre-coloured defensive tower on a long curved jetty that protected the harbour. She could easily imagine the hoards of tourists that must flock here in high season – with a swimming beach just over the wall from where she'd parked, the coastal path snaking invitingly up over the headland and a string of restaurants right along the promenade overlooking it all, it was an ideal spot. That was the kind of place people liked to see on cards, somewhere that fulfilled their aspirations of the perfect holiday, somewhere that combined the magic ingredients of water and sunlight. The latter might require a little artistic licence, but she could feel the special qualities of this place and was itching to convey them.

She watched a small sailing boat making its way into the harbour and wondered where it had come from. Was this a holiday, an adventure in wintry seas for those on board, or had they come from a mile up the coast to do some routine shopping? Thinking of travel always turned her thoughts to Lucas and she could not help, for all her resolutions, wondering where he was. The banana trick had stopped working. The problem was that her mind had been filled for so long with these constant images that the habit was excruciatingly hard to break. She imagined him stepping off this little blue boat and striding towards her along the quay...

A young woman with a baby at the next table leaned over.

'An interesting perspective,' she said with some amusement.

'Sorry?' Zena spoke in English without thinking, surprised by the sudden interruption and unsure that she had understood properly.

The woman laughed and replied in almost accent-less English.

'Your drawing is unusual.'

Zena had been aware of her hand moving methodically over the page of her little sketch book, but her mind had been filled with Lucas and she had hardly known what she was doing. Looking down now, instead of boats in a calm harbour scene, she saw a familiar image: before a line of dark mountains was a hooded female figure. So far Zena's errant pencil had only produced two spilt cups for her to gaze at.

Overcome with embarrassment and an odd rush of self-pity, Zena tried to smile.

'Sorry. I was thinking about something else.'

'Why apologise? You are an artist and I suppose artists draw what they feel as much as what they see.'

'That's true. But I am supposed to be making sketches here. That was the point of coming, but sometimes other things just seem to take over.'

'There is no need to explain.'

The woman looked about thirty. Her most striking

feature was a well-cut bob of chestnut hair, glossy and thick enough to take the style that hung longer at the front than the back, softening a rather bony face.

She shifted the sleepy baby from one knee to the other. 'When this one is asleep, I take the opportunity to think of many things that are not about him.'

'He's lovely.'

Zena stared, fascinated by the little yellowish face under its blue knitted cap. She rarely found herself at close quarters with babies, and felt the instant attraction of this one, all puffed up like a profiterole in his warm winter suit. Large blue eyes suddenly opened wide to meet hers as she leant forward towards him and she had a split second's anxiety that he would screw up his face and yell his disdain for this stranger intruding in his limited vision. But he just crinkled a smile and waved a hand in her direction.

'We've been visiting his Nana. He's tired from all the attention and I always like to come down here after and get my temper back before going home.'

'Is it that bad?'

'It is very bad, but she is my husband's mother and she loves Tomas very much.'

'I'm not surprised,' Zena said with feeling, holding out a finger for the baby to bat with his mitten. 'How old is he?'

'Eleven months. Not a baby much longer! Do you have children?'

It always seemed to come to this very quickly in France. After a couple of weeks, Zena was becoming inured to it.

'Unfortunately not.'

Where had that come from? Why on earth had she made such an admission to someone she didn't know at all, when she'd kept it back from all her nearest and dearest, including Lucas. The point where she'd begun to feel the subject had to be aired between them before she got any older was almost exactly the moment when he announced his imminent departure from her life. Perhaps it wasn't the coincidence she had always imagined. Maybe she had given off subconscious signals and it was the dreaded ticking of her body clock that had woken up his need to leave.

'Are you OK?'

Zena nodded dumbly and tried to recompose her face to hide the distress she felt all over again. The baby's head nodded back into sleep as his mother looked at Zena with concern.

'Hold him a moment. I'll get us some coffee.'

Before she knew it, the woman had gone into the café and she was sitting with a solid mass of baby in her arms. She shifted her arm slightly to support the lolling head and felt his warmth spread through her like a fire.

The coffees were small, black and steaming hot.

'My name is Laure. I can see that you have made friends with Tomas.'

Her eyes were understanding and Zena tried to relax. No-one was judging or criticising.

She began to tell Laure why she had come to Brittany. Lucas popped out in edited highlights as 'someone' she had lived with in England. When it came to describing her present position, alone in the countryside near La Folle, Laure laughed.

'That's where we live. La Folle. My husband works in the mairie, the town hall. And I think your neighbour must be Monique Bougeard.'

Zena's instinctive feeling that she and Laure could be friends made her take a risk.

'Afraid so.'

They both laughed. Laure had been a teacher at the primary school in La Folle before Tomas's birth. Monique had not been an easy parent to deal with, full of criticism and idle complaints. Her children were surprisingly sweet, however, and Laure liked Jean-Yves, who knew her husband well.

'I never know quite how seriously to take him,' Zena said.

'Not at all, I would say,' Laure replied firmly. 'He likes to play the great lover with women, but he is quite harmless, I think you could say. He will not bite you unless you want to be bitten.'

'That's the last thing I want,' Zena said with some feeling. 'I just want to be me for a bit. Without complication.'

'You are right to make your own life. No-one can live only for another person, not even this little one.'

A faint grisly noise heralded Tomas' return to the world, and Laure made ready to take him home. She gave Zena her telephone number and squeezed her shoulder briefly as she left. It came as a welcome touch of friendliness, the first unthreatening physical contact since her brother Stephen had hugged her goodbye.

Zena sat on in the café a while longer, cheered by the encounter with a potential friend. She had never been very good at close friendships. She enjoyed both male and female company for going out, but the party scene held no attractions for her and at the other end of the scale she seemed to shy away from the intimacy of one-to-one contact. She found it hard to talk about her emotions or even to analyse them for herself, which was why relationships with men tended just to fizzle out. It might take a month or two – on one occasion, her record before Lucas, very nearly a year – but it always came to the same thing in the end. It was easy to see why Lucas had been different. Love had animated her from the start, filling her with a rapture that fired her mind and body and energised the connection between them. There was no need to discuss their relationship (the aspect at which she had most conspicuously failed in the past) – it just was.

She instinctively sensed that emotional demands would cut no ice with Lucas, but it suited her too not to feel the pressure of verbalising her feelings. It had never been asked or expected of her as a child, growing up in a family of remarkably self-contained individuals. Stephen was always absorbed in some mechanical toy or, later, computer problems, whilst her father, before his death, had been forever locked away in his study, almost hidden behind a towering mass of books and paper. Her mother had always been peculiar, motivated by bizarre fancies and completely inconsequential to others in conversation. Zena had never voiced her anguish over Lucas in their regular phone conversations, and if her mother thought Zena was thin and pallid when they met, she never raised the subject with her daughter, nor enquired about Lucas' prolonged absence from the scene. Whether she had ever noticed his existence or not was debatable.

With her brother, Zena came closest to expressing her true feelings, but usually in side-swipes of humour or sarcasm rather than emotional effusion. Her anxiety about Stephen's relationship with Hermione came out in similar vein. He had never responded with revelations of his own, but she knew he would always be there to provide a sympathetic ear if she was in need. A lot of the time she welcomed the restraint that kept a lid on feelings that were too powerful to handle.

Most of those people she had kept contact with from school and college drifted away during the preoccupation of the Lucas years. None had really survived the stormy emotional aftermath of those times, when Zena's life had descended into dismal depths of loss and she felt even less ability to connect with the outside world. It had seemed like a bereavement, his sudden and absolute disappearance leaving a gaping hole in her sense of identity and personal assurance. For this last year she'd been almost a recluse, refusing invitations and resisting friendly advances from colleagues who were daily witnesses of her withdrawal. In the end, when even she herself was fed up with this morose introspection, she had thought it easier to get away and try something different in a place where no-one knew her and she would have to buck up her ideas about relating to others and involving herself in life again.

But now she was surely on the road to recovery – new surroundings, new occupation and new people in her life, people who had no knowledge of Lucas and her relation to him, but just took her at her own valuation. It was a good start.

It hadn't long been light when Zena turned up at the square in La Folle ready for her stint on Llewellyn's market stall. The sky was a clear pale blue, with a crescent moon still poised high behind the church. The temperature hovered around freezing. It had taken a while to de-ice the car and then drive slowly along the slippery minor roads towards the town. The street-lights were still on and a single floodlight picked out the spire of the church.

At first she wondered if she'd come at the wrong time. A few stalls were half set out and there were plenty of white vans parked up, but there was little sign of the traders themselves. She recognised Christian and gave him a tentative greeting which was cheerfully returned. He had already erected the stall from the components dumped by Llewellyn at crack of dawn and now handed her a stack of boxes from under his table. Whilst she was still fumbling with them, he dumped a few more on the ground behind her stall, smiled and unleashed a veritable torrent of French. Zena had no idea at all what he'd said, but thought it expedient to smile and agree with whatever it was as brightly as she could. He seemed perfectly satisfied, and ambled off towards the brightly lit bar. The noise as the door swung open solved the mystery of the missing traders. Zena sighed. It looked like she was on her own now.

An hour later she had arranged all Erin's beautiful artefacts on the broad black velvet cloth, propping up the necklace and earring boards as Llewellyn had shown her. She had also sold a couple of items, not without some difficulty over the money, as Llewellyn had neglected to supply her with a float and she had little change in her own purse. The customers had both been French and Zena was finding it a struggle to be convincing as a salesperson in a foreign language. It was fortunate that the quality of Erin's work made up for her own ineptitude. People would want to buy it no matter what blunders of syntax she made.

As she waited for more customers, Zena sat and watched in fascination the extraordinary parade of human interest on offer. The range of physical appearance was matched by the range of clothing each had deemed suitable for this winter morning. A couple of young girls were in T-shirts and hipsters that left a large slice of exposed flesh in between. The older generation were almost invisible behind up-turned collars, hats and headscarves. She could see at once who was happy with their bodies and wore what they liked regardless of rolls of flesh or those who had dressed to try to disguise whatever aspect they were self-conscious about.

She was pleased to see Laure, easily distinguishable by her lovely hair, edging through the crowd with Tomas in a pushchair. After the four traditional kisses of greeting and a game of peek-a-boo with the baby, she was able to fetch some coffee from the bar and then look on in admiration whilst Laure expertly dealt with a couple of elderly French women who were blocking the front of the stall and fingering almost every item, clearly without any intention of buying a thing. When they'd moved on, business was brisk again, with Tomas proving a useful attraction with his beaming smile. Women could not resist stopping to admire him and Laure was quick to engage them in conversation and point out the fine quality of the jewellery. Zena was happy to take the money and wrap the pieces, but she tried to listen and learn from the French approach.

It was certainly a place to meet everybody. She saw the man she had met on the hill at the vegetable stall opposite. He was selecting produce from the vast array available even at this lean time of the year. He exchanged a few words and a smile with the woman who served him at the till and then caught Zena's eye as he turned away.

After a second's hesitation he took a tentative step in her direction but Zena's view was suddenly blocked by the large apparition of Jean-Yves, complete with woven shopping-basket and black beret. He planted a positive flurry of kisses on her cheeks in his delighted surprise at seeing her in this unexpected setting, shook Laure's hand like an old friend and patted Tomas' head good-naturedly. Full of praise for everything, he bought an extravagant silver collar of roses twisting together with their thorns and then, to Zena's horrified embarrassment and Laure's amusement, tried to present it to her as a token of his affection. Flustered and annoyed for being put in such a situation, Zena's mortification was complete when she realised Ian had witnessed the entire episode as he appeared to be studying Christian's scarves with far more attention than they merited. When she eventually got rid of Jean-Yves, having secured an unlikely-to-be-fulfilled promise that Monique would receive the necklace, Ian had gone. Laure was still laughing at Jean-Yves.

'You can tell he's not from round here!'

'What do you mean?'

'He's a southerner, from Marseilles if I remember rightly. Monique's family are from the other side of Brittany and they came here when he bought the printing firm from a local family. That was about fifteen years ago, but he hasn't changed, hasn't...'

She stopped, searching for the right English word.

'Toned down at all?' Zena suggested. 'He certainly seems a lot more expansive than most people round here. More like the sort of Frenchmen you meet in books!'

'It's the sunshine,' Laure said. 'In the south you live outside, but here we stay at home, each in our own house, with our own family. We take our time to welcome people from outside perhaps.'

'It's true people here are not so demonstrative, and they don't volunteer very much information, but everyone's been helpful when I've needed it.'

'I'm glad.' Laure kissed her goodbye as Tomas began to show signs of restlessness. 'It will encourage you to stay here with us for a long time, I hope.'

Zena was sorry to see them go, but they'd made an arrangement to meet for lunch later in the week at the restaurant where Poppy worked.

On her own again, she resumed her observation of the market, amazed at the range of things people bought. Many gathered to admire the cheap plastic offerings of watches on the stall the other side of her, and she watched the owner's money-belt grow fuller and fuller as the day wore on. She began to see that one customer browsing or buying inevitably attracted others like a magnet. Even little old ladies had been jumping up to peer over Jean-Yves' shoulder when he appeared engrossed in her wares.

Now that he was well out of range, Zena felt a moment of affection for Jean-Yves. For all his ridiculous declarations and expansive gestures, he had a good heart and had already been helpful with practical problems at the house. Being married to Monique must be quite an endurance test, if her curt communications with Zena were anything to go by.

By the time that she had packed up all the gear and loaded the boxes into her own car in the rapidly emptying square, Zena felt exhausted but also triumphant. Her icy cold feet and general weariness counted for nothing against the fact that she had taken what seemed to her a good sum of money and was in cheerful anticipation of Erin and Llewellyn's approval. She felt the happiness of someone who is habitually solitary suddenly being a part of something, having a role and function outside of themselves. I wouldn't mind doing this again any time, she thought, as she carried the boxes carefully inside her house.

She lit a fire in the wood-burning stove, made herself tea and toast and curled up on the sofa with a hot-bottle for her feet, glad to rest her legs after the unaccustomed standing about in cold weather. But she couldn't stop smiling to herself and desperately wanted to tell someone about her day. That was the trouble with expanding your horizons and letting a bit of life in – you needed someone to share it all with. She decided to phone Stephen, but put the phone down at once when Hermione answered. A few words with that woman would dissolve her good mood as quickly as sugar in hot tea. She tried her mother's number.

'Who's there?' a voice said sharply.

'It's me, Zena.'

'Do you know what time it is?'

'Nearly six here, so about 5 o'clock with you in London.'

'Six o'clock? Time for a drink, thank God. Did you want something?'

Now here was the perfect invitation: all she had to say was, I just need someone to talk to in a normal friendly way and you're my mother after all – what was so hard or unreasonable about it?

'No,' she said, conditioned still by painful childhood lessons of not making demands or expecting too much. 'Just rang to see how you were getting on.'

'I'm fine. Rather busy just at the moment. May is being particularly stupid about the coq au vin.'

Poor long-suffering May, Zena thought, more the paid companion these days than the childhood friend who came to live with her mother after Zena's father died.

'Any tips?'

'What?'

'Coq au vin. Sniffed out any secret ingredients over there?'

Zena laughed.

'It's more crêpes and sausages in Brittany, and I'm not exactly eating out every night.'

'Pity. Well, mustn't keep you. Bye.'

Sitting alone in renewed silence, Zena reflected that these inconsequential conversations with her mother were getting more and more common. They left her feeling torn between amusement and frustration depending on her own mood. She got up and stretched. Maybe it was better to occupy herself than to rely on other people.

Despite her tiredness and keen anticipation of an early night, she spent the evening making cards, decorating a forest green background with beads, ribbons and scraps of fabric and exotic paper from what she called her resources bag. She loved working with different textures, mingling disparate shapes into a recognisable form, as mini-collages of hills and trees and stones began to emerge.

As she worked she felt calm and happy for the first time since – when? Loving Lucas had made her light-hearted in the beginning. For a year of their relationship she had been bubbling with pleasure and anticipation of their meetings, but after he came to live at the flat, things had gradually changed. Little by little she became fearful and uncertain, her good humour suppressed by the anxiety of failing to please. Each time he left for a trip, her life fell into abeyance. She sat in the painfully quiet house, the unthreatening neutrally coloured environment she'd created, which felt for one person as impersonal as a waiting-room. Which was all it was after all.

It was ironic that over time her fear of turning out to be not what Lucas wanted had made her behave more and more unnaturally. As her fingers worked busily, Zena looked back and realised she had spent much of the time waiting to be found wanting, anticipating his departure to the arms of someone more entertaining, more alive than she had ever been. That must be why she just accepted the quiet ending of their relationship without raging and yelling or chucking one of her very tasteful vases at his head. In a way that she could only now admit, there must have been an element of relief deep inside her, relief that the axe had finally fallen and she need no longer fear the worst but live with the pain of reality. If she had been less uptight, less cowardly all along perhaps things would have been different. She had a source of joy and fun inside her that had been shut off like a tap by her wariness and a determination to do nothing so positive that she could be judged.

Zena went outside to search for tiny slivers of slate in the yard. She wanted to blend their solidity and sharp outline with the softness of some silver-grey cloth she had found at the bottom of the bag. Perhaps with some of the shiny beads for stars. Flipping off the outside light, she looked up at a huge black sky full of bright points of light from all the constellations she had ever learnt in childhood and the thinnest arc of a new moon presiding over them all like a master of ceremonies. This was the first time since then she'd seen a sky so dark and clear over an empty land with no light or noise pollution to spoil the perfection of a cloudless winter night.

For a moment she remembered the excitement of being outside well beyond her bedtime, of feeling her father's hand on her shoulder – look there, Zena, the great bear, and over there Orion and the Hunter's Belt, Cassiopea, the Plough – the names and the sharing of this grand experience making her swell with love beneath the vast starry sky, until she felt at one with the stars in their courses. She felt it again now, that she was part of it all, of the greatest show on earth, and not just some solitary, insignificant thirty-nine year old woman alone in a foreign country in the middle of winter.

Chapter 6

The path to the standing-stones was tortuous to say the least. After trailing up hills and down into muddy stream valleys, Zena ended up on a broad farm track which led through what would have been beautiful mixed woodland at any other time of year, but now remained unrelieved firs under the grey skies of winter. A rough wooden board to the side of the track pointed the way and granted access onto this private land for the purposes of seeing the stones only.

The land dipped abruptly as she left the path and slithered down an earth bank to the glade where the stones had stood silently for thousands of years. The sight of the first one took Zena's breath away. The wide granite shaft rose to a height of about 10 metres, tapering at the top to a rough point. Lucas had told her that the Breton name for these megaliths was menhir or long stone. Close by another, more delicate and graceful, leaned longingly towards it. A narrow stream rushed past a few feet away, the only sound in what Zena felt at once to be a magical place. Last night's sense of contentment seemed to spread over her again in this calm setting where she was truly alone and at peace with the world.

'Wooooooooof!'

Damn, she knew that bark anywhere. It was bloody Fido again!

Zena turned quite crossly, feeling that her privacy was

being invaded by this second encounter.

'Shut up, Fido,' she said harshly. 'Shut up, you stupid dog!'

The dog gave a strangled yelp at this insult and turned his head towards his master in the hope that retribution would somehow be exacted.

Ian smiled tightly at Zena.

'His name's Frodo actually, and you've hurt his feelings by calling him stupid.'

'Truth always hurts, does it?' she said childishly to the dog, who shot her a brief look of contempt before leaping into the stream and wading about, tail aquiver, with noisy slurps at the water.

'We haven't followed you, if that's what you think.' Ian looked worried as if she really might think it. 'It's just a coincidence. We must like the same sort of places.'

'Quiet, peaceful ones, you mean?'

He disregarded her sarcastic tone.

'Ancient places. You can't go far here without running into one. The concentration of Neolithic sites in the area is extraordinary. How did you know about this one? It's not in any of the guidebooks.'

'I'm not a tourist.' Zena was struggling with her desire to be rude and a certain curiosity about this man and what exactly he was doing here. 'I looked at a local map and saw the menhirs marked. I thought they might make a painting.'

'You're an artist?'

Well, why not, she thought. It's what I'm doing here, after all. It's what I'm trying to turn myself into.

'Yes I am.'

'That's interesting...'

'Isn't it? I'll get on with it now, if it's not disturbing you?'

Christ, why was she being so rude? It just seemed sort of natural with him.

He was about to answer when Frodo rushed back up to them. Before Ian could say 'Don't you dare', the dog shook himself all over Zena. She gave a little scream as jets of water splattered her from head to foot.

'I'm sorry,' Ian said, trying not to laugh at the mixture of shock and fury on Zena's face, despite the fact she was wearing old frayed jeans and Wellingtons and was pretty muddy already. He made an abortive attempt to apprehend the culprit, but Frodo squirmed out of reach and rushed off again.

'I expect you trained him to do that,' Zena fumed, 'just to pay me back for shouting at him.'

'You don't know Frodo very well yet or the idea that was possible would never have entered your head.'

She couldn't help smiling.

'He's not exactly Crufts' obedience material, is he?'

'I tell myself it's a language problem. He's Breton through and through. Doesn't even seem to understand my very limited Gaelic. They told me at the rescue centre he was a quick learner, but kept his special subjects very quiet.'

Frodo hurtled back though the glade at that moment, tail up and ears flapping, hell-bent on the chase of nothing whatever as far as Zena could see. He dodged round them, raced up over the bank and disappeared. After a few seconds of cracking undergrowth, silence fell once more.

Ian moved over to the largest stone and laid his hand

on it. It was almost a caress, Zena noticed, as if he was touching a human being. He stepped back when he saw she was watching him and put his hands into the pockets of his jacket.

'How long do you think they've been here?' she asked.

'Five or six thousand years.'

'Do you think people have been coming to visit them all that time?'

'Certainly. It will have been a sacred spot for many generations. Still is for some people.' He held up the metal casing of a night-light candle which had been placed in a crevice on the side of the stone. 'The legend says they're two lovers turned to stone by a priest who found them here. He tried to lead the girl home to her family but she broke away from him and was running back to her man when the priest's curse fell on them both.'

He laughed uneasily, as if unsure about having shared the story, but Zena looked at the two menhirs again and saw the scene vividly in her mind's eye.

'It seems rather an excessive punishment for something quite natural!'

Ian shrugged. 'Slights to the moral authority of the church couldn't be ignored. They were always on guard against the old paganism with its 'natural' forces.'

'So is it modern pagans who still revere this spot?'

She was half-joking.

'Why not? It has a very special atmosphere, don't you think?'

Something stirred in her memory.

'And do you think there's still a connection – a living one, I mean – between the past and now? Something that can be sort of tapped into?'

He looked at her in surprise.

'Yes, I do. I've experienced it myself around the stones sometimes. Why do you ask?'

'Something strange happened to me the first day I arrived here.'

She laughed deprecatingly, a little embarrassed now it came to it.

'Go on.'

'There's a cave in the woods just across the river from the house I'm renting. I thought I saw a young girl dancing among the trees but then she disappeared. I went on up to this cave and heard the oddest noises there, as if I had fallen into another time... it only lasted a couple of seconds. I know it sounds stupid.'

Ian looked at her searchingly.

'Hardly. You're highly receptive to certain atmospheres by the sound of it. Artists, creative people often are.'

'I don't think I am. Nothing like that's ever happened before.'

'It's this place,' he said. 'The earth energies are so strong here that memories – no, more than memories of the past linger. Tiny pockets of ancient reality. I don't know about the cave, but one theory is that the megaliths were constructed with sound vibrations in mind - sort of neolithic accoustics. It might have been some prehistoric echo that you heard. Where did this happen?'

'The hamlet - all two houses of it - is called Kerroch. Do you know the roadside calvaire about five kilometres from La Folle in the Morlaix direction?' He nodded. 'Turn right just before, past the dead end sign, and I'm at the bottom of the hill by the river. You cross on a footbridge and the woods are right there.' She hesitated. 'So you don't find this sort of thing... well, extraordinary.'

'No, I don't think it's extraordinary at all. It's perfectly natural, this connection between man – and woman – and the land, so certain places bring out responses from our unconscious, if we're sensitive in that way.'

'I'm not going mad then?'

He laughed.

'Maybe, but I'd put my money on the land. It's alive, every inch of it...'

At that moment Frodo lunged back down the bank, took a flying leap and planted two paws filthy with yellow mud on Ian's chest, knocking him to the ground. Ian leapt back up at once, cursing and brushing great clods of mud from his clothes, but Zena could see how embarrassed he was and tried to conceal the laughter that had risen spontaneously at the ridiculous sight.

The dog, suddenly calm and quiet, stood watching them both.

'Are you OK?'

'I'm fine.' He rubbed his chest gently. 'Probably just a few broken ribs.'

'It's a variation on dog bites man anyway.'

'Oh, he's certainly original. I'll say that for him. It was what made me get him actually. The others were climbing over each other to jump up and lick me through the wire, show how affectionate and lovable they all were.'

'And Frodo?'

'He sat at the back of the cage staring at the wall. He was shaking too. I noticed that.'

Ian ran a muddy hand over his hair. 'It was a terrible

place. I mean, the people there obviously love the dogs and give their time and all that, but all those animals packed into cages, all desperate to be rescued, to be chosen by someone...' He turned away, so she couldn't see his face. 'It's very sad.'

'But you chose the one who didn't want to go?'

He turned back to face her momentarily.

'I chose the one who wanted to go more than he could express. But it's freedom he was after, I think, not being some foreign idiot's pet.'

'Nonsense.' This picture was more than Zena could bear. 'I'm sure he's deeply grateful.'

'That's why he knocked me over, you mean?'

He was smiling now.

'Of course. He just needs to learn how to express his gratitude and devotion a little less boisterously. Why did you call him Frodo?'

Ian clipped the lead onto Frodo's collar.

'It seemed like a good idea at the time. I wanted something original.'

'You've certainly got it. I'm sorry about the Fido bit.'

'Sometimes I feel he does have some sort of manic Frodo-type quest going on. Maybe his former master is out here somewhere, although from the physical state of him when he was brought into the rescue centre, I hope not. Come on, boy. Enough excitement for one day. We'll leave you in peace now.'

'I've enjoyed talking to you.'

Zena meant it as she smiled and said good bye. She even patted Frodo's now docile head as they passed and received a surprisingly shrewd glance from the sad brown eyes.

Alone in the glade, she sat down on a fall of granite stones and began to sketch, but her mind was still on this latest encounter with Ian. She had been pleasantly surprised by the warmth beneath that rather stiff and polite exterior. His sensitivity towards the stones and Frodo's pitiful history was revealing of interesting depths.

Llewellyn was supposed to be decorating the kitchen, but there was no sign of it when Poppy came down to have her breakfast. She was washing up all the dirty dishes from the night before when Llewellyn crept up behind and gave her a good slap on the backside. Soapy water flooded over the edge of the sink as she swung round in surprise and flushed when she saw his large grinning face at such close proximity.

'Couldn't resist it, sweetheart. Luscious big bum like that just asking for a smack, I'd have said.'

He was only inches from her, running the tip of a very red tongue round his bearded lips as if in preparation for a further assault. She felt her heart skip wildly as Erin came into the room and stepped past them to put the kettle on, without appearing to notice any tension in the air. Llewellyn moved away casually and began a conversation about paint colour with his sister, whilst Poppy silently finished the washing up and ran up to her room. Here she closed the door and then leant against it, breathing heavily. What had he meant by that? It was the first time he'd shown any physical interest in her – could it be a sign of what was to come?

The influence of the landscape was beginning to

penetrate the under-used instinctive right side of Zena's brain. She found herself drawing jagged outlines of granite ridges, lone menhirs rising from the gorsy scrub and sunken tracks inviting passage between their tree-lined banks. She had sent off a batch of more conventional subjects to the agent and now felt free to indulge her own inclinations while she waited for a response. The discipline of drawing every afternoon and often into the long dark evenings was paying dividends in her technique and confidence.

As she worked, Zena felt comfortable and relaxed. She didn't know what was going to happen in six months time when this Breton interlude was over and at the moment that thought did not alarm her as it would have done a few weeks earlier. Worrying about what would happen after, before she'd even begun the adventure, had been typical of her state of mind over the last year but things were definitely changing.

She wondered how the people who were renting her flat were getting on in their search for a house in the countryside around Bath. They were down-sizing from London. How long before they turned up over here in search of even cheaper property, and the British who had colonised so many corners of France moved on to... where? Poland? Romania? She could almost hear Lucas' voice talking about the irony of today's shifting populations.

What her next move would be, Zena had no idea. She might even think about giving up the flat in Bath, which had been her security for so many years. It had made her too secure. It was too easy to run and hide, to hole up and keep other people out. It had been a sort of secret place, not a meeting place. In all the time she had shared it with Lucas they had never once had friends in for a drink or a meal. Those kinds of meetings – with her colleagues or his editor – had taken place outside of their home environment. As a result the flat had become not only a sanctuary but a sort of shrine to their dead relationship after he had left. It was true that she had parcelled up his few remaining things and stuffed them in the minute loft space, but that was not to banish his presence – if she'd felt she could bear to see them without breaking down, the books, scarf and odd item of clothing would still be there on display to preserve the memory of what had been. She had almost drowned the scarf in tears initially as she clutched it in bed alone those first few terrible nights, and had to dry it out on the radiator in the mornings. It had taken a couple of months to gather the strength to put the things away out of sight to give herself a better chance of living normally again and arriving for work without a ravaged face and the temper of exhaustion.

Zena could smile at herself over that now. It was still painful to think of it, but she could now almost face the inevitable and maybe let go altogether in time if she could just continue gently here in this unthreatening environment. Strange that a territory so wild and barren could be so comforting.

Ian's mind was restless since his meeting with Zena. He gave up trying to concentrate on writing and went outside to chop a bit of wood and mend a fence panel that had splintered when Frodo hurled himself at it for no apparent reason other than that it was there. All the time he wielded the axe and the hammer, Ian was going back over their conversation, wondering if he had given too much away, talked too freely to this woman he hardly knew. It was not like him to be so forthcoming, but the novel experience of finding someone who seemed interested in discussing the things that fascinated him had loosened his tongue.

It was true that he believed in magic, in cycles of time that retained some past energy in the fabric of the present — hell, he even believed in the spirits of the forest, though he had had the sense to keep that particular nugget of information to himself. On the rare occasion in the past when he ventured what people liked to dismissively call 'alternative' views, his colleagues would react with disbelief that someone from a scientific background could countenance such irrational opinions. 'Stick to the facts' was an especially infuriating favourite phrase bandied about by those he suspected had never had a deep emotional, much less spiritual experience in their lives. He himself had always retained an almost childlike connection with his surroundings, untarnished by the scientific knowledge he came to possess in the course of his career. No amount of analysis and rational explanation could nail the natural world down nor divest it of its power and wonder for him. Yes, he understood the principles of woodland management and water purification, but this could never remove the mystery of the living spirit of the forest or the moon-fed emotional power of the ocean.

The dichotomy between his inner life and outer professional role had been an increasing strain over the last couple of years, and only this hard-won sabbatical had given him the chance he needed to explore the possibilities of bringing the former out into the open, to live according to his beliefs. The only problem was, it seemed to make going back look more and more impossible.

Zena was looking forward to her lunch with Laure, but she decided to call on Erin first. She was pleased with the cards she'd made and decided to take a bold step whilst this positive mood lasted.

It was a bitingly cold day and the wind swept through La Folle like a nasty rumour. She huddled in her thick coat on the doorstep for what seemed an age before Erin came, but they sat down together at the little table with its purple cloth as naturally as old friends bound by shared experiences. Zena asked about the fair, which had apparently led to a bunch of new commissions, and Erin thanked Zena for her handling of the market stall.

'I wanted to ask you something about that.'

Now the moment had come, Zena felt nervous and tongue-tied.

Erin spoke first.

'I'd love you to do it again any time, but we can't afford to pay someone regularly. I'm sorry.'

'No, it's not that. Though I'll do it if you're stuck anyway.' Deep breath. 'I wondered if you'd consider selling some of my cards on the stall. For a percentage, of course,' she added quickly.

Erin leaned back in her chair, her gaze never leaving Zena's face.

'Have you got any to show me?'

Zena fumbled in her bag, scattering the cards over the

worn carpet.

'Wow!' Erin had picked up one of the menhirs. 'Yes,' she said, before looking at any of the others. 'Definitely yes. They're brilliant. Cards over here are usually so trashy, these should do well. How many have you got?'

'Only ten, to see if they work or not. They're quite labour intensive, but I was thinking of getting some black and white outline drawings of this sort of thing printed properly. I thought 2.5 euros for the collages? And I'd give you 40 cents of that.'

Erin smiled.

'It's a deal, and you can ignore Llewellyn when he asks for more. Leave these with me and I'll do a little sign for them before Thursday.'

Zena stood up.

'Thanks. Well, I'd better be going.'

'Didn't you want a reading?'

Of course she did, that had been her motive for coming as much as showing Erin her own cards. She wouldn't have asked, but with the opportunity offered she could accept without needing that courage.

'I'm meeting someone for lunch, but... why not?'

She felt ready for it this second time, unafraid and ready to get to grips with whatever message the cards might have for her. After the positive steps she had been taking lately, she now felt in need of direction, some pointers to what she should take as a destination. Something of substance to put in place of Lucas, a goal. She felt a strange core of confidence that this sprite-like figure could help her.

'Three cards,' Erin said, as she shuffled the deck.

Not just one. That felt like a promotion to Zena, a

reward for all her efforts to move on and get her life in some sort of order. She sat up a little straighter and tried to keep a smug smile from her lips.

'First card – what's passing.' Erin laid the card face down on the table.

'Second card – what's with you now.'

Zena gulped. Her confidence was dwindling in the face of these rectangles of cardboard. And that's all they are, she tried to tell herself. So what the bloody hell are you here for then? That was her rational self, being snotty. She was starting to feel really nervous as the third card went down.

'What's approaching.'

That was the one! That was what she needed to know. The other two didn't matter. She wanted to turn over that third card and see a picture of Lucas, dark hair all over the place, arms outstretched...

Erin was reaching for the first one.

'The Four of Pentacles.'

'Is that bad?'

'Zena, tarot's not a school report. The card can mean lots of different things, it depends what's relevant to you now. Pentacles are related to down-to-earth stuff usually – money, work, family, property. I'd say this card means you've a certain amount of financial and material security...'

'But you said it's what's passing. Am I...'?

'Wait,' Erin said firmly. 'Don't jump at everything! It looks to me as if maybe you've been clinging on to this type of security too carefully and it might be time to loosen up a bit.'

'That's exactly what I was thinking earlier! It's incredible!'

A brief spasm of weariness passed over Erin's little face.

'I'm not a mind-reader, Zena. I don't want to be. It's down to the cards you attract from your energies, my intuition and experience with reading – that's all.'

'Sorry. Sorry, I'll be quiet.'

Erin grinned.

'We need to look at the other cards, anyway, and see how they relate to each other. OK. Second card.'

There was no need to name it.

Oh God, not again. Zena wanted to knock the table over and run out into the street screaming. Only an effort of will kept her in her seat, but she closed her eyes tightly against the sight of those five gold cups. It must be some sort of trick. Far from being on her side, far from being an innocent, sensitive little fairy person, Erin was trying to drive her mad in calculated stages, like some Svengali in an old black and white movie.

She felt a hand on her arm.

'Zena, it's OK. Come on, think about it. This relationship has been such a big thing for you, how could you expect it to disappear in a puff of smoke? You are doing a lot of new stuff now and getting things together, but you can't clear your head like a kitchen cupboard and just chuck everything in the bin.'

'But I'm trying!' The tears of self-pity were welling up now to Zena's horror. 'I've stopped thinking about him all the time, stopped expecting him to come back, stopped hoping...'

Erin leaned forward, interrupting her.

'Have you really? Isn't there still some part of you that looks for him round every corner? Every time the phone rings?'

The questioning was gentle and kindly. It prevented Zena from lying in self-defence. Perhaps dissembling wasn't the way to protect herself after all.

'Yes.' She nodded. 'That's still true. But for at least 5% of the time, he doesn't exist for me anymore.'

Erin laughed and eyed the third card.

'Perhaps we should focus on the future. This will tell you what's coming towards you.'

Probably a great big truck, Zena said to herself, as she closed her eyes again.

There was a pause.

'The King of Cups.'

Zena's eyelids shot open as she picked up the hesitation in Erin's voice.

'What's that?'

She peered at the card. Someone in a silly hat sitting on a throne which seemed to be floating in the sea. Another of those hated golden cups was in his hand. There was a kind of vacant look on his face as if he didn't realise where he was or what was happening.

'Hope someone calls the lifeguard.'

Erin gave her a puzzled look.

'He's sort of drifting away out to sea.' Zena was aware that she'd got it all wrong somehow and shut up before her nervous frivolity put an end to Erin's reading.

'The Kings usually represent a person, a man.'

Zena sat forward and began to take notice.

'What sort of man?' Her excitement was mounting again despite her attempts to suppress all signs of it.

'A man of great feeling and sensitivity, perhaps creative.'

Zena's hand was over her heart at once.

'Is it Lucas? Is he coming back, do you think?'

There was a long silence as Erin gazed at the cards, her green eyes unfocused. The long wispy tendrils hung down from her short black hair, enhancing the waiflike appearance that made Zena feel like an elephant in comparison.

Erin gave a little shrug at last.

'I don't know,' she said. 'Tell me a bit more about Lucas.'

This was Zena's special subject. She was used to going over and over a description in her head, pretending she was giving a thumbnail sketch to someone else, impressing them with his perfection. She'd start with his physical presence - slim, dark, slightly tousled look, lean in the face, intelligent eyes but an air of reserve. It was true he gave little away and rarely expressed strong feelings. Even in bed she felt something of him withheld from her, a deliberate barrier behind which he maintained his separateness. That was probably his own form of security and she'd respected it rather than trying to hammer the wall down. If he needed that small area of privacy inside his head, who was she to question it? At the same time, she'd often wished he didn't feel it necessary with her.

She couldn't put this into words for Erin. It was too intimate, a piece of secret knowledge about Lucas she felt the need to cling onto.

'He's quite a private person,' she said cautiously. 'Very clever, knows about everything although you don't realise that at once. He sort of reveals it as you get to know him. He has a way of focusing on you and listening. Yes, he's a good listener.'

She felt pleased to have given a positive picture of Lucas.

Erin said nothing.

'Do you think it's him?' Zena said eventually, her mouth dry with the fear of longing.

'There's definitely something there,' Erin said finally. 'but it feels new to me. I have the sense it's something you don't know about.'

Zena leaned forward anxiously to study the picture again.

'But surely, it would be like new, in a way, if he came back now?'

Zena despised the pleading tone in her own voice, but Erin didn't seem to notice her words at all. She rocked gently in her seat, one finger tapping lightly on the last card.

She looked at Zena.

'Keep aware,' she said. 'Don't…'

'Don't what?'

Erin collected the cards up carefully and wrapped them in a silk square.

'Don't make up your mind too quickly. Leave room for other things, Zena. That's all.'

'You don't think he'll ever come back, do you?' Zena asked eventually, trying to keep her voice neutral.

Erin smiled and went over to the door to signal that their time was up.

'Do you?' she said, but Zena sensed no answer was expected as she sidled out, trying not to knock a thin red vase from its perch with her bag or any bit of protruding anatomy. Erin's tiny figure slipped through the gap with ease and followed her to the door.

Zena was a few minutes late, but Laure and the baby were already well-established in the pretty restaurant. Although the great swathes of vines and blooms around the walls were certainly plastic, there was a bright little pot of early daffodils on their table. Tomas sat in his high-chair grinning gummily and waving a spoon as if he was conducting a particularly frenetic orchestra.

Laure's hair gleamed in the rather dim light. She greeted Zena warmly, looking as relaxed as ever, and Zena wondered if this ease of manner was something you had to be born with, a genetic gift that she was wasting her time hankering after. She was nearly ten years older than Laure, but felt gawky and incomplete beside her.

Poppy herself peered out from the kitchens and then came over to take their order. Whatever it was that had been bothering her still cast a shadow over her plump face. She didn't know Laure, and Zena felt her own confidence boosted by the act of introducing people to each other only three weeks after arriving in the area herself. However, she didn't have much follow-up information when Poppy had gone.

'She lodges with Erin and Llewellyn, the ones with the stall. I don't really know anything about her except she's unhappy about something and always looks as if she's just been crying.'

'It must be a man,' Laure said.

'Probably. Perhaps she's hankering after the chef here. Apparently he's teaching her to make chocolate.'

'Now that is a useful skill!'

They both laughed and chatted easily about this mutual love until their food arrived.

Zena couldn't help thinking what a nice life Laure must have, at home with a beautiful baby, husband returning from work at the end of each day, a perfect family unit...

'Do you want to have children?' Laure was asking in that very direct French way that Zena both feared and admired.

'It might be a bit late, whether I want to or not.'

'Nonsense. How old are you? 36? 37? There's plenty of time these days for late families.'

Zena didn't see any need to be specific about her age. After all, she wasn't forty yet. Not quite.

'I know. But I wanted to do it as you've done. I thought it would all just happen for me – marriage, children – in some mysterious natural way. The family all growing together, that sort of thing. But it didn't. Then I met the man I told you about and thought that although I'd been late, I was finally catching up with everyone, all my contemporaries who were married and producing the required number of children. I used to think that then life would begin. Now I'm here on my own, envying you like some old maid.'

Laure was surprised. 'Why would you envy me?'

'Your life is sorted out in a way mine isn't. You know what you're going to be doing and who with for years to come.'

Laure laughed.

'It does not sound so appealing, put in that way. And life is never so simple. It can be a sort of ending, giving up your independence to settle down with one man. And a child is another restriction, of course.'

'Is that what you felt?' Zena was surprised, but Laure remained totally matter-of-fact.

'Certainly. Oh, I loved Thierry and of course I love Tomas now, but it has changed my course in life and I wonder what would have been different if I had not married. Marriage is not the end of wanting, Zena.'

'No, I know that. It just seems that the main issue is sort of settled.'

'But you have to learn how to make that 'main issue' work. It's not easy to live with another human being day after day, to be cleaning and washing when you'd rather be in a working environment with other adults.' Laure shrugged. 'Sometimes I think I'd prefer that. We all need some personal freedom. Don't look so anxious, Zena. I am not about to run away and leave Tomas and Thierry. But no marriage is so perfect that it cuts out everything else. At first, certainly, but after five years or ten years, no man will remain the perfect god who rules your life.'

Poppy came over to take their plates.

'I've made chocolate tart for dessert — would you like that?'

Zena and Laure looked at each other.

'I think I could manage a small piece,' Zena said with a straight face.

The great god who rules my life, she thought as they ate and Laure called her congratulations over to Poppy, who blushed with pleasure. Was that a fair description of her attitude to Lucas? Did she still think him perfect (except for his rather major lapse of behaviour in leaving her)? Another thought came in behind the first so swiftly that Zena was taken unawares. Did I ever really know him that well at all?

Chapter 7

When Zena woke up the next day, the atmosphere felt ominously quiet and heavy. She opened the bedroom curtains to a white world, every contour of tree and meadow blurred by a thick mounting of snow. She ran downstairs, put on wellingtons and a coat over her nightie and went out into the yard.

The virgin spread gleamed across the earth like the beginning of new life. She ran here and there, crunching happily into the bright crystal layer. By the time she'd finished, it looked as if a demented herd of cattle had done a war-dance, but she collapsed onto a kitchen chair, flushed with the childish excitement, grinning her pleasure and an unfamiliar sense of exhilaration.

A knock on the door made her start guiltily, as if someone might be coming to complain about her mad cavorting. The snow had started to fall again heavily as she opened the door to Jean-Yves with the radiance of this vitality still all over her face. She instantly switched off the enthusiasm and heavy breathing when she saw the response in his eyes.

'Zelda! How beautiful you look!'

He on the other hand looked rather ridiculous in an enormous fur-hat with ear-flaps.

'Thank you. What on earth are you doing here at this time? Aren't you going to work?'

'My dear, my first thought at this awful time is for you. I must save you!'

'Why, what's happened?' She peered nervously past him for some lurking calamity.

Jean-Yves flapped his gloved hand skywards as the thick flakes began to come down even faster, jostling each other in their eagerness to meld into the depth.

'The snow, of course! You will not be able to get out. I do not think your little car can manage such a hill.'

Zena hadn't thought of that, but after all she had enough food and there was no absolute need to go out except to enjoy a walk in the snow later on perhaps.

'It's fine. I don't have to go anywhere.'

'But you can not stay here all alone!'

He really did look concerned.

'Why not?'

'If you have a fall, who will be there to 'elp you?'

'But that could happen any time. I'm OK, honestly.'

'What about your fire – you will be very cold!'

'There're plenty of logs in the wood-store, I ...'

'No, no,' he said firmly, 'you must go inside and Jean-Yves will bring the wood.'

He plunged off, scarf ends flying.

She sighed and went in to put the kettle on, trying to think of polite ways to get rid of her visitor. In fact it took a whole pot of coffee to reassure him that she would survive and a hard-won agreement that he should call in later to make sure no catastrophe had befallen her. He reacted with horror to her idea of going for a walk and extracted a promise that she would not stray into the woods but keep to the main paths if she was determined to be so foolish as to leave the ring of warmth around the stove. She had to endure a great bear-hug, and shook him off quickly, feeling slightly vulnerable about having on only a nightie beneath the thickness of the coat. He finally stamped off up the hill and Zena could barely make out his bulky figure through a storm of snow as he turned for a final wave and nearly fell over.

She was reading by the fire an hour later when there was another knock at the door. It looked like a blizzard outside and she felt slightly apprehensive about opening the door. To her surprise, she saw Ian standing on the step, hunched into his coat and well on his way to becoming a snowman.

'Come in!' She waited while he stamped and shook off the worst of the snow, then took his wet coat and gave him a seat by the fire.

'The hill's like ice! I didn't risk bringing the car down, but the top road's not too bad, so if there's anything you want or anywhere you have to go, I thought maybe I could help.'

'That's extraordinarily nice of you!'

Zena meant it. It seemed a lot of trouble to take for a casual acquaintance.

'I do have an ulterior motive, to be honest. Two, in fact. I was intending to come and see you anyway.'

He smiled at her over the rim of the steaming coffee cup she'd handed him. She felt the smallest twinge of disappointment.

'What can I do for you?' She tried to sound bright and positive.

'The first thing is more the other way round. I've found out something about your little girl and the Forest of Souls.'

Zena leaned forward with interest.

'The Forest of Souls? What's that?'

'It's a sort of ghost story, I suppose. A local legend, although it only dates back to the mid 19th century.'

Zena settled down like a child waiting for a bed-time story.

'I'm sitting comfortably,' she said, 'now tell me.'

Ian laughed.

'Let's hope it doesn't send you to sleep! A little girl, Marie Pouliquen, disappeared whilst playing in the forest here behind your house. She came home a day later, saying she'd been playing with the spirits of the forest, who were very kind to her.'

'She was...' Zena hesitated, '...unharmed?'

'Yes, no question of anything like that. She was fine. Always a dreamy child, apparently, and the rational explanation was that there were travellers of some sort about who took her in for a bit but then sent her home.'

'Did she describe these spirits? Like people, I mean.'

Ian shook his head.

'No. But she said they sang for her. When the wind was strong she used to say it was them calling her. Her parents stopped her from returning to the forest and everyone shunned the place after that.'

Somehow Zena knew there was more to it than that.

'What happened to Marie?'

He frowned.

'It's a sad story. She went into a sort of decline. Kept seeing visions and claiming she could hear the souls of the forest. Doctors couldn't find anything wrong with her, so put it down to a sort of nervous hysteria. She died a few weeks later.' He stopped and looked worriedly at Zena. 'Ever since then there have been sightings of her ghost in the forest.'

She looked at him, round-eyed.

'You mean I saw a ghost?'

He shrugged.

'I'm just telling you the story. But they do say that if you see Marie's ghost it means you belong here and are bound to this land forever.'

Zena laughed nervously.

'I'm not sure how to take this. The child I saw seemed so happy and carefree, a real spirit of the forest herself. I've seen more nervous hysteria in Tesco on a Saturday morning. But what she said about the spirits singing to her, that made me think of the cave and what I heard there, as if it was singing to me.'

'A siren song. A way to bind you.'

His tone was light, but serious. They looked at each other for a moment before Zena's eyes slid away.

'There's a very powerful atmosphere around here,' she said.

'It's a wild land, still full of magic and mystery. By some quirk it hasn't lost that, despite the farming and occasional hideous development. The magic remains.'

'Do you believe in magic?'

He nodded.

'Certainly. Go out on the hills here and you can feel the energies, the power in the earth and the air.'

'I know what you mean,' she said thoughtfully. 'I've felt it, but I hadn't thought of it as magic, like spells and all that kind of thing.'

'They're connected though. The energies are there and can be harnessed if you have the power of intention within yourself. It's a sort of alignment, becoming part of the flow.'

'And then you can have whatever you want?'

She was teasing him, gently, but he didn't mind, nor feel the need to become defensive.

'I believe we can make our own destinies, yes. The human will is an extraordinarily powerful instrument, but it takes a lot more determination and focus than most of us have on a regular basis.'

'Once everyday life has finished with us! But being at one with what's around you, I can see that. You can't be here long without coming up against the elements, especially the earth, and water that seems almost a part of it.'

She spoke very earnestly and he felt the desire to tease her in turn.

'Water's the element of feelings. The Celtic soul needs rain to feed on and give it expression!'

She laughed.

'Even the rain - it all makes you feel alive in a different sort of way.'

His heart jumped as she said this. He'd never imagined talking about such things with anyone. Something made him brave.

'Don't forget the fifth element.'

'The fifth?'

'Spirit. If ever there was a place filled with the spirit of the universe, this is it.'

She looked at him with sudden understanding.

'Is that why you're here?'

It was too strong a bond for him to try to forge at this moment. His mind and heart were in a whirl. He pretended to take it lightly.

'You mean not just for the cheap housing like most of

our compatriots? No, I actually came for the place's own sake!' He grinned. 'Which brings me to my request. It may not be your sort of thing at all, so just say if you think it's a terrible idea.'

He smiled at her again. Less comfortably than a few minutes before.

There was a little silence.

'I will,' she said. 'Of course.'

'Good,' he said, as if something was settled.

'I will say if I think it's a terrible idea when you tell me what it is.'

He put his cup down in some confusion.

'Sorry. I need some illustrations for an article I'm writing and I wondered if you'd be interested. I was going to send photos back to England and then get a friend to make some sketches, but with you being here on the spot and knowing the look of the land, it just seemed like such a good idea...'

'What's it about, the article?'

'Sacred sites, pagan sacred sites, that is, in this area.'

'So this is your interest here — the megalithic monuments? Are you an archaeologist or something?'

'More of a something. I'm a lecturer in environmental science but with a sabbatical for good behaviour, so it's a chance to pursue my own interests for a change.'

'Like the menhirs?'

'Exactly, and the dolmen where we first met, if you remember.'

'I remember. Where's Frodo?'

'I left him in the car.'

'I'm surprised he hasn't forced his way out yet and slithered down to join us.'

Ian laughed.

'There's still time. The article is just a trial really. I'm planning to do a book called Stone Stories, putting the sites in the context of their landscape and legends. I've just been waiting for a solid bit of time over here to get into it properly.'

'Is your wife over with you?'

Where did that come from? Zena felt embarrassed as soon as she saw Ian's discomfort.

'No, it's a bit cold for her at this time of year. Doing some work on the cottage is supposed to be my main project.'

'But it's too tempting to get out and walk here, don't you find? I could be doing a lot more painting if I wasn't drawn out onto the hills most days.'

She liked the way he was looking at her with a sudden quickening of interest.

'Yes, it's exactly like that for me,' Ian said.

They shared a moment of happy silence.

'You may not like my style, of course,' she said finally, thinking that a joint project might be quite enjoyable.

'You may not like mine,' Ian replied. 'We'll just have to see.'

Poppy was in her room. It was her day off, and after slithering up icy pavements to the little self-service shop for some candles, she was ensconced on the floor on a large beaded cushion, concentrating for all she was worth. The ingredients were laid out before her on a silk cloth and she had an open book precariously balanced on one knee. It was the likeness to cookery that had encouraged her to try this out. She had to do something.

She could cope with cooking and feel some achievement in the end result, but this constant simmering of emotions with no outlet was really getting her down. There couldn't be any harm in trying this. The book had come from Erin's own collection on a painted wooden bookshelf on the landing. Poppy had locked her door, so no-one could surprise her, although the knock on that door she so often hoped for had never come yet.

She went through the list again. Two candles, one red, one white in pottery holders, a cheap silver ring with a heart symbol, an apple, red ribbon, a lump of modelling clay, a little pot of earth, matches and an incense cone of ylang-ylang fragrance. She was ready. All she had to do was start. Her legs were aching already from sitting in this uncomfortable position, but she had placed a ring of tea-lights in a circle around her, for protection or something, and any movement was likely to dislodge one of these and ruin the whole thing. She lit the two candles in front of her and the incense cone, releasing a cloud of pungent smoke that made her eyes water. Trying to ignore the discomfort, she reached for the clay, and began to mould it rhythmically like dough in her hands whilst gazing at the flames, her lips moving in a silent incantation. From time to time, when her memory failed, she gave a darting glance at the book beside her. Then she shaped the soft dough into two rough, ill-proportioned figures and pressed their hands together so they were linked. She wound the ribbon round them and placed them between the two candles, with the ring beside them. Now she had to concentrate really hard and bring the full power of her most fervent wish to this ritual. She squeezed up her face and spoke the words internally, fearing that someone in the house might hear. Only one thing now remained. She must cut open the apple, extract the pips and plant them in the earth. She looked around for the knife. Had she remembered to bring it up from the kitchen?

She longed to get up and stretch her legs and she was beginning to feel distinctly hungry. It was hard to concentrate, to maintain the focus the book said was required. There was no sign of the knife, and when she lifted the pot to look for it, all the earth trickled out of the hole in the bottom which she'd so carefully blocked with a finger earlier. Putting the pot down again, she knocked over the white candle and at once the smell of singed fabric filled the small room. She leapt up, wincing at an excruciating spasm of cramp, and stamped on the burning cloth. The other candle went out very suddenly in the breeze, and Poppy sank down on her bed disconsolately, wondering if this sloppy ending would negate the whole thing.

She ate the apple and felt marginally better. If this didn't work, she could always give the onion spell a go. All you had to do was scratch the loved one's name on an onion bulb and plant it in a pot, then put it somewhere facing where the person lived. That bit wouldn't be too difficult at all.

Zena was thinking about Ian and how his face lit up from ordinary to something rather special when he was talking about legends and magic. His feeling for the land touched her, the way he spoke about it as if it was a person of instinct and sensibility.

It was obviously a passion for him, and he'd come to

Brittany to live it, rather than for the negative reason of escape as she had done. She always secretly admired the expression of strong feelings - something she herself had tried to avoid from childhood, where such things were not encouraged – and worried that it might denote a depth of character she lacked.

That was something she had sometimes wondered about with Lucas, whether he didn't view the subjects of his photographs and his interviewees a trifle too coolly. They were part of his purpose, but not a focus of commitment. When she'd once asked him if he'd want to be part of their cause if Russia ever had new designs on eastern Europe, he'd dismissed it as a romantic question which showed little grasp of the political situation. They'd both laughed then and gone on to something else, but she'd have liked a hypothetical answer, even so.

She thought again of Ian's self-conscious laugh after telling the story of lovers turned to stone, as if he feared he'd foolishly betrayed his vulnerability. She wondered for a moment about his wife and what their marriage was like, but was soon interrupted by the return of Jean-Yves, jealously demanding to know who had been down here bothering her in his absence.

'I'll be getting off now. Got loads to do.'

Llewellyn heaved himself up out of bed and started getting dressed, while Dominique still lay with a cigarette in her hand, moaning about her colleagues at work and how unfair almost every other aspect of her miserable life was. God, he was getting sick enough anyway of coming here on the odd morning she was not at the office and her husband was far away, but today was the last straw. He'd already had to put up with being bored witless by Erin's little chats about money and responsibility recently: he really did not want to listen to any more female whinging.

'You will stay for coffee, yes?'

She got up and pulled on a tatty polyester wrap he particularly loathed.

'No, darling, I've got to make a move.' Five more minutes and he'd feel like strangling her. And it wasn't as if she was such a good lay after all, very much one of his reserve list when nothing better was on offer. But maybe there was something needing his attention closer to home. He'd been thinking about Poppy a bit lately, especially since that little slap this morning when her big face had flushed as red as a tomato. A nice ripe, juicy tomato that no-one had yet bothered to pick...

Dominique was trying to get between him and the door, hands with chipped nail-varnish pressing playfully on his chest. She was a good foot shorter than he was. He decided it was time to concentrate on larger women.

'I'll be here on Friday,' she said, looking up coyly through her lashes.

I won't, he thought as he pushed her aside almost roughly and went out through the back door. He always kept his instinct for rough stuff close enough to the line of playfulness for him to protest innocence and feign offence at any hint of complaint.

There shouldn't be any worries of that sort with Poppy. She'd enjoyed the little game that morning, he was sure. She was probably up there in her room every night just longing for him to burst in and rip her clothes off. He'd have to try it some time. Not straight away though. It wouldn't hurt to keep her guessing for a bit. And if Poppy didn't work out, there was always Zena. Llewellyn really rather fancied her, despite her age. At least she was a woman, and probably one with a lot of experience. It might be rather fun to find out what was behind that reserved exterior.

Ian's car slithered up the long gentle slope of the track to the cottage. He'd stacked the stove up with logs before leaving, and a welcome plume of smoke from the chimney greeted him. Frodo fretted and fussed around in the back of the car, hating the confinement as he did any form of constriction. Ian understood that only too well. For the last few years he had felt trapped in his own life, hopelessly entangled in an empty marriage, treading water at work with only early retirement to look forward to. The thought of returning to the suburbs of Birmingham, with just the occasional precious walk in the Peak District snatched from his humdrum routine, was depressing in the extreme.

What made him alive was this place, the lines of the hills that opened their histories to him, the density of woodland around the cottage and the vast unpopulated spaces all around. Just being on his own had done a lot of good over the last few weeks, but he'd enjoyed being with Zena, feeling his natural reticence thawing in front of her fire and the interest she'd shown in what he was doing. And he'd loved her work. The cards and sketches she'd shown him were full of life and energy. They conjured up places he knew in much more than just their physical detail. He marvelled at how she could make a single line convey a sense of movement and atmosphere. The simplicity of her approach was also just what he wanted – a delicacy of shading that made the outlines alive and breathing. He was rather alarmed at how much he was looking forward to working with her.

He opened the post box by the gate and sighed as his wife's familiar hand-writing glared up at him from the top of the pile of circulars and free magazines. At this moment, he really didn't want a reminder of that other half-life over there across the Channel, with its routine tediousness and banal exchanges over the meal table.

Frodo was running about in the snow like a being possessed, tongue lolling and saliva dripping from his open mouth. Was he chasing or running away, Ian wondered? Was he happy to be free to bound about as he pleased? If only I was, he thought sadly, and took his letter inside.

It was worse than he'd imagined. Leah was intending to come out for a visit as soon as the weather improved. Maybe Easter, if he was unlucky. She dropped it in casually between complaints about the quality of a repair to her best shoes (Ian spared a thought for the poor cobbler) and descriptions of curtain material she was planning to inflict on the spare bedroom. He wondered idly what the latest colour scheme recommended in My Own Beautiful Home magazine might be – lilac with orange highlights, perhaps? Anything was better than the lime green with coconut (was that really a recognised colour these days?) accessories that now adorned the bathroom.

He looked around at the natural fabric of his cottage, rough schist walls, the granite fireplace with its oak lintel, a floor made from slate dug out of the hillside not far away. It was simple and genuine. Those were the qualities he responded to best, in his environment, in people, in himself even. And he thought he could see them very clearly in Zena too.

It was icy cold in the workshop. Erin's mittened fingers could hardly accommodate the small movements necessary for the woven bracelet she was making, but she could not afford to waste money by putting the electric heater on. Sales from the market stall were well down at this time of year and they could expect little more than to cover their costs with the bad weather of February looming. She didn't really need to be out here producing yet more stock, but the question in her mind was whether they could live off just her commissions, the intermittent tarot readings and Poppy's rent for a couple of months. Llewellyn contributed nothing in the way of finance, although he had made quite a good job of decorating the kitchen, which had been in a very bad state before. She was sure he could find work painting or doing small repairs around the town if he tried. The cost of feeding his enormous appetite was quite a drain on their meagre resources, even before his increasingly regular visits to the bar. Another twenty euros had disappeared from her tarot donations box yesterday and she did not believe for one moment her brother's casual suggestion that Poppy was 'borrowing' from her.

This was certainly the lowest time since they'd come to Brittany, and, although it was not in Erin's nature to worry about things, she'd felt a growing uneasiness in the house lately. There was a definite atmosphere building, and she hoped she was wrong about the cause of it. She wasn't ready to move on yet and had been given no signs that she should do so. She would simply have to trust in the universe to provide as it had always done, and listen to the promptings of her inner guides.

When she managed to get rid of Jean-Yves at last, Zena put on her boots and went out, crossing the slippery bridge over the river and making her way up through the deep snow into the woods again. Hearing Marie's story had made her curious to return and make another connection with the place.

Not knowing what to do or expect, she stood awkwardly beneath the trees in a dome of complete silence, as if even the birds were quietened by the thick fall of brilliant snow. There was no sign of a child, no dance or song, and she began to feel foolish and fanciful, lingering here in severe weather hoping to meet a spirit, for want of a better word. It was all too real, too normal – a wintry forest, nothing more.

After a while, she closed her eyes and almost immediately began to sense something outside of herself nearby. Suddenly frightened, her eyelids snapped open but there was nothing to be seen, no print or track in the unblemished snow. She tried again, and again the feeling came to her that someone else was present. This time she held the moment and waited. The vibration around her grew and grew until a rush of warmth seemed to suffuse her whole body from head to foot, and she felt her toes tingling with sensation as if they longed to sprout roots and anchor themselves here in the earth. The moment passed quickly, and she opened her eyes slightly dizzily. The little clearing looked exactly the same, without any sign or clue that anything untoward had taken place. Zena wondered if she had simply imagined it, a kind of wish-fulfilment because she wanted to re-establish contact with the child she'd seen.

She decided rather ruefully that this was the most likely explanation and wondered if it was even worth mentioning to Ian next time they met. Probably not. She did not want to make herself look like some mild hysteric in front of him. Anyway, it was far too cold to hang around any longer. Kindly spirits or not, she did not fancy still being out here when darkness fell. As she crunched back towards the path, however, Zena found herself whispering, thank you, thank you, Marie.

Chapter 8

The snow lasted for three days before succumbing to the rising temperature and turning to slush. On the first day of the thaw, Zena drove into La Folle to buy bread and post off some more designs. She passed the cemetery on the way in and thought that she must get some flowers for the anniversary of Lucas' mother's death, only days away. She felt that the gesture might be helpful for her now in getting some kind of closure on that aspect of her life. Everything else was going so well. She'd enjoyed this brief period of enforced solitude, discounting the intermittent appearances of Jean-Yves, and was very pleased with the work she'd achieved. Now she was happy to be entering the world again, exchanging the same pleasantries about the weather in the boulangerie and the post office.

On her way out of the latter, she saw Poppy coming round the corner from Erin's house. She looked as if she'd been crying yet again. There was something seriously wrong with the girl and Zena, in her new-found state of contentment, felt moved to try to help.

Poppy eyed her defensively.

'I'm alright,' she said. 'Got shampoo in my eyes, that's all.'

'You've been crying,' Zena said in a sympathetic tone. 'Come and have a coffee with me, tell me about it.'

She sensed little resistance in Poppy and took her arm decisively, leading the way into the café on the square. A couple of old men in caps and working boots were leaning against the counter, full glasses of eau de vie awaiting their attention. The owner was reading a paper at the end of the bar. He brought them over large milky coffees with tiny bars of bitter chocolate in the saucers. Poppy ate hers before touching the steaming cup.

'How's the restaurant?' Zena asked neutrally.

'It's great. I really like working there.'

So it wasn't that. And it rather ruled out a torrid passion for the chef, as she had spoken quite unselfconsciously. Zena watched Poppy taking a great gulp of coffee and tugging at her fringe, recently dyed a lurid magenta colour.

'And do you like living at Erin's? I never enjoyed sharing accommodation much when I was a student. It can be difficult fitting in with other people and putting up with their little foibles.'

Poppy said nothing, but her eyes looked suspiciously moist again.

'Come on, Poppy. You look as if you could use a friend. Talk to me. I can keep a secret and at my advanced age, I might be able to give you some advice. Not that the state of my love-life exactly qualifies me for that.'

She was trying to lighten the tone and make the girl laugh, but Poppy began to cry, first silently with tears running down and plopping into her coffee and then with a great snorting sob that attracted the attention of everyone in the room. Zena smiled around brightly as if nothing untoward was happening, and people looked away, renewing their conversations.

Poppy was breathing deeply, holding back another sob, and Zena leaned across to speak to her in a low voice.

'Please tell me, Poppy,' she said simply. 'I can't bear to see you so upset. Surely it would help to let some of it out?'

Apparently it would, but the words were jumbled and twisted so that Zena struggled to understand the half of them.

'.... took some notice....... like they really cared.... I want to stay close to them but...... it's so hard......... and then he......... and now........ I don't know what he's thinking about me, but........... and I can't help what I feel......... love..........'

Suddenly Poppy leapt up mid-gurgle and rushed out of the bar.

Zena paid quickly and hurried out into the square, but there was no sign of her and she did not feel able to go and knock on Erin's door to ask how Poppy was. There was obviously a serious problem which was causing all this anguish. The hallmark of young love was shining out clearly from Poppy's besotted state and Zena had an awful feeling that she knew the object of her affections, if mention of the house had brought such a violent reaction. Poor Poppy. Zena could see that Llewellyn had a certain animal attraction, but she wouldn't like to be dependent on him for any sort of emotional well-being. Personally she wouldn't trust him one little bit...

It was strange how your body could let you down sometimes with no apparent explanation. Laure felt the tiredness spreading through her like the slow creep of a tide. She had done nothing more than tend to Tomas, shop and tidy the house, but by midday she was longing for sleep rather than food.

She stood looking out of the sliding French window to the back garden. Brightly coloured swings and a slide stood on the neatly manicured lawn and all the shrubs in the new hedge they had planted last autumn looked trim and ready to flourish at the first sign of spring. How long would that be? She longed for an end to the cold and the long dark evenings when there was little to do but sit in front of the television once Tomas was safely in bed. They had even started to eat whilst watching the news at eight o'clock rather than sitting silently at the dining table at the other end of the lounge. She knew that Thierry was tired too at the end of the day, but he seemed to want nothing more than a few glasses of wine and a good meal. The habit of talking had somehow fallen away from them almost unnoticed and their exchanges were increasingly limited to what had to be done and arranged and put into motion for the smooth running of their family life.

It hadn't always been like this. She remembered their first years in this house as a time of sharing and laughter. With help from their parents, they had purchased this small plot of land and had a house built almost to their own design. After their marriage, they had camped in the finished shell, tackling the décor and the tiling themselves from start to finish. It had been a lot of fun, and when friends came round to help, there were long picnics at a wooden table on the stone terrace, ending under the stars. The conversation was always animated, with the zest of young adulthood, confident and carefree, all the huge potential of themselves ahead.

But things had changed gradually. The house became routine, a source of niggly jobs and extra shopping trips. You take your home for granted after a bit, she thought, as well as your partner. The exciting discoveries of early married life inevitably give way to habitual patterns of behaviour and reaction. Then you have a baby and everything is new and different and exciting again. Does that determine when couples try for pregnancy, when they begin to be bored with marriage? No, she was a realist, not a cynic. She loved Tomas with the fierce pride of any mother and she was glad to be married to Thierry. She was not unhappy, just very, very weary.

Unable to sleep again after a strange dream about her mother on a cross-channel ferry with a white poodle, Zena felt too restless to stay in bed. She got up before dawn and drove up the hill, hoping not to wake Jean-Yves and Monique. The world was totally silent and deserted as she took the narrow route up over the ridge of the Monts d'Arrée and then pulled off the road at the foot of Menez Kador. The dark summit of the hill with its sharp boulders rose massively against the clear sky, and a near full moon still hung against its navy backdrop. She climbed the rough path snaking right up to the top, and then perched on a rock to watch the sun come up in the east. It was like taking one's seat in a theatre for a grand performance.

As she waited, she found herself thinking of Laure, picturing Tomas on a swing somewhere, with his mother pushing him back and forward, laughing at his shrieks of delight and then sweeping his padded little body out of the plastic seat and whirling him round in her arms, their faces almost touching, separated from the rest of the world by their unity, their shared essence. It must be a sensation you could get from no-one but your child and

Zena felt a momentary pang of her old sadness in the face of that one glowing image. She tried and failed to imagine how her own life would have been if she'd managed, like most others, to settle down and have a family ten years earlier. The need to love, to have someone depend on you for nurture was such a powerful one. It had found some fulfilment in her relationship with Lucas, but the next step, the becoming a family was what she had really longed for to feel her life complete. Now she didn't even have a dog or cat to shower with affection and buy dinky Christmas presents for.

As she thought of dogs, Zena cast her eyes across the wide expanse of heath, half-hoping to catch sight of Frodo's ugly form or hear his strangled bark in the distance. It would be nice to see Ian again and talk more about his book. There was no reason why they couldn't become good friends, despite him having a wife and she herself loving Lucas as much as ever. Because she did, if she was honest. She knew that she was better than before, that the all-embracing involvement of Lucas in her thoughts and feelings had passed to some more manageable plane and a level of acceptance had been reached. From this plateau she could see the bigger picture, a wide perspective of her whole life stretching out before her, full of possibilities and diverse directions. She was becoming curious again, interested in things outside her obsession. She wanted to develop friendships and learn new things, but at the back of her mind, he was always there and she didn't yet see how this would leave room for anyone else.

The sun was nearly above the horizon now. When light rose above the range of Brittany's highest hills it gradually illuminated the vast bowl of their interior, from the chapel of St-Michel on its windswept perch to the low brume-covered lake, wreathed by swathes of mist and shadow so that it was impossible to tell what was semi-land of marshy bog and what water. The sudden revelation of the whole scene was like magic. She began to understand what Ian meant: it was both entirely natural and yet at the same time full of unseen power and vibration. The life force of the elements pulsed around her in the gentle fire of the wintery sun, the air's cool currents, the soft flow of water and the solidity of earth beneath her feet. She felt curiously at one with them, herself a part of this mystical landscape. Despite the early morning cold she was warm inside, sitting between the moon and the sun, both evident, two halves of a whole, a rare moment of peaceful unity.

As she set off back down the track, she experienced a new sense of exhilaration, a burst of vibrant energy that allied her with the buzzard riding the breeze, the pair of deer kicking their way up the rocky slope beyond the stream and all the smaller animals that scuffled and shimmied through the long coarse grasses of the moorland.

Seeing the land fall away sharply to her left, Zena made a detour from the path through the gorse and found herself on the sheer edge of an old quarry site. A small lake filled part of the crater and someone had laid out a huge spiral of stones, like a maze on the earth beside it. She scrambled down a steep track, slipping and then sliding the last few metres before reaching the bottom. The water was a deep luminous green, the kind of depths in which she could easily imagine archaic monsters and undines dwelt.

Under the lip of the cliff she'd first stood on, Zena could now see another smaller circle, marked out with boulders at the quarter points and small pebbles in between. As she went closer she could make out the remains of candles around the edge of the circle and a fire-pit in the centre. Its ashes were still warm, so people had been here recently, performing some kind of ritual. A wilting bunch of grasses and early daffodils lay on a slab of stone which had been placed on the northern rim. She looked around, trying to imagine the... what? Chanting? Dancing? It was certainly a secluded spot: although the moon was no longer visible, it would have flooded the quarry with light when overhead. She wondered what the ceremony would have been in aid of – presumably some sort of earth ritual by the modern pagans Ian had talked about. It was a little early for spring rites at the beginning of February, but perhaps the full moon was all the occasion required. She had no knowledge of such things beyond televised shots of Stonehenge binges with long beards and oak wreaths predominating over multi-coloured crowds. This was so different, a world away in its simplicity and integrity, remarkably natural in this landscape which retained such a vibrant expression of man's bonds with the earth over many thousands of years.

Feeling a strange sense of intrusion, to pick over the bones of someone else's beliefs, she turned away and took the old quarry access road back towards her car. She squelched along through the tiny streams crossing her path as they forced their way downhill, and felt the earth expanding beneath her feet with all the moisture of the thaw and relative warmth of the restored winter sun. There are so many things I don't know about, she thought.

So many things to discover and experience – and it seems as if I've come to the right place for that.

The jewellery shop in Brest had accepted Erin's samples without hesitation. They had even paid her upfront for them, and although she knew the items would be in the window next day with a huge mark-up, she was simply glad to have the money and a new avenue for earning in the future. Erin had no doubts about the quality of her work: it was an extension of herself, as the tarot reading also was, both outlets for the creative imagination.

When she got back to La Folle, she found Llewellyn lounging morosely in the sitting room reading an out of date copy of the Daily Mail someone had left in the café.

'Fancy a glass of wine?' she said, waving the bottle at him.

'Not especially.'

'Come on, I sold the stuff OK, let's have a celebration. We can pay the rent this month.'

'Some fucking celebration that is!'

'What's the matter with you?'

He sat up straight and glared at her.

'There's nothing the matter with me. I'm just sick and tired of you going on and on about money and the rent and the sodding electricity bill all the time. It's like living with some old woman who's got nothing better to think about.'

Erin met his gaze calmly and he turned away at once, making a pantomime of folding back a new page of the newspaper.

It was the same pattern that had dominated their childhood when she was forced into an early role of protector and organiser for her older, less sensible brother. Their father had drunk himself to death at the age of 52 and within a year his wife gave up a long struggle with cancer to join him. Erin was 16, Llewellyn 19 when they inherited the two bed-roomed terraced house in Swansea, now let to students. For the last eleven years this had provided a basic income which they shared between them equally. Without that money Llewellyn would have long since been forced to exert himself to earn a living but he preferred survival and living off the efforts of others whenever possible. Erin had always smoothed his path where she could, never reacting with anger to his furious outbursts and ferocious temper. He had always backed down in the face of that calm, serene exterior. But while Erin never got annoyed, nor did she try to change him, just accepted him for what he was as she dried the tears of rejected girlfriends and married lovers, offering them camomile tea and tarot readings on the way to acceptance of their fate.

'Come on, have a drink. There's nothing to get worked up about.'

'I don't want a drink, OK? Just leave me alone, will you?'

'With pleasure,' Erin said with a smile. 'But I'll need the room at five, I've got a reading.'

'That's just wonderful!' He threw down the paper and lumbered to his feet, glowering at her. 'Can't have a moment to myself in my own house now, is it?'

'You've got your own room, and there's the kitchen.'

'What, and have bloody Poppy taking up half the room and looking longingly at me with those big cow eyes all the time. I'm sick to death of women everywhere, if you want the truth. I'm going out.'

She knew he'd slam the front door for maximum effect and stood still until the house had finished shuddering. Then she went to the kitchen and put the wine away in a cupboard. Perhaps tea would be a better preparation for helping someone with their problems anyway, but she had wanted to make the gesture to Llewellyn, to try to restore some of his former jollity that seemed in such short supply these days.

She had always felt it was up to her somehow, to keep the peace and maintain his equilibrium as best she could, but these were old ideas and, here in Brittany, she was beginning to see things differently. He was relying on her too heavily, to make money, to make things right with individuals he rubbed up the wrong way, to sooth any emotional upsets he caused. After all these years it was becoming too familiar and too easy for him. Erin began to long for her own space, a life without the adverse influence of brotherly love and a bit of peace and quiet. Reluctant though she was to admit it, because she herself had played a part in the development, she was starting to believe that in fact, Llewellyn was simply not a very nice person. But how to give up feeling responsible for him was another matter.

Zena laid her flowers on the grave and then spoke inwardly to Lucas' mother. Her unspoken wishes for the future seemed safe in the hands of the dead, and Zena was sure that if Thérèse could hear she would understand her feelings for Lucas and her inability to come to terms with his loss. If only she had known this woman, she might have been able to get closer to Lucas, to forge a deeper bond. God knows, she'd tried to nurture him, to create a home where he'd feel comfortable and at ease, but maybe he'd have preferred a challenge, an intellectual discussion or political debate when he came home instead of the home-cooked meal and unadventurous baroque music in the background. In fact, she'd been giving him the sort of things that made *her* feel safe and secure: it was probably not at all what he had wanted. No wonder he was relieved to escape her clutches, get away from the cloyingly controlled atmosphere of the flat into the free air of whatever underdeveloped country was claiming his attentions now. Or whichever lively, laughing woman was providing a less onerous shelter for him.

Her heart felt almost as cold as her knees at that thought. She straightened up, feeling a twinge of stiffness in her joints. She was nearly forty, after all, and had little else to look forward to physically except decline. Everything would start to dry up soon, although the good side was that this constant urge to cry might disappear when her body no longer had the fluid to spare. It was the thought of no baby that usually got to her. Spending time with Laure and Tomas, pleasurable though it was, was serving to remind her of all she had failed to achieve for herself, all that she had lost when Lucas left her...

She turned away from the grave, half-blinded by tears of self-pity. Someone was standing a few yards away, watching her intently. Zena blinked and swayed slightly on feet that seemed to have forgotten their function. She struggled to speak, but her throat fought the attempt.

She could only manage one word and that in a funny squeaky tremble.

'Lucas?' she said.

Chapter 9

It really was him. She could hardly believe it, as if she'd conjured up some spirit which would vanish before her eyes if she tried to touch it. He looked solid enough, in a long black overcoat. In his hands was a bunch of flowers.

'What are you doing here, Zena?'

His tone was neutral, and gave no hint of his reaction to seeing her.

She laughed a little crazily.

'I live here.'

He raised an eyebrow.

'Not in the cemetery, obviously,' she added.

He was un-amused.

'But near La Folle,' she went on. 'In a hamlet. At the bottom of a hill. Near a very scary cave.'

She found herself looking at the ground like a naughty schoolgirl.

Lucas shook his head from side to side as if avoiding a cluster of flying insects.

'I don't understand. What are you doing here?'

It seemed a good question now someone actually posed it, twice in one minute. What was she doing here? All her feeble little plans and hopes of the last few weeks didn't really amount to much when faced with Lucas' tall, lean presence. She could tell that he was being careful, not hostile, just very, very careful while he weighed up the situation.

Go on, a voice said inside her head, tell him. You're an

artist now. Independent. And free to go where you like whatever anyone else thinks. It's none of his business.

'I'm having a few months off work, looking around.'

'But here? Why here, Zena?'

'Why not? I liked this place if you remember, I always wanted to come back and I have. That's all there is to it. I wasn't expecting to see you here, if that's what you think!' God, she was a terrible liar, but her belligerent tone seemed to have worked.

'Sorry,' he said. 'It was quite a shock, seeing you there. I am sorry. It's good to see you, just so... unexpected.'

He lifted his shoulder in a bemused shrug and Zena watched the carmine red petals of his flowers moving up in the air and then falling against the grey stone background. They held her gaze, an easier focus than looking into Lucas' eyes and seeing the rejection she did not feel she could bear again.

'You'll want to be alone,' she said quietly in the direction of the flowers. 'I'd better go.'

This was all she could say whilst keeping her voice steady, but Lucas seemed to have roused himself and be in possession of his feelings again.

'Why don't we meet in the café and have a drink? I won't be too long here.'

Her readiness to leave him so easily seemed to have earned her a reprieve. She nodded without saying anything and left, picking her way through the tightly packed graves, noticing tiny details as she passed. A tear on the cheek of a marble cherub, a row of crosses like kisses, almost invisible, on a dead baby's plaque... After a minute of paralysis, her mind and heart were starting to run faster and faster. She forced herself to believe in the reality of the encounter, to marvel at the dream coming true as if she herself had shaped her destiny with her own longing. Was this the true nature of magic, as Ian had said? In a sudden blinding sweep of emotion she was back in the full throes of her love for Lucas, and Zena could not help the ridiculous hope, as she gently closed the tall iron gates, that here in a place of endings she might have found a chance for a new beginning.

When Lucas entered the café, the guarded look of the cemetery was gone, and he smiled as he sat down opposite her. Zena's heart lurched at the familiarity of that smile which triggered a machine-gun effect of memories from their shared past. She was as much in thrall to his physical presence as ever, drawn to the lean lines of his face, framed by long unruly dark hair and his tall, slim body, a slight tension denoting the careful control of considerable physical energies.

'How have you been?' she said, wanting to initiate, to try to keep on top of the situation. She realised now in all her longings for Lucas' return that she had never thought beyond the initial rushing back into each other's arms - a point of the script which seemed to have got overlooked here.

'Busy!' Lucas now looked quite at ease, drinking his coffee and looking around the square from their vantage point by the window. 'Nothing here seems to have changed very much, except for the inevitable new housing schemes springing up everywhere. What's the unemployment situation like?'

'I've no idea.' Zena immediately felt guilty for whiling away the last six weeks on painting and making friends when she could have been reading the French papers and studying the local economy. Her old instinct to please him and live up to his expectations revived all too quickly.

But Lucas was smiling at her indulgently, as if he knew what was going through her head.

'It doesn't matter. I'm not supposed to be working here! Tell me about you – how are you finding it over here? And what are you doing with yourself? Are you.... alone?'

For an instant he looked a little uneasy at the significance of this last question.

'Yes.' Zena skimmed over it quickly. 'I've rented the house for six months, until the end of June, to get some peace and quiet to work on my painting. An agent has taken some designs for a card company, so it seemed a good idea to give it a serious try.'

'Zena, that's fantastic!' He leaned across the table and briefly touched her hand in a spontaneous gesture that moved her greatly. 'You've got real talent – it always seemed so wasted at GPE. Although I bet they were sorry to lose you.'

'I may go back yet,' she said, laughing. 'They've got a temp in to cover for me. She's having a baby, so the six months suited her fine and it means I can go back if I want. We agreed I'd let the MD know by the end of May.'

'You won't go back, will you?'

Their eyes met in a moment of total understanding and accord.

Zena shook her head.

'I don't think so. Now tell me what you've been doing.'

She wanted to break the sense of intimacy that was rearing its dangerous head between them. It was too much, too difficult for her to adjust to so quickly. She had been through a long period of grieving for Lucas and now it was as if he had risen from the dead, and a complete revision of the whole process was required of her.

'I was in Russia for a couple of months last year, then the Ukraine. And in and out of Paris a fair bit. I left there very early this morning and haven't really stopped since.'

'Have you eaten?' She looked across at the blackboard, now wiped clean with lunch long over, before she could stop herself. Damn that nurturing reflex!

He laughed.

'It's OK, I'll survive. I'll get a meal this evening on my way back.'

The words fell like a stone into Zena's heart. She couldn't bear to let him go so soon. They went on talking, about the places he'd been and the book that would come out of it all. She was interested, and genuinely wanted to know what was filling his mind in the way she knew only too well, but all the time she was thinking of a way to keep him, or at least delay the terrible moment when he was going to leave her again.

When the conversation moved on to her work and all her hopes for establishing herself as a commercial artist, he unexpectedly handed her the opportunity she'd been frantically searching for.

'I'd love to see what you've been doing. If you've time, of course.'

It was a perfectly natural suggestion, there was nothing of significance to read into it, Zena told herself sternly, but her heart leapt at the thought of this continuance of their time together.

'OK. Good idea. I'd like to show you.' This was like saying she'd like to keep breathing, so greatly did she feel the need to stay in his company, to look at him whenever he was looking elsewhere and feel their old connection re-established by simple physical presence. But she mustn't give herself away so easily. 'I've even got some left-over lasagne if you're really starving!'

He grinned.

'Sounds good. I seem to remember your lasagne was pretty sensational.'

This was too intimate, too cruel, almost more than she could bear and still keep up a neutral appearance, but her instinct for survival seemed to kick in and save her. She had at least suppressed the inclination to suggest he stayed the night with her – there was a spare bedroom after all. But there was also far too great an element of risk attached to this, and fear of rejection, either at once or later, kept her quiet.

He was looking at his watch.

'Can you give me a couple of hours? There's something I want to do first.'

'Of course,' she said, trembling inside. 'About half-five would be fine. The house isn't much, I warn you now.'

But I'll be so happy to see you in it, she thought.

Ian saw Zena coming out of the café with a man he hadn't seen before and turned quickly away so she wouldn't spot him. He went to the car feeling rather despondent that she was involved with someone else. They clearly were involved from their body language, moving easily together, although Zena kept her head down and seemed to be trying to keep her waves of hair in some sort of order as if she was unusually self-conscious.

That's me, Ian thought, a natural observer. When they line up for the new ark when the big wave comes, I'll be the one standing at the side watching couple after couple stroll up the gangway. And it's not as if I'd really thought of Zena as anything other than a nice person and someone to work with. Or had I?

He had begun to think that married life with Leah had killed his sexual instincts stone dead, but he knew there had been a real flicker of attraction towards Zena when they were looking at her drawings and enjoying that fireside talk. Now it seemed just as well he hadn't allowed himself to get too worked up about it...

There was no denying a feeling of disappointment as he drove the few miles back home. Frodo seemed to pick up on his master's mood and howled pitifully all the way on his smelly rug on the back seat. He then came into the house quite docilely and sat down against the chair Ian had slumped in, leaning his head back to be stroked. This kind of gesture was becoming more frequent as the dog settled, and Ian appreciated his company more and more. It was as if the dog was beginning to take an interest in his master and their shared routines, to be forging a real bond of belonging at long last. There was no way that Ian would be able to leave him behind, whatever happened in the future, but on the other hand, he couldn't imagine Frodo acting the domesticated pet back in suburban England, even if Leah had been prepared to let him set foot in the house.

Christ, what was he going to do about everything? He had to talk to her, try to gauge the real state of her feelings about their marriage. They had each avoided this sort of talk for so long – he really hadn't a clue how to start, how to breach the great wall of silence about any subject of real import that had separated them for the last ten years.

But something had to give. He couldn't imagine going back to England and picking up the old routines, having had this taste of freedom and autonomy.

If Leah was really coming out to Brittany as she'd threatened in that letter, that would be the time and he'd decide what to do on the basis of her reaction. He had the cowardly thought that perhaps if she was determined to keep up the pretence of their partnership, he'd be unable to refuse. Was he that unselfish? It wasn't so easy to overturn so many years of habit and familiarity. But he had other considerations too.

Ian stroked Frodo's ears and bent down to whisper.

'If it comes to you or her, mate, don't worry, I'll never let you go.'

After a frantic burst of tidying up and then deciding not to worry, Zena lay in a hot bath, dreaming. All the stern warnings she had given herself about not indulging in romantic scenarios had evaporated in the steamy perfumed atmosphere of the room. She was anticipating a whole succession of possible conversations she might have with Lucas that evening over dinner, and most of these were peppered with little touches and lingering looks that gradually made clear the overwhelming power of revived attraction between them. Then they'd sit by the fire and suddenly it would be too late to go back to Paris and he'd have to stay and then he'd say he was glad to and he'd stroke the back of her neck gently with his long fingers, pushing her hair back from her face and saying how much he'd longed to see her and then...

She sat up with a great splash that sent a wave of water over the side of the bath. This was madness! She'd met Lucas completely by chance. He hadn't come to La Folle looking for her, but to honour the memory of his dead mother. He certainly wasn't looking to rekindle an old, dead relationship – his visit was just a natural courtesy to take an interest in a friend's progress. They had never quarrelled after all. There had been no words of bitterness and accusation to sour the memory each had of the other, or to threaten the idea of friendship between them in the future. And here they were now, meeting again in that future with all the pleasant enquiries and un-intrusive curiosity of friends who had not seen each other for quite a while. There it was, all perfectly reasonable and understandable.

The only trouble was, friendship was no substitute for what she wanted. And all Zena's deepest feelings, five years worth, were filling her heart again, even as she towelled herself dry and prepared to dress carefully for an evening with the man she had loved for so long.

'What sort of man?'

Erin looked up from the cards she was laying out in an elaborate spread.

Llewellyn shrugged.

'He was French was all Michel said, and well-dressed in a casual kind of way. But he's not been in the café before, he was sure of that. And he and Zena were obviously well-known to each other, if you know what I mean.'

'It could be a relative. I'm sure she said she's got a brother who's visiting some time. Though he wouldn't be French.'

He shook his head very slowly from side to side.

'It didn't sound like that to me. I think it's someone from her murky past, turned up here at the end of the world to find her out. We know she's been running away from something.'

'Do we?'

'You, my little Erina, know far more than me about the secrets of Zena's heart, I'm sure. Is there nothing you'd like to share with me that might throw some light on the mysterious stranger in our midst?'

'Nothing at all,' she said, turning over another card. 'But I wonder if you can shed any light on the money that's missing from my box – and before you even think of mentioning Poppy's name, she hasn't been in the house all day. Someone left 10 euros this morning and it's gone now.'

'Someone? Why do you always say 'someone' in that prissy way, when we all know it's that batty English woman from Landivisiau who probably wants your advice about communing with her dead cat or getting rid of those enormous warts on her chin...'

'Shut up, will you?' The savage tone of his mockery had got to her as he had hoped it would. She calmed herself instantly and turned over another card before speaking again. 'Confidentiality is important for what I do. No-one wants their business discussed in the town or even the fact they've been to see me maybe.'

'Well, people must think you've an extraordinary number of strange friends just dropping for the odd half-hour. If they weren't mostly women, I think some would begin to wonder exactly what is is you get up to in the allotted time.'

The front door opened and Llewellyn stuck his head into the hall.

'Here she is, pretty Poppy, back from a hard day's graft at the pit face!'

He stepped in front of her as Poppy tried to get past, and catching her by the arms pretended to dance in the narrow passage.

'Ow!' Poppy's shoulder slammed into the wall as he swung her round, nuzzling his big head into the nape of her neck.

'Let her go!' Erin's uncharacteristic look of anger seemed to register even with Llewellyn. He released Poppy, who fled upstairs in a state of some distress, and turned to face his sister's wrath with a provocative smile.

'Come on, it's just a bit of fun. She's longing for a bit of my special attention.'

'Then she's got less sense than I thought. Leave her alone, Llewellyn. She's not happy here and I'm beginning to see why. If we lose her rent, we'll...'

'Find someone else,' he cut in. 'Preferably someone who takes better care of herself than Miss Piggy up in her lonely room.'

Erin laughed as she shut the door of the front room in his face.

'Look in the mirror some time, brother dear,' she said.

They stood on the bridge in the fading light watching the water flying along below, its level much higher since the snowy spell. A small herd of cream Charolais cattle squelched around the field which had been churned to a sea of mud by their heavy perambulations. Some were little more than babies, winter-born and already miniature square and solid versions of their parents. Water dripped from the pines in the forest and a jay whipped past them into the trees, a flash of blue and mushroom pink against the darkening grey sky. Zena thought of the cave, concealed up there and hiding its secrets as it had for thousands of years. Even if it was not too late for a walk, she wouldn't have proposed it to Lucas. She couldn't remember ever walking in the countryside with him and found it hard now to associate something so aimless and full of abstract reflections with his quiet purposefulness.

The noise of the river was enough to prevent easy conversation, but silence between them had never been a problem. He would often work at his desk in a corner of the living room in the flat whilst she read or sewed or idly sketched the back of his head or his serious profile. It had been an undemanding relationship, she saw clearly now. It couldn't be that they were both totally satisfied with things as they were, or he'd never have left and she would not have felt the longing for a child to cement their bond and make a family out of a partnership.

Now Zena was finding herself tongue-tied and nervous at the thought of going into the house with this man, at once so achingly familiar and so hopelessly remote. He would see all the personal things from the flat re-set in a new environment. But would he remember them at all, she asked herself? It was a year ago and he had never shown any great interest in décor or inanimate objects. She was glad that she'd taken the Polish forest photograph down – he would certainly have noticed that she still wanted to look at his work and be reminded of his existence.

They walked back into the yard.

'Has the house ever flooded?' he asked.

She laughed.

'Not since I've been here, but that is only six weeks.'

'It was always this time of year that the weather was worst when I was growing up just down the road.'

'Thanks' she said. 'I'll put my wellingtons by the bed just in case!'

They were laughing as they went into the house and suddenly Zena felt a whole lot better. Lucas was here with her and everything felt good and easy. It was amazing how quickly you could fall back into familiar patterns, and they had always got on well together in a friendly kind of way. It was just the bigger stuff that had somehow slipped away, but he surely wouldn't have come to the house now if he was determined to avoid a potentially intimate situation? He must be reluctant to leave, he must be glad to have found her again... No! She was just going to make the most of his company and not keep running ahead in her mind about what might or might not happen between them.

Jean-Yves was home early. He'd had a frustrating day of difficult customers and lazy employees and the last thing he wanted was to listen to Monique carping about the quality of education provided by the perfectly adequate local school.

'The girls are happy,' he said. 'They are learning with their friends and enjoying their lives. Why would you wish to change this?'

'Madame Bonneau is a rude and arrogant person!'

'No wonder you feel so attracted to her then.'

It was so easy to send Monique into outrage mode. Hardly surprising that he sometimes longed for greater challenges.

'I'm not attracted to that woman!' she shouted.

'Then why are you always writing to her and trying to make appointments to be with her?'

'My God, you are so disgusting!'

She ostentatiously moved to another chair further away from him.

Jean-Yves smiled sardonically. Now he would get some peace in his own home. Otherwise he might go down the hill and see Zelda. She'd been out the last time he tried and he missed seeing her. He was beginning to regard her house as a haven where at least for the duration of a cup of coffee or glass of wine he could look at her attractive face and imagine the pleasures concealed beneath her rather dowdy clothes...

'Your little friend has grown tired of your elderly advances, then?'

He'd hardly heard his wife's words. If she discovered the trick of invading the privacy of his thoughts, life would become truly unbearable.

'What?'

'That Zelda. She has a man of her own at last.'

'What!'

Monique shrugged her skinny shoulders.

'A very good-looking man. Much younger than you.'

'What are you talking about?'

He felt surprisingly wounded by her barbs.

'I saw him going down to the house in a car. All alone. And he hasn't come back.'

She turned her smirking face in his direction as she said this and he had to suppress a strong desire to leap up and slap it. He did get up and leave the room, a feeling of bitter disappointment and jealousy rising from his stomach.

He didn't at all like the sound of this. Zelda might be in danger. He would have to go and see for himself.

Zena and Lucas were sitting together on the sofa in front of a lively fire in the stove, patiently coaxed by Lucas from some damp kindling and a couple of enormous oak logs. The remains of their meal were still on the table and the second bottle of wine, half-full, on the floor beside them.

He had admired her card designs as she knew he would, but it was her personal paintings of hills and ancient stones that had caught his attention and drawn warm words of encouragement. Lucas had practical ideas about exhibitions and sales which she had not even begun to think about for herself in these last few dreamy weeks, and she suddenly felt inspired for the future by his enthusiasm and support. Filled with happiness and gratitude for this confirmation, by someone she totally trusted, of the quality of her vision, she gazed into the flames with a rare sense of contentment on the one hand and longing on the other. Being in such close proximity to Lucas for so long without touching him was almost causing her physical pain.

The abrupt knock at the door made her jump. She experienced a brief moment of alarm when the handle began to turn, and then Jean-Yves' head appeared around it. Lucas had sprung up and stepped between Zena and the door, almost before she realised what was happening.

'It's OK,' she said to Lucas, 'it's my neighbour. But he usually waits for an invitation before coming in.'

Jean-Yves was now inside the room looking suspiciously from Lucas to Zena.

'I saw a car on the 'ill,' he lied, 'and I want to be sure you do not 'ave trouble.'

'No, of course not,' she said quite sharply, feeling angry at the arrogance of his intrusion, whilst also wondering whether in fact Lucas might not be classed 'trouble' with this dramatic reappearance in her life. 'I'm fine. A friend is here for dinner. There's no problem at all.'

Jean-Yves stepped forward towards Zena like a welcome guest, but Lucas was too quick for him, filling the gap himself. He greeted Jean-Yves swiftly in French, offering a brief handshake before turning to stand by Zena's side. A current of bodily electricity ran through her as he placed one hand lightly on her shoulder.

Faced by their solidarity, Jean-Yves shifted uncertainly from one foot to the other, taking in the nest they seemed to have created in the sofa cushions and the un-cleared table. He gave a hopeful glance at the wine-bottle, but Zena was certainly not in the mood for indulging him tonight.

Reluctant though she was to move away from Lucas, she went to the door and opened it, ushering Jean-Yves out firmly.

On the step where Lucas was out of earshot, he turned to speak privately to her, but Zena pre-empted him.

'Thank you,' she said in a tone that implied no such thing, 'but please don't ever do that again.'

'But I am thinking of you...'

'Bollocks,' she said, and closed the door in his face.

Lucas was standing in the same spot as she went back into the house. His mouth was twitching as if he was struggling to keep a straight face and they both burst out laughing as soon as their eyes met. In that moment she just knew that he must still want her and everything, after all she'd been through, was finally going to be OK.

Chapter 10

Laure rang the bell of the doctor's house, entered the hall and opened the door to the waiting room. Most of the chairs were already full and a handful of toddlers played in a corner with plastic toys and wooden puzzles. She was in for a long wait, despite deliberately coming at the end of the evening session in the hope that others would have preferred to be at home eating their family meal.

As the minutes passed she flicked restlessly through the pages of a recent edition of Ici Paris, read the notices about diet and nutrition on the walls and eyed up all her fellow patients, wondering what had brought them to the surgery. She wasn't sure why she herself was here, except that her weariness continued to plague her each day and she was starting to be impatient over trifles with both Thierry and even poor little Tomas who did nothing to deserve it.

It was fully dark outside. Car headlights passed the waiting room window spasmodically, but mostly the streets of La Folle would be quiet as families sat around the dinner table discussing the events of the day and sharing all their ups and downs as families did. She had not felt able to talk to Thierry about her irrational fears of a problem with her health. She was just over-tired, which was hardly something to bother him about when he himself worked hard and endured the daily frustrations of a busy administrative job. He had noticed her fatigue, which some husbands wouldn't have done, and tried to do some extra domestic chores to help out whilst she concentrated her efforts on Tomas. But something held her back from sharing a growing sense that there was a real problem underlying this malaise, and the weariness that seemed to seep right into her bones was merely a symptom of a much more serious cause.

She looked at her watch. It was quarter to eight and she was the only remaining person waiting. It was deathly quiet since the three children had been hauled off into the doctor's room by their harrassed mother. She hoped that none of them were really ill and that it was a routine visit. She wished the same for herself, of course. It was a rare occurrence for Laure to sit in this small room enlivened by its yellow walls, bright posters and trailing plants. She knew the doctor well: he had been in the town a very long time and his son had been a contemporary of her husband's at the local college.

At last she heard the noisy departure of the children. After a minute the waiting room door opened and she was greeted with a warm smile and handshake. For some reason, this friendly greeting made tears prickle in the corner of her eyes.

After the departure of Jean-Yves, Zena and Lucas returned to the sofa and refilled their glasses. The incident had bonded them in some mysterious way and they now moved and looked like a couple instead of the two wary individuals of five minutes earlier.

Lucas replenished the logs on the fire and then sat down again even nearer to her. Now she accepted this as a natural progression, not a worrying development.

Everything seemed natural and comfortable, with the warming heat of the fire on her face and the wine inside her body. She relaxed into the cushions as they continued to talk easily about neighbours in general and then the strange old man in the flat below them in Bath who always said 'Good Evening' regardless of the time they met him on the outside steps. Zena rocked with laughter as Lucas reminded her how they had rung his bell to speak to him about something one hot summer morning and he'd opened the door wearing a dinner-jacket and a bobble-hat.

'And what about when he came in carrying that celery wrapped like a bunch of flowers?' She could hardly speak for mirth and Lucas too was laughing with her. And then suddenly they were so close, inches apart, just looking and looking and looking into each other's eyes. He made an infinitesimal movement towards her and then sat back quickly as if to break the magnetic field that had held them so near for the last few minutes. The laughter was over.

Zena's heart lurched madly. He had nearly kissed her! She was sure that he had thought of it, wanted to, but just stopped himself at the last minute. Maybe meeting her again by chance had been just the right thing to trigger his true feelings. He must have realised what he had lost and be considering whether they might start again. Of course it was a big step and he needed to be sure, but it was going to work out this time. She'd make sure of that. Miraculously, suddenly the world had changed, turned upright again and her life was going to be restored.

Lucas stared at the carpet, apparently lost in thought.

She watched his profile dreamily. Everything was just as she'd imagined so many times. He was sorry that they'd parted, he had wanted to see her again. She was going to touch him again, to know the feel of his skin and the lines of his body. She knew it, just as clearly as she saw the twitch of a muscle in his cheek, representative of some inner tussle that embroiled him. Was it possible, could she even dare to imagine that he still loved her?

He looked up at her again at that moment, with signs of struggle in his face.

'I do love you, Zena,' he said.

They did kiss then, fast and passionately, clinging together with an urgency that was at odds with Lucas' usually calm desire.

But just as she felt she was drowning in the deluge of emotion released by the touch of his lips and the pressure of his arms around her, he pulled away abruptly.

'I've really got to go.'

Zena looked at him with frantic bewilderment.

'What do you mean go?'

'Leave here, now, at once, get back to Paris. I must go, Zena, God help me, I have to.'

'I don't understand. What's wrong? What have I done this time?'

His face crumpled at her distress and she realised he was struggling as much as she was.

'It's not you. You're lovely, I've missed you such a lot... but I can't do this now. I'm sorry.'

She was horrified to see tears in Lucas' eyes. He who always seemed so much in control of his feelings was finally at sea with how to cope with what was happening between them. She couldn't help him. It was too much to expect that he could leave her a second time and be allowed to go without a fight.

'What's the matter with you?' she yelled with all the force of the pain inside her. 'How can you treat me like this? I can't bear it again...'

He held her then, as he had done a year ago outside the flat in Bath when he drove off out of her life, as he intended to do again now. She saw what was in front of her. The long empty Lucasless days reaching away into a barren future. How could he say he loved her and behave like this? The anger went out oh her like a balloon deflating and she felt icily calm. Some internal defence mechanism clicked into motion and contained the liquid force of her despair.

She pushed him away, quite gently, and stood up.

'Goodbye, then,' she said simply.

He looked wretched.

'No, don't say that, Zena. It's not goodbye. I just need some time. Seeing you again was so unexpected and there're things to sort out in Paris. I can't just...'

He turned away and began to pace about the room. She saw as she watched him that he had become a separate person again and all the closeness they had so easily recreated had vanished under the pressure of time and these unspecified 'things' in his life that seem to take precedence over any reconciliation with her.

'How can I ask you to be patient?' he said finally.

'That would be more than last time,' she said quickly and cruelly, wanting him to suffer, to share some of the anguish she had felt a year ago when he left her with little more than a brief word of goodbye.

'Listen,' he said, taking her wrist and pulling her down

beside him on the sofa again. 'A lot of things have happened since then. I realised, well, I thought a lot about you and what we had. I wanted to see you...'

'But you weren't looking for me, were you? You haven't been to Bath and followed me out here, have you?'

He looked steadily at her.

'No, I haven't. It seemed a complete chance when I saw you in the cemetery but now I'm not so sure.'

'You mean in an anticipatory sort of way I followed you?'

'Not at all. It's more as if we were meant to meet again. I'd been thinking a lot about you lately since I... well, anyway it was almost as if I'd conjured you up.'

'I thought that about you! I did have a sort of fantasy about us meeting there, I can't deny it. But it hasn't turned out as I imagined.'

Her voice wobbled at the folly of her imaginings.

'Did you really hope to see me there?' he asked earnestly. 'You remembered what it meant to me?'

His face was soft and almost vulnerable for a moment.

She nodded dumbly.

'You wanted to see me?'

'Of course I did,' she almost shouted. 'But I wouldn't have wanted to if I'd known it was going to lead to this! I'd have preferred never to see you again.'

'Oh, Zena.' He pulled her into his arms and held her close, stroking the unruly waves of her hair. 'Don't say that!'

'Even if it's true?'

'I'm so sorry. Truly I am.'

'But you are going to leave me again, aren't you?

They stared at each other in miserable silence for a

minute before he nodded.

'I have to go back. A lot of things have happened...'

'So you said,' she interrupted curtly.

He clutched her hand tightly.

'Please be patient. Give me a chance to sort things out. Please.'

She could no more have refused him than denied she still loved him. It was a bleak admission to herself, almost a failure of self-worth to make herself so vulnerable again so soon. But he knew it in her face, and in the passion of her embrace on the door-step and in the desolate resignation in her eyes as he drove away.

Poppy lay on the bed in her dark room with the curtains drawn. She was visualising. So far, in her mind, she had walked along a path through a forest, crossed a small river in a conveniently waiting coracle-type boat and passed through a meadow bright with flowers. Now she had only to climb the hill to the round temple-like building at the top and there she would meet her inner guide who would resolve all her problems for her and put an end to the misery she'd endured for what felt like most of her life already.

She had got the idea from something Erin said when they were together in the kitchen a few days earlier. In fact, she was feeling a whole lot better since that conversation, not crying or feeling overwhelmed by everything. It was so relaxing just sitting and talking, not being on tenterhooks in case Llewellyn came in, because she'd waited for him to go out to the bar as usual before she came down to stick her pizza in the microwave. Erin was there, just finishing a vegetable stew, and they'd sat down to eat together at the little yellow table, chatting easily about nothing very much until the subject of meditation and the power of the mind came up.

It wasn't something that Poppy had ever given much thought to, but Erin told her how many people used it to take control of their lives and find answers to their problems and it seemed like something she ought to take more interest in. She'd searched for another book and found it this time on the bathroom shelf, between 'How To Be Who Other People Think You Are' (a concept Poppy found alarming) and 'Why Witchcraft and Not Wicca?' (a question she couldn't begin to understand). Her find was simply called PathWorkings and it had a pretty purple labyrinthine pattern on the front like one of those designs that a 3D picture of a dinosaur suddenly jumped out of if you looked for long enough. Until you were almost comatose, in Poppy's case.

She'd read the short book right through once just to get the hang of everything and tried to spend a few minutes now and then thinking about nothing, not even the someone very close to her whose breathing she liked to imagine she could hear on the other side of the wall in the stillness of the night. But emptying her mind did not come naturally and as often as not her thoughts strayed to food – the stock of chocolate in a drawer of her bedside table, the massive strawberry tart she'd brought home from the restaurant which Llewellyn had already eaten most of, but very appreciatively. She had decided that something more structured like the path-workings with their visual journeys would suit her and enable her to develop these mental powers that would change her life.

This was the first time she'd tried properly and

although it had been OK so far, her concentration was beginning to flag as she struggled up the slope by its winding path, round and round the hill, towards her goal at the top. At last she stood in front of the doorway and ready to put the key in the lock and turn the bronze handle to open the door. Wait a minute! What key? She hadn't brought a key! After a moment she remembered it wasn't real anyway so presumably she could just pretend the key had been in the pocket of this long robe thing all the time, whip it out and get in there...

Poppy sat up suddenly and fumbled under the bed for the book. She couldn't quite remember what was supposed to happen once she was inside.

Ian was talking to Frodo.

The dog was becoming quite responsive and picking up a reasonable vocabulary. His ears shot up almost vertically at the sound of the word 'biscuit' for example, and it was proving a useful decoy to get him back to his master's side on a walk. That particular four letter word he had mastered from the very first day of his new life with Ian. He was definitely a dog for the great outdoors, a free spirit and a free thinker too, for all I know, Ian thought.

He'd been reading a finished chapter of his book aloud to Frodo, trying to gauge the sound of the paragraphs to a reader's ear. Possibly the dog would not turn out to be a great judge of creative achievement, but he was all Ian had to work with at the moment. He longed to jump in the car and shoot down to Zena's house to ask her to read it through and give him some critical comments (and a bit of praise too, he hoped). He really would value her opinion and it was important she understood what he was trying to do if she was going to illustrate his book. But was she? Would he find next time they met that all had changed with the advent of this stranger, who certainly looked the part of Zena's lover?

'What do you think?' he asked Frodo, who was sitting on the floor nearby, ears up, head cocked on one side as if pondering this eternal question. He didn't look very happy about it.

'So you think it's a waste of time going to see her in the morning?'

Frodo gave a strangled sort of bark, leapt up and head-butted Ian who had been bending down to give the dog a reassuring pat.

'Ow!' He touched his forehead to see if Frodo's hard skull had actually drawn blood. 'You obviously feel very strongly about this. So shall we go tomorrow or not?'

Frodo began to dance around the room, up on his hind legs and down again, lips drawn back in a disgusting grimace, a high-pitched whine punctuating his jerky movements.

Ian had never seen this particular manoeuvre before and watched in morbid fascination.

'Good grief,' he said finally as the dog began to calm down. 'I'll take that as a yes, shall I?'

The fire was burning out slowly but Zena did not feel she could rouse herself to fetch more wood, given the listless state of her body and the weight in her heart that kept her fixed to the point where, only an hour before she and Lucas had kissed and he had said that he loved her. She was numb and weary, in the state of shock and first grief before the pain sharpens and penetrates all the mind's protective layers, rocking gently on the spot to lull and soothe her spirit.

And yet, and yet... She went over and over his words, his expressions and each touch of his hand. Without thinking, she stroked her own hair as she gazed into the embers, re-seeking the comfort and security of that caress. Hadn't he said he just needed time to sort things out? She knew only too well what he was like with work, how projects absorbed him totally, and all his emotional energies were wrapped up in the development of an idea or new direction. He could hardly drop whatever it was and just stop with her in Brittany – whatever would he do? He didn't seem to have any papers or a lap-top with him, so this had just been the briefest trip to visit his mother's grave and do whatever he had gone off to see to in the afternoon before coming to her house.

Of course he had to go back and get something organised. Maybe she could go to Paris if he preferred, but knowing how Lucas cared so little about his surroundings, she imagined he was probably renting just a room and bathroom as he had once before when working on a programme for French television. There'd be no kitchen or sitting room even – it was hardly the sort of set-up she could just slot into. They needed time and the right space if they were going to get back together again.

Just the thought of that sent a shiver through Zena's body and her physical longing for him reared up again before all else. Why hadn't he stayed the night with her? He could have left early enough to reach Paris in time for whatever commitments were waiting, or put them off a few hours. What could be more important? But he had seemed so torn – yes, that was the word – she'd seen it clearly on his face. Perhaps it was all too much for both of them, this sudden encounter and the ease with which old ties resurfaced after a long, long silence. Would it have helped just to rush into bed together (yes, something inside her shouted) as if the last year of torment for her had never happened? If they'd made love and then he'd leapt out of bed and said he had to go, wouldn't she be feeling ten times worse than she was now? That was true, if she was brutally honest. Lucas was right to put off such a binding reunion until they had a clear space together without other pressures and constraints. She had no idea what these were for him but she had to try to understand. It had all been so sudden, neither of them were mentally or emotionally ready to dive back in too quickly. He loved her, he'd said so and she would hold on to that now.

Zena had tried very hard not to consider the possibility of the other relationships he must have had along the way of their year apart. Especially now, after this tentative reunion, she could not cope with jealous thoughts and stark imaginings. Of course he wouldn't have been celibate for the last year as she had been, but she must hold on to the thought that he wouldn't have behaved as he did on seeing her again if he had found what he was looking for elsewhere. Hadn't she made any progress in self-worth over the last two months?

No, enough of this. Lucas was back in her life. He had said he'd sort things out. He loved her. He had asked her to be patient. And she would be. She was good at that.

Chapter 11

When she woke up the next morning, Zena felt both worse and better. The dreary drizzle outside suited her mood only too well. She'd cried quite hopelessly when she went to bed, thrown back into the loneliness she'd started to keep at bay quite successfully in the last few weeks, but then fell asleep, tumbling into a dream about Lucas. She saw him standing in a field, talking to the camera as if on a newscast, but she was the only audience and all his unheard words and tender smiles were for her alone. She'd tried to step towards him but it proved impossible, although she could see no obvious impediment. The experience could only mean that he was trying to communicate with her on some deeper level, to send her messages of encouragement and love.

She lay for a while replaying this reassurance and determined that she would think only positive thoughts until she heard from Lucas again. She did wish he had given her an address or telephone number so at least she would feel in touch with him in the physical world even if she didn't make use of the information, but there was no point dwelling on such little details. The answer was to keep herself busy, to carry on with all the progress she'd made since coming to Brittany and maybe act on some of Lucas' advice about her career so he'd be impressed when he returned. Which was what she hoped would happen.

To be honest she found it quite difficult to imagine herself settling into a Parisian world of eating out two or three times a day and gadding about meeting all sorts of people who might be helpful with sponsorship or publicity or marketing. She had been quite happy staying in Bath when he got on with all that in London before. Lucas always made it sound like a chore, necessary but not particularly enjoyable for its own sake and she knew quite well that he was no more a natural socialite than she was. They both liked space and calm and a quiet atmosphere to be at their best. Maybe it would work again in France if they found somewhere to live here in Finistere, a place which after all had such family memories for Lucas and had already become very important to Zena herself. She would create their home again and provide the base from which he could operate in the wider world, but this time she'd be sure to continue her own interests and develop her friendships with people like Laure and Ian rather than keeping to herself in the house.

Trying to be rational about the situation, Zena told herself that she wasn't any worse off than she'd been this time yesterday morning when she got up oblivious to what or who the day would bring. She must surely be much better off for having seen and touched Lucas again even if so very briefly? She had an emotional direction again, something to aim for. Waiting for Lucas was a condition she was more than used to but this time it would be with purpose and hope for the future.

Zena felt less grim as she turned over the new avenues of possibility in her mind. This was the hardest time now, without him again, but it would be worth it in the end. She wouldn't spoil everything by making the same mistakes again, and she was still only thirty-nine...

plenty of time for a family these days. She remembered what Ian had said to her about magic, about the power of will and self-determination — now if ever was the time for her to put that into practice and believe that her dearest wishes would come true.

Poppy heard the shouting downstairs and crept onto the landing. Part of her didn't want to listen at all because she hated quarrels, having been brought up in a house where nervous tension was sometimes relieved by scarily explosive releases of pent-up frustrations from both her parents. But she had to hear this because anything that involved a certain person concerned her too.

It was Llewellyn's voice, of course, that had reached up two flights of stairs to break into her sleep, whilst Erin's sounded like a faint murmur in comparison. Poppy crept down to the mezzanine floor landing below so she could hear both sides of the argument.

It was unfortunate that the first words she heard were 'that bloody girl!' She was tempted to stick her fingers in her ears as she'd done as a child, but that was the problem really — she couldn't do that any more. It was time to grow up properly and face up to things. They probably weren't talking about her at all.

'I tell you, I'm sick of all of it! It's time to move on, except you're too pigging stubborn to admit it...'

That was him again. Poppy didn't like the sound of those particular words one little bit. She strained to hear Erin's response, but something was banged down with a metallic din at the same time. And then she heard Llewellyn blundering through the hall and shrank back against the wall in case he saw her, but he just wrenched open the front door and went out, giving it a great slam. There was no further sound from the kitchen. Poppy wondered about going down, but she was still in her nightie and she suspected that Erin would go straight out into the yard to her workshop.

Up in her room she got dressed clumsily, trying not to give in to the sense of panic aroused by the thought of Llewellyn's words about moving on. Was it possible, could she hope even in her wildest dreams, that they'd consider taking her along too?

It was still raining persistently as Ian drove into the yard. He let Frodo out of the car to sniff around whilst he knocked on the door. The first thing he noticed about Zena when she opened it was that her eyes looked red and puffy, but before he could take in anything else or even return the welcoming smile she gave him, Frodo shot past them both into the house, did a mad circuit of the downstairs, rushed out again and veered off wildly over the bridge towards the woods.

Zena did a double-take.

'Was that a dog or just my imagination?'

Ian laughed.

'I don't know what you're talking about. I see no dog.'

They went inside and shut the door against the rain and cold wind that eddied across the yard. Sketches of Tomas, intended as a present for Laure, littered the table where Zena had been sitting.

'I'm sorry for disturbing you when you're working,' Ian said. 'I've finished a chapter of Stone Stories and just wanted to talk a bit about the illustrations if you've time.'

He watched her as she poured him out some coffee. She was looking tired, with the sort of underlying weariness of spirit that comes from an emotional dip. He knew the feeling well himself. Whatever had happened with that chap yesterday had been at best bitter-sweet and as there was no sign of him about the place, Ian assumed he'd gone back to wherever he'd appeared from. He was tempted to say to Zena that he'd seen her in the town to get some sort of reaction, but that would be a cruelly selfish thing to do if the unknown visitor had made her unhappy.

'Why don't you read it to me?' Zena said as she sat down again. 'I'm just doodling here.'

To his surprise, Ian didn't feel the least bit self-conscious. Zena was a more attentive and calmer audience than Frodo. He could see that she was listening intently, giving him her full concentration, even as her pencil moved over the paper.

'It's just a draft,' he said apologetically at the end.

'I love it,' Zena replied with a warm enthusiasm that made him want to weep. His own wife had never shown the slightest interest in any of his research, and here was this lovely woman who hardly knew him praising his work and treating it as if it was important and worth doing.

'Thank you,' he said with some feeling. 'Do you feel you'd be able to do anything with it, in terms of line drawings, I mean?'

Zena looked down at her sketch pad.

'What about something like this?'

Ian held the pad in front of him in astonishment. There it was, exactly his concept of the story and the way he wanted it visually portrayed. And she'd done it simultaneously with his own words giving birth to this creative response. There on the white page in a few black lines, were the lovers, almost petrified, their stony eyes still yearning for each other as their faces began to turn to granite, and the priest already moving away, one hand on the brim of his wide hat, an expression of smug satisfaction bringing ugly lines to his fat features.

He had to swallow hard to suppress the power of his emotional response. He wanted to give her a calm, objective reply but the paper trembling in his hand was quite a giveaway.

'It's perfect.'

'Do you mean it? It needs a lot of work on the shading obviously. But is that the sort of thing you want for the book?'

She sounded tentative and uncertain.

He nodded and swallowed again.

'Exactly like that.'

He risked a quick look at Zena and she too seemed moved by the moment, blushing and smiling with pleasure at the same time. He wondered if they were both so unused to anything going smoothly or having a natural affinity with other people that a successful collaboration on this book might really be an emotional issue for each of them.

Frodo chose that moment to explode through the door which had been left on the latch for him and hurl himself at Zena. She fell back onto a chair almost obscured by a dirty wet grey brown mass of wriggling limbs, tail and ears that seemed intent on smothering her.

'Just as well you like dogs, isn't it,' Ian said as she

struggled to extricate herself and restrict Frodo to the floor, and he then ducked quickly as a cushion sailed in the general direction of his head.

Ian stayed for more coffee and some lunch-time sandwiches, and by the time he left they had worked out a plan for the next drawings and discussed the finer points of optimum sizes and page lay-outs, based on the text he had brought. Frodo snoozed happily in front of the fire after gobbling down a hard-boiled egg by way of refreshment, and let them talk without further interruption apart from the occasional thump of his wiry tail on the carpet during an especially exciting dream hunting scenario.

Ian drove away from the house thoroughly happy about the future progress of his book and thoroughly miserable at the realisation that he was totally smitten with Zena, who clearly had someone else altogether on her mind.

For Zena it was a strange juxtaposition to spend such an easy, worry-free time with Ian in this room less than twenty-four hours since she had experienced a very different encounter here with Lucas. She liked Ian very much, more and more with each meeting in fact. She suspected, from the lack of reference to his wife and a sort of contained sadness about him sometimes, that his marriage was not a brilliantly happy one. He'd hardly be out here all alone for months, even to write his book, if that were the case. It was a shame that she'd never met anyone like Ian earlier in her life.

She found herself interested in his thoughts and what he had to say, moved by the sudden glimpses of enthusiasm, clearly habitually restrained, which lit up his face when he talked about the stones and their settings. He struck her as someone of emotional depth and sensitivity, despite a certain shyness of manner, and rarely had she felt so at ease and comfortable with anyone she'd known for so short a time. She found him attractive too, the more time she spent with him, but it was impossible for Ian's fair, open features to remain long in her mind's eye without being displaced by Lucas' dark, lean profile and shrewd brown eyes.

She'd felt the urge to confide in Ian about Lucas, but something had held her back. It was not that she didn't feel he'd understand, far from it, but it seemed a sort of presumption to draw him into her emotional world to that extent. Their relationship, although certainly friendly, was to be about work and she did not want to make things awkward between them on that score. She was really looking forward to a productive creative partnership with Ian.

She went out for a walk in the afternoon, putting aside all her resolutions about committing to work to fill her empty time with useful activity. She felt the need to be outside, not trapped with her thoughts in the draughty attic of a dreary house. She walked fast, driving herself on, filling her lungs with great gasps of fresh air. The February sky was grey but no rain threatened and there was little wind to ruffle the long reedy grass. She soon felt warm inside her fleece and very much better for the physical exertion. She wanted to be tired enough to sleep easily and avoid the long lonely hours of lying awake wondering where Lucas was.

She met no-one on the tracks up to the hills and as she

turned along a rough path that linked the sharp granite peaks along a wide, flat ridge, she began to regain that feeling of integration, of being part of some greater whole, out here where mental horizons expanded with the vastness of the views. It was impossible to be alive up here and remain trapped inside one's head by worries and anxieties. No-one could help breathing more freely and feeling the rousing call of all their senses in crossing this brumal moorland and climbing the rocky summits of the Monts d'Arrée.

For a while she even forgot about Lucas as she scanned the waves of countryside on both sides of the ridge, making out places she knew, thinking about Ian and his stones secreted all over this landscape, each in their own particular setting, each unique in alignment and orientation. Each with its own story. It was a great project and up here she felt a genuine sense of thrill to be contributing her own skills and creative responses to it.

She didn't understand the force of her physical reaction to the stones, the way she seemed to fall outside her own boundaries into another sphere like the first day at the cave, or the echoing sound waves of the dolmen filling her head to the extent that her own rhythms were obscured and lost in the primeval tug of their past history. It was like bursting some biological barrier which opened her up to their emotional energies. The whole experience was beginning to teach her something about the extraordinary powers in the atmosphere, something that Ian found natural and unthreatening, a force that could be harnessed and directed in accordance with will, if she had understood him properly. She really wanted to talk to him about it again and probe deeper into the mysteries of this extraordinary place. Were there spots outside time? Was it possible? How could it be proved? Or was it just a state of mind?

Zena wondered what Lucas would have to say about such an esoteric subject. He was very much a man of the modern world, a political animal, socially and economically aware. She somehow suspected he wouldn't have any more time for the esoteric than he did for nature for its own sake. Maybe he was right. It was all a bit hard to swallow - except that out here on the hills, it was so very simple to believe.

Laure was not enjoying her morning at all. She had driven to Morlaix to get a blood test done at the laboratory and had to wait nearly an hour with a restless Tomas wriggling and fretting in her arms. She left him with an assistant when she went into the little room and heard him crying outside as the needle went into her flesh and she watched the deep ruby liquid filling the first tube. Then she turned her head away and gazed out of the window into a little garden surrounded by a stone wall and planted with small shrubs and herbs in raised beds. There was not much to see there at this time of year but she looked carefully for any signs of new growth that might herald the arrival of spring. As she did so, it suddenly came into her head that this might be the last one she'd ever see.

It was a crazy thought, she told herself. She was thirty years old, a young mother in good health. This was just a blip, some enervating virus that would play havoc with her energy levels for a few weeks and then move on, leaving her hale and hearty again. From having a blood test to dying swiftly of some nameless disease was an irresponsible fantasy, an indulgence of melodrama quite unlike her usual down-to-earth outlook on life and its possibilities. And yet, as she stared blankly at an ornamental bay tree, its leaves blackened by frost damage, she just knew inside in a moment of cold certain horror that these were not idle fears and she was very, very ill.

Chapter 12

Time was starting to drag for Zena as more than a week passed and no word came from Lucas. Inevitably she began to wonder if he could have said what he did to extricate himself from making another mistake and get away without recrimination, never seriously intending to contact her again. She didn't really believe this. He was not weak or cowardly and she was not such a poor judge of what had happened between them. Certainly there were things she didn't understand about the situation, but Lucas' integrity was never in doubt. She had to trust to that. There was nothing else she could do. Was there?

When Llewellyn opened the door and leered at her invitingly, Zena was tempted to make some excuse and not go in, but he yanked her over the threshold before she could formulate a suitable excuse and she found herself alone with him in the colourful sitting room.

'This is a pleasant surprise, my lovely lady,' he said. 'So what can I do for you?'

'I was looking for Erin.'

'Another reading, is it? You must be going through a torrid time, cariad.'

'Is she here?'

Llewellyn looked round the room and bent to peer under the sofa.

'I don't think so, precious. You'll have to make do with me, but I'm very good at giving advice on matters of the heart, you know. I can give you better help than any old tarot cards — coloured cardboard's not a lot of use in life really, now is it?'

Not quite liking his suggestive expression, Zena took a step towards the door, but there was little room to squeeze out round his bulk.

'Gone off, has he? The boyfriend?'

This startled her.

'Who?'

'You were seen, my little firebird. Nothing happens in this dump without Llewellyn ap Gryffud hearing all about it. So come on now. Tell me all your secrets and then we'll see how I can be of service to you.'

'You can get out of the way for a start!'

'Not so fast, Zena!'

He was enjoying her discomfort and pretended to lunge for her as she reached for the door. Zena gave a startled squeak, side-stepped into the plinth on which Erin's blue bowl stood and sent it crashing to the ground.

Llewellyn laughed nastily.

'Now look what you've done, you naughty girl.'

He came up behind her as she frantically scrabbled around for the broken pieces of pottery, but she was saved by the door opening and Erin's arrival on the scene. She almost fell over Zena in the process, and Llewellyn had to catch his sister to keep her upright.

'I'm sorry,' Zena said in embarrassment. 'It was an accident. I was just...'

'Escaping, I expect,' Erin said calmly. 'Don't worry about it.' She turned to Llewellyn. 'Those pieces on the bench are ready for delivery. You can take the van, I'll be here for the rest of the day.'

He kissed her hand extravagantly. 'Your wish is my

command, sister of my heart. Expect me when you see me. I've a delivery of my own to make.'

He left, whistling, with a loud wink in Zena's direction.

The two women smiled at each other.

'Are you OK?' Erin said.

'I'm fine, but what about your bowl, I'm so sorry.'

Erin shook her head.

'I've a dozen more like it out in the shed. I used to make nothing but back in Wales when I first took up pottery. Honestly, it's no problem.'

'But what am I going to put my money in?' Zena said, taking out her purse.

There was something hypnotic about Erin's shuffling of the cards and Zena waited in a state of suspended animation, feeling listless and withdrawn from this action she hoped would help in some mysterious way - for they were after all, as Llewellyn had said, just pieces of cardboard.

Erin seemed to pick up on her mood. She was unhurried in her movements and her eyes were dreamy.

'Is there something specific this time?' she asked eventually.

Zena gave a big sigh.

'So everyone really does know!'

'What? You had a coffee in the bar with a friend was all I heard. Could be your brother or could be Lucas. I feel it might help to know for the reading, but it's entirely up to you.'

It was a shock for Zena to hear Lucas' name spoken so naturally by someone else. She had almost forgotten telling Erin about him. Of course she would think the stranger in town might be Lucas.

'It was Lucas,' she said. 'He turned up unexpectedly, not to see me, his family used to live here, but we met by chance.'

'And?'

'And something seemed to reignite between us, but then he went off again without an explanation, and I haven't heard from him since, despite me getting the impression he would be coming back.'

Put like that, she felt cold bleakness of her situation as if for the first time. She pressed her lips together tightly to keep the tears at bay. There was to be no more crying. She was here for answers.

Erin's face was full of sympathy.

'I'm sorry. That's so hard for you. And I expect you're assuming the worst right now.'

'I go up and down, but the longer this waiting goes on the harder it is to hold on to the thought he's coming back, and if he isn't... well, I don't know what I'll do this time.'

Erin was dealing out the cards, face up into two piles. She then handed the smaller one to Zena. She noticed it was a different deck this time.

'Look at those court cards carefully and choose the one you feel represents you, and then one to do the same for Lucas. Don't dwell on it too long, just trust your instincts.'

Puzzled, Zena leafed through the cards. Each had a single figure, man, woman or adolescent. She felt instantly drawn to one of the women, the Queen of Wands, with her long red hair. The male figures were harder. She hesitated long and hard before handing the

King of Swords to Erin, who placed both cards side by side, with an empty card's width between them. 'Here you are,' she said softly. 'You and Lucas. This card...' she pulled one from the reshuffled deck and placed it face down in the lower part of the space between the pair, 'is what binds you, and this' – she drew another and set it above, still between the two court cards, 'is what separates you. OK?'

Zena nodded dumbly. She was prepared for a well-known scene to surface from the latter. It was with a kind of fascinated dread that she watched Erin turn the first card.

'The Four of Swords unites you.'

And the second.

'The Seven of Swords comes between you.'

At last, a reading with no sign of that wretched Five of Cups. She wasn't doomed to a life of disappointment and regret after all!

'There's a lot of swords,' she said.

'Three out of four's not bad!' Erin smiled. 'I don't think we can ignore the significance of the suit.'

'And it is?'

'Mental force, the intellect, reason, logic, justice, truth...'

'Sounds OK...'

'... and their negatives, like dogmatism, domineering behaviour, intolerance.'

'Those don't sound like either of us at all.'

Erin ignored this.

'Swords indicate troubles and difficulties too.'

'Well, that makes sense. Although the guy in the Four looks peaceful enough.'

The card showed a figure asleep, leaning against a rock, surrounded by the swords. 'Is that what binds me and Lucas, sleep?'

Erin, as usual, didn't respond to Zena's nervous babbling. For a minute she stayed silent, fixed on the cards.

'I think perhaps you and Lucas each used your relationship as a form of emotional escape, a quiet time of non-engagement,' she said at last.

The shock Zena felt was like a deluge of icy water. She saw the truth of it at once. They had created a safe zone, without total passion or total commitment, a place that was satisfactory but not fulfilling for either of them. She wanted a child, a family. And Lucas wanted, well, obviously something else as he'd left her. Was it possible that he saw things differently now, but still balked at the final step?

'And the Seven of Swords?'

She wanted to get it all out of the way, for the reading to be over. She didn't have the sticking power for Erin's insight and the painful feelings it aroused.

The last card showed a man walking uphill on his own, five swords held over his shoulder, two left in the ground behind.

'It seems to me that what separates you is Lucas' desire for going it alone. Look at him, gathering up as many swords as he can and going off with them for his own purposes.'

'I don't see him like that,' Zena said sharply.

Erin was unperturbed.

'From what you told me Lucas is very involved in his projects, doing whatever that takes, following his own path about the world not just physically, but in his head too. These things, these mental things, take priority over an intimate relationship. He values the whole picture but the detail eludes him. Like someone collecting paintings because they're worth a lot of money without actually exploring what the pictures mean.' She shrugged. 'There's often an element of dishonesty in this card — something you might like to think about.'

Zena was genuinely shocked.

'But Lucas is not like that!'

'I know you don't see him like that. This is your perception' — she tapped the King of Swords — 'upright, honourable, truthful. But life isn't always as simple as that. I think the King of Swords would have told you why he had to rush off and what was really in his head.'

'So you think he was pretending to be in love with me again?'

'The cards don't speak of strong emotional involvement to me, but they do have an important message for you.'

'Meaning what?' Zena said without bothering to disguise the scepticism of her tone.

'Meaning, THINK about it, Zena! Stop looking for clear-cut answers from outside and search within. Consider what this reading has offered you and reject it if you like, but be honest and look inside yourself for the truth. I think it's an issue in this relationship.'

They sat in silence for a moment, Zena trying to contain her reactions, trying not to burst out with angry arguments and an instinctive, passionate defence of Lucas' character.

'Do you want another card for an overview?' Erin asked at length.

'No, I don't think so. You've certainly given me a lot of difficult things to think about.'

She got up to go, fixing a brave smile on her face.

After Zena had left, Erin went back to the table and drew another card.

It was the Five of Cups.

That figures, she said to herself. It was either that or the Three of Swords.

After delivering Erin's commissions, Llewellyn took himself off to a bar on the main road beyond La Folle where he went occasionally to avoid the usual acquaintances. He had several whiskies in quick succession, standing at the counter, and for once did not try to strike up conversations or to insert himself into already existing ones. He felt rather sorry for himself and still angry with Erin and her calm acceptance of whatever crap he threw at her. She always had the upper hand with her iron self-control, whereas he had none whatsoever and needed a constant outlet for all the great mass of disappointments he'd accumulated over the years. He wanted to provoke her, to fracture that hippy mask of good will, to pay her back for all the years of amused tolerance he'd had to endure from her. He had no doubt of his own superiority: his mind was quick, if relentlessly superficial, but he could not suppress the gnawing restlessness that drove him and everyone who got involved with him crazy. He was incapable of self-motivation or the inner life that Erin enjoyed. He had to stir things up to feel alive, force a reaction from others to give himself something to play off. But where it was once humour, music, laughter, he now felt the recurring impulse to hurt, wound and pierce the equilibrium of those around him. Part of him feared this tendency, and feared the unknown doom to which it was leading him, but self-indulgence had wrecked the mechanisms that might have saved him and all he could think of now was provoking the final row that would send him away, out of the orbit of the only person who cared about him, to be free of the burden of that care and free to go to hell in whatever way he chose.

Ian swore when he saw another letter from Leah lying in wait in the post-box like a ticking bomb. Something must have happened to set her writing again within days of the last – or was it weeks? Time out here did not hold the same significance as in his old life across the Channel. It was not an issue at all: he rarely knew what day of the week it was, weekends were a thing of the past, and he had given up wearing his watch as he had nothing to be on time for or to anticipate. All he felt was the bliss of a clock-less freedom, and a constant awareness of the changing season around him, the nights now quickly drawing out, so he could sit outside between six and seven in the evening, his favourite time of day, and watch the birds' last fidgets before settling down, as they bid him goodnight in precise, mellow voices.

He didn't want to go in and read the letter. There was a long raft of brambles by the gate that he'd been meaning to cut back for ages, so he went to fetch his secateurs from the shed and spent a good five minutes taming the beasts that would soon completely over-run the garden given half a chance as the year turned. He threw a stick for Frodo and then gave up after fetching it himself a few times. The dog either completely ignored its swift arcing course, or would run after it eagerly enough, taking a huge leap and dive onto his prey, but then invariably fall over and prove completely incapable of working out that he was actually lying on the stick. His head would flick round from side to side, ears twitching in bewilderment that a sizeable chunk of wood could vanish so mysteriously.

'Come on, then,' Ian said finally. 'Let's not put it off any longer.'

Frodo trotted in obediently and sat in his basket by the fire watching his master thoughtfully. Ian was tempted to give him the envelope and later justly claim the dog had eaten it, but as Leah was totally unaware of the presence of Frodo in her husband's life and would have had a great deal of unpleasant things to say if she did know, he decided against it.

'I suppose I've got to face up to... oh, shit!'

He leapt up in consternation, causing Frodo also to leap wildly with an ululating howl that went right through Ian's skull.

'Shut up, you silly mutt, you're making things worse!'

If they could possibly be so. He looked at the thin blue paper again.

'... so as Tom and Betty are going down to their place next week, I've taken advantage of their kind offer to drop me on the way. I'll take the boat with them and we'll all be with you about half-past seven... I can leave the car at Plymouth, so if you take me back to Roscoff I'll go back as a foot-passenger too, so we'll save money... make sure there's some food in so we can offer something to the Parkers, maybe a bottle of sherry too... and try to have the cottage looking smart, won't you Ian?'

No, I fucking won't, he thought savagely. Christ, all these arrangements and tedious minutiae hurt his brain even more than Frodo's yelping had done. He couldn't bear it, having his wife in this place that he'd come to regard as his own, suffering her complaints about the practical work that remained unfinished (most of it, now he thought about it), experiencing her inevitable rejection of the dog.

He looked at Frodo whose expression was now decidedly anxious as he watched Ian pacing, uncharacteristically tetchily, about the room. Ian went down on his knees by the basket and stroked the mottled head firmly.

'No-one's going to separate us, mate. Don't you worry about that.'

But Ian was worried. Leah arriving with the bloody Parkers in tow was the worst possible scenario. Frodo hated strangers at the best of times, but a load of yakking fuss-pots crammed into this tiny space where the two of them co-existed perfectly happily didn't bear thinking about. It would give him no chance to explain or prepare Leah for Frodo's appearance. He absolutely refused to think of locking the dog in the barn for the ghastly evening, although knowing Frodo he'd batter the door down anyway or set up such a din that the slates would fall off the roof.

No, he had to avoid this initial confrontation. He was too cowardly to face a tussle of wills in public after quite a long separation from his wife. My God, Leah in the flesh with her permed hair and carefully co-ordinated leisure wear would actually be here in a week's time. It was the most awful prospect he could have conjured up even in a nightmare. He'd just have to hope that Zena — he couldn't bear to contemplate a meeting between Leah and Zena - would understand and provide a temporary refuge for Frodo.

Tomas really wanted to stand up. Everyone else did it and he was tired of a world limited to floor-level. He hauled himself up by grasping the arm of the sofa, did a half-turn and then let go, wildly flapping his hands as if about to soar into the air. Instead he plumped down on his bottom with a little bounce on the soft carpet. Mummy was just a few feet away in the kitchen preparing his lunch. He could smell food and had a vague sense of some desire stirring, but this was soon forgotten in another attempt to lever himself off the floor and stand unaided. Some instinct told him it was a very important, life-changing goal. This time he did it and gave a loud squeaky gasp to attract Laure's attention, but she turned on the liquidiser at that very second and neither heard the sound nor saw Tomas totter a few paces before falling back onto the soon-to-be despised safety of the floor. So she did not know that her little son had just taken his first real steps and Tomas didn't know that his Mummy was now convinced that she really was dying.

It was a couple of weeks since Zena had seen Laure. She wanted to give her the sketches of Tomas and she also wanted to talk about Lucas.
Since Erin's reading, Zena had suffered an inner turmoil she hadn't experienced before, even in her worst lows in England, after Lucas' first departure, when all the focus of her mental agonising had been on what she

had done wrong or whether he would come back. She had not dwelt at any length on their relationship as a whole and considered its true merits, but just accepted as a given that it was what she wanted. She was blinded by her physical thrall to Lucas and her infallible belief in his intelligence and completeness. He was not an arrogant man, but she never thought of criticising him or questioning how their joint life worked, never thought it odd that he didn't suggest taking her along on one of his trips. Neither was he ever apologetic about going off for a month here and there – that was how he was, how his working life functioned – it was a fact of life rather than something up for discussion. She felt naïve and stupid now to think she'd never even realised this at the time. None of these new thoughts were directed against Lucas but more against herself and her meek acceptance, her lack of self-examination in the last analysis. She could only think that she hadn't wanted to rock the boat, and anyway, she really did like time on her own. At least in those days he had written or phoned from time to time, not simply disappeared as he seemed to have done now.

She rang the bell at the white-rendered house and waited in the porch. No footsteps came, and at first she wondered if Laure was down in Camaret again enduring the criticism and indulgence of her mother-in-law. Then she put her ear to the door and caught the unmistakable sounds of a young child crying. She rang the bell again.

Laure finally opened the door looking exhausted and uncharacteristically vague for a moment before she rallied and greeted Zena with surprised pleasure. She led the way into the living room, picking up toys and discarded shoes as they went, apologising for the mess. It all looked quite organised to Zena, but, even though they did not know each other very well, she realised that Laure was not quite herself.

Tomas greeted Zena with delight and whacked the sketches of himself enthusiastically, making noises like a donkey braying as his mother tried to coax him to say his own name in response to them. There was no doubt that Laure's admiration and gratitude were sincere, which pleased Zena enormously. She lifted Tomas onto her lap and began to pull faces that made him laugh and then throw his head backwards to return the favour of entertainment and amusement.

Laure watched them.

'I wonder if you would have time to look after Tomas next week for a couple of hours on Tuesday afternoon. I have an appointment and it is much easier to go without this little one.' She leant over to poke him in the stomach affectionately.

'I'd love to,' Zena replied. 'It'll be fun.'

'He usually sleeps for one or two hours after lunch, so you may be lucky and not have to occupy him at all.'

'That would be a shame - I'd much prefer to give him a good tickle!'

She did so as she spoke and made Tomas scream in ecstasy. Laure laughed as she went to the kitchen to make coffee and listened to the happy sounds of her little son. She wondered for a moment about telling Zena the truth about her appointment, but decided against it. There'd be time enough for that if the worst happened.

When Tomas' attention was briefly absorbed by a Franklin video, Zena related to Laure her surprise meeting with Lucas in the cemetery.

'Lucas?' Laure looked startled. She pronounced the name in the French way, without sounding the final 's.' 'That's the name of your man, the one you lived with in England?'

'Yes, Lucas, why?' Zena was suddenly afraid. 'Do you know him?'

'No, no, it is not I who know him, but my neighbour, Madame Le Gall. She was a friend of his mother's. He came to visit her last week.'

'Ah.' So Zena now knew what his afternoon business had been and it was hardly a big mystery. He must enjoy talking about his mother to someone remaining from her generation and who had presumably known him as a boy here in La Folle.

Laure was looking puzzled.

'But, Zena, he can't be the same one surely?'

'Of course, he is! It would be a bit of a co-incidence for two different Lucases to be here in La Folle on the same day!'

Laure didn't laugh. She began to play abstractedly with Tomas, who had grown tired of staring at the screen and was now busily arranging and destroying piles of wooden blocks on the floor.

'But why shouldn't they be the same?' Zena persisted, her heart thudding with anxiety and a sense of deep foreboding.

Laure looked up at her strangely.

'I'm sorry,' she said.

'What is it? What's happened?'

'Perhaps she got it wrong, but I don't think so,' Laure said. 'She's still very sharp for her age and the detail was quite precise.'

'What detail?'

Zena was increasingly distraught. She knew that something awful was coming. Laure was looking at the floor again.

'He told Madame Le Gall he's getting married.'

'WHAT!'

The word shot out of her like a flame.

'I'm so sorry, Zena. He's about to get married. To a Russian.'

Chapter 13

Zena didn't remember driving back to the house.

Rigid with the numbness of betrayal, she sat down at the white melamine table and stared blankly at the dirty wall, imprisoned by the turmoil of her thoughts but lacking the strength to get up and do something else. There was no distraction powerful enough to deflect this reality. No wonder Lucas had rushed off to get away from her, with his prospective bride to get back to. Taking another lover just before getting married was going it a bit for anyone, and Lucas was not at all that sort. She had never worried about his fidelity during all those long absences – perhaps she had been a naïve fool in that respect too? Had the whole thing, all those four and a half years of her life, been an utter sham and a complete waste of time? Had he been pretending then as he must have pretended the week before, in this very room when he said he loved her. But why, why, why? She had not tried to force him, to re-entice him in any way. It was sad to think how low her true expectations had been, and it was only when he put his hand on her shoulder – voluntarily – in Jean-Yves' presence that she had dared to imagine any sort of reunion might be possible.

But this was it now, this was over the brink, off the edge of the precipice, into the void. Lucas was going to marry another woman and there was no chance of a future with him for Zena. She must look at the reality and accept it. There was no other way. She felt no desire to cry or rage, but dully got up and forced her heavy limbs up the stairs to the attic. She had plenty of work to do for Ian's book and the agent had phoned to say the card company wanted more of her designs. There was a new life in all this to be built and planned for, and even though she would really have liked to chuck herself in the river or become entombed for ever in the depths of the cave, she had better forget about the past and get on with the future right away.

She worked like a zombie for the next few hours and then grabbed her lifeless sketches, put on a coat and went out to the car in the dark. She knew where the track to Ian's cottage forked off the road past La Folle, but this was the first time she'd bumped what seemed like endlessly uphill along the uneven surface. Oblivious to the jolts and bounces, she went forward steadily, making for the only lights visible on the fringe of the forest in its deeper darkness.

Ian heard the car coming. For a moment of horror he thought it was Leah and the wretched Parkers arriving a week early. He dragged an uncomprehending Frodo into the bathroom and slammed the door shut. The dog was so stunned he stayed quiet. Ian put on the outside light and stood nervously in the open doorway. When he saw Zena get out of her little car, he could barely resist the urge to rush out and throw his arms round her. That was before he saw the expression on her face.

Inside it was even worse. He looked anxiously at her frozen features, a cold mask on the usually mobile face and knew that something awful had happened. He refrained from questions and busied himself with settling her by the fire, then making hot coffee laced with brandy. She smiled at him so sadly when she took the cup that his heart lurched as if he'd slipped on ice and could not prevent a fall.

Frodo suddenly let out a great roar to remind them both of his presence and on release from the bathroom threw himself at Zena, nearly sending the mug flying. Ian mopped up the spills and tried to calm the dog.

They looked through her sketches in silence.

Zena rubbed a hand roughly over her face as if to stir herself back into life.

'They're no good, are they?'

'You couldn't do a no good drawing if you tried, but they are different. I can't quite explain why, but the lines are sort of heavier. It makes the figures feel enclosed somehow.'

'I'm sorry.'

She sounded so desolate it was hard not to enfold her in his arms and comfort her like a child.

'Do you want to talk about whatever's happened?' he asked gently.

'How did you know?'

He laughed.

'Zena, I'm delighted to see you but it's not the usual hour for visitors, and, well, you look awful, as if your light has gone out.'

She said nothing.

'I saw you last week with someone in the square...' he began tentatively.

'Good grief, is there anyone on this side of the channel who didn't see me?'

'Sorry.'

'No, it's just funny really. I was completely oblivious to my surroundings when every single person I know in Brittany was watching me.' She gave a small rueful smile. 'I ran into someone I used to live with back in England. He didn't know I was here.'

'That's quite a coincidence.'

'He's from here, originally. That's why I came here, to be honest. After he left me. I know it doesn't make sense…'

'You wanted to be as near as you could be without him.'

She looked at him in gratitude.

'Exactly. Do you really understand that? Anyway he came back and now he's gone again. From what happened last week, I was expecting to hear something from him about getting back together, but I've just found out, by chance' – her voice wavered – 'that in fact he's about to get married. To someone else obviously.'

Ian was both pleased this man was on the point of marriage and keen to kill him for hurting Zena so badly. She was still talking.

'I never was any good at the whole relationship thing. All I wanted was to be normal - get married, have a family, be part of something bigger than just me. All my friends did the conventional thing and have partners of one sort or another. I feel as if everyone's at some great party I haven't been invited to and I'm home alone like an outcast.'

Ian stared into the flames of the wood-burner.

'Have you ever considered it might be the world's most boring party?'

She managed a little smile.

'In my mind, they're always having a wonderful time.'

'But isn't that always the case? You look in a lighted

window, see a family watching television and think how happy and cosy they must all be, whereas in fact the husband's planning undetectable ways of murdering his wife and she's worried to death about the daughter's anorexia. And the couple in the restaurant look so romantic, but he's slipping out the back to phone his girlfriend on the mobile...'

She was looking at him with a real flicker of interest. He felt embarrassed to have given himself away so easily.

'I just mean things are rarely as they seem to an outsider,' he finished lamely.

Zena was thoughtful.

'So you don't think marriage is necessarily the be all and end all in other words.'

'No, I don't.'

'Or children?'

'I've survived without them.' Unfortunately, he thought, but didn't say. 'We have to make our lives out of what we've got.'

He wasn't going to say more, out of loyalty to Leah as much as anything. They were still very much married and she had no idea that he was here in France enjoying an intimate conversation with someone he was falling in love with. The fact that it had been a sexless marriage for nine long years was not something he'd care to discuss with anyone. In his heart, he knew that an end of the marriage had to come, whether or not Zena was to play any part at all in his future life.

'Thanks.'

'What for?'

'You've made me see outside my miserable head for a minute,' she said. 'And I feel better for it. I'm sorry to have invaded your space like this though. I was so wrapped up in myself I didn't think about the time at all.'

'I'm always glad to see you, Zena,' he said with obvious sincerity. 'Actually I've a big favour to ask you. Could you have Frodo at your place overnight next week?'

She was surprised by the underlying anxiety in his voice.

'Of course I will. Are you going away?'

'No. It's a bit difficult to explain.'

'There's no need. I'll be happy to have him. The company will be good.'

If he had been on the brink of loving her before, he was right there now. With Zena there was no need for all the tedious explanations and endless what ifs and but whys that characterised every move Leah ever made. Just the acceptance he had always craved.

Erin was sitting in her workshop staring into space. She wasn't in the mood for creating anything this morning. Pressures building in the house around Poppy and Llewellyn with their different problems were beginning to get to her. She saw quite clearly what those problems were and that she was powerless to intervene, even if she had believed it right to interfere with another's will. Something she must do, however, was to protect herself. All the festering frustration and lack of fulfilment was beginning to sour the atmosphere in which she lived and invade her own mental space which she had once regarded as inviolate.

She sat on a cushion in the corner near the old stove, back straight, legs crossed, her usual meditation pose, and began to draw deep breaths through her slight body until the rhythm soothed her mind and led her down a tunnel of light into a dark absence of thought. She remained motionless for the next fifteen minutes, lost to the conscious world, unaware of Poppy peering through the dirty windows and watching her for some time, anxiety and despair written on her big face.

When Erin had finished, she walked a little unsteadily over to the house and made a sandwich. She needed to eat to ground herself again after the deep meditation. She felt so much better: in touch with her emotions and with a clarity of thought that had temporarily deserted her.

Perhaps Llewellyn was right and a change of scene was needed. She'd been given enough hints lately. Almost every time she went out, she seemed to bump into one or other of the couple with the pottery stall in the market. She liked them both and admired their work. They divided their time between creative art and restoring what amounted to an entire hamlet of little houses and stone outbuildings just outside La Folle. Their intention was eventually to open a fully fledged craft centre during the six months of the tourist season and carry on their own work in the winter. Maybe she had something to contribute there. They had certainly been in her thoughts a lot lately and there was nothing accidental about these connections. She had always paid attention to such promptings in the past and recognised the signs, or signposts as she liked to think of them.

There was a light drizzle of rain through the pines as Ian took Frodo for a walk before sitting down to work on his book. He found it hard to settle his concentration as the day of Leah's arrival inched nearer. Everything he'd been doing and feeling out here seemed increasingly vulnerable, and liable to crumble to nothing under the sharpness of her tongue and the weight of her expectations. He still didn't know if he would have the courage to say what he wanted to when the time came, or if the power of convention would drag him back into the fold even now when he had glimpsed the possibilities of a life that had seemed closed to him for so long.

Frodo dashed about sniffing the aromatic damp floor of the forest, oblivious of the terrible threat hanging over them both. He revelled in his freedom, far less inclined to run off now that he became more confident of staying with Ian and having a home and life of his own. He actually kept one eye on his master, ready to bound after him in a new direction or respond to the sound of his voice. He could no longer remember what elusive thing he had chased so wildly on first being released from the constraints of the rescue centre.

As usual, a buzzard was hovering on a current of air above the wild ridge. Ian watched its apparently nonchalant poise and the elegance of movement even in the vicious swoop before it mounted again triumphantly, a tiny animal skewered in its claws. He admired its freedom of movement, the independence of fending for oneself and managing with whatever resources you could produce by your own efforts. Not relying on other people. He sighed as he remembered the advent of Leah and the Parkers. He'd have to get on with cleaning up the house a bit whether he liked it or not. Old habits were too hard to break in a moment of defiance. Thinking of Zena might have helped his resolve a week ago, but now it all seemed hopeless with the re-appearance of her old love, who clearly still retained his power over Zena's heart. She was gripped in the vice of past emotional patterns every bit as much as Ian himself was. And anyway, would he want to start a relationship with someone when he would always be wondering when the other chap would turn up again and take away all his happiness?

Back in the cottage he made a desultory attempt to tidy away a few things, but was soon enticed away by the siren call of his manuscript and books, settling himself contentedly for a few hours of oblivion of all the hard things he was going to have to face in the coming week. He wanted to do some preparation for a visit he was going to make later in the day, which had arisen out of a chance encounter with his nearest neighbour. Assuming the farmer was a local man, he'd asked about the dolmen where he'd first met Zena.

The family of Bernard Le Guen had lived on their farm, about a kilometre from Ian, since the mid 19th century. His grandmother, who was 86, still inhabited the single storey original farmhouse, just across the yard from the modern house where another three generations of the family were established. Like so many, this was built in the 1970s when the lot of farmers began to improve financially with the development of the European Union. Bernard had invited him to go and talk to the old lady who apparently knew stories about the dolmen that he wouldn't find in any book. Despite the warning that she was liable to lapse into Breton, Ian was hopeful that he'd come away with some original material for the book.

The book was becoming more and more important to him now, a symbol of what he wanted to be and do in his life and a connection to the wild landscape of Finistere that he felt must always have been lurking in his bones. He was not going to let it go so easily. Going back to England, to the run-of-the-mill college, dreary colleagues and dead marriage was unthinkable. There had to be a way.

'What do you think?' he asked Frodo, who appeared to be asleep with his eyes open. 'Shall we stay here in this cottage for ever?'

A single bark seemed to confirm that the plan was a good idea. From that moment it became fixed in Ian's head as a desirable goal. Having voiced the notion, it became a plan and one he was determined to fulfil. He might even ask Bernard if he ever had need of an extra pair of hands. There must be some busy times of the farming year when some casual labour was needed, and Ian was pretty much on the spot. There were always possibilities, he must remember that and stop assuming the worst.

'Do you think love spells work?'

Erin went on with peeling vegetables while she considered her answer to this question.

'If they're done properly, yes.'

Poppy looked worried. It had been hard enough to steel herself to ask the question.

'What's properly?'

'Not interfering with someone else's will. Not expecting something to happen that's impossible. Not thinking you can make someone love you if they don't. That sort of thing.'

Poppy's face was flushed and she did not look at Erin.

'What's the point then if you can't do any of that?

Erin smiled.

'Magic is the art of putting yourself in harmony with positive energy. You can attract love into your life with a love spell, without saying I want A or B or even C. Ask for love itself, be open to it and let the universe bring you what you need.'

'But what if it's A or B you need?' Poppy persisted stubbornly.

'Then if it's right for A or B too, I expect you'll find yourself getting what you want. But maybe you should think about whether A or B have given you any sign that they were interested in you in that way. Consider if your expectations are realistic before you start asking for the gods to weigh in too. It's easy to misread things when we want something a lot.'

Seeing Poppy's wobbly lower lip, Erin decided to change the subject. She'd given Poppy the best hint she could without causing an open fuss that would disrupt the whole household. It really was time that the girl grew up a bit and took some responsibility for her life.

'Have you heard from your parents lately? Any plans to go back and pay them a visit?'

'I did have a letter last week.' Poppy looked sulky. 'They're always asking me to go home for a bit and look for a job. My mum's friend Mary says I could have some work at the local hotel this summer.'

'Good idea.'

'Do you think so? But what about everything here?'

Poppy nervously scanned Erin's serene face. The green eyes were cool and clear.

'What everything? Look around you, Poppy. Your parents will be keen to spoil you. Give yourself a chance to take stock and make some choices. Get in control of your life. It's time.'

Chapter 14

Tomas was still asleep when Laure left for her appointment. Zena had helped to put him to bed so the shock of finding himself alone with her later wouldn't be so great.

'Don't worry,' Zena reassured his mother. 'He'll be fine with me. We'll have fun.'

She noticed that Laure seemed unusually anxious, and wondered if it was the doctor or hospital she was attending. Perhaps she was pregnant again? It wasn't the sort of thing she felt she could ask, but Laure's usual mask of competence had certainly slipped lately.

She sat glancing through a French newspaper, alert for sounds of restlessness from the little bedroom at the top of the stairs. It was strange to be in a modern, smart and well-ordered home for a change and she looked around at the leather sofas, large flat-screen TV and sleek metallic open kitchen as if they were manifestations from another world compared with what she had become used to in the shabby house by the river. It was not a style she hankered after, but it represented something she very much wanted – a family unit, a partnership for planning and regulating a joint life, rather than making decisions by oneself, when it somehow didn't seem quite so important and things just happened in random sequence in response to outside circumstances. Maybe this was just an illusion born of her depressed state, because she had tried to create something special at the flat in Bath. But she had done it alone. She could not imagine discussing a suitable type of new sofa with Lucas or going out to buy curtain material with him. The supermarket was about the only place they had shopped together.

A muffled cry came from upstairs and Zena leapt up to go and fetch Tomas. He cried even more when he saw someone other than his mother and at first refused to hold up his arms so Zena could lift him from the cot. He clutched the wooden rails, his face bright red and streaked by large tears, peering past her in the hope of seeing Laure's beloved shape in the doorway.

'Mummy's coming back soon,' Zena said to him in French. 'There's nothing to worry about, she'll be here soon.'

She picked up a stuffed rabbit from the cot, gave it a big hug and kiss and started to whisper into the rather matted fur of its blue ear. She turned away from Tomas and then back, making the rabbit mime her movements and continuing to talk softly to it. Intrigued and then enraged at being left out as she stepped towards the door, Tomas roared to be picked up, waving his arms in angry demand.

Downstairs he began to cry again as soon as he realised there was no Laure and nothing Zena could do seemed to distract him from his abandoned plight. He struggled to be put down on the floor and then crawled miserably around, looking in vain for the only thing that would offer him true security. Unable to bear his distress, Zena scooped him up again and sat down, holding him tightly towards her. Eventually the sobs subsided and Tomas fell into the deep sleep of nervous exhaustion. His head rested under her chin and she kept one hand securely on his bottom, stroking his head and back with the other. She was not in a comfortable position herself, but she dreaded waking him, so she sat on, smelling his skin and hair, feeling his solid weight against her chest. Feelings of longing swept over her for the child she'd never had, for all the hope and promise of the little life encircled by her arms and all the parental love he embodied. She tried to imagine Lucas as a father – would he roll around on the carpet playing silly games to entertain and amuse his son spontaneously, or would fatherhood have to be fitted in amongst his other commitments so that its time was limited and rationed to a timetable that suited him? She imagined him here with her now, handing him the soft bundle of Tomas, sharing a look of pride and complicity at the wonder of their potential child. But then she remembered that Lucas was going to marry someone else, some beautiful Russian girl – the thought of Lucas having children with anyone was too much to bear and she struggled to blot out the image. She thought of Ian, for some reason, also childless, and wondered if he had wanted a family and if so what had happened to prevent it. Now he would make a good father. Out of nowhere came a picture of Ian and a toddler on a beach, throwing spadefuls of sand at each other as Frodo gambolled madly around them. She could hear the toddler's eager shouts and see the devoted smile on Ian's face...

This was mad. None of that was going to be for her now, she knew inside. It was all too late and the sooner that little voice stopped saying there was still time, still time for her..... the better.

Poppy was walking along the road. She'd been out

longer than she realised and now it was raining. Her cotton fleece was damp as well as warm from the unaccustomed exertion of exercise. Erin's words had really made an impression on her, sort of opened her eyes to a lot of things. Today she was determined to make a new start, to stop thinking about her usual obsession and get on with being in control of her own life. She'd put on a lot of weight lately and knew she looked a mess in general so it was time to take action. Walking was fine, she quite enjoyed looking at the countryside. It was pretty and unthreatening so she could relax, away from the house. It was amazing how things looked different when you got right away from a bad situation physically.

She wished she'd had a bigger lunch though. Two crispbreads with sliced tomato followed by an apple was not really enough to sustain her through the six kilometre circuit she'd followed via wooden signposts from the centre of La Folle. Funnily enough she'd been thinking a lot about her parents on the route. They were always trying to get her to go on country walks, and then tried not to look too upset by her rude reactions. They'd given her too much freedom and she had hardly used it wisely. She could see that now and rather regretted that she hadn't been up to that sort of challenge. Miserable seemed to be her middle name then as a moody teenager and if she was not careful she'd go right through life crying for the moon and expecting everything to work out as she wanted without putting in the effort herself.

A car passed her and then drew up a little ahead. It was a long way to the nearest house and her first thought was anxiety, although she'd rashly hitched lifts many times back in England. She was wondering what she could do if the situation turned tricky when Zena's head appeared out of the window and Poppy ran up gratefully to get out of the rain.

They talked about nothing very much for the short distance back to the town, but when Zena drew up opposite Erin's house she put out a hand to keep Poppy from leaping out.

'I'm sorry if you think I'm interfering but there's something I must say to you.'

Poppy felt alarmed. She had nearly told Zena all about it once, so perhaps she'd guessed and was going to express her horror and be all judgmental now.

'I must get back...'

'Just a minute, please. It's important, Poppy. It's easy sometimes to be, well, taken in by people, sort of overwhelmed by their personalities.'

Poppy gave her a puzzled look. This was not what she'd been expecting. Zena seemed nervous, not about to lay down the law or give her a lot of grief. Perhaps in her new spirit of growth and maturity Poppy would listen to what she had to say.

'It's just, I'm sorry, it's none of my business really, but don't do anything you don't want to, will you, Poppy? Lust is fine, of course it is, but love is something else, if you understand me.'

Poppy looked at her in astonishment.

'I don't think I do.'

Zena was covered in confusion.

'You having a thing about Llewellyn, I mean. He's really not such a nice sort of person, you know, and...'

'Llewellyn? I know! He's horrible and slimy!'

'But aren't you in love with him?'

'You must be joking. He's a colossal prat who can't keep his hands to himself.'

Zena put her hands over her face.

'I'm sorry. I've got this all wrong. I thought that being at the house was so difficult for you because of unrequited love...'

'That's right.'

'But... ' She took her hands away and looked at Poppy's blushing face. 'Oh, I see. I'm very sorry, Poppy.'

'No problem. Well, I'm going in now unless you want to have a go at me about being a sad and disgusting cow.' Her lips were trembling as she spoke. 'Thanks for the lift.'

She slammed the car door and rushed across the road to let herself in.

'Shit,' said Zena, and drove away quickly.

The house was empty. Poppy went out to the workshop hopefully, but the door was locked and a glance through the window showed no sign of Erin. She scuffed her feet back across the yard and heard the front door slam as she entered the kitchen. Llewellyn had a black eye and was clearly in a furious temper. He ignored Poppy at first and flung open cupboard doors looking for a bottle of whisky he always kept ready. She held out a glass from the draining board silently to him and he dashed it out of her hand with a sneering grin. It shattered on the tiled floor. He slugged back a huge mouthful from the bottle.

'Want some, do you?'

Poppy shook her head.

'That's bollocks, my pretty, and you know it. You might as well get down on your knees and beg me for it sometimes. I see that look in your eye.'

She tried to get past him, but he grabbed her wrist and pushed her back against the sink.

'What's happened to your eye?' she tried to disguise her sudden fear in a normal question, but her voice gave her away.

He put his face up close to her so the fumes of alcohol washed over her hot skin.

'Excitable these Frenchmen when their wives are playing away. He should try giving her a good hiding instead. She really enjoys that, I've found.'

He was squeezing against her now so she could hardly breathe. Suddenly she felt rage rather than fear.

'You're disgusting. Keep your hands off me!'

He laughed at her feeble attempts to struggle out of his grasp, and holding her firmly with one hand, tipped whisky down the front of her T-shirt with the other. Then he threw the bottle down in the sink and began to massage her chest hard, rubbing the wet fabric all over her breasts. She tried to scream, but one big hairy hand stopped her mouth. The other ripped the T-shirt right away and tore her bra half off.

'Look at the size of those!'

He took his hand away from her mouth, but Poppy felt herself powerless to raise a sound in her throat. She was frozen and helpless, watching him pawing and licking her breasts as if it was happening to someone else in a film.

Suddenly he yanked her tracksuit trousers down and then half threw her onto the table. Before she could even take a breath, he was between her legs, fumbling to open his jeans. This is where it all ends, Poppy felt herself thinking. I won't be able to get over this, I'd rather die.

No-one will ever love me or treat me as if I matter... She squeezed her eyes shut waiting for the final humiliation, the final proof of her worthlessness.

Nothing happened. She heard a chair fall over and opened her eyes to find the room empty. She hauled herself off the table, and pulled her tracksuit up with difficulty as her legs were almost too weak to support her. The stink of whisky was everywhere. She splashed cold water on her face and body and then used the kitchen towel to wrap around her naked upper half. She was not going to risk going to her room. She could hear Llewellyn upstairs, banging about. What should she do? She couldn't run out into the street like this. In England she might have done, but here, how could she explain? In the end he hadn't gone through with it, so what could she accuse him of? She had no friends and she knew the restaurant would not appreciate a half-naked, wholly hysterical visit from their employee. If only she knew where the workshop key was she'd lock herself in there – was it in that old flour tin?

She was clumsily searching when heavy footsteps crashed down the stairs and Llewellyn burst into the kitchen again. She snatched a knife from the drainer and held it shakily in front of her, but he didn't even meet her eyes. He was wearing a coat and carrying a couple of holdalls. He picked up his bunch of keys from the dresser and turned away without even looking at Poppy.

'Tell Erin she'll find the van at Morlaix station,' he said over his shoulder, and was gone.

Poppy sat down at the table and wondered if she would ever stop trembling for long enough to go upstairs and lock herself in her room.

Zena was trying to take herself in hand. She felt foolish and insensitive about Poppy, jumping to conclusions without any real evidence. She had this sense of getting things wrong a lot of the time lately, like badly misjudging her recent meeting with Lucas. A new perspective was what she needed. She went for a walk along the river, watching the rain fall on the water and the storm clouds gather over the peaks of the Monts d'Arrée. She was part of all this, part of the trees and the water and the force of the coming storm. All the energy was inside her, to be tapped and directed, focused onto what she wanted. That was the big question, the nagging, gnawing worry underneath it all. She had to scrap all her old entrenched ideas – she wanted a loving relationship with someone and the chance of a family, that much she knew, but the new equation she came up with no longer automatically had the tag of Lucas' name.

There were other men in the world and it was time she stopped thinking of herself as still half of a couple. She was alone and herself, not part of any unit. She might well remain this way too, so what did she want out of life on her own? Somewhere congenial to live was top of the list. The flat was so much part of her old life that she'd already made the inner decision to sell it as soon as she went back. Then she'd have capital to look around for somewhere else. Here in Brittany was beginning to feel right more and more, but she would have to earn money and that was not so easy.

She could not go back to GPE, and keep plodding on in that office, trapped in a mesh of dissatisfaction, like water by pond weed.

There must be ways of exploiting her talents that she hadn't yet thought of. That was going to be her priority now, looking to the future. She'd wasted enough time waiting around for Lucas. Seeing him again had been such a shock and she could not deny the desire and longing the sight of him produced, but Laure's revelation had been an even bigger shock and she could see no point in continuing to dwell on a futile prospect. The last year on her own had somehow strengthened her after all.

She hurried back to the house as the rain began to fall more heavily. The ground was muddy and slippery, forcing her to tread carefully and loading her boots with the weight of the earth. She heard the phone ringing and scrambled to get inside in time to catch it.

It was her mother, in remarkably communicative mood.

After a few routine remarks about Stephen's folly and May's inadequacies, she asked Zena if she was painting.

'It's going very well. I've been asked to illustrate a book. Brittany's a very inspirational place.'

'Good. Stay there.'

'What? Permanently?' Zena was taken aback by such a prescriptive statement. 'You wouldn't mind?'

'Why ever should I? I always thought that flat and dreary job were crushingly limited for you.'

'You never said anything.' Zena heard her own voice trembling at the implied criticism of what she felt had been a sane and sensible life.

'You never asked. If you'd said, what do you think of my life, mother dear, I'd have said. Dull. Dreary. Dismal.'

Zena was wounded.

'But I had Lucas!'

As the silence lengthened, she wondered if her mother

was still there, but somewhere in the background she could hear May's plaintive voice.

'Hello?' she said weakly.

'Must go, dear,' came the brisk response. 'Your father's just back from the war.'

She sat down weakly, her earlier attempts at positive thinking severely undermined by her mother's demolition job on the past. And yet, didn't it really fit in with what she'd been thinking herself? And wasn't the encouragement for staying in Brittany and making it work somehow an endorsement for her own feelings?

If only it were couched in more loving terms, Zena thought miserably.

When the phone rang next morning, she was surprised to hear Erin's voice.

'Is there any chance you could take me into Morlaix this afternoon?'

'No problem. Something wrong with the van?'

'Only that it's it in Morlaix and I'm here.'

'Oh.' Zena didn't know quite how to respond to that cryptic statement.

As they drove out of La Folle, Erin was marginally more forthcoming.

'Llewellyn seems to have taken himself off. He dumped the van at the station.'

'I'm sorry,' was all Zena could think of to say.

'No need. I'm glad he's gone. He's been making Poppy's life a misery lately and done no work at all. Which reminds me of another favour...'

Zena grinned.

'Ask away.'

'The stall on Thursday. Could you manage just an hour in the morning for me? I need to shoot into Morlaix about ten with some deliveries. I won't be long.'

'No, that's fine.' Zena forgot momentarily that she'd have Frodo in her care then.

They sat in silence for a few kilometres, Erin calm and introverted, Zena worrying over what she really wanted to say.

'About Poppy...' came out finally.

Erin looked at her at once.

'Yes?'

'It's just... well, she's been very unhappy lately.'

'Yes.'

'I wondered if she ever, um, confided in you, if she had anyone to talk things over with properly.'

'Poppy's decided to go back to England to see her parents and think about getting some kind of training.'

This was surprising news, but all for the best, Zena thought to herself.

'That's good. A purpose in life is what she needs.'

'Isn't it what we all need?' Erin asked wryly.

Zena laughed.

'I'm not very good at this, am I? It's just Poppy led me to think that she... well, you... oh, nothing really.'

'If you mean all that stuff about being in love with me, it's OK. She's attracted to women, that's all, and she tends to fall madly in love with anyone who's nice to her. I mopped up the tears from a fall-out with some girlfriend at the festival last year and let her sleep in my arms in our tent and that brought her here, running after someone who'd look out for her. Unfortunately it also brought her the attentions of my lecherous brother. She had an unpleasant experience with him yesterday and it's kind of brought about a major change of heart about everything. Now she wants to go home.'

'So you don't feel at all responsible for her?'

Erin's green eyes were candid.

'No, I don't. She's twenty years old and perfectly able to make her own decisions if other people stop doing it for her. She thought she was being independent, living in a foreign country, but I think she's just realised that emotionally she's still her own prisoner here.'

'You're a very strong person, Erin,' Zena said.

Erin shrugged.

'We all have our own problems,' she said, 'we all have control over our own destinies. Poppy has chosen to make a positive step after a nasty jolt – that's progress, that's taking control over her own life. We can all choose how to react to what comes at us. If she's tired of being Poor Poppy, object of pity and sympathy, she'll be free to move on and learn to ride her luck as it comes.'

'You're talking about inner strength.'

'You've got it,' Erin replied.

If only I had, Zena thought as they pulled up next to the van in the station car-park.

Chapter 15

Ian waited in dread for the lights of a car coming up the track. He felt like a doomed man, next in line for the executioner, a precious part of his life about to come to an end. How he was going to handle this superficial social evening when all he wanted was to tell his wife their marriage was over was hard to fathom. He was not a good actor, better at mute suffering than active pretence, but these next few hours of chit-chat and bonhomie had to be endured and, in a way, would furnish a welcome delay to being left alone with Leah and coming up hard and sharp against the emptiness of their reality.

The rich wine smell of the casserole he had prepared filled the cottage, and he had done his best to tidy and clean up or 'make the place respectable' as Leah always said. Respectable was a word he had come to loath with passion: it seemed to him the epitome of narrowness and the stifling of spirit. He thought of Zena's place with its splashes of colour, neither tidy nor a mess, just a living space where one could breath easily and feel relaxed. The house in England where he lived with Leah oppressed him as soon as he opened the front door on the pink hall and moved into the egg yellow kitchen which he was convinced had an adverse affect on his digestion. He felt imprisoned by all the dots and striped wall-paper like prison bars keeping him confined. Supposedly at home, he would roam restlessly from room to perkily co-ordinated room searching for a single spot of calm energy, a natural resting place. Even the garden shed where he'd found refuge for a while now had natty gingham curtains and a frill along the tool shelf, which he was required to keep in a pristine state of cleanliness. He knew his wife's frenetic decorating and primping was a sign of frustration and emptiness, but nothing he had tried had penetrated that inner desolation and he had simply given up. Now it was much too late.

They'd be here soon. He wanted to get it over with. He missed Frodo's presence with a great sharp pang, at the same time envying the dog's billet with Zena. For a second he was tempted to leap in the car and rush to join them, begging Zena to hide and protect him. It was the sort of thing he felt he could ask her and be sure of support with instinctive understanding and no endless stream of questions.

When he had taken Frodo down to Zena's place at five o'clock, it was hard to say which of them was the more anxious, as the dog seemed to have absorbed all the crackling tension that was in his master, but Zena's welcome was soothing. Despite his own pre-occupations, Ian thought that she seemed calmer, or perhaps just more resigned to the new absence of her great love. He was moved just by seeing her again and tried to cover it by fussing about dog biscuits, Frodo's bed and his usual routine. He was relieved that Zena seemed to take it all seriously and realised without being told how important it was that Frodo didn't feel abandoned again.

Ian heard a car approaching and got up with the stiffness of an old man to open the door to the jovial boom of Tony Parker and the shrill greetings of the two women, like schoolgirls on an outing. How much worse could things get, he wondered?

The market was busy on this sunny spring day. People emerged from winter hibernation in colourful clothes, smiling and ready to linger, a marked contrast from Zena's last stint when shopping was something to be done as quickly as possible before a speedy return to the warmth of the hearth.

She was enjoying herself being at the heart of the town again and selling several of her own cards to appreciative English and French customers made her determined to expand her range and look into the possibilities of getting larger numbers printed for sale here in Brittany. She might even go round some of the local shops and try for new outlets, if she really wanted to make a future in Finistere.

She looked at her watch, anticipating Erin's return, and when she looked up again, it was to see Ian at a nearby stall apparently in the company of a short, plump woman in a pink leisure suit. She realised at once that this was his wife, and that something inside her hurt to see this theoretical partner made real before her eyes. The fact that she disliked the other woman on sight was not entirely linked to jealousy either. There was something so carefully safe and restrained in the highlighted perm and overall neatness of her appearance. They were moving towards the jewellery stall now. Please let them not notice, Zena prayed, and - a wild biblical thought - let them pass by on the other side. She turned to smile at a couple of teenage girls who were admiring the earrings, but as soon as she tried to engage them in talk, they giggled – at her poor French, she imagined – and wandered off, just as Ian and his wife drew level with the stall. There was no place to hide as Ian's miserable eyes met hers with surprise.

'Hello Ian,' she said as friendlily as possible. 'Hello.'

The woman's instincts were obviously sharp. She put her arm through her husband's at once, drawing him close to her side and glared disapproval at Zena.

'Hello, Zena.' Ian's voice was tight and full of tension.

Zena determined to pull them both out of a difficult impasse.

'Can I interest you in any hand-made jewellery? We've got some lovely new brooches.' She held out the tray of delicate silver pieces fashioned from loops and twists in fragile versions of Celtic style.

Leah wrinkled her nose.

'Not at all my sort of thing, thank you.' She managed to instil a large dose of contempt in those few words. Zena was torn between anger at her rudeness and amusement as she looked at the painted shell earrings the ghastly woman was wearing, earrings which bobbed bright yellow with every bird-like nod and dip of her permed head.

'How's business?' Ian asked quickly and in some embarrassment. His eyes looked pleadingly at Zena. 'Is everything alright?'

She wouldn't let him down. No wonder Frodo had needed a safe house.

'Not bad at all. My cards are doing well. But I'm only here for an hour until Erin gets back. I've got a friend staying at home to get back to.'

She tried to smile a message of reassurance about Frodo to him and he could not keep back an answering smile which Leah certainly spotted.

'We're rather busy ourselves, so don't let us keep you,' she said icily and with a last superior glare at Zena, dragged her reluctant husband away

Zena turned away, her face flushed with anger, only to see that Erin had returned and was watching her closely.

'That was Ian's wife,' she said by way of explanation. 'Rude bitch of a wife, in fact.'

'You certainly seem upset by seeing them together. Did you know she was here?'

Zena shook her head. Ian had not confided in her, just used her as a hotel for Frodo, who was, poor sod, presumably a secret from the wife. She'd thought that she and Ian had got closer than that, even that maybe... well, that was all nonsense now, she could see that. It had been a mad idea anyway, just because Lucas was going to marry a Russian she had wanted to throw herself into someone else's arms and Ian was the only likely candidate, excepting Jean-Yves, of course.

'You really like him, don't you?' Erin said quietly.

'He's a nice man,' she replied brightly. 'He asked me to illustrate a book he's writing about the stones around here.'

'I know. It's very good.'

Zena looked up in sharp surprise.

'I didn't realise you knew Ian?'

Erin shrugged.

'Why not? I know most people at least by sight.'

'It's just you never said.'

'I don't gossip – that sort of goes with the job, if you like.'

'Of course. I didn't realise he was a client, I mean...'

Erin laughed.

'I didn't say he was. It's just my habit to keep things to myself, I suppose. But going back to Ian – he didn't look very happy.'

'I'm not surprised if that's the sort of woman he's married to,' said Zena shortly, and began getting her things together to go back to Frodo.

'That's a strong reaction,' Erin persisted in her gentle, even voice. 'You only saw her for a minute.' Then she gave a light laugh. 'What's it to you, after all?'

Zena drove home rather quickly and tried hard not to think about it at all. She felt suddenly embroiled again by all the complications of life, and her emotional life in particular. First seeing Lucas again, then losing him, getting close to Ian, then seeing him today and realising that nothing could happen between them... it was all so wearying and depressing. She just hoped Frodo hadn't trashed the house to put the cap on her woes.

She expected a volley of frazzled barking to rend the air as she stepped from the car, but there was silence. She went up to the door and peered in through the glass. Frodo was curled in his basket by the fire, eyes wide, staring at her mutely. When she opened the door and went over to him, his ears dropped with pleasure and there was a faint flicker of the feathery tail. She stroked him lovingly and was rewarded by a sudden bound which knocked her sprawling backwards on the floor as Frodo cavorted round the room with a delayed reaction of delirious joy. It was as if he'd had to be sure she was back, sure that he was still loved and wanted before he could give vent to his true feelings. He did run to the door and look out hopefully for his master, but in the mean time, Zena would clearly do, once she'd picked herself up and towelled off the exuberant licks.

She let the dog out into the yard to sniff around whilst she collected the post from the box, and then stood with the pile of circulars and letters in her hand as she breathed in the mossy tang of the spring air and felt the freshness of moisture from the tumbling river waters. Life couldn't be quite so bad when all this growth and budding promise was going on around, she thought, trying to be positive and cheer herself up.

This new spirit of optimism lasted all of two minutes until she'd put the kettle on and sat down at the table to look through the post. She flicked through the supermarket publicity material and then stopped, the movement of her hand suspended. There, on top of some bills and bank-statements, was a letter from Lucas.

I am sorry for leaving so abruptly. There were many things I should have talked to you about, but seeing you again was a great surprise – a wonderful surprise – and I needed time to take you in, as it were, and to assimilate my own feelings. I wanted to stay, more than anything to make love to you and lie close in the same bed together comfortably as we once did – it brought me such peace, but I was not sure of myself, of the future, mea culpa, Zena, and it was cowardly to leave you as I did then, and you may think more cowardly still to do the same thing again. You are right. I lacked the courage, the words to explain what has happened in my life since we were together.

I know that I have told you of my friend Vassily, my one true friend in that great bleak country of Russia. Hearing he was very ill, I went to Moscow last June and was able to spend some time with him before he died. He asked me to do something for him – I hope you can understand that it was like a sacred duty to me – to help someone he cared for very much, Irinia, daughter of his brother. Anatoli has been involved in some serious trouble in Russia – I have spoken to you of the gangs and protection rings that riddle society in Moscow now, for all its new 'freedoms' – and Irinia had been sent to Paris for her own safety. No-one had heard from her for a while, and Vassily begged me to find her and then to see that she could remain in France, out of reach of the criminals who have already wounded her father twice.

I did this for him, Zena, out of loyalty and indeed I am not ashamed to say out of love also. But when I found her, she was not in good circumstances, so I took her to live with me in an apartment and tried to find her proper work, which is not so easy for a Russian girl if she is not to end up dragged into prostitution. I thought that perhaps we could marry, simply an arrangement of convenience for her to take French citizenship and remain in Paris, but it is not so straightforward and the rules are strict, so now we just exist without any progress or purpose. I think now that I was a fool to get so involved, but at the time it did not appear such a difficult thing to give her a home, with the memory of Vassily in my mind. What did it matter to me - until I met you again.

I have thought of you often, of course, in this last year, but it truly seemed to me that I had lost my chance, and perhaps my pride prevented me from returning to England to ask you to take me back into your life. I had no confidence that your answer would be yes – Zena, you let me go so easily. Without protest even. I think now it was from your goodness and generosity, but then I convinced myself it was indifference. Forgive me for all I have got wrong about this, and for the bad decisions I have made. Now that I have seen you again and realised fully what you mean to me, I feel strangely that I have betrayed you by this arrangement with Irinia. There is no question of a long-term commitment between her and me now. When I came back from La Folle I told her about you and that I must be free, in the hope that you will want to resume our relationship. Already she has her own 'amusements' here in Paris, so it is not so difficult for us to resume our separate lives, although I must make some provision for her.

Zena, I do love you, this is truly a letter of love from my heart. I want us to live together again. Although we have never talked about it, I would like us to have a child and be a family. Do you think you could want this too, my Zena? I remember when you picked up the child who had fallen in the park and gave him words of comfort that stopped his tears. I have often seen that picture of you with the boy in your arms in my mind's eye, knowing that you will be a wonderful mother and that we can be very happy in the future. Together.

I will return to Brittany next month, so you have time to consider what I have said and I can organize my separation from Irinia. Expect me on the 12th. I hope fervently that we can enjoy a proper reunion on that day.

with my love, Lucas

Much of this letter had blurred before the fall of Zena's

tears. The rather formal English which always brought home his foreignness to her was so familiar from their separations over the years when he had written regularly. She had a stash of such letters - articulate, rational and full of astute observations of what was happening around him. And yet this one was different. He had not lied when he said it was a letter of love. She felt it, and the power of the feeling behind the words was like a revelation to set against the usual quiet calm of his affection. She was overwhelmed by evidence of his lasting, romantic memory of their time together, amazed at the detail of their walk in the park remaining in his consciousness as an image of their potential together. She had so often dreamt of this sort of response from Lucas and longed for words as warm and passionate as these – the reality made her weak with longing and tense with uncertainty. Here was all she had desired, offered by the man she loved. There was no need to struggle any more on her own to make her mark and find her own niche. They could settle here in the land she had come to love and she could continue what she had begun with her own career, creating a new kind of warm and loving home for Lucas and their children... if it was not too late.

But even in the midst of this euphoria, something niggled at her happiness, some crack in the smooth surface of Lucas' words opened before her into a dark place and made her fearful of easy acceptance, of trying to recreate a past that had not sufficed for either of them. She would wait and see. Let the dust of this sandstorm of emotion settle before she took a long, clear look at the permanent features of the landscape that remained.

Frodo had sidled over to her as she smiled and cried

over the pages of the letter and now he placed his muzzle in her hand. Whether he wanted to comfort her or gain reassurance for himself, she couldn't tell, but she fondled the mad ears tenderly and whispered gently to him of the loving home he would always have and the certain loyalty of his master.

At that moment, Ian was driving full-pelt towards Zena's house, filled with a rage he had never known before. The scene at the market had been enough, but Leah's constant sniping throughout the afternoon had put paid to any thought of the civilised discussion he had been planning, the careful lead-in to a frank exchange of views about their marriage and the hopelessness of continuing as they were. She was dissatisfied with everything - his demeanour towards the Parkers, the state of the cottage, the time he had clearly been wasting on his silly book, his friendship with that woman at the market and finally the inexplicable doggy smell that had penetrated every item of furniture and inch of carpet. She accused (that was the only word) him of having someone who owned a dog in the cottage for god knew how long to give everything such a canine pong. It was the use of the word 'pong' that broke Ian's resolve to act calmly and rationally. A mad, animal urge rose up in him to defend Frodo from this woman's stupidity and he began to yell at Leah incoherently about love and loyalty and her total ignorance on both subjects. Then he had run out of the house, shouting 'I'll show you!' at the top of his voice and driven off like a maniac.

Reaching Zena's yard, he strode from the car to the door and barely stopped for a brief knock before flinging it open and finding himself in Frodo's hairy paws-on-shoulders embrace. Zena came quickly down the stairs to see what the commotion was about. She was red-eyed and her hair dishevelled as if she'd been running her hands through it in frustration. For once the sight of her only made him angrier still, though he couldn't explain why.

'What's the matter?' she said in some alarm at his wild expression.

'I've just come to get Frodo,' Ian replied, grabbing his bed with one hand and a bag of dog-biscuit with the other.

'I thought he was here for a few days. Presumably whilst your wife was around.'

There was an unmistakable hint of rebuke in her voice that made Ian see red.

'Change of plan,' he responded savagely, trying to accommodate all Frodo's possessions in his arms and cope with the dog's cavortings at the same time. 'And you can be quiet,' he snapped as Frodo's whines of pleasure at seeing his master rose by a few hundred more decibels.

Zena leant against the banister and folded her arms defensively across her chest.

'What's the matter, Ian? Your wife's rudeness was enough for one day without you behaving like this and treating me and my home like dirt.'

Although there was undeniable anger there, Ian also heard the undertone of bewildered disappointment and felt a sudden clutch in his gut.

'I'm sorry...' he began.

'No, you carry on, don't worry about me, but try not to blow so hot and cold with Frodo's feelings, because whatever I've done, he certainly doesn't deserve it.'

Ian dropped all he was carrying and strode over to her. He caught her in his arms and kissed her with all the passion of his nature and current overwrought state. For more than a minute their mouths locked together, stirring every nerve-ending he possessed and exploding all other thoughts from his brain.

When he finally let her go, Zena too was visibly shocked by the kiss, but before either of them could speak, there was a rap at the door. They turned to see Jean-Yves' inquisitive face pressed up to the glass, peering through at them.

Frodo shot out as soon as the door was opened and Ian followed him directly without another word, ignoring Jean-Yves' attempt at interrogation as he passed. Frodo leapt willingly into the car and Ian drove away marginally more sedately than he had arrived.

Zena didn't know whether to laugh or cry. The effects of Lucas' letter and Ian's kiss had left her feeling weak and inclined to giggle feebly in the face of Jean-Yves hurt disapproval of her liaison with yet another eligible male.

'You really have got to stop checking up on me,' she said.

'I have to be sure that nothing bad happen to you. I care for you, Zelda. It is something important for me.'

'Jean-Yves, we are neighbours and friends, yes, but I have my own private life that has nothing to do with you.'

'That is what Monique, she say.'

'She's right. You know it. You have helped me and made me welcome here and I'm grateful, but that's all. I've far too many complications in my life now without worrying about you too. Please understand.'

He looked at her miserably.

'I want you to be happy. I wish that I had married someone like you, with spirit and talent...'

'Please. I can't cope with you as well now. I've lots to think about. I need to be on my own.'

'But why, Zelda? Why is it not me that you want?'

Despite her profound emotional confusion, she looked at him in fond exasperation.

'Jean-Yves, come on. That's completely different. Even if I wanted to, and I don't' – she quickly put up a forbidding hand, 'it just wouldn't be possible. After all, you're m...'

She stopped. The hand that had admonished him went up to her mouth as she realised what she'd been about to say. Wasn't Ian married? Wasn't Lucas living with Irinia? She began to laugh inwardly and then suddenly aloud with a great snort of mirth that seemed to frighten Jean-Yves out of his wits. Once she'd started there was no stopping her – all the tension and uncertainty of her recent emotional roller-coaster bubbled up and over until she was weak with laughter. The onslaught proved too much for Jean-Yves, who removed himself from the unseemly scene before she had finished, his pained expression on departure far from making the desired impression, only causing Zena to laugh the more.

She dreaded stopping because she knew that when she did, there was nothing but a hell of a mess to think about.

Laure lay in the hospital bed, numb and exhausted. Despite her physical state, she hated the enforced inactivity and longed to be at home again, to take her place as the fulcrum of the household, essential to the daily well-being of her husband and son. She felt useless here, useless and resentful. The sooner she could get back into normality the better. She had refused to let Tomas come and visit her here and missed him terribly, but tomorrow she would go home, all being well when the doctor made his morning round. It would seem like freedom after the mental prison she'd inhabited for the last few weeks, despite the repeated doses of poison she would have to endure in the coming days. It would be worth it just to be outside again, to feel the fresh air on her face and see ordinary life going on all around. It would even give her pleasure to sit at the window and watch the routine activities of her neighbours, anything as long as it affirmed life and the possibilities of health and a future with her family. There was every chance that the operation had been a complete success. She would hold on to that and build her strength by making plans for the future. There was Tomas' first birthday to think about. That was what mattered, all the hope and potential tied up in that little boy that she had brought into the world. She'd never leave him. Never.

Leah was fussing about at the stove when Ian came in with Frodo on his lead.

'What's that,' she squeaked, holding a saucepan out between them as if Frodo was threatening her physical safety.

'It's a dog,' Ian said, putting the basket down and willing Frodo to go into it docilely.

Instead he could feel the dog bristling beneath his hand and sounding a low growl in the back of his throat.

'Frodo, it's OK. There's nothing to worry about. You're

home now.'

'Home! I'm not having that dirty, smelly thing in my house!'

Her voice was like the screech of a parrot, something Ian had never identified until this moment. He went on trying to force Frodo down into the basket, stroking him and murmuring quietly in his ear as he did so. But the dog was not to be soothed. His hackles were up and his thin body trembled with the awareness that his territory and household position were at stake. He was prepared to fight this hellish apparition for it if he had to. He knew his master didn't want her here, he could sense all the resistance and tension in Ian's body. That decided Frodo. He made a great lurch forward in the hope of lunging at Leah, but Ian was too quick for him.

'No, you don't, boy. I'll have to tie you up, if you can't settle. Just for a while.'

Frodo whined his distress as his basket was dragged over to the far wall and he was firmly secured to an iron ring that had once been used to tether horses in a stall at one end of the room.

'I mean it, Ian. I'm not staying here with that... that beast in the house.'

'I'll phone the hotel then, shall I?'

The determination in his voice alarmed her.

'Don't be silly, darling. You know perfectly well how I feel about dogs. You can't expect me to put up with it in the house.'

'And you know perfectly well how I feel about dogs and I don't expect you to 'put up' with Frodo but to get to know him and like him.'

Her face twisted in disgust.

'That's ridiculous. Dogs are dirty and dangerous.' Frodo's whine had changed gear to a steady growl now. 'I'll never allow a dog in my house.'

'Just as well this is my house then.'

That did shock her.

'What do you mean? We're married, it's our house.'

'A second ago it was yours, now it's ours, make up your mind. Anyway, technically it is mine. If you remember I alone signed for it and I paid with money my father left me. It's also been my home for the last few months and I intend to spend a lot more time here in the future.'

'And what will happen to the dog when you're in England, may I ask?'

'Frodo goes where I go.'

'No, I'm sorry Ian, but that's out of the question. You're being totally unreasonable.'

She sounded on the verge of angry tears. 'I come out here to find you've done no work on the house except to make what we decided was to be my utility room into some sort of office for yourself, you've obviously been wasting your time socialising, given the familiarity of that girl in the market and now you tell me this thing' – a sneering gesture in Frodo's direction which produced a fearsome bark – 'is going to be part of our lives – I won't put up with it! You'll have to choose between me and that scruffy apology for a dog!'

Ian went over to the phone and flicked through the local directory.

'What are you doing?'

He ignored her, dialled a number and spoke to the hotel. Leah had never managed to pick up any French beyond Bonjour, which she annoyingly insisted on pronounced bon-jaw, so she didn't understand what the call was about until Ian told her to pack her bag so he could take her into La Folle.

She puffed herself up like a little bantam-cock.

'This has gone too far! You're not seriously suggesting I should leave here tonight? Look, take the dog out to the barn and we'll talk about it in the morning when you've had a chance to calm down.'

She was not used to seeing him so forceful and angry and did not know how to handle it. Nothing except tears and abject apologies could have swayed Ian at that point and he knew Leah would never give in and allow herself to be beaten over the issue of an animal she despised. In the end she went up the ladder-stairs to the bedroom where the night before they had slept apart in the single beds, with only a distant peck goodnight on the cheek — after more than three months of absence. When she returned, Leah was carrying her neat suitcase and matching monogrammed vanity case.

They drove to La Folle in stony silence. Ian led her into the hotel, got her key and carried her bags to the room.

'You'll be hearing from Gerald, I warn you,' Leah snapped, as he left without a word.

The thought of divorce proceedings initiated by soupy Gerald, the family solicitor, brought Ian nothing but pleasure on the drive home.

It was extraordinary how one short row out of nowhere could put an end to a twenty year marriage, and yet the marriage had only lasted so long precisely because of the avoidance of any sort of openness and plain speaking between them. Although he knew it was inappropriate, given what Leah must be feeling in her lonely hotel bedroom, Ian could not help glorying in the surge of freedom that ran through him as he drove up the long track under a clear starry sky. Frodo's joy at his return brought tears of happiness to his eyes, and, when they went outside to enjoy the silvery light and crisp air, the memory of kissing Zena and the utter rightness of that compared with the travesty of affection between him and his wife made him hope that the future despite its inevitable complications and wranglings might be something to savour after all. He had to believe in the possibility of happiness.

Poppy chattered away as Erin drove her to the ferry terminal at Roscoff. All uneasiness between them was gone since Poppy had sobbed her heart out over Llewellyn's assault and confessed all her feelings to a totally unsurprised Erin, who soothed and comforted her in a matter-of-fact manner that soon had Poppy admitting that she'd like to go home and see her parents. For all the quarrelling between themselves, they had always shown affection and concern for their only child's welfare.

As they crossed the wide Penzé estuary, Poppy outlined her plans for catering college and work experience in the local hotel and Erin wondered how long it would be before another emotional upset interrupted this march of progress.

She herself was all set to move, with the lease on the house coming up for renewal and her own distaste for staying in the place where things had turned so sour with her brother's dreadful behaviour and Poppy's earlier misery. She blamed herself a little for not sorting things out earlier and for underestimating the depth of Llewellyn's malaise. Not a word had come from him since the day he left and she had made no enquiries among their mutual friends for news. One day he'd turn up again wherever she was and it would be time enough to think about their relationship then. She had asked Poppy if she wanted to involve the police, saying she was quite within her rights to do so, but with the relief of escaping what she had most feared, the girl wanted to forget the incident above all else and move on into a new life somewhere else without loose ends and bitter memories. The incident seemed to have burst a bubble of unreality she had been hiding in. Erin knew that Poppy was a generous person, who would forgive and forget quite easily as she became absorbed in new things and made firmer friends she could rely on and share her problems with.

'I'm sorry I got carried away,' Poppy said suddenly, keeping her eyes fixed firmly on the fields of artichokes and cauliflowers grown all around on the high plain of Léon. 'It was a bit mad of me.'

Erin looked at the plump, now almost pretty profile and smiled.

'There's nothing wrong with being attracted to women, Poppy. It's nothing to be ashamed of or to hide. When you find the right person, everything will work out fine.'

'But don't you want a relationship? I don't mean with me,' she added quickly, 'but a partner you love back.'

Erin lifted a hand from the steering-wheel and twirled a trailing ribbon of hair into a ringlet.

'Not really,' she said.

Chapter 16

In the clear light of day, Ian felt remorseful at the way he had treated Leah.

It must all have been a hell of a shock for her, finding him so changed from his months in Brittany, so determined to go against the previously accepted patterns of their co-existence. No wonder she didn't have any answers except to try to lay down the law, a tactic which had worked well enough for her in the past. But he had the energy now, the energy and the purpose to resist her will and stand up for himself.

He'd never challenged her like that before in all their silent, sexless years, keeping his anger in check, giving in to her because he felt guilty about their childlessness, regardless of whose 'fault' it actually was. He would have used the word misfortune himself, but he knew that Leah's views were totally different. She needed the certainty of black and white, right and wrong, guilt and innocence. The results of any tests, whatever they showed, would have polarised the two of them, but non-communication and diverging interests had done the job well enough anyway over the years. He could not believe that Leah was any happier inside than he was.

Knowing that he could not leave her alone in a foreign country to fend for herself, he drove down to the town after an early breakfast and caught Leah just leaving the hotel dining room. She was stiff and hostile, but allowed him to lead her into a small lounge area where they would not be overheard.

'We need to talk about things, Leah,' he began reasonably enough, carefully resisting the customary urge to apologise for the previous evening.

'I don't see there's anything to talk about,' she said primly. 'You made your feelings plain enough last night.'

He swallowed hard to keep his tone calm.

'And what about your feelings? I'd like to hear what they are. This is our marriage that's at stake here, we ought to be able to discuss things, surely?'

She snapped her head towards him like a clockwork toy responding to the turn of its key.

'What marriage?' It was a sneer that took him completely by surprise. 'You've not exactly been the world's greatest husband, you know.'

Ian took this in silently for a moment.

'No, you're right.' He was not going to stoop to say she hadn't been a brilliant wife either, although it was tempting. 'So what do you want to do?'

'I'm going back to England this afternoon. I shall talk to Gerald about a divorce. He's been saying for a while it would be a good idea.'

'What?'

She looked smug and slightly pink in the cheeks.

'Gerald's been a good friend to me whilst you've been living it up over here. He knows how hard it is to manage alone and it's nice to be appreciated by a man. Makes a pleasant change.'

So that was how it was. Gerald was the most conventional and stuffy of all their acquaintances. He and Leah probably were two of a kind. Since his wife died he'd been round for meals occasionally – it was true on reflection that he'd lavished praise on Leah's predictable cooking and taken an unlikely and avid interest in the tedious details of home furnishing that she loved to talk about. Ian had been rather grateful for these interludes that allowed him to give up contributing polite host-like remarks, and he had gladly left them to the sort of suburban exchanges he loathed.

He had almost laughed when Leah described his stay in Brittany as 'living it up' but in a way she was right. Being close to the land, leading a simple, natural life with his dog for company had brought incredible peace and strength to his spirit. He'd found what he wanted over here, and maybe his absence had given his wife a chance to do the same.

'I don't have any problem with a divorce, Leah,' he said firmly.

'I'll expect what I'm entitled to you know,' she responded quickly.

'I don't have a problem with that either and nothing I've ever done should make you think so.'

She had no answer to that, just pushed her mouth into a thin grudging line.

'What time's the ferry? I'll take you to Roscoff.'

'There's no need for that. I've already ordered a taxi.'

'Did you intend asking me for a divorce anyway?' he asked out of sudden curiosity. 'Is that why you came out here all of a sudden?'

Her face flushed.

'It's obvious we're no longer suited, Ian.'

'That's been obvious for years. I suppose it's Gerald popping up out of the woodwork and giving you a nice, easy alternative that's made the difference.' It was harsh, but he felt a spurt of anger to think of all his wasted years. Then he remembered Zena and his own hopes and relented. 'Fair enough. It's a relief to stop pretending anyway. Should do us both a lot of good.'

'I don't know what you're talking about. But then I never was clever enough for you, was I?' She sounded bitter and resentful.

Ian sighed.

'It's nothing to do with being clever, Leah. It's about openness to new ideas, different ways of looking at things. You've never been prepared to listen to anything like that or to take any interest in my work.'

'Your precious work! That's all you ever think about. The environment, all those bloody stupid old stones – what sort of a contribution to a marriage is that?'

She was full of righteous anger now: all the years of suppression were now stripped bare to this deep resentment and harsh dismissal of all he held dear.

He stood up, having no intention of prolonging the pointless argument.

'Well, that's all over now. You'll never have to hear another word about those bloody stones. And I'm free for the rest of my life from stripy wall-paper and stencilling. Sounds like a good deal to me. Have a good trip. Give Gerald my regards and tell him I look forward to hearing from him.'

He gave her a nonchalant smile and strolled out of the hotel into the spring sunshine feeling twenty years younger and as if his life was just about to begin all over again.

On leaving La Folle, Llewellyn had taken a train to Rennes. There he headed for the nearest Irish bar and was soon among the sort of friends that leavened most of his existence. He drank himself into a state of near oblivion, using up the last of Erin's money which he'd taken from her room, then staggered off upstairs in search of a bed or something more entertaining. He tried to push his way into the room of a girl from behind the bar who'd seemed accommodating enough in front of a crowd, but now shunned him with a contemptuous indignation that made him wild with anger. It was still there, the rage that filled him from childhood, unbroken and increasingly hard to contain.

The first night of dossing down on the floor of a flat that stank of alcohol and unwashed bodies, he closed his eyes to images of Poppy's terrified face as he tried to force her into sex, and then the knife shaking in her hand at the very sight of him. His initial remorse on running away had been short-lived, so had the kind of shock at discovering what he was capable of. It rather pleased him in retrospect and the thought of how Erin would take the news from Poppy gave him a moment of sick satisfaction.

Despite the self-control he had apparently summoned up then in his own home environment, Llewellyn now seemed to have passed a barrier of self-restraint, the pivotal moment that would either put an end to his journey of self-destruction or plant his foot more firmly on the path. There were reasons and answers, even some excuses lurking in the undergrowth of his upbringing and subsequent drifting, but he chose not to look at them too closely. He could not bear that sort of self-scrutiny that women indulged in so often. He thought again of his sister, so measured and calm, just like their mother had been, so lacking in the greed and need that dominated his own wretched life.

So now in bar after bar he found companions to share his complaints against women and the unfairness of life that gave so much to so few whilst deserving cases like himself were almost reduced to begging to survive. He scrounged money, food and fags where he could. The charm still worked if he could be bothered to make the effort. There was always some poor sad cow in need of a good seeing to who was grateful enough to slip him a few quid, if only to keep his mouth shut. By the time that supply ran out, he'd be able to go back and face Erin again. Although he'd never acknowledge it, that was the thought that kept him going, some notion of redemption lingering from their upbringing and his emotional reliance on his sister. For the moment he needed to keep his anger against her well fuelled with alcohol and distorted memories, because when it died, he feared there might be nothing left but abject self-pity.

He stole the motorbike in a mood of defiance after being taunted by a group of passing youths. He was stumbling about the cobbled streets, much the worse for wear, when he fell into their path. He didn't understand all the French insults, but the gist of fat old git was plain enough. Taking a swing at one of them only led to uproarious laughter and a few not so gentle shoves that left him slumped in the gutter as they moved on towards the city centre. Llewellyn could hardly haul himself up, not from any damage, but his own unwieldy bulk and shortness of breath. Christ, he was so out of condition! He felt old then for the first time, leaning against a wall, listening to the fading taunts of the next generation of young bloods who had pushed him aside. He comforted himself with the thought that if his head was clearer he'd have taken on any of those boys or better still banged their heads together, the lot of them. It was unthinkable that he had passed from being a young buck himself to a faded has-been at the age of thirty!

When he saw the bike in a dark side alley seconds later, an irresistible urge for power and freedom surged through his veins. Getting astride gave him a few moments of bother, but then the engine started up sweetly enough and he eased out into the main road. This was better, although his vision was a little hazy. He had to swerve to avoid a group of girls crossing the road and gleefully yelled obscenities at them as he lumbered past.

Soon he was on the motorway and moving at high speed. The bike shuddered and groaned beneath him. He must have been about half his current size the last time he rode one. He couldn't seem to settle his balance, shifting and lurching in an attempt to keep upright. After a while he got the hang of it again and kicked up his speed, faster and faster along the empty road. This was glory, this was the sharp edge of excitement he craved. If only the easy motion and thrusting exhilaration could go on for ever and ever. He wished everyone who had ever known him could see him now, sweeping through the night air like a guided missile. He wanted to go on like this for ever, pulsing through the night, free of ties, free of himself in the wild ecstasy of breakneck speed.

He didn't bother to make allowances for the bend until it was too late to judge shifting his bulk with the necessary finesse. The ground came up towards him like lightening: he felt a searing pain in his leg and then he was sliding, sliding, sliding into total oblivion.

Jean-Yves was sitting at the breakfast bar with a glass in his hand watching his wife outside gardening. Every time she bent over to pull up a miniscule weed from the well-tended beds, he admired the shape of her little behind in the clinging lycra trousers. Life was not so bad after all when there were such small pleasures to enjoy at the end of a working day, with the anticipation of a good meal to come and maybe even a little indulgence in the bedroom if he played his cards carefully.

His two daughters came running in to interrupt this languid mood.

'Papa, Papa, come with us!'

He got up good-humouredly and allowed the girls to drag him into their playroom, where they began to dress him up in an old cloak and hat with a feather. This was a favourite game, a prelude to a mad chase around the garden, the sort of rough and tumble that their mother thought unsuitable for girls and usually prevented. Jean-Yves, on the other hand, was always amenable to their pranks, and enjoyed the childish rituals of make-believe and invention. He entered into it fully, bellowing like a stage villain as he chased them round the garden brandishing a plastic sword that had somehow lingered on from his own childhood, and swirling his cloak in pantomime flourishes.

They ran out now, screaming with fake fear, ignoring their mother's sharp rebuke at the noise level.

'But who can hear?' Jean-Yves asked as he neatly feigned a slash at her with the sword.

'That English woman for one,' Monique replied. 'Is it not bad enough that you run after her like an animal?'

'All the better for her to hear the sounds of our joy then, my little dove. So she will know what she is missing by living alone in that miserable run-down house.'

Monique managed a half-smile. It was an enjoyable picture that her husband was painting of Zelda the have-not and she, Monique Bougeard, at the centre of her loving family, secure and enviable. Yes, she liked that image very much.

Jean-Yves took advantage of this momentary thaw to clamp a warm arm round her shoulders. He gestured at the girls, ill-concealed behind a bush and giggling fit to burst at their parents' moment of physical closeness.

'Will you not admit that we have done well, cherie? They are good girls, are they not?'

Monique considered. She knew perfectly well where this sort of expansive mood was leading. She met his eye. It was rare for them to look at each other calmly without impatience or rancour. After many years of marriage, he understood that code. All thought of strolling down the hill to see Zelda after supper faded from his mind. What need did he have, after all?

He chased the girls around the garden until they were tickled half to death and weak with laughter. That should tire them out, he thought with satisfaction, and as they went back into the house, took the risk of patting Monique's bottom without undue fear of a swift rejection.

There was no-one in the house by the river. The phone rang on and on and then finally stopped, leaving an echo of failed contact in the shabby room.

At the other end of the line, Zena's mother sighed and wondered.

Was it better to leave her daughter alone? Should she maintain her own rule of non-interference? It had kept the two of them on good terms for so many years, but this was obviously a time of crisis. She could hear that in Zena's voice, the strain and weariness of emotional stress. No, it was never any good to offer advice to your children – look at Stephen and that fool Hermione - and when it came to comfort, what was there but platitudes? There was no habit between them of asking for help: their relationship was based on the unwritten rule of independence and lack of expectation. She loved her daughter, regretted the limited life she seemed to have settled for in Bath and revelled in her new-found freedom in France. But there was something else there now, some man who would spoil it all, she feared. That was something they had not discussed. They had no shared emotional currency to exchange. But Zena was never a complainer, even as a child, battling through her problems quietly, emotions kept in check beneath the surface. Was that our fault, her mother wondered? Perhaps we should have actively brought her out of herself, but we agreed, her father and I, from the start that the children would grow up as they wished. It hasn't been such a failure of policy either. Any parent would be proud of such a son and daughter.

Well, she'd phoned. There was nothing else to be done. It was better for Zena to make her own way through the maze and come to the centre by her own efforts. However long it took.

Zena had no expectation of seeing Marie's ghost again, but she felt her presence from the moment of entering the wood. The familiar scents of the forest floor triggered her memory of the little girl swinging round under the trees and the light notes of her song echoing in the branches.

She pressed on uphill to the cave, finding the climb much easier without the element of the unknown, and again put her hand on the rock at the entrance. It seemed to grow warm under her touch, to respond to her presence. Although there was no repetition of the earlier hallucinogenic experience, Zena had a clear sense that she was not alone. Filigree strands tightened to bind her in the centre of a giant web of connection: for a split second she felt she knew everything and held the whole world in her grasp before the air seemed to sigh and release her with a shiver.

As she gazed into the darkness of the cave, Zena wondered whether she was now tied to this place, as the legend said. Had it chosen her, fed on something in her psyche to establish the bond? She didn't know. It was something too large for her to comprehend when all her thoughts were filled with the emotional uncertainties that threatened to drown her. She didn't know anything until she had seen Lucas again and found out if there really was a chance of getting what she wanted.

Chapter 17

A few more days passed before Zena encountered Ian again. She was lost in thought, walking slowly on one of the narrow earth paths through scrubby undergrowth near Roc'h Tredudon. It was Frodo who saw her first, bounding across the gorse like a motley wave in his desire to greet an old friend. Ian remained on his path, which ran parallel with Zena's for a while and then merged on a patch of open stony ground.

'How are you?' he asked.

'Fine. Who wouldn't be on a day like this!' she said, suddenly alive to her surroundings. It was a truly glorious April afternoon, the clear blue sky and confident sunshine bathing the rough moorland all around them in a glow of promised warmth.

They stood in silence for a minute, watching the hawks swooping and hovering at the edge of the ridge, lords of their land, following their simple, savage routines.

Zena was wondering if what had passed between them on that last afternoon at her house was to be forgotten or if it required some acknowledgement to get it out of the way and make things easy between them once again. She wanted to ask if his wife was still here, but couldn't find the neutral tone the words would require.

'I've decided to finish the book out here,' he said suddenly.

She turned to him, her face full of pleasure.

'That's wonderful!'

He looked away.

'But first I'm going back to England, next week in fact, to finish my contract at the college and sort everything out. Then it's back here as soon as I can.' His lips twisted in what seemed a painful smile. 'Probably for good.'

'And... your wife? Is she going to live out here too?'

'We're getting a divorce. She keeps the house in England, I make my home here. That suits both of us.'

'I'm sorry. I didn't realise... it must be very hard for you.'

He shook his head.

'It's been a long time coming, but I was too cowardly, too lazy to admit it. And I didn't have any particular reason before to want my freedom.'

Their eyes met and held.

'And you, Zena, where will you be in the summer?' he asked softly, as if in dread of the answer.

She looked away.

'My lease on the house is up at the end of June, although I'll be going back home to sort things out too before that, I expect.'

'You don't want to stay on here then?'

'I don't know. Part of me wants to, but I have my flat and technically still have a job to go back to, so there are lots of practical things to consider. Making a living out here is a bit uncertain for me. I like to know where I stand.'

Ian moved closer to her.

'Would you...'

She started speaking at the same moment.

'And I'm...

They both laughed, each urging the other to continue.

'I was wondering if we could meet up in England?' Ian said. 'I'd like to have a look at Bath again.'

'And we'll need to talk about the book, won't we?' she asked.

He had completely forgotten about that in the moment of panic that maybe they'd never see each other again. Now he could relax a little.

'You were saying about wanting to know where you stand, when I interrupted you!'

Zena shook her hair back out of her eyes and looked away.

'It's just that I'm waiting for Lucas,' she said.

At once the small space between them took on the proportions of an abyss.

'Waiting for him?' Ian echoed sarcastically.

'He's coming back here next week.'

'Is he bringing his prospective wife?'

'Ian, stop it, it's none of your business about me and Lucas, and you're still a married man yourself, or have you forgotten already? Lucas has been sorting things out in Paris. He's explained everything to me and he's coming here so we can talk properly about the future.'

'So it's all on again, is it? In spite of everything?' he asked bitterly.

'I don't know why you're being like this. What has there been between us to entitle you to sneer and scoff at my relationship with Lucas? You don't even know him!'

'I know how much he's hurt you. That means something to me. Hell, that hurts me too! Zena, you know how I feel about you. I was hoping now I'm free that we could find out what there is between us – openly, honestly, without Leah or Lucas or anyone else casting a shadow.'

'Ian...'

He went on recklessly.

'And there's Frodo to think of too. A dog needs two parents, you know.'

Right on cue, the dog leapt up to try and lick Zena's face in mid-air, but missed and raked a couple of muddy paws down the sleeve of her jacket. She couldn't help laughing, but her heart was heavy.

'You're taking him to England?'

'Where I go, he goes,' Ian said simply.

She turned away to look across the great vista of Breton countryside stretched out before her. She could make out the large white blob of the ferry in dock at Roscoff waiting to set out for Plymouth.

'You don't understand,' she said at last. 'Lucas and I have a long history, there are more things between us than I could ever explain. I have to see him again, to talk properly...'

'And let him come back into your life again. You're mad.'

'I am not mad,' she shouted, shoving at him in sheer frustration. 'I have a right to find out, haven't I? You can't control my life, there's nothing between us...'

'Nothing!' He was yelling now too. Their angry words echoed around the granite rocks. 'Was that kiss nothing?'

'Ian, one kiss against nearly five years!'

He grabbed her then and kissed her hard again, unable to bear hearing a comparison of his fading hopes with Lucas' prior claim on her. The kiss went on and on and on, harsh and soft, greedy and forgiving, until they broke away from each other in surprise for a moment before stepping again into each other's arms. They stood there for a long time, Zena's head on his shoulder, both with eyes closed and bodies pressed tightly together.

She was the first to break away.

'I'm sorry, Ian,' she said and turned away down the hillside, touching Frodo's ugly head as she passed and then stumbling on the uneven path as her eyes filled with tears.

The air of gloom in Laure's house seemed to have lifted a little. Her latest results were good, showing that youth and good health were on her side as the doctor had anticipated. She looked tired and thin, but in her eyes at least was a definite glimmer of hope which had been absent when Zena last saw her.

They hugged emotionally and settled down on the leather sofa with Tomas wedged between them waving a yellow plastic lorry at the antics of Franklin the turtle on the television screen. Zena alternately stroked his soft hair which was starting to show the red of his mother's and tickled his ribs when he demanded her attention.

'So what happens next?' she asked, unsure how much Laure wanted to talk about her illness.

'I have five more sessions of this terrible treatment and then we wait for the results. The doctor assures me there is reason to be positive now, but of course I am afraid of what might happen in the future.'

For once Laure felt in herself the need to confide and draw comfort from a friend's support. Zena held her hand lightly and let her talk, enabling Laure to express some of her fears, and to push them away in the process. She shed a few rare tears with the unexpected relief, but kept her voice calm and her mouth ready to smile so that

Tomas would not be alarmed by his mother's distress.

'And how's Thierry?' Zena asked.

'Thierry is fine. Worried, but trying very hard to be a good strong man! In fact, we have been able to talk because of all this, to be close again, like when we were first married.'

'So it's true that troubles bring you closer together?'

Laure shrugged.

'For me, yes, but we are all different. It is not possible to judge our own lives by what happens to others.'

Zena sighed.

'I know, but it's natural to look for answers in other people's experience. It's something to measure your own acceptance against.'

'Live your own life, Zena. Every relationship has its own way to work or not work. You must find out for yourself. Is this about Lucas?'

Zena smiled.

'It's about me now.'

Tomas let out a shriek as she swept him up into the air and danced around the room making him scream with excitement as he soared towards the ceiling and then dropped almost to the floor, dipping and climbing as she whirled round and round.

Although she didn't usually approve of such wild games, Laure smiled indulgently as she watched her happy son, so full of life and energy, and, cheered by Zena's visit, allowed herself to hope that she might actually see him grow to be a man.

Her heart lurched as she heard Lucas' car draw up outside. She had taken a lot of trouble with her appearance, brushing and brushing her buoyant hair into some sort of order, and wearing the well-cut deep tan suede jacket he had always liked over her usual jeans and T-shirt. It was important to be herself today, even if it was the best possible impression she could give of that.

Lucas himself looked as cool and casual as he always did. In the few seconds before he was at the door, she admired his lithe movement, the simple bodily confidence he enjoyed which seemed to her so masculine an accomplishment. There was no sign of insecurity in Lucas, and this had made his letter even more appealing with its touch of vulnerability, the glimpse of a Lucas who had self-doubt, regret and weakness.

All this went though Zena's mind as she opened the glass door and watched him approach. The smile they exchanged held the new depth of all that had happened lately and she felt the familiarity of his arms around her with a new sense of potential and discovery. She noticed, however, that he left his suitcase in the car.

At first they talked of nothing other than the usual banalities about the weather and the journey from Paris, but the big heavy topic of his pseudo-marriage hung silently in the air between them like an enormous weight, capable of crashing down and destroying all in its wake. She thought of many evenings they had spent together in the flat in Bath, speaking about nothing very much – had a similar weight of omission hung over them then? Was there always something missing in their communication?

'Thank you for the letter,' she said at last when no cue came from him.

He looked relieved that she had opened the real proceedings.

'I had to explain to you. It was stupid of me not to do it last time I was here, but it was a very confusing time... if you can understand that.'

She nodded and he seized both her hands in a tight grip.

'I am ready to commit, Zena, I promise you. There was a great resistance in me to that before, I admit it, but freedom can seem pretty empty too. I couldn't forget what we'd had, what I was sure I'd lost...'

'You could have tested that theory,' she said mildly. 'Just a friendly phone call or a postcard with your address, so I could ignore it, if you were right I'd lost interest, or follow it up if I wanted to get back together.'

'And you would have? Followed it up?'

'I would have, Lucas. Don't you realise I spent a year of utter misery before coming out here? I didn't know where you were or how you were thinking about us, or if I'd ever lay eyes on you again! I imagined so many different scenarios – the one that never occurred to me was that you might marry someone else...'

Even the words hurt. She bit her lip to stop tears coming.

He leant towards her.

'I can't say I wish I'd never gone to see Vassily before he died. You must understand that. And I had to keep my promise to him.'

'I do understand that, of course I do. But you didn't have to plan to marry her!'

'I told you that was just an idea, it never would have worked out.'

'But you told Laure's neighbour you were getting married!'

He looked confused.

'Who is Laure?'

'Just a friend. Never mind. You visited her neighbour, an old lady who was a friend of your mother. You told her you were getting married.'

His eyes hardened.

'I did no such thing. She pressed me about when I'd get married, certainly. That's always the main theme of my visits. I told her there was someone around, it was just to keep her happy. That we were to marry must have been an assumption on her part. I swear to you! She's an old lady, Zena. It is a natural wish for her that all the world should be married.'

She knew he was telling the truth, but couldn't help persisting.

'But you did think about it! About marrying this girl.'

He looked away then and stared at the floor.

'You're right. I was foolish, but it didn't seem to matter. I'd lost you, another relationship was not on my agenda...'

'But you hadn't lost me! I'd lost you. You don't seem to understand that at all. One day we were together, the next you'd gone without trace. I lost you! I was lost! Until I came out here and began to make a new life for myself, I lived like an empty shadow, not responding to the world, just existing. It was terrible. I want you to understand, to acknowledge this somehow, I don't know...'

'You mean that it was my fault? I did this awful thing to you?'

She laughed in surprise and got up.

'I suppose I did mean that... well, once maybe, but now,

no. It's up to me what happens in my life, I've begun to see that here.'

'It's up to us now, Zena,' he said urgently, pulling her down to the sofa again. 'We can do whatever we like, make plans for the future, there's nothing to stop us having what we want!'

'Just the minor detail of your current living arrangements.'

'Oh, yes, that of course,' he waved a dismissive hand, 'but that's all being taken care of.'

She changed tack.

'I think I might like to settle here – not here in this house, but in Finistere, around La Folle. What do you think?'

He looked surprised and then thoughtful. When he said nothing, Zena went on.

'Surely it would be a good base for you? You can easily fly to Paris or England from Brest!'

He gently patted the hand she'd placed on his arm.

'I suppose I could, yes. It is just that I hadn't thought of living out here quite yet, maybe in ten years time, but... if it is what you really want, then we must consider it. Paris is certainly very expensive, it is true.'

'I don't want to be here for a negative reason like that though. There are far too many who come here for cheap housing and nothing else. It's the landscape, I've... well, I've sort of grown into it.'

He laughed.

'It suits you, Zena. You look very beautiful.'

He kissed her. She had to concentrate hard to keep the conversation on track, but there were things that had to be established and understood, before she'd let her body's demands distract her completely.

She took a great inward breath.

'And were you thinking of us getting married at any time?'

He looked at her tenderly, the sharp lines of his own face still softened from their kiss.

'If that is what is what you would like.'

He kissed her again then, long and slow, without pressure or urgency. She thought fleetingly of Ian and his tense determination, but then surrendered herself, mind and body to the pleasure of Lucas' familiar touch.

She was disappointed again that he could not stay the night because of a breakfast meeting in Rennes, but at least they had made love, slowly and tenderly, in a long afternoon, with the spring sun, full of new life and promise, slanting in between the shutters to illuminate the bed on which they lay, rediscovering each other. She watched him now, pulling on his clothes with constant pauses to kiss her again and coil her hair around his hands as he had always liked to do.

She finally got up to prepare an early dinner for them before he left and the atmosphere between them was just as it had been for all those meals in the flat, easy and measured at the same time. It was something she recognised as strongly as a scent from childhood, with the same power to conjure up another way of existence, another phase of life.

The feeling of warmth and security seemed to part with him, however, and the house suddenly felt chilly. It was only April after all, and Ian had warned her that she'd probably need a fire well into May. As she brought in logs and snapped up twigs for kindling, she wondered what Ian was doing now, up in the cottage with Frodo, maybe working away at his book. It was hard to imagine two men more different – at their core, au fond, as the French say – than Lucas and Ian. It was not something she wanted to dwell on at this moment, when her bed and body still held the warmth of Lucas, just as she had longed for through so many nights.

No, she thought. Nothing has changed for me as far as Lucas is concerned.

Chapter 18

A week later, Zena was on Erin's doorstep again. She made her way into the familiar sitting room by stepping over cardboard boxes and packing cases in the hall.

'You're not going far though, are you?' she asked. Suddenly it seemed important to her that Erin would still be around.

'It's only just outside La Folle, on the Plouneour road. There's a sign for the pottery on the roadside and lots of delphiniums along the bank. You must come and see as soon as I'm in.'

'I've decided to go back to England next week to sort out a few things,' Zena said quickly. 'Not quite sure when - or maybe if - I'll be back.'

'Is that what your question is?'

'No. Well, not directly. I want to know about relationships, about what I should do.'

Erin raised her eyebrows.

'Forget the should,' she said. 'Advice is the most tarot will go for. At that, though, it's very good indeed.'

They both laughed, although Zena could not entirely conceal her nervousness and the store she was setting by this reading. She waited tensely, determined to be quiet and to listen carefully this time, both to Erin and to her own inner responses to the cards. A week had passed since Lucas' departure, but this time he had phoned her every day, gradually re-building their shared memories and bringing their separate presents into some kind of alignment. She had not seen or heard from Ian again. Part of her was disappointed, part relieved to escape any more emotional pressure. Walking and thinking for hour after hour had convinced her that the answers to the future lay with her, not with the actions of others. She tried to think about the sort of person she would become in any of the various future scenarios that filled her imagination. All that seemed certain was she needed to know how to proceed for herself, not just react to overtures presented to her. If only she knew what she wanted and the path ahead was clear!

This time, she was presented with a deck to draw ten cards from. They went down on the table with Erin's steady incantation naming each one and their positions, so it felt like a sequence of cause and effect:

'The Heart of the Matter – Ten of Pentacles
What crosses you – Two of Swords
The root cause – Ace of Wands
What's leaving you – Five of Cups'
She ignored Zena's gasp and continued steadily.
'Your beliefs – Eight of Cups
What's coming – The Lovers
As you see yourself – Eight of Swords
Expectations of another – Nine of Pentacles
Guidance – Judgement
Outcome – Ace of Cups

The spread seemed to animate Erin.
'Wow! Choices, choices, choices, Zena. Looks like you've got some major decision-making on the agenda.
Zena groaned.

'You did once say 'Tarot only tells you what you know already' – very true in this case!'

Erin laughed, but her concentration was fixed on the cards, eyes darting back and forward, weaving patterns of connection.

'There's a lot of other things here. We need to look carefully, not rush into assumptions, OK?'

Zena grinned.

'Not my forte, but OK. I'll try.'

She looked at the cards, absorbing the detail of the pictures and the grouping of figures. Inevitably it was the card of the Lovers that held her attention. A man stood between two women, clearly in a state of indecision. He didn't look too happy about making a choice. It was a card she could relate to.

Erin began.

'The heart of the matter is about being part of something, establishing a family, making a home. Security is important to you, isn't it? Interesting contrast between these two cards' – she pointed at them – 'you see yourself as trapped and powerless to take control of your life, whilst others see you as independent and pretty clear about what you want. Breaking out seems to be a bit of a theme too – you're deeply creative but it's been kind of suppressed, you've invested a lot in an old emotional situation but it hasn't served you well and yet moving on hasn't exactly been a bed of roses either. And far from having lost, you seem to have the chance of great love within your grasp.' She touched the Ace of Cups lightly. 'Here's the beginning of it.'

'But? I'm waiting for the but.'

Erin gave her an impish grin.

'Don't worry, it's coming. Look at her.'

The card showed a young woman sitting with her back to the sea, blindfolded, two large swords held crossed against her chest.

'You've come a long way from the Five of Cups, Zena, but there's still a blockage, something holding you back from dealing with all the traumatic things that have happened. It's as if you don't want to face up to some reality that will be hard to handle.

'That one's a bit the same,' said Zena, pointing at the Eight of Swords.

'Exactly. I don't think we can ignore the significance of two blindfolded female figures in one reading! And there's this too – it's the key to the whole reading. The card of Judgement. The people are stripped naked – no cover, no pretence, no hiding.'

'But they're waiting to have their sins judged. Isn't that what the angel is trumpeting about?'

'It's symbolic, Zena. Forget sin and guilt and all those wretched Christian notions. This is something else. Your card of Guidance. Use the lessons of the past, think karmically if you like.'

'You mean it's all come back to haunt me now?'

'No, I mean something positive and hopeful. Listen to your inner voice – you don't have to do things the same way all over again. Learn from what's happened and then move on. This is a chance for a new start, but you must choose it, make a real decision about what you want and then act on it – don't just take what comes along.'

Zena put her finger on the Ace of Cups.

'That's my route to happiness, is it?'

Erin smiled. 'That's the advice tarot is giving you. How

you respond to it is up to you.'

Zena gave a big sigh.

'A challenge then!'

'And choices. That doesn't just mean about love and a partner either. You might decide the best course is to continue on your own...'

She saw the sheepish look on Zena's face.

'Ah, things have moved on, I see. I did wonder if the King of Swords was back on the scene.'

Zena's eyebrows shot up.

'What made you think that?'

'I don't have to be psychic to know your body language has changed. Always means sex in my book. Simple as that. No magic needed. And that secretive grin is a dead give away too!'

Zena blushed and they both laughed until Erin rapped the table lightly to restore order.

'Right. To work!'

'What?'

'Well, it's not as straightforward as that, is it? You wouldn't be here if you had everything sewn up in your mind. There's a lot to think about here, some real emotional dilemmas. We need to go through all the cards in detail and think how they apply to your situation and what resonance the reading has for you.'

Erin touched the picture of the Lovers. 'I'd like to start here,' she said. 'In the future.'

Before leaving for England, Zena went one last time up onto the Monts d'Arrée and sat on the rock where she had first danced her pleasure in the landscape nearly five months earlier. So much had changed in that time, for her and those around her, that she could barely recapture the sense of fear and initial isolation of her arrival. She had achieved so many things in terms of confidence, not only with establishing a small start in her new career but also the friendships she had made in a foreign environment. It was peculiar how quickly the strange could become familiar – she would feel a wrench to leave this place, but what would she feel when she turned the key of her old flat and re-entered the most familiar territory of all. Was it still her ultimate place of safety? Somehow she felt that had shifted, as if her inner landscape had been reshaped. Looking at all that was before her eyes, Zena began to fully understand the power of the unique environment here that she had discovered by chance. But it wasn't chance that had brought her here in the beginning. It was the connection with Lucas. He was there at the root of it all, even if it was Ian who had helped open her eyes to the secrets of the landscape.

A note from Ian had come through the post. He had been back in England for some weeks now, continuing to go to work and give his classes, working on the book in his spare time. He had an invitation for Zena, a suggestion for meeting on a particular day outside the Roman baths, to take her out to lunch and talk about the illustrations for Stone Stories. His phone number at the college was given as a contact - she did not know if he was trying to protect her from speaking to his wife, or if he was staying somewhere else.

What Ian did not know, unless he was psychic, was that the day he proposed for their meeting would be her fortieth birthday. She was starting not to believe in coincidence, and realising that everything was somehow part of a big pattern, but how could he have known? It would be good to see him again. She smiled as she wondered if Frodo would be coming too. Perhaps they could take a picnic to the park rather than sit in a stuffy restaurant...

She must go back and load the car if she was to get to the over-night ferry on time. Then it would be home the next morning, back to the flat, her old sanctuary. There'd be lots to do and organise before Lucas arrived from London where he had meetings with a publisher about a project which would take him off to Tibet for a few weeks. She sensed his excitement about this new venture and hoped the terms would work out as he wished.

She wanted to overhaul the flat, even if it was only to be a temporary resting place, to bring in some brightness and shake up the staid energies of the place. She wanted Lucas to come back into an environment that was newly and positively hers.

One thing she did know was that any new relationship she had would have to be on very different terms from her old limited expectations. She must impose herself more, make some demands, have some expectations that required a response from a partner. It would no longer be satisfactory for Lucas to come and go, leaving only a shadowy presence in her everyday life between visits, even if they set up home in Finistere. She needed more. To give more and to take it too. Hell, she deserved it!

A little note of nervousness, however, crept into her thoughts at the prospect of this self-assertion. She watched the soft grey banks of clouds settling over the lines of the hills and woodland. Mile after mile of empty land punctuated by little pockets of occupation. The mild early evening air was like cool silk on her skin. She remembered all the weathers she had walked in on these hills, all the thoughts that had jumbled and jangled as she wandered in countless ancient footsteps. The pull of the past would hold her here so easily if she let it, if she clasped the hand of legend and accepted the bargain of belonging. She already knew she would return, in some guise, but the circumstances, the time and the means remained concealed from her. There was so much to be faced and assessed in her old life.

The late sun streaked out unexpectedly from behind the clouds and shadows skimmed across the landscape like racing horses before its capricious appearances.

Instead of stabilising her thoughts, she felt even more unsettled up here, overwhelmed by the awareness of decisions she had to make. How to arrive at a decision about the future? How to find the formula for choosing or rejecting?

An old mental puzzle from her university days pushed its way into the forefront of her mind.

You are in a cell which has two doors. One door leads to freedom, the other is a dead end. Each door has a guard: one of them always tells the truth, the other always lies. To escape you must find the single question which, put to each guard in turn, will enable you to discover the safe way out. What is the question?

Annoyingly, she could only recall the situation, not the answer, but was that really how she felt, like a prisoner? And would one way, one choice, really lead to freedom?

She mulled it over for a minute. What was the wretched question? What was it? What was it she needed to ask?

She closed her eyes. Stone chats were merrily singing nearby and after a moment there came the distinctive cry of a single curlew above the ridge, just as she had heard it on her first walk in these hills. She let the sounds wash over her and felt the gentle but insistent power of the life in the ground beneath her feet, as if the earth was reminding her of something. She sat on, letting her body relax and, with this, she sensed her mind gradually shedding its habitually anxious buzz. She felt unresistant and open. Ready to believe, ready to trust.

And suddenly, magically, out of the fog of all her confused loyalties and mixed messages, an image came into her mind, a shape she recognised began to emerge, and in a moment of total clarity, Zena knew what the question was.

Epilogue

In fact it was autumn before Zena returned to Finistere.

She had even gone back to work at GPE in Bath for a few weeks in the summer as holiday cover for a variety of administrative jobs. Everyone commented on how well Brittany seemed to have suited her and tried to wheedle out details of what she had been up to. She just laughed and refused to be drawn by jokes about Breton bagpipes and cider drinking.

Now she was back in La Folle. As the car laboured up the hill, it seemed like only a few days that she'd been away. She sent a silent message to Lucas' mother as they passed the cemetery. Given all that had happened in the interim, all the arrangements they had had to make, everything seemed strange and yet familiar at the same time. She recognised various people as they drove through the centre and restrained herself from calling out to Laure, whom she glimpsed disappearing round a corner to the car-park. Time enough to catch up with her friend and fill in the details of their spasmodic email contacts during the summer. No, it was Erin she was keen to see before decanting all the remnants of an old life into a new home. The car passed straight on through the town.

Erin was unchanged by her new location. She came out of one of the barns in a complex of old buildings at the sound of the car, wiping her paint-covered hands on a colourful cloth.

'This has worked out well for you?' Zena asked after they had hugged each other happily.

'It's great. We all get on without any problem and my painting is turning out to be something else.' Erin looked at the loaded car. 'But I'll show you that another time. Come in the cottage for a moment.'

She led Zena by the hand into a minute converted stone storehouse which was now her one-up one-down residence, with its own little private garden out of double-doors at the back and a kitchen in a recess past the oak-linteled granite fireplace.

After admiring the little house, Zena's eyes were drawn irresistibly to the familiar round table, just the same, with its purple cloth and tarot deck. One card lay separately, face down, ready and waiting, like a gauntlet, cast down between the worlds of intuition and reason, setting its own challenge.

Erin smiled.

'I drew that for you after you phoned this morning,' she said. 'It's one card for where you are now.

'And is it appropriate, do you think?'

'Of course. Now I've seen you I can see it's perfect.'

Zena turned the card over.

A golden haired woman was sitting on a throne in a corn-field, a cornucopia of fruits at her feet.

'That's me,' Zena said. 'I can feel that smug expression on my face'.

'The Empress — the lady who has it all. You are pregnant, aren't you?' Erin asked.

Zena nodded in pleased amazement.

Erin's green eyes never left hers.

'When did you know?' she said.

'Last week.'
Erin shook her head.
'I didn't mean that.'
Zena hesitated.
'You'll think I'm crazy.'
'Try me.'
'It was the answer to a simple question. About magic.'
'And?'
'Lucas gave me the answer I was expecting.'
Erin reached up and kissed Zena warmly. They squeezed each other's hands so tightly it hurt.

Zena went back out to the car. It was so packed with their possessions she could hardly see in, but there was the beloved face barely visible beneath a mass of duvet. It grinned up at her lop-sidedly, spraying saliva on the window pane and emitting a high-pitched whine of delight.

'Be quiet, you stupid dog,' Ian said from the driver's seat. 'We're nearly home.'

About Tarot

I hope this book gives some indication that I do not regard tarot as an exercise in either fortune-telling or melodrama. I have been studying and practising tarot for ten years now from an original connection inspired by my interest in Jungian psychology and symbolism. It has never failed me as a source of support and insight, and I have tried to offer those same things to others in my readings.

If you are interested in finding out more about tarot, I recommend TABI (Tarot Association of the British Isles). Their website (www.tabi.org.uk) also offers free online readings, carried out by experienced tarotists.

Note
Tarot readings by the author of this book can be arranged - see www.wendymewes.net
or email startarot@wanadoo.fr for details.

If you enjoyed The Five of Cups, you'll love
Moon Garden...

Rufus' life is a mess. Can the mysterious moon garden save him from total disaster? Will its legend prove true? It seems so when he meets Lily, the woman of his dreams...

"...a witty, intuitive story with vivid characters and lively relationships"

"...delightful read combining enchantment, love, life, humour and natural magic"

Also by Wendy Mewes

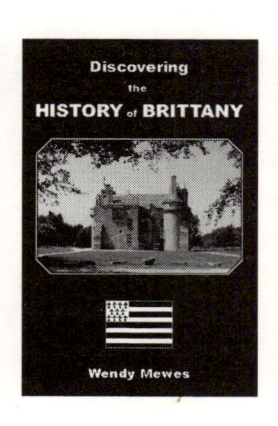

**Discovering
the History of Brittany**

A concise account of this extraordinary region of France presented through the people and places that have coloured events from prehistoric times to the present day

"...enlightens the reader on the indispensible elements in understanding Brittany today"

www.reddogbooks.com

BIO

Modern biology covers a wide field, ranging from the study of cell chemistry and genetics, through anatomy and physiology, to evolution, ecology and the study of animal behaviour. This book aims to provide an introduction to biology as it is now understood by surveying its main divisions. It begins with an account of the way in which animals and plants 'work', which leads on to a consideration of the biochemical basis of life. The author, in imagination, divides the living cell into smaller and smaller components, eventually explaining the nature and function of the essential macromolecules. He then goes on to discuss the variety of forms to which this biochemical mechanism has given rise, describing representatives of the major divisions of the plant and animal kingdoms. Ecology, genetics and evolution are next discussed, and the final chapter looks briefly at animal behaviour.

Written in a simple style and well illustrated throughout, this book will prove a valuable introduction to biology for the interested layman and for mature students just beginning O or A level work. It may also be useful as a basic text for non-specialist sixth-form courses.

TEACH YOURSELF BOOKS

BIOLOGY

John Ruthven Hall

B.A.

TEACH YOURSELF BOOKS
Hodder and Stoughton

First printed 1974
Second impression 1975
Third impression 1977
Fourth impression 1978
Fifth impression 1979

Copyright © 1974
J. R. Hall

All rights reserved. No part of this publication may be reproduced or transmitted in any form or by any means, electronic or mechanical, including photocopy, recording or any information storage and retrieval system, without permission in writing from the publisher.

This volume is published in the U.S.A. by David McKay Company Inc., 750 Third Avenue, New York, N.Y. 10017.

ISBN 0 340 18265 2

Printed and bound in Great Britain for
Hodder and Stoughton Paperbacks,
a division of Hodder and Stoughton Ltd,
Mill Road, Dunton Green, Sevenoaks, Kent,
(Editorial Office: 47 Bedford Square, London WC1 3DP)
by Richard Clay (The Chaucer Press), Ltd,
Bungay, Suffolk

Contents

Introduction *ix*

1 The Flowering Plant 13

The factory organism. Raw materials. The source of energy. Products. The release of energy. Structure and functions. Patterns of growth. The factory that manufactures new factories

2 The Mammal 57

The automobile organism. The heart and circulatory system. The lymphatic system. Foods and digestion. Release of energy. Regulation and control. The nervous system. Cells, tissues and organs. Reproduction

3 Biochemistry and the Cell 107

What organisms are made of. Carbohydrates. Proteins. Enzymes. Biochemical systems. The function of the nucleus and nucleic acid. Chromosome number

4 The Variety of Organisms 134

Phylum Protozoa. Phylum Algae. Phylum Bryophyta. Phylum Pteridophyta. Phylum Spermatophyta. Phylum Coelenterata. Phylum Platyhelminthes. Phylum Mollusca. Phylum Echinodermata. Phylum Annelida. Phylum Arthropoda. Phylum Chordata. Fungi. Bacteria. Viruses

5 Ecology 207
Natural communities. Food chains. The circulation of material in nature. Utilisation of natural resources. Effect of physical and biological factors on the environment. The struggle for life—population control

6 Genetics 237
Mendel's breeding experiments. Human heredity. The practical application of genetics

7 Evolution 252
The evidence for evolution. The mechanism of evolution. Human evolution

8 Animal Behaviour 273
Automatic behaviour. Learned behaviour. Learning in humans

Further Reading 288

Glossary 290

Index 299

List of Plates

1 The result of a water culture experiment using barley seedlings. The plant on the left has been grown in a solution containing all necessary elements. The others lack respectively (*above*, in order from the left), sodium, sulphur, molybdenum (*below*, left to right), phosphorus, iron, copper, potassium and nitrogen

2 Transverse sections of (*above*) a sunflower stem and (*below*) a buttercup root, as seen under the microscope. The cells may be distinguished as rounded or polygonal objects of varying sizes. The small cells in the centre of the root are those concerned with the conduction of food and water (xylem and phloem), whereas in the stem these tissues are found in the veins at the periphery

3 Model of a molecule of protein (myoglobin, a substance found in muscle and similar to haemoglobin). The small spheres represent atoms, of which there are about 2600. 150 amino acid units go to make up this particular molecule

4 Model of part of a DNA molucule. The objects looking like matchsticks are the links between atoms, which are represented by the match heads. The simplified diagram on the right shows how the molecule consists of two 'backbones' twisted around each other and linked by 'side pieces'

Introduction

Modern biology covers a wide field, ranging from the study of cell chemistry and genetics, through the more traditional physiology and anatomy, to evolution, ecology and the study of animal behaviour in laboratory and field. In spite of this diversity, it is a unified subject, held together by a connecting theme, the consideration of how living systems perpetuate themselves in the face of an ever-changing environment. This book is an attempt to introduce the subject by surveying some of its main divisions. A number of pages are devoted in the first two chapters to the biology of the flowering plant and the mammal—traditionally the core of elementary biology—but, of necessity, these cannot be treated as fully as is, perhaps, usual. The interested reader is recommended to consult other titles published by Teach Yourself Books, such as *Botany* and *Human Biology* which provide a more detailed treatment. A more comprehensive list of books for further reading is given on page 288.

To the American reader

Most of the examples mentioned in this book are of plants or animals well known to British readers. In many cases similar or identical species are to be found in North America, but the author is confident that American readers will find the explanations perfectly intelligible even where unfamiliar examples are involved.

Acknowledgements

The author and publishers wish to thank the following for permission to include photographic material in this book: Rothamsted Experimental Station for Plate 1; the Longman Group Ltd. for Plate 2 (A) from *Photomicrographs of the Flowering Plant* by Shaw, Lazell and Foster; Sir John Kendrew for Plate 3; and R.J.M. Exports Ltd. for Plate 4, which shows a model of DNA built in the Minit system made by Cochranes of Oxford Ltd., Leafield, Oxford, OX8 5NT.

1 The Flowering Plant

The factory organism

When a seed germinates and grows into a plant, a very remarkable thing occurs. The seed may be very small and seem to be a simple object, but it gives rise to a complex, highly organised structure, in some cases weighing many tons. Just how remarkable this is will be realised if it is compared with examples of growth in the non-living world. Think of a stalactite growing from the roof of a cave. Limestone dissolves in water flowing through the rocks and is deposited on the stalactite as the water drips from it, slowly making it bigger. Or think of a crystal growing in a solution of copper sulphate. Copper sulphate comes out of solution and is added slowly to the crystal. In both cases growth is just a matter of getting bigger by the addition of more stuff. There is no increase in complexity and the material added is just the same as the matter originally present. In a plant this is not so.

Plants are made of very complex chemicals, but the raw materials needed for growth are surprisingly simple: carbon dioxide, water and a few simple salts such as are present in a packet of garden fertiliser. Mix these things up and put them into a test-tube and nothing much would happen; but add one little seed and this would get to work, taking the simple chemicals and making them into the organised, complicated thing that is a plant.

The plant is like a factory (a very strange and beautiful factory) that requires raw materials. To make a ship a shipyard needs steel plates, rivets, wood for decks and furnishings, cable for rigging, paint and much else besides. It also requires a supply of energy in the form of fuel or electricity for working cranes and other machinery. Likewise, nature's factory requires energy as well as raw materials.

Raw materials

What is a plant made of? Supposing we took a plant, weighed it and then dried it in a warm oven. Then its weight would become less, because of the water loss. So we could discover the amount of water in the plant at the beginning. This is surprisingly large, water often making up as much as 85% of vegetable matter.

If we now heated the dried material more strongly, it would begin to burn and blacken because of the formation of carbon. Stronger heating would cause this gradually to burn away and eventually we should be left with a white ash, like that left after a bonfire has burnt out. This would consist of salts of various metals, especially potassium, and its weight would be very small, equivalent, perhaps, to only 10% of the original dry matter.

Thus a large part of a plant is water. The remainder consists principally of carbon, but chemical analysis shows the presence of hydrogen, oxygen, nitrogen, phosphorus and sulphur, as well as the metals mentioned above. The exact composition varies, but analysis would show proportions by weight approximately as follows (in dry plant material):

carbon	40%
hydrogen	6%
oxygen	45%
nitrogen	3.5%
phosphorus	0.4%
potassium	3.4%

calcium   0.7%
other elements 1.0%

Where do these elements come from? Long ago in the seventeenth century a Dutchman, van Helmont, thought that plants were made only of water and he performed a simple experiment to prove it. He took a branch from a willow tree, weighed it accurately and planted it in dried soil which had also been weighed. He then watered this with rain water. The branch took root (a thing that willow branches do readily) and van Helmont allowed it to go on growing for five years. He then carefully separated the small tree from the soil, dried the latter and weighed both. The original branch weighed 5 lb, but the tree that grew from it weighed 169 lb. The soil, on the other hand, which weighed 200 lb at the beginning, lost only 2 oz during the five-year period. Van Helmont assumed that this small loss was due to experimental error (some of the soil had been lost by mistake) and concluded that, since water was the only other thing supplied, the increase in weight of the plant was due to this alone. Hence, he thought, plants are composed only of water.

Today we cannot accept van Helmont's conclusion. Water is composed solely of hydrogen and oxygen. What was the source of the other elements? Perhaps he was wrong about the loss of soil being due to experimental error. In fact, we now know that all the elements below oxygen in the list given above come from the soil. They make up only a small percentage of the whole plant and consequently only small amounts are taken from the soil. Van Helmont's methods were probably too crude to detect this with certainty. However, his biggest mistake was to forget about the air. This contains carbon in the form of carbon dioxide. The amount is tiny (0.03% by volume), but it is always there and plants absorb it all the time. It is their only source of carbon.

The raw materials of the plant are, then, water (in large amounts), carbon dioxide (large amounts absorbed slowly) and certain elements from the soil (small quantities). The last-named substances are obtained in the form of mineral salts. These are simple compounds of the class called salts by chemists because they are chemically similar to common salt. The term *mineral* indicates that most of them, in the first place, come from the rocks that form the soil. Since these salts and water are the only things that are taken from the soil, it is possible to grow a plant in a suitable solution of them. This is sometimes done commercially, usually with greenhouse plants such as tomatoes. In the laboratory plants may be grown in jars, as shown in Plate 1. The solution in the jars is called a *culture solution*. Air has to be bubbled into it from time to time to supply the roots with oxygen, and the jar is covered with black paper to keep out light and to discourage the growth of microscopic green plants which would otherwise appear.

By varying the composition of the culture solution it is possible to discover what salts the plant needs. The absence of any essential element will result in poor growth and signs of disease, as illustrated in the photograph. In this way it has been possible to show that all plants need six major elements:

>   nitrogen
>   phosphorus
>   sulphur
>   potassium
>   calcium
>   magnesium

The first three must be in the form of nitrates, phosphates and sulphates, and the remainder as their salts. There are also other elements, such as iron, zinc and copper, which are required in very tiny amounts (a few parts per million, or less) and these are called the minor elements of plant nutrition.

This knowledge has led to the development of artificial fertilisers, consisting of chemicals containing the essential elements, which are added to the soil to make it more fertile. Normally there is likely to be a shortage of nitrogen, phosphorus and potassium, and commonly used fertilisers are, for example, potassium sulphate, sodium nitrate and basic slag (which contains phosphates of calcium). Calcium is also sometimes lacking and may be added in the form of lime (calcium hydroxide) or gypsum (calcium sulphate).

Note that, although carbon compounds are usually present in the soil, none of the carbon in the plant comes from this source. It all comes from the air. The way in which carbon dioxide is absorbed from the air is described below.

The source of energy

The sun provides the energy needed by plants in the form of light. It is well known that plants must have light in order to grow properly. House plants must be placed on window sills; greenhouses have roofs and sometimes walls made almost entirely of glass; few plants grow in the dense shade of trees in a thick wood. The leaves are the organs that absorb the light, and as the plant grows they are spread out and exposed to it as much as possible. A plant growing near a window bends so that its leaves face the light.

The light energy absorbed by a leaf is used to manufacture food. This takes the form of sugar at first but is very often converted into starch immediately. The presence of starch can be demonstrated very easily by treating the leaf with iodine after it has been killed by boiling and had the green colour washed out of it with methylated spirit. This gives a blue or grey colour if starch is present. If a plant is kept in the dark for a day or two, any starch becomes used up and a leaf when tested will give no colour. If a stencil is now attached to another leaf, so that part of it is covered and part not, on exposure to light for a few hours starch will be formed in the parts that are not covered. If the iodine test is then applied, the leaf will be stained in such a way that the pattern of the stencil is reproduced (Fig. 1.1).

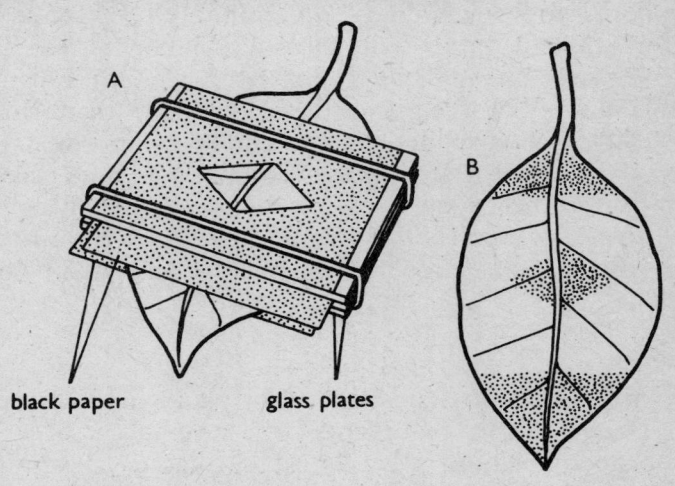

Fig. 1.1 Starch formation in a leaf: (A) leaf with stencil attached; (B) result of testing the leaf for starch after exposure to light

The process by which sugar and starch are formed in this way is called **photosynthesis** (from the Greek word *photos* = light).

Both starch and sugar are fairly complex chemical compounds composed of carbon, hydrogen and oxygen (they are carbohydrates), and raw materials are, of course, needed to make them. The raw materials are carbon dioxide and water. The latter is taken from the soil by the roots and travels to the leaves via the stem. The former is absorbed directly by the leaves, entering by minute holes, or **stomata**, in their surfaces. It can easily be shown that leaves cannot photosynthesise if carbon dioxide is removed from the air surrounding them.

The Flowering Plant 19

Like many manufacturing processes, photosynthesis, as well as making useful products (sugar and starch), also results in the formation of a waste product. This is the gas, oxygen, which escapes from the leaves through the stomata. In water plants bubbles of oxygen may be seen coming from the plants when they are exposed to bright light. Canadian pond weed, often used in aquaria, is a favourite material for laboratory experiments on the formation of oxygen. A simple experiment is illustrated in Fig. 1.2.

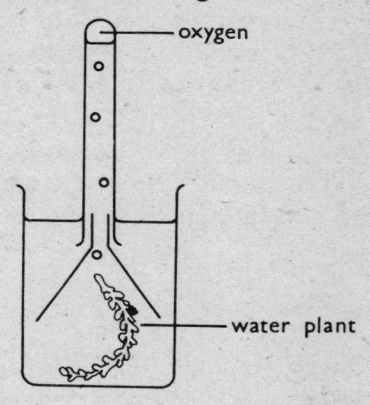

Fig. 1.2 Production of oyxgen by a water plant exposed to light. The water contains dissolved carbon dioxode

Although it is a very complex process, the net effect of photosynthesis may be represented simply as

light energy + carbon dioxide + water ⟶ carbohydrate + oxygen

The light energy needed for the process is absorbed by the green pigment in most ordinary plants. This pigment is called *chlorophyll* and actually consists of a mixture of substances. It is quite easy to make a solution of chlorophyll by grinding leaves with a little sand (to help to break up the leaves) and a suitable solvent, such as acetone. If a drop of the solution is put on blotting paper, it spreads out and yellow and green fringes appear at the edge of the spot, due to separation of four pigments.

If white light (which consists of a mixture of the colours seen in the rainbow—red, orange, yellow, green, blue and violet) is allowed to pass through a chlorophyll solution, it is found that the light that emerges contains less red and a little less orange and green than ordinary light, and hardly any blue or violet. Thus the chlorophyll has absorbed some of the red, orange and green, and most of the blue and violet light. When chlorophyll is in a leaf the energy of the light absorbed is used to split water molecules (H_2O). The resulting oxygen eventually escapes from the leaf as oxygen gas (see above) and the hydrogen is used in a process that converts carbon dioxide into sugar and other carbohydrates. All this can be represented simply as follows:

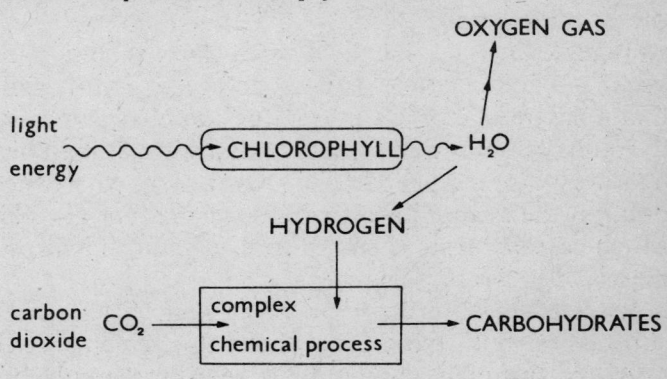

Fig. 1.3 Photosynthesis—an outline of the process

Products

What happens to the carbohydrates produced by photosynthesis? Broadly speaking, they may (i) be stored for future use, (ii) be used to make new material required for

The Flowering Plant

growth of the plant or (iii) be used to produce energy. We shall consider these three uses in turn.

Starch is the form in which plants often store carbohydrates. In the pure form it is a white powder. The housewife uses it for stiffening collars and suchlike. It is also found in an impure form in many foods, for example flour, rice, oats and potatoes. It does not dissolve in cold water, but it absorbs hot water to form a sticky paste or solution. This property is often used in cooking, as when flour is used to thicken gravy or oatmeal is made into porage.

The starch formed in leaves by photosynthesis represents a temporary store of carbohydrate. Not much of it can be kept in the leaves and it is moved to other parts of the plant for more permanent storage. Before it can be moved it is converted into sugar, which is then transported through the veins in the leaves, stem and other parts. When it arrives in the storage organ it may be reconverted to starch. The storage organs are usually special parts of the plant which become swollen to accommodate the stored carbohydrate. Examples are the tubers of potatoes, dahlias and carrots, and the bulbs of onions, hyacinths or daffodils. Sometimes carbohydrate is stored as sugar, as in sugar cane, where the storage organ is the stem, and sugar beet, where it is a swollen root. Much carbohydrate is stored in seeds, and this is one of the reasons for the importance of grains as food.

Plant tissues are made up of a great variety of chemical substances, but, apart from the water which makes up so much of the plant, as we have seen, these substances are practically all compounds of carbon. Carbon is a unique element which is capable of forming an unlimited number of compounds with other elements, some of these compounds being very complex indeed. Life as we know it depends upon such compounds (see Chapter 3). The source of all the carbon in the plant, and in all other organisms for that matter, is that absorbed during photosynthesis.

Some of the substances in the plant are composed of the same elements (carbon, hydrogen and oxygen) as are the carbohydrates manufactured in photosynthesis. Examples are fats, oils and related compounds, and cellulose. The latter may make up the bulk of the material apart from water. These substances are made more or less directly by chemical transformation of the carbohydrates. Other substances contain various additional elements. For example, proteins play a very important role in the life of the plant, as we shall see, and they always contain nitrogen and frequently sulphur and various other elements, in addition to carbon, hydrogen and oxygen. These other elements come ultimately from the mineral salts obtained from the soil. As the plant grows, more and more of the various compounds have to be manufactured, and it is clear that photosynthesis has a key part to play in providing essential raw materials.

The release of energy

The sun's energy is absorbed by chlorophyll in photosynthesis and is used to drive the process that results in the formation of sugar. You may wonder how the plant's other needs for energy are met. Plants do use energy. Sometimes one sees a tree that has grown in some tiny crack and split a great rock apart, and it is obvious that an enormous amount of energy must have been required. Less obviously, materials are always being moved about the plant—sugars are transported from leaves to storage organs, for example; mineral salts are being absorbed from the soil; leaves, stems and roots are being slowly moved, and complex chemicals manufactured. All these processes need energy.

The required energy is obtained from the sugar made in photosynthesis. This contains the energy of sunlight as stored chemical energy, which may be released and made available when the sugar is broken down chemically. The process may be compared to the release of energy from fuels, such as petrol or coal. We know that energy is obtained by burning them. This results in their chemical breakdown. The petrol in a car engine, for example, combines with the oxygen in air drawn into the engine (i.e. the petrol burns), and carbon dioxide, carbon monoxide, water and some other substances are produced. Heat energy also appears and this is used for driving the engine.

The process by which the energy of sugar is released is called *respiration*. Usually (although not always) it is like burning, in that it involves chemical reaction with oxygen from the air. Carbon dioxide and water are produced as well as energy, which may appear as heat or in various other forms.

The normal type of respiration occurring in plants may be represented as

sugar + oxygen ⟶ water + carbon dioxide + energy.

This represents the net effect of a very complex process.

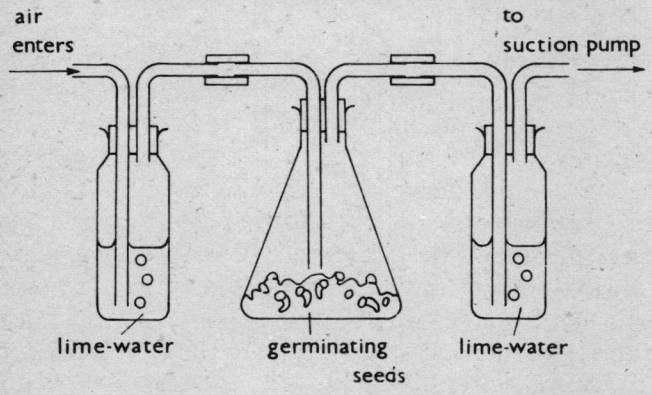

Fig. 1.4 Production of carbon dioxide by germinating seeds. The lime water in the flask on the right soon turns milky, due to the presence of carbon dioxide coming from the seeds; that on the left does not, because the amount of carbon dioxide in ordinary air is very small

Germinating seeds carry out respiration quite rapidly and it is easy to show that they give out carbon dioxide (Fig. 1.4). They also produce heat at the same time, but this is more difficult to demonstrate because the amounts are so small. However, if seeds are soaked in water, so that they start to germinate, and then placed in a vacuum flask, a rise in temperature may be detected (Figs. 1.5 and 1.6). Two vacuum flasks are used in the experiment illustrated so that

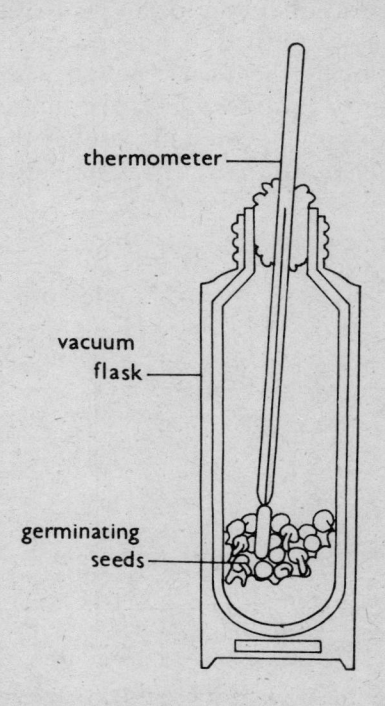

Fig. 1.5 Apparatus to investigate heat production by germinating seeds. *A second identical flask is set up containing seeds which have been killed by chemical treatment*

the effect of changes in temperature in the air surrounding

the flasks may be allowed for. The vacuum flasks allow the heat produced by the seeds to escape only very slowly, so that this heat causes a small rise in temperature. However, heat can enter or leave the flasks to some extent and the fluctuations in temperature shown in the graph (Fig. 1.6) must have been due to changes in room temperature. It will be noticed that, nevertheless, the temperature of the living seeds was consistently higher than that of the dead ones. The energy released in respiration was appearing as heat.

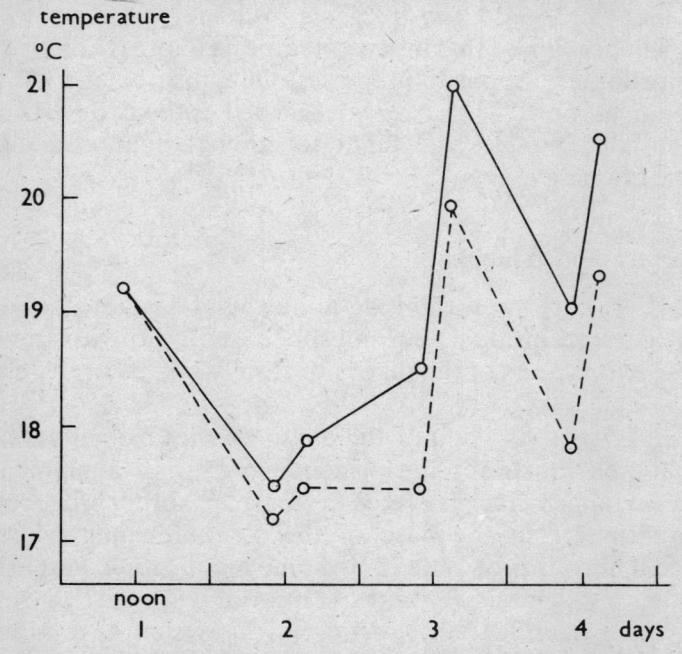

Fig. 1.6 Result of experiment on heat production in germinating seeds. The continuous graph line shows variations in live seeds, the dotted line those of the dead ones

It is more difficult to show the occurrence of respiration in the fully grown plant because the process is slower. At the same time, in the green parts, the effects of respiration are masked by photosynthesis. Thus, when the plant is exposed to light, any carbon dioxide resulting from respiration is immediately used up in photosynthesis. At the same time, the amount of oxygen produced by the latter process is usually greater than that used up by the former. In the daytime, in other words, photosynthesis predominates, and the overall effect is consumption of carbon dioxide and production of oxygen. At night the position is reversed: carbon dioxide is produced and oxygen consumed.

It will be realised that in several respects photosynthesis and respiration are opposite processes. One absorbs energy, the other gives it out. They may be regarded as the two parts of a system that enables the plant to convert light into other forms of energy.

Structure and function

So far we have been thinking about what a plant does and what goes on inside it, but not much about how it is made. These two aspects of the plant are closely related, as we shall see.

Fig. 1.7 is a drawing of the common meadow buttercup, which well illustrates the principal organs of a plant and their arrangement. There is a mass of branching roots originating from the base of the stem, forming what is called a fibrous root system. (In some plants, for example the dandelion, there is a central tap root with lateral roots branching from it.) The function of this system is to absorb mineral salts and water from the soil and to anchor the plant. Frequently starch or other food reserves are stored in the roots. Above the ground, the stem and its branches support the leaves, which might be regarded as the most important organs because it is in them that photosynthesis mostly occurs. Branches of the stem are formed by the growth of buds. These are normally found in the angles (called **axils**)

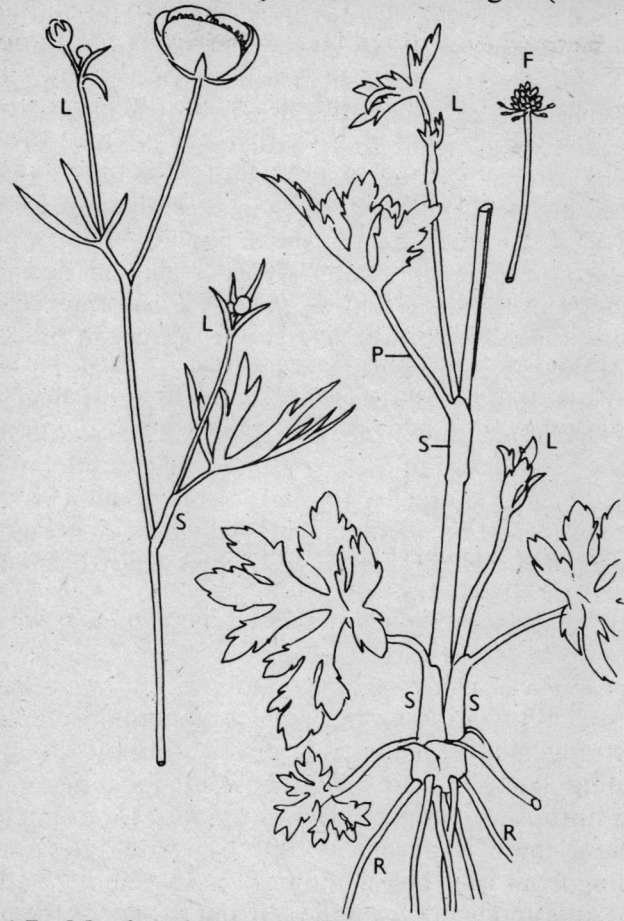

Fig. 1.7 Meadow buttercup, *Ranunculus acris*. R, R—roots; L, L—lateral shoots in axils of leaves; F—head of fruits developing after loss of petals from flower; P—petiole of leaf. The petioles have sheaths (S, S) which enclose axillary buds and the bases of lateral shoots

between leaves and the stem. A new stem, bearing leaves, may grow from any of these axillary buds. In the buttercup such lateral shoots generally end in a flower. In other plants this will not necessarily be so, and especially in long-lived plants, such as trees and shrubs, the laterals will themselves develop shoots growing from axillary buds and repeated branching results. The leaves in the buttercup have a regular spiral arrangement on the stem, but other plants may differ from this. A common arrangement has leaves in opposed pairs alternately at right angles (decussate arrangement). This is seen in the dead nettles, the horse chestnut and the sycamore, for example. The leaf stalks present in the lower leaves of the buttercup are called **petioles**.

If a plant stem is cut across with a sharp razor blade and the cut surface examined with a magnifying glass, it looks as though it is made up of a large number of minute bubbles. These bubbles are in reality the cells of the plant. The whole organism is made up of them, rather in the same way as a house is made of bricks. Plate 2 (A) shows a slice (section) of

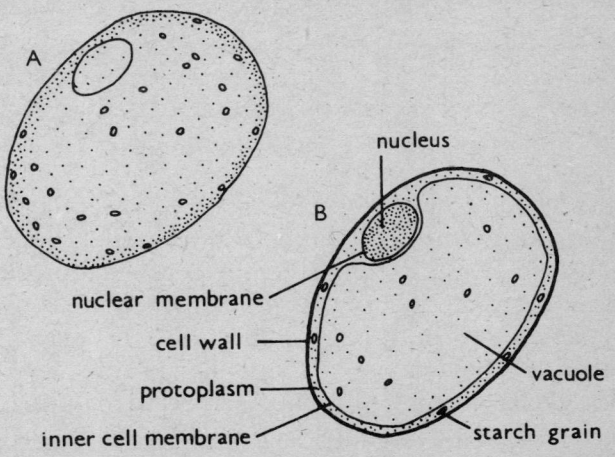

Fig. 1.8 A plant cell: (A) entire cell; (B) cell shown as if cut in half

a sunflower stem as seen under the microscope. The cells are clearly visible. It will also be seen that there are various kinds of cell, some larger, some smaller.

A single cell, separated from other cells, is illustrated in Fig. 1.8. It is something like a transparent balloon, or, more aptly perhaps, a football. The outer cover, corresponding to the leather part of a football, is made of a thin transparent layer of cellulose, a tough fibrous substance something like cellophane or polythene. This part is called the **cell wall**. Inside this, corresponding to the rubber bladder in a football, is a thin layer of a jelly-like substance called **protoplasm**. Protoplasm is the living substance of the cell. It may contain various things—grains of starch, for example— but there is always a round body called the **nucleus**. This consists of a special kind of protoplasm separated from the rest by a thin membrane (the **nuclear membrane**). There is also a **cell membrane** covering the inner and outer surfaces of the protoplasm and separating it from the cell wall on the one hand and the liquid that fills the centre of the cell on the other. This liquid is a solution of various substances in water called **cell sap** and the space containing it is the **vacuole**. The cell sap corresponds to the air in a football and, like it, is normally under pressure and pushing out against the protoplasm and cell wall, so maintaining the shape of the cell.

Usually, of course, the cells are not separate from one another. In fact, they are often tightly packed together, so that instead of being rounded they become polygonal with flattened sides. In section they are frequently six-sided and look like the cells in a honeycomb (Plate 2). They are stuck together by a glue-like substance called pectin.

Plant cells are not all alike. The kind described above (called parenchyma) compose the soft parts of the plant— as, for example, the pith that sometimes occupies the centre of the stem. Other kinds differ in shape, very often in the nature of the cell wall and sometimes in other respects. For example, some have very much thicker walls and are long and thin, forming fibres, bundles of which help to strengthen various parts of the plant. Such fibres from the stem of the flax plant are used in making linen. In another kind, **xylem** vessels, the cells are cylindrical and joined end to end. The partitions between each cell and the next disappear, so that a chain of cells forms a long tube. At the same time, the side walls become thickened and strong, so helping to prevent the collapse of the tube and also strengthening the plant as a whole. The living protoplasm disappears. Xylem vessels are found in the veins of the leaf and in the stem and root. They carry water from the roots to the leaves. **Phloem** cells are another tubular type. In this case the walls are not thickened, protoplasm is present and the partitions between the cells remain, although perforated by a number of holes, making them like little sieves. Phloem vessels are often found near the xylem vessels, and they carry sugar and other food substances about the plant.

It must be clear already that the different cell types are designed to carry out various special functions. The way several different kinds of cell make up an organ that is beautifully constructed in order to carry out a particular complex function most efficiently is well illustrated in the leaf. Fig. 1.9 shows the microscopic structure of a typical leaf. The centre of the leaf is occupied mostly by two kinds of tissue, the upper **palisade layer** and the lower **spongy layer**. Their cells contain numerous green bodies called **chloroplasts**, which contain the chlorophyll needed for photosynthesis. Chlorophyll is always contained in such chloroplasts, which are present in all the green parts of the plant. There are many air spaces between the cells, especially in the spongy layer. Veins are present in this part of the leaf, forming an extensive network, so that no cell is very far from a vein. The veins contain both xylem and phloem cells. Covering upper

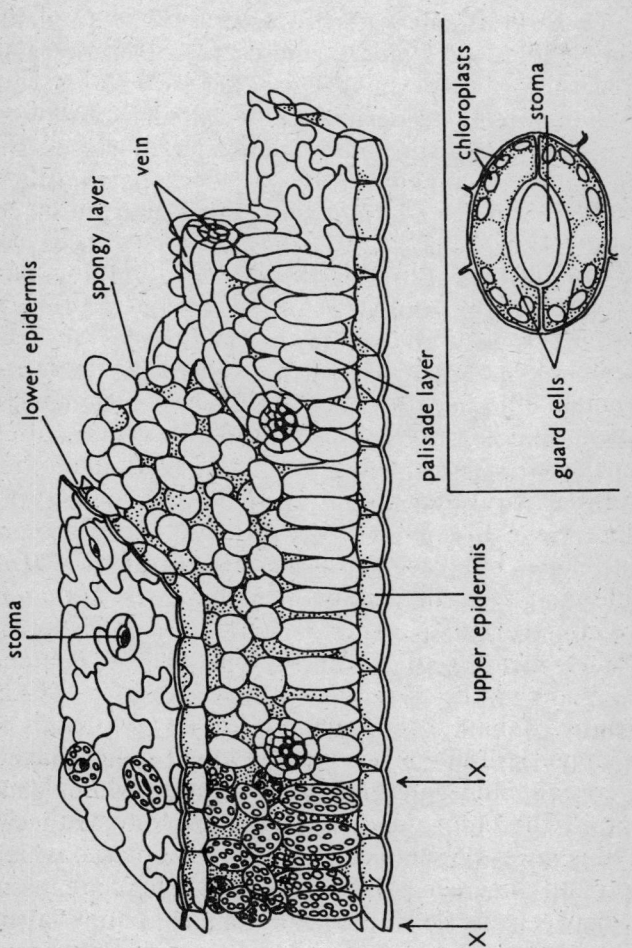

Fig. 1.9 Leaf structure—stereogram showing small portion of leaf *upside down* in order to show stomata on lower surface. Chloroplasts are shown only towards the left of the figure (X–X) and otherwise cell contents are not portrayed. Inset—a stoma with its guard cells

and lower surfaces is a skin, or **epidermis**, composed of a single layer of cells. These cells contain no chloroplasts. Their outer walls are thickened and covered with a waxy **cuticle**, which makes them waterproof. In the lower epidermis are many holes, or **stomata** (these are sometimes also present in the upper epidermis). On either side of a stoma there are two special epidermal cells called guard cells (Fig. 1.9, inset). They can cause the stoma to close as a result of a change in shape when they lose water from their vacuoles. Unlike other epidermal cells, most guard cells do contain chloroplasts.

The function of the leaf is to carry out photosynthesis. We have seen how the chlorophyll essential for the process is contained in the palisade and spongy layers. It is clear that the chloroplasts are spread out in such a way that they are exposed to the light most effectively. Light can reach all chloroplasts at almost full intensity, since none is masked by many other chloroplasts above it, as would be the case if a leaf were a thick organ like a stem. The flattened shape of the leaf means that it has a relatively large surface area in contact with the air. This is obviously an advantage, because the rate at which the leaf can absorb the carbon dioxide needed for photosynthesis must depend upon this surface area: a large area will result in a high rate of absorption.

The carbon dioxide is actually absorbed through the stomata and travels within the leaf through the air spaces. This comes about by a process known as diffusion. This is a very widespread effect which causes gases or substances in solution to spread out and fill any space evenly. An example may help to make this clear. Suppose a spoonful of sugar is put in the bottom of a teacup and tea is then added but *not* stirred to dissolve the sugar. At first there would be a little sugar dissolved in the tea, but most of it would still be at the bottom. Gradually this would dissolve but still remain near the bottom, so that there would be a strong sugar solution below and a weak sugar solution above. Slowly, however, the sugar would begin to spread upwards, and after some time—long after the tea had become cold—it would be evenly distributed throughout the tea. This happens because the molecules of sugar, indeed the molecules of all substances, are moving hither and thither in a random fashion because of their heat energy. The random motion causes them gradually to spread out, rather as a crowd of children running about in one corner of a playground will eventually spread out to fill the whole of it. Note that the effect is to cause a substance to move from a region of high concentration to one of low concentration. Diffusion also occurs in gases. Thus an unpleasant-smelling gas released at one end of a chemistry laboratory is soon smelt at the other end, even if the air is quite still.

Returning to the leaf, we can understand how diffusion ensures a supply of carbon dioxide to the inner leaf cells. When they carry out photosynthesis, they use up carbon dioxide. As a result, the concentration of the gas inside the leaf falls. Its concentration in the air outside the leaf remains the same as it was and therefore greater than that within the leaf. Diffusion, however, tends to even out the difference, and so carbon dioxide spreads from the region of relatively high concentration outside the leaf to the region of relatively low concentration within it. As fast as the chlorophyll-bearing cells use up carbon dioxide it is supplied from outside.

Diffusion happens much more rapidly in gases than in liquids, and this explains the presence of air spaces in the leaf. Carbon dioxide passing through the stomata enters the air spaces and travels through them to the cells in the spongy and palisade layers. If there were no air spaces, it would have to dissolve in the water of the cell sap of the leaf cells and then diffuse in solution, which would be a very slow process. As it is, only the very last stage of the journey

—from the cell surface to the chloroplast—takes place in solution.

The other raw material for photosynthesis is water, and there is an abundance of this in the cell vacuoles. It is supplied to the leaf through the xylem vessels in the veins, as explained below.

Of the two products of photosynthesis, oxygen diffuses out of the leaf along the same pathway as carbon dioxide entering it. Sugar, after temporary storage, is carried away by the phloem tissue of the veins. The pathways travelled by the various substances involved in photosynthesis are illustrated in Fig. 1.10.

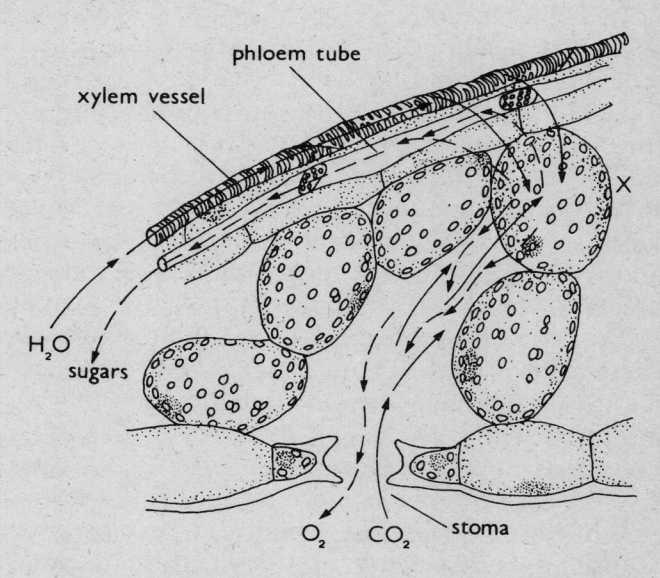

Fig. 1.10 Pathways of raw materials for and products of photosynthesis in the leaf

So far nothing has been said to explain the fact that the stomata are capable of opening and closing. They are generally open during the day and closed at night. Obviously they must be open in the light to permit carbon dioxide to enter and oxygen to escape so that photosynthesis may occur, but, although this is not necessary in the dark, it may not be clear why there is any need to close them. What harm would there be in leaving them open?

The explanation has to do with the fact that, besides allowing exchange of carbon dioxide and oxygen with the air, the stomata also permit water vapour to escape from the leaf. The vacuoles in the leaf cells are full of water, and this can pass quite readily through the protoplasm and cell walls. Where the cells are in contact with air spaces the water evaporates, and so the spaces come to contain a great deal of water vapour. This diffuses through the system of air spaces and out of the stomata. As a result, water vapour is constantly lost from the leaf. The leaf does not dry up because of this, since more water is, under normal conditions, constantly being supplied from the roots. However, there is always a danger that the supply may not be enough: there may be an insufficient reserve of water in the soil, for example, so that the roots are unable to obtain enough to replace what is being lost from the leaves. In the extreme case this could lead to the plant drying up and dying. The function of the stomata is to reduce loss of water (i) by closing if the leaf begins to lose too much water and (ii) by closing at night, when there is no need for them to be open, so that loss of water vapour is reduced and the supply in the plant and in the soil surrounding the roots is conserved.

The closure of the stomata is effective in reducing water loss because the cuticle of the epidermal cells prevents, or at any rate reduces, evaporation from them. However, it is clear that the stomata and cuticle cannot always stop loss of water altogether, since, as is well known, the leaves of most plants dry up quite rapidly when removed from the stem, thus cutting off their supply of water. Nevertheless, some plants growing in dry situations are able to reduce water loss almost completely.

All this suggests that the main function of the epidermis, with its cuticle and stomata, is to protect the leaf from drying up. As far as the function of photosynthesis is concerned, it plays no part and the leaf could work perfectly well without it.

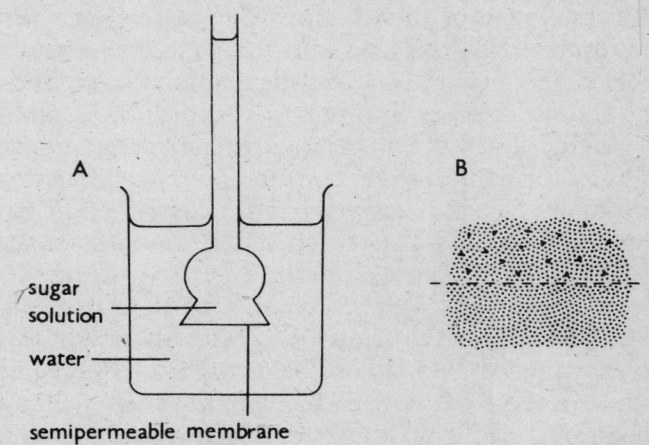

Fig. 1.11 Osmosis: (A) apparatus to demonstrate osmosis; (B) diagram illustrating action of the semipermeable membrane: sugar and water molecules are represented by the larger and smaller dots respectively, the semipermeable membrane by the broken line. See text for explanation

To understand how water is absorbed and transported within the plant it is necessary to consider a process called **osmosis**. This causes water to pass into or out of cells, or to move from one cell to another. It can occur in non-living systems, and the apparatus illustrated in Fig. 1.11 (A) is commonly used to demonstrate it. The glass funnel has a skin or membrane stretched across it. This can consist of various substances, for example plastics, such as cellophane, or part of the bladder of an animal or the skin lying under the shell of an egg. The essential thing is that it should be **semipermeable** (i.e. partly permeable); that is, it should allow water to pass through (i.e. be permeable to water) but not be permeable to substances dissolved in the water. Thus in the apparatus shown water can diffuse into or out of the funnel, but the sugar cannot: it remains inside the funnel.

The result of this arrangement is that water passes from the beaker through the semipermeable membrane into the sugar solution. This is shown by the fact that the solution begins to rise up the stem of the funnel. We may understand why this happens if we realise that there are fewer water molecules per cubic centimetre in the sugar solution than in the water in the beaker, simply because sugar molecules take up some of the space that would otherwise be occupied by water molecules (Fig. 1.11 (B)). This means that the concentration of water molecules is greater on the beaker side of the membrane than on the other. Diffusion results in the movement of substances from regions where they are more concentrated to those where they are less concentrated (p. 32), so in this case water moves from the beaker into the funnel. Although there may be a high concentration of *sugar* in the funnel and none outside it, the sugar cannot diffuse out of the funnel because of the semipermeable nature of the membrane.

The movement of water through a semipermeable membrane in this way is called osmosis.

Osmosis would still take place if sugar were dissolved in the water in the beaker as well as in the funnel, as long as one solution was stronger than the other. For example, if there were a strong solution in the funnel and a weak solution in the beaker, water would still pass into the funnel, since the *water* molecules would still be more concentrated in the beaker (see above). On the other hand, if the strong solution were in the beaker, the position would be reversed and water would now flow out of the funnel and through the semipermeable membrane into the beaker.

When water flows into a solution it naturally dilutes the solution and makes it weaker. On the other hand, if water is removed from a solution, exactly the opposite happens: the solution becomes stronger. So during osmosis the flow of water causes the stronger solution to become slowly weaker and the weaker solution slowly stronger. This goes on until both solutions have the same concentration, when osmosis ceases.

To sum up we may say that osmosis is a flow of water from a weaker solution to a stronger one through a semipermeable membrane. Notice that it is only the water that flows. The sugar (or whatever the dissolved substance may be) cannot pass through the membrane.

Osmosis occurs in plant cells because the protoplasm acts as a semipermeable membrane, separating the solution in the vacuole (the cell sap) from any water or solution outside the cell. Imagine that the cell illustrated in Fig. 1.8 on p.28 is placed in pure water. The conditions would exist for osmosis to take place: a stronger solution (in the vacuole) separated from a weaker solution or water by a semipermeable membrane. Water would therefore pass into the vacuole, causing it to swell. It would not, as a matter of fact, swell very much, because the cell wall would prevent this from happening, although it would stretch slightly, so allowing some expansion. Soon, however, the cell wall would be stretched as far as it would go and prevent any more water from being taken up by osmosis. If, on the other hand, the cell were placed in a sufficiently strong solution of sugar or some other substance, water would flow out of the vacuole, which would shrink. Consequently, the cell would collapse. In fact, in these conditions, the protoplasm shrinks away from the cell wall so that spaces appear between the two layers.

The Flowering Plant 39

Note that the cell wall plays no part in osmosis. It is completely permeable, allowing both water and dissolved substance to flow in and out of the cell freely.

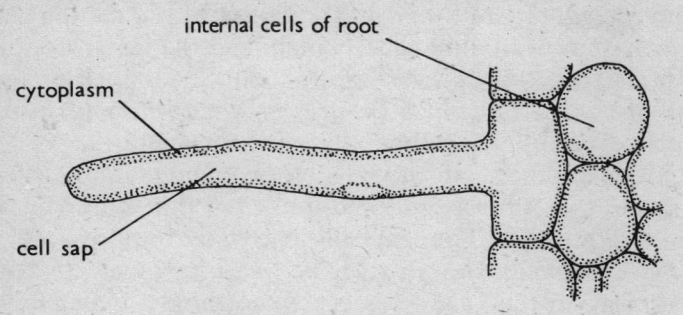

Fig. 1.12 A root hair

We are now in a position to understand how roots absorb water from the soil. Near the tips of the roots there are a large number of **root hairs** growing out from the surface (Fig. 1.15). They are best seen in the roots of seedlings that have been grown on blotting paper or in water, since in the natural state, in the soil, the root hairs usually become so closely attached to the soil particles that they break off when the plant is uprooted. Each root hair is a single cell (Fig. 1.12). Since it is in contact with water in the soil and this, although not pure water, is a much weaker solution than the cell sap, the conditions exist for osmosis to cause water to enter the root hair. The process does not stop here, however, because the entry of water has the effect of making the cell sap more dilute than it was. The result is that there is now a difference between the concentrations of cell sap in the root hair and the neighbouring cells in the root. Even if these concentrations were the same at the start, the cell sap in the root hair would now be weaker than that in the other cells. Consequently, osmosis will now cause a flow of water from the root hair to these other cells. The same process will then be repeated as the cell sap of the neighbouring cells becomes weaker than that of cells still further inside the root, and so the water flows from cell to cell. Eventually it enters the xylem cells which are found in the centre of the root. These form a system of minute tubes which lead the water up into the stem. Here the xylem vessels continue upwards and eventually branch out into the leaves, where they form the network of veins which has already been mentioned. The veins are in contact with the cells of the spongy and palisade layers, and there a process the opposite of that occurring in the root takes place. The leaf cells lose water by evaporation into the air spaces and so their cell sap becomes stronger than the sap in the xylem vessels. Accordingly, water flows by osmosis into the leaf cells.

The net effect of the process described above is to cause a flow of water through the plant, so that as fast as water is lost from the leaves it is replaced by water absorbed by the roots. The loss of water from the leaves and other aerial parts of the plant is known as **transpiration** and the resulting flow of water through the plant is the **transpiration stream**. A great deal of water—much more than that required for photosynthesis—is needed for transpiration.

Besides taking up water, the root hairs also have the function of absorbing mineral salts from the soil. This has nothing to do with osmosis and the uptake of water; the two processes are independent. However, the transpiration stream does carry the salts absorbed to other parts of the plant.

It has been explained that the cell sap is normally under pressure and pushes the protoplasm of the cell outwards against the cell wall. This is because the tendency for all the cells of the plant to take up water by osmosis, as described above, is normally greater than their tendency to lose it as a result of transpiration. This pressure of the cell sap plays an important part in making the softer parts of the plant rigid, as can be seen when wilting occurs. This happens if the water supply becomes insufficient to replace losses by transpiration. For example, if a plant is pulled out of the soil, it continues to transpire but can no longer absorb water. Consequently, the pressure of sap in the cell vacuoles falls and so the cells become soft, just like a football that has insufficient air in it. The result is that the whole plant becomes soft and floppy—it wilts. It can be revived, of course, if it is placed in water soon enough, so that water is taken up and the pressure restored.

The loss of pressure in cells also explains why the stomata close if too much water is transpired. In the guard cells the pressure of the cell sap causes them to swell slightly and to change shape in such a way that the stoma between them opens, but it can be shown that if water is withdrawn from the guard cells the stoma closes. Naturally, if the plant is losing water so fast that it is in danger of wilting, the guard cells, along with all the other cells, lose water and so cause the stomata to close.

The rigidity of the plant also depends upon the presence of special strengthening tissues, especially xylem and fibrous tissue (p. 30), in which the cell walls are thickened. In the stem of a plant such as the buttercup, these tissues are to be found towards the outside, whereas the centre is hollow or contains soft pith. This arrangement makes for maximum stiffness. In the root, by contrast, the strengthening tissues are central: hence roots are flexible rather than rigid. The actual arrangements of tissues in a stem and a root are shown in Plate 2. In the stem there are a number of veins (vascular bundles), each of which contains xylem, the tissue that carries water, and phloem, which conducts food materials. (The phloem cells do not have thickened walls and the tissue is therefore soft, except in some cases where strengthening fibre cells are present.) Just outside each vein is a strand of fibrous tissue (appearing as an oval patch in the section). In the root, xylem and phloem are concentrated in the centre.

In woody plants the amount of xylem is much increased: the wood, in fact, consists entirely of xylem tissue, and in a woody stem there are no separate veins. The stiffness of the stem depends entirely upon the xylem. Indeed, it is the strength of this tissue that makes the trunk of a large tree capable of sustaining the enormous weight of the branches and foliage.

Patterns of growth

We commonly think of the starting point for the growth of a new plant as the seed. However, the seed already contains a miniature plant, or embryo, before it germinates. This may easily be seen in a large seed, like a pea or bean, especially if it is soaked in water for a few hours to soften it. The seed coat, or **testa**, may then be peeled off easily and inside will be found two rounded organs, called the **cotyledons** (Fig. 1.13 (B)). Where they are joined together is a rudimentary root, or **radicle**, and a minute shoot, the **plumule**. The last is hidden between the cotyledons. The cotyledons themselves are leaves that are much swollen with stored food (especially starch) and have no chlorophyll at first. They do not, therefore, look much like normal leaves. However, in many cases, when the seed germinates, the cotyledons are raised above the surface of the soil, turn green and function as ordinary leaves.

When germination begins the root is the first part to grow (Fig. 1.14 (A)). Moisture is necessary for the process to start and, as it is absorbed, the seed swells. Then the radicle starts to grow and, splitting the testa, emerges from the seed. Only after the root has grown some distance into the soil does the shoot begin to appear. In some seeds (e.g. broad bean, pea) the plumule begins to grow into the first shoot,

The Flowering Plant 43

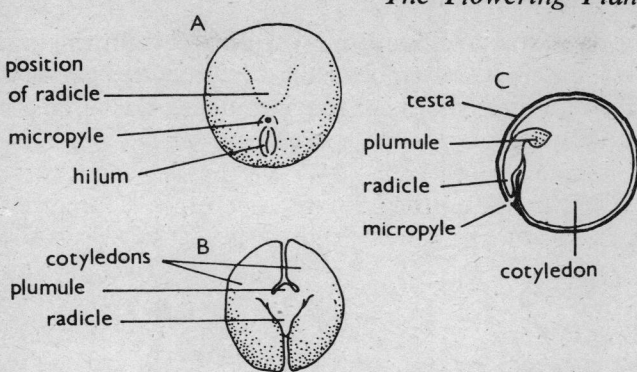

Fig. 1.13 Structure of a pea seed: (A) entire seed; (B) testa removed; (C) seed cut in half

the leaves of which unfold when it appears above the soil. In others (e.g. runner bean, sunflower, mustard) a portion of the stem just below the cotyledons starts to grow and raises the cotyledons, still covered by the testa, above the soil surface. The testa falls off and the cotyledons, becoming

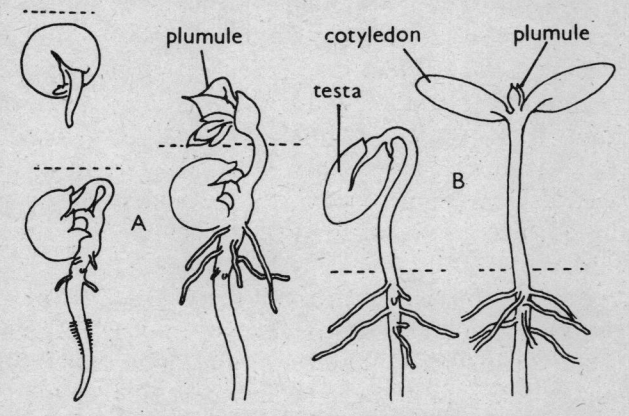

Fig. 1.14 (A) three stages in germination of a pea seed; (B) two stages in germination of a French bean. Broken lines show the position of the soil surface in each case

green, open out and continue to photosynthesise (Fig. 1.14 (B)). Later still, the plumule, between the cotyledons, grows into the first shoot, producing more and more leaves.

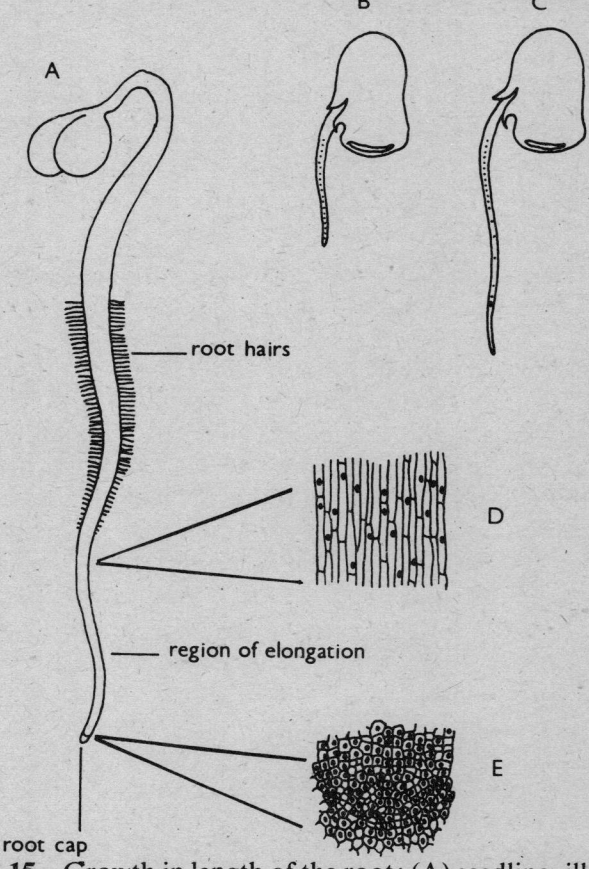

Fig. 1.15 Growth in length of the root: (A) seedling, illustrating different regions in the root; (B) germinating broad bean seed with root marked at equal intervals; (C) the same after two days; (D) cells from the upper part of the region of elongation; (E) cells from the region of cell division and the root cap

The Flowering Plant 45

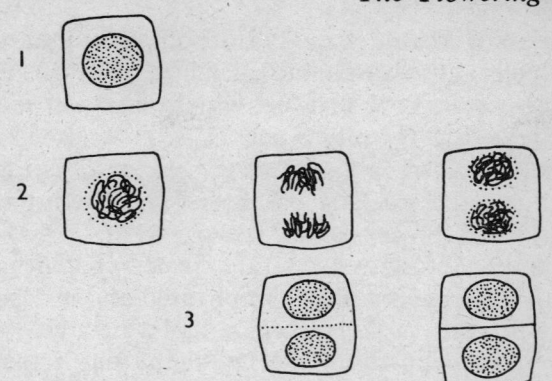

Fig. 1.16 Cell division: (1) the cell before division; (2) first stage of division—chromosomes appear in the nucleus and become separated into two groups; (3) second stage of division—a new cell wall is formed between the new nuclei

Clearly there is a stage in germination when the young plant cannot carry out photosynthesis, and even when the first leaves have appeared the amount of photosynthesis cannot be very great. This is why food must be stored in the cotyledons. (Sometimes it is contained in a special tissue which surrounds the cotyledons.) When germination begins this stored food is moved to the growing points to make possible the manufacture of new material and to provide energy. Only later does photosynthesis provide enough material to supply the needs of the plant.

How does growth occur? If a growing root is marked at regular intervals and observed after a day or two, it will be seen that the marks have become further apart in a region just behind the root tip (Fig. 1.15 (B) and (C)). Clearly this is where growth is taking place. There is no increase in length further up the root. More information about growth is obtained if a thin slice of the root is examined under a microscope (Fig. 1.15 (D) and (E)). The cells near the root tip are very small, have extremely thin cell walls and, unlike most plant cells, have no vacuoles. These cells are undergoing a process called **cell division**, which results in each cell becoming divided to form two new cells.

Cell division takes place in two stages, as illustrated in Fig. 1.16. First, the nucleus breaks up into a number of thread-like parts (chromosomes, see p. 111, 127) and these then gather together into two separate groups which form two new nuclei. This stage is rather complicated and is described in more detail later. In the second stage, a new cell wall is manufactured between the nuclei, with the result that two cells are formed. The new cells start to grow larger and then division may be repeated. The result of this process is that the number of cells in the region immediately above the tip of the root is constantly increasing.

Some of the new cells are added to the **root cap** (see Fig. 15 (A)), which protects the end of the root as it is forced through the soil. Cells on the surface of the root cap are rubbed off by the friction of the soil, and so there is a need for constant replacement. Other new cells come to form part of the region a little higher up the root. Here there is less cell division and the cells are growing rapidly, mostly in length. This is brought about chiefly by the uptake of water into the cell vacuoles that form in this zone, so that most of the increase in size of the cell is due to an increase in the volume of the vacuole. This is, of course, the part of the root where maximum growth in length takes place.

In this process the cells are at first all alike, but after they have finished growing they become specialised. So the different kinds of cell—xylem, phloem and so on—can be distinguished above the growing region.

Growth takes place in a similar way in the shoot, but the process is complicated by the presence of leaves. When a shoot is growing it will be noticed that the leaves are crowded together towards the tip of the stem. They are also smaller and, in fact, the very tip is usually covered and protected by young leaves. Here there is a region of cell division similar to that in the root. A little lower, growth in length is taking place, so that the leaves come to be spaced apart more and more. At the same time, the young leaves expand rapidly. Finally, all increase in length ceases in the lower parts of the stem.

Growth in thickness begins only after growth in length is complete, either in the stem or in the root. Once it has started, however, it may go on indefinitely. Thus the trunk of a tree may continue to get gradually thicker for hundreds, even thousands, of years. The height of the tree, on the other hand, is increased only by new growth at the top.

The direction of growth is controlled mainly by light and gravity. At the same time, the effect of these influences depends upon what part of the plant is considered: the tap root grows downwards but the main shoot upwards; lateral shoots, however, grow at an angle to the vertical.

The effect of light on growth is well known. House plants often have a rather annoying habit of bending towards the light coming from a window, so that they tend to grow crooked. It might at first be supposed that this bending is brought about in rather the same way as the bending of a human limb, but careful examination of the way it happens shows that this is not so. The shoots of oat seedlings have often been used to study the effect. This is because in the very young seedling the shoot and its leaves are completely enclosed in a sheath, so that there are no leaves to complicate matters. If such a shoot is marked at equal intervals, kept in the dark and then examined after a few hours, it will be found that the marks become spaced further apart in a region between about 5 mm and 15 or 20 mm below the tip (Fig. 1.17 (A)). This is the region of growth in length. If the experiment is now repeated and this time the seedling is exposed to light coming from one side, instead of being kept in the dark, the shoot will bend, and it will be observed that the bending occurs exactly in the region of growth (Fig. (1.17 (B)). In fact, bending is caused by uneven growth: the shoot grows faster on the side that is away from the light. This is shown by the fact that

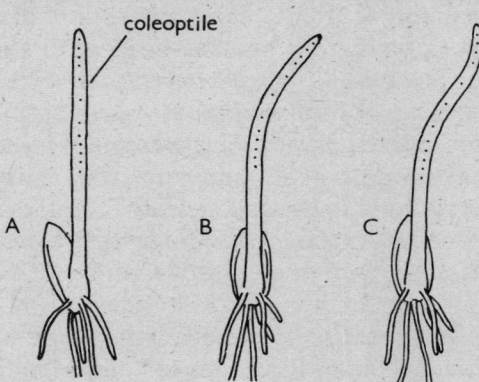

Fig. 1.17 Phototropism in an oat seedling. (The coleoptile is a sheath enclosing the shoot.) See text for explanation

the curvature produced is permanent, so that if the seedling is allowed to go on growing in the dark the tip of the shoot continues to grow vertically upwards but the bend remains (Figure 1.17 (C)). It is impossible for it to become straightened out.

This effect is due to the presence of a chemical called **auxin**, which is manufactured in the shoot tip. It passes downwards and has the effect of stimulating growth in the region below. Thus, if the top 1 mm is removed, auxin is no longer produced and growth ceases. On the other hand, if some of the chemical (which can be made artificially) is applied to the shoot, its growth is speeded up.

Light can cause bending because it slows down the production of auxin. Thus, if light is shining from one side, less auxin is produced on that side than on the other.* Conse-

* It is possible that light also causes auxin to diffuse sideways away from the illuminated side.

quently, as the auxin travels downwards, more rapid growth occurs on the side that is away from the light and therefore has more auxin, and so the shoot bends towards the light.

The effect of light on growth which has been described is called **phototropism**. Where growth causes an organ to move towards the light, as above, it is known as **positive** phototropism. Roots commonly grow away from the light, exhibiting negative phototropism.

The effect of gravity on growth (**geotropism**) is not as well understood, although it appears to work in a similar way. Thus if a seed is allowed to germinate and the radicle to grow until it is about 25 mm long, and it is then placed in a horizontal position, the root will bend until the tip is pointing vertically downwards. It can be shown, just as in phototropism, that the bending takes place in the region of elongation and is caused by uneven growth. However, it it not known how gravity brings this about. Roots that grow downwards in the direction of gravitational attraction are said to be positively geotropic, whereas shoots, which usually do the opposite, are negatively geotropic.

In these ways the main directions of growth are controlled, so that the root grows into the soil, where it can carry out its principal functions of absorbing water and mineral salts, and the shoot grows upwards into the air and light, where it can perform its main function, photosynthesis.

The factory that manufactures new factories

We began by likening the plant to a factory that takes in raw materials and converts them into various products. Photosynthesis manufactures sugar and starch, and these are used to make other complex chemicals. These are then utilised in the manufacture of new cells in the processes of growth that have been described above. The plant therefore continues to increase in size and so the factory gets bigger. It is rather as

50 *Biology*

if the bricks made in a brickworks were continually being used to build extensions to the works. However, the process does not stop at that, because the plant eventually gives rise to new individuals. It makes copies of itself. This is reproduction.

In ordinary flowering plants reproduction is achieved in two ways: (i) by the production of seeds and (ii) by the splitting off of parts of the plant, in what is known as vegetative reproduction.

Reproduction by seed
If any plant that has a large number of flowers on the same stem is examined when it is in bloom, it will be discovered that the younger flowers are at the top and the older flowers lower down the stem. In fact, very often the flowers near the stem apex will still be in bud, a little lower they will be starting to open and lower still they will be fully out. Even lower than this the flowers may be fading and losing their petals, and here it will be noticed that the seed-containing organs, or **fruits**, begin to appear in the middle of each flower. Thus in a tomato plant the young tomatoes are present, in a pea

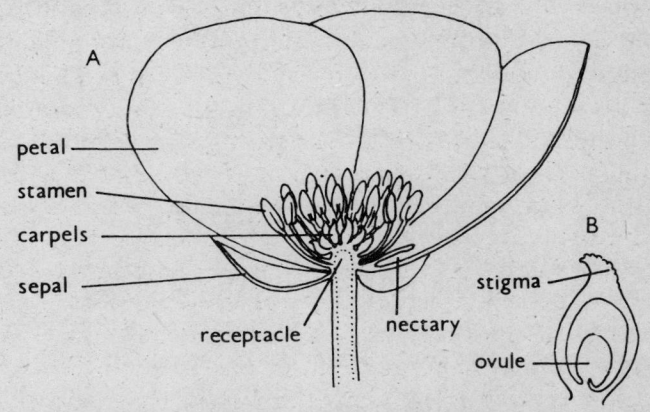

Fig. 1.18 Structure of the buttercup flower: (A) flower cut in half; (B) carpel in section

The Flowering Plant 51

the beginnings of the seed pods. These enlarge and eventually ripen. So on one plant it may be possible at the same time to see all stages in development from the flower bud to the ripe fruit with its seeds. The whole function of the flower is to produce these seeds.

The buttercup illustrates the essential features of a flower in a very clear way and it is shown in Fig. 1.18. In the centre of the flower are a number of green organs, the **carpels**, in which seeds later develop. A more familiar example of a carpel is the pod of a pea or bean. In those flowers there is but a single carpel, instead of the many present in the buttercup. In other flowers there may be several carpels joined together, so that the fruit has several chambers in which the seeds develop. Surrounding the carpels in the buttercup flower are many yellow **stamens** which, when they are ripe, produce the yellow powdery pollen. Outside these are about five yellow **petals** and finally, under them, the smaller and duller **sepals**. These form the outer cover of the bud before the flower opens.

In each carpel is a small, round organ, the **ovule**, joined to the inside of the carpel by a short stalk (Fig. 1.18 (B)). It is the future seed, but it cannot develop further until pollen has been transferred from the stamens to the carpel. The upper rather pointed end of the carpel, known as the **stigma**, is sticky and designed to catch the pollen grains. The latter are specialised cells. They are spherical in shape with a tough wall, somewhat roughened on the outside. When a pollen grain becomes stuck on one of the stigmas, part of its cell wall grows out to form a tube, which penetrates the stigma and grows through the wall of the carpel towards the ovule. Eventually the end of the tube enters the ovule by a small opening (the micropile) at its base. At this point the pollen tube contains three nuclei. One of them seems to be concerned with forming the tube and the other two are equivalent to sperms, or **male gametes**. Inside the ovule is an egg cell, the

female gamete. The end of the pollen tube dissolves away, so that it becomes open, and the male gametes enter the ovule. One of them fertilises the egg cell—i.e. it fuses with it—to form a single new cell, termed a **zygote**.

Fertilisation of the egg cell, then, results from **pollination**, the transfer of pollen to the stigma. In brightly coloured flowers such as the buttercup, this is brought about by the visits of insects. They come to the flower in search of nectar, which is a sweet fluid produced, in the buttercup, in a nectary at the base of each petal. The nectary is covered by a small flap. In obtaining nectar an insect cannot avoid brushing against the stamens and, if they are ripe, picking up some of the pollen. This is likely to be transferred to stigmas in the same flower, or it may be carried to those on another flower visited later. In the latter case cross-pollination, and therefore cross-fertilisation, results. This means the fertilisation of egg cells in one plant by male gametes coming from another. Often (in other flowers) there are quite complicated arrangements to ensure that only cross-pollination can occur. However, in some cases self-pollination is the rule.

Once fertilisation has occurred the ovule begins to develop. The zygote inside it undergoes cell division and the resulting cells divide repeatedly, so that a mass of cells is formed. This is the beginning of the embryo plant. It grows, and the ovule also grows to keep pace with it. Soon the cotyledons, radicle and plumule develop, and eventually the embryo comes to fill the ovule completely. Meanwhile, the outer wall of the ovule has become tough and thickened to form the testa, and so the complete seed is formed. It is still contained in the carpel, which has also become much enlarged and is now known as the fruit. By this time the sepals, petals and stamens have fallen off and the carpels are all that remain.

The fruits of the buttercup are simple and unspecialised. The kinds of fruit that we eat usually have some part of the ovary (i.e. the part of the fruit that contains the seeds) enlarged and succulent. Typical examples are the tomato, orange and blackberry. However, sometimes some other part of the flower is concerned. Thus the juicy part of a strawberry is the swollen end of the flower stalk (the receptacle) and the hard 'seeds' covering it are actually the carpels. In an apple the ovary is sunk into the lower part of the receptacle, which completely surrounds it. (If the apple flower is examined, a swelling, marking the position of the ovary, will be noticed just below the sepals.) The flesh of the ripe apple consists of the swollen receptacle.

Succulent fruits are produced so that the animals that eat them will scatter, or disperse, the seeds. Dispersal is important because it enables the plant to colonise new areas and helps to avoid the overcrowding that could result if the seeds all fell near the parent. Other means of dispersal are the production of fruits armed with hooks or spines, so that they become attached to fur or clothing and so transported; the formation of wings or hairy projections which enable fruits to fly or float through the air and be dispersed by the wind (e.g. sycamore, dandelion); the development of fruits which burst suddenly when ripe, so scattering the seeds (e.g. gorse, balsam or 'touch-me-not'); and, less commonly, the production of floating fruits dispersed by water. The classic example of the last kind is the coconut, the fruits of which may be carried considerable distances in the sea.

The buttercup is a good example of an insect-pollinated flower. Some flowers, however, are pollinated by the wind, i.e. pollen released by the stamens is carried to the stigmas by air currents. Such flowers are very different in appearance from the other kind, chiefly because they lack bright petals. Clearly these are needed in insect-pollinated flowers to advertise the presence of the flower and to attract insects. Flowers are frequently scented for the same reason. Wind-pollinated flowers are typically green, small and inconspicuous. So much so, in fact, that many people do not realise that they are flowers at all. The most important examples are the grasses and cereals. The flowers of the latter may be grouped together in a head which later becomes the ear when the grain ripens. Another familiar example is the hazel tree. This is a little unusual because it has separate male and female flowers. The male flowers form the catkins, and the clouds of pollen released by them when they are ripe are well known. The female flowers appear like small buds with bright red feathery projections. These are the stigmas. The nuts, which are the fruits, develop from the female flowers. In spite of the differences, the essential parts of the flower—the stamens and carpels—are similar in both wind-and insect-pollinated flowers, as are the processes of fertilisation and seed production.

Vegetative reproduction
The creeping buttercup provides a good example of a simple form of vegetative reproduction. Unlike the meadow buttercup, the stems of this plant grow along the ground instead of being upright. Roots grow from the stem (or stolon, as it is called) at the points where the leaves are attached and so anchor it to the ground. Soon shoots develop from the axillary buds. The effect of this is to produce a number of little buttercup plants, each complete with roots, stem and leaves, joined to one another by the horizontal, creeping stem (Fig. 1.19). It is because of this method of growth that the creeping buttercup spreads about untended gardens so much. Sooner or later the connections between the little buttercup plants become destroyed—older parts die off, the stolon becomes broken and so on—and reproduction has occurred: one individual has given rise to a number of new plants like itself.

Notice that in this type of reproduction there is no sexual process: there are no gametes uniting to form a zygote. It is said, therefore, to be **asexual** (i.e. non-sexual). Also there is no special reproductive part or organ. The parts of the plant that become separated have leaves, roots, etc. with the ordinary non-reproductive functions, such as photosynthesis, absorption of water and salts, and so on.

Many cases of vegetative reproduction involve food-storage organs. An example is the potato. The potato tubers develop as swellings at the ends of slender stolons which grow out from the main stem of the plant below the

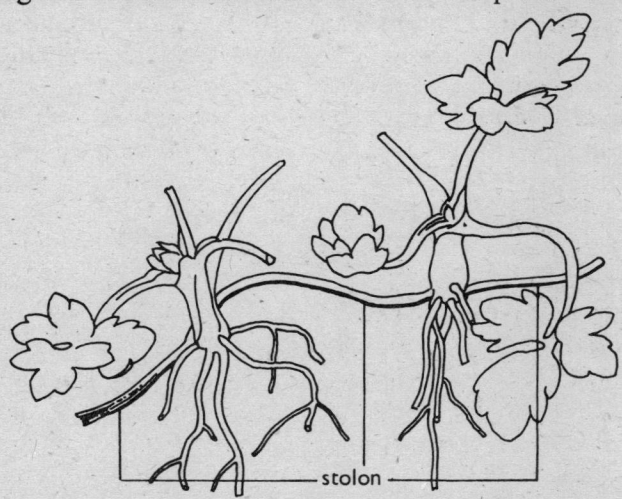

Fig. 1.19 Creeping buttercup, *Ranunculus repens*

surface of the soil. When the tubers are fully developed the stolons wither away. Under natural conditions the parent plant also dies and decays at the onset of winter, but the tubers remain protected in the soil. In the spring shoots begin to develop from the 'eyes' (really buds) on the potatoes. (This is often seen in potatoes that have been kept in the house too long.) In this way each tuber is capable of giving rise to at least one new plant, so bringing about reproduction of the original parent.

Similar examples of vegetative reproduction involving underground food-storage organs are seen in many garden plants. For example, there is the dahlia with its root tubers, the daffodil, hyacinth, tulip and snowdrop with their bulbs, and the iris with its rhizome (a horizontal underground stem). In each case the storage organ enables the plant to survive the winter, because it is protected from frost by the soil. The food it contains makes rapid growth of shoots possible in the spring, and the production of several shoots, which eventually give rise to separate plants, leads to reproduction.

2 The Mammal

The term *mammal* refers to all those animals that feed their young with milk. They have hair or fur, are warm-blooded and breathe air. In the majority (but not quite all) the young develop inside the mother before being born, instead of developing from eggs outside the body, as in the case of birds and most lower animals. Most domestic animals—dogs, cats, sheep, cows, horses, goats—and many familiar wild animals—mice, elephants, kangaroos, hippos, foxes, for example—are mammals. Typical mammals have four limbs and live on land, although some, such as whales, live entirely in water and others (bats) are capable of flight. Man is a mammal and, since we are all quite familiar with our own bodies, we shall consider the human species as our example in this chapter.

The automobile organism

If a plant can be compared with a factory, then an animal may be likened to a motor car. Like a car, the animal moves about and requires fuel to make this possible. In the machine fuel is burnt inside the engine to produce mechanical energy. Oxygen from the air is required for combustion of the fuel, being taken in through the carburetter, and waste products (smoke and gases) are formed and passed out through the exhaust pipe. In the animal the fuel is in the form of food, which is broken down to yield energy in the process of respiration, as in the plant. Respiration requires oxygen, which is taken in from the air in breathing, and produces waste products (carbon dioxide and water), which are given out at the same time.

This comparison is only true up to a point, of course. One big difference is connected with the fact that animals grow and repair themselves, so that food is needed not only to produce energy but also to make new living matter, repair injuries, and compensate for wear and tear. A wide range of materials is therefore required in the food. By contrast, a car uses only oil and petrol. Both of these have to be highly refined if the car is to work properly. The food of an animal, on the other hand, is varied and contains much material that the organism cannot use. To cope with this it has to have its own built-in refinery, the digestive system, which extracts the useful substances.

The heart and circulatory system

Raw materials are absorbed by the digestive system and oxygen by the organs of breathing (the lungs), but these substances are needed in every part of the body. At the same time, waste products are being formed all over the body and have to be removed. Hence there is a need for a means of transporting substances, and this is provided by the circulatory system.

At the centre of the circulatory system is the heart, a muscular pump that causes blood to flow through the system. From it lead a number of thick-walled blood vessels, the arteries, which branch out and carry blood to every corner of the body. If any branch of this system is followed out, it is found to split up into an ever-increasing number of smaller and smaller vessels, which finally end in a network of microscopic capillaries. These are to be found in every tissue of the body. The blood does not actually flow out of the capillaries into the tissues, but it is separated from the latter only by the very thin walls of the former, so that substances such as oxygen can easily diffuse from the blood into the tissues, or in the reverse direction. If we continue to follow the flow of blood through the capillaries, we find that it is collected up by the finest branches of a system of veins. These join up to form larger and larger veins, which eventually lead the blood back to the heart. The heart then sends the blood on its way again and it flows once more through the system.

The circulatory system thus consists of four main parts: the heart, the arteries, the capillaries and the veins. The arteries are the vessels that carry the blood away from the heart and the veins those that carry it back again. The two kinds of vessel also differ, in that arteries have much thicker and stronger walls than veins, whilst veins, unlike arteries, are provided with valves (Fig. 2.1). These prevent blood from flowing in the wrong direction.

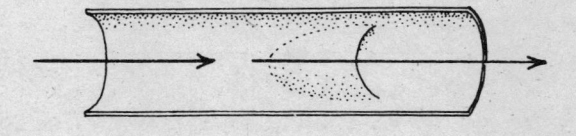

Fig. 2.1 Pocket valve in vein. Arrows show direction of flow of blood

In mammals the blood flows through two main circuits and there is said to be a double circulation (Fig. 2.2). Thus blood flows first of all from the heart to the lungs, where it picks up oxygen, and back to the heart; then it flows to the rest of the body, where it gives up oxygen to the tissues, which need it for respiration, and finally back to the heart

60 *Teach Yourself Biology*

again. The effect of this arrangement is to keep the circulation to the lungs, which is concerned with picking up oxygen, separate from the main circulation, in which oxygen is given out.

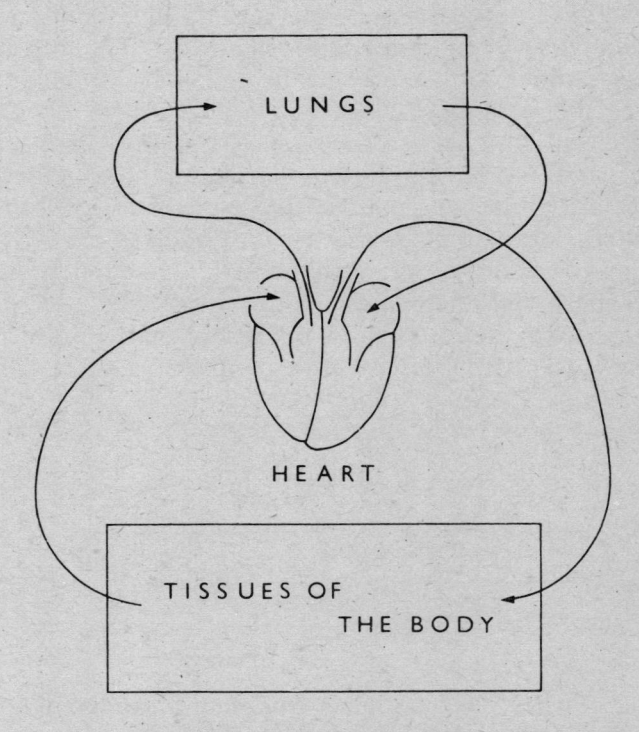

Fig. 2.2 The double circulation

The structure of the heart is illustrated in Fig. 2.3. It is something like a closed pocket divided into left and right halves by a vertical partition and having each half again divided into upper and lower portions. The lower halves are called ventricles, have very thick muscular walls and are the chief pumping organs. The upper halves are the atria singular atrium), which have much thinner, although still muscular, walls and receive blood from the veins. Between each atrium and the ventricle below is an auriculoventricular valve in the form of a thin flap attached to the heart wall and hanging downwards into the ventricle. The free edge of the

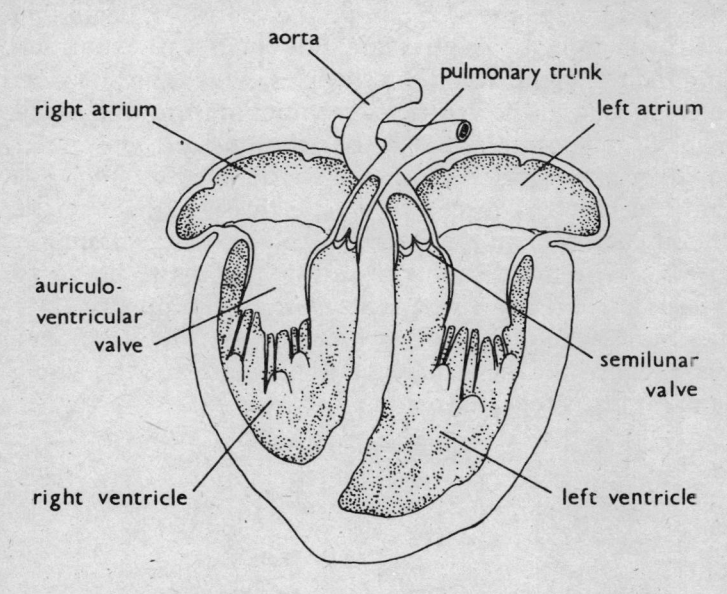

Fig. 2.3 Heart with front half removed

valve is joined to the ventricle wall by a number of cords, the cordae tendinae. A single large artery leads upwards from each ventricle. That from the right ventricle (Fig. 2.3 shows the heart from the front, so that the right ventricle appears on the left side of the diagram) is the pulmonary trunk, and this branches into the left and right pulmonary arteries, supplying the lungs. The artery coming from the left ventricle is the aorta and carries blood to the rest of the body. At the base of each main artery are three pocket valves, the semilunar valves. They open upwards and prevent blood from flowing back into the heart from the arteries.

Blood flows from the veins into the atria, causing them to swell as they fill up, and also on into the ventricles, beginning to fill them. When the atria are full their walls contract, forcing their contents into the ventricles, which thus become full of blood. Next the ventricles contract in turn. The blood in them flows upwards and causes the auriculoventricular valves to rise, closing the entrance to the auricles (Fig. 2.4) so that the blood is forced to escape through the arteries. As blood enters them, the arteries swell and the pressure in them rises. The increase in pressure would cause blood to flow back into the heart when the ventricles completed their contraction were this not prevented by the semilunar valves. Meanwhile, the atria begin to fill again and the whole cycle of events is repeated.

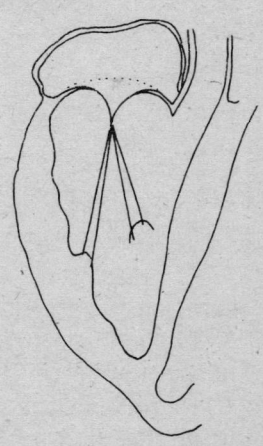

Fig. 2.4 Auriculoventricular valve in closed position (compare with Fig. 2.3)

The Mammal

If we could follow the path of a single drop of blood through the system it would be as follows, starting in the right ventricle. First, the blood would flow through the pulmonary arteries to one of the lungs. There it would pass through capillaries in contact with air in the lung and pick up oxygen. Next it would return to the left atrium, pass into the left ventricle and thence into the aorta. Passing into one of the arteries branching from the aorta, it would be carried to capillaries in some part of the body, where it would give up oxygen. Lastly, our drop of blood would enter veins through which it would be returned to the right atrium and then finally back to the right ventricle.

The blood itself is a watery fluid, plasma, containing a vast number of minute cells, the blood corpuscles. Plasma consists mostly of water (about 90%) in which are dissolved proteins, salt (sodium chloride), small amounts of glucose and various other substances. It is yellow in colour, the redness of blood being due to the corpuscles.

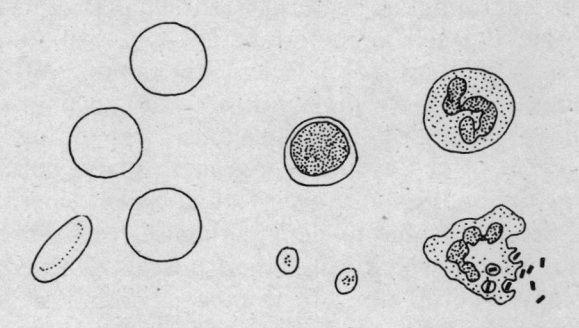

Fig. 2.5 Red blood corpuscles (left), white corpuscles (centre and right) and blood platelets (lower centre). The white corpuscle at the lower right is shown engulfing bacteria

The corpuscles are of two main kinds, red and white

(Fig. 2.5). The red corpuscles (erythrocytes) are unlike most cells in that they have no nuclei. They are discs which are slightly thinner in the centre than at the edges. Inside the cell membrane the contents are made up mostly of a protein called haemoglobin, containing chemically combined iron. Haemoglobin is red and is responsible for the colour of the blood as a whole. It is capable of combining with oxygen to form a loose compound, oxyhaemoglobin, so that the red corpuscles act as oxygen carriers and vastly increase the capacity of the blood to take up oxygen. There are about five million of these cells in every cubic millimetre of blood.

The white corpuscles (leucocytes) are colourless and contain nuclei. There are several different kinds, some of which are illustrated in Fig. 2.5. They are much less numerous than the red corpuscles, there being only about 8000 per cubic millimetre.

One of the chief functions of this second kind of corpuscle is to destroy any bacteria that may get into the body. This they do by engulfing the bacteria, as shown in the illustration. Once inside the cell a bacterium is quickly digested and destroyed. The white corpuscles are capable of moving independently by a creeping motion and can pass through the walls of capillaries to enter the surrounding tissues. Similar kinds of cell are also present in many parts of the body and they collect in any infected organ. The infecting bacteria are often able to defend themselves by producing poisonous toxins which kill the corpuscles. The dead corpuscles may accumulate to form pus. This kind of infection is often signalled by an increase in the number of leucocytes in the blood.

The blood also helps to prevent the entry of foreign materials and bacteria by the formation of clots to seal up wounds and the cut ends of capillaries or small blood vessels. This is brought about through a change in the nature of some of the protein dissolved in the plasma. It comes out of solution to form a jelly-like mass containing a network of microscopic threads of protein. Blood corpuscles become trapped in this network and the whole forms what is known as a clot. This is familiar in the form of the scab that forms on a cut or graze. Clot formation is the result of a rather complicated series of chemical reactions started by injury to the body. Bodies called *blood platelets*, much smaller than the corpuscles, are thought to be concerned with the process.

It will be realised that the blood system has two main functions: (i) to transport oxygen and other substances, and (ii) to protect the body from harmful agents, especially bacteria, which might enter it.

The lymphatic system

As blood passes through the system of capillaries, some of the liquid part of it leaks through the thin capillary walls into the surrounding tissues. The liquid that escapes in this way is known as lymph. It is similar to plasma in composition but contains much less protein. Although some of the lymph finds its way back into the capillaries, this is not enough to balance the loss of fluid, and to prevent accumulation of lymph in the tissues there is a system of branching vessels, the lymphatic system, which has the function of collecting excess lymph.

The lymphatic system does not form a circuit like the circulatory system. Instead, the finest vessels, found throughout the tissues, have closed ends. They join together to form progressively larger ducts which, finally, are connected at two points with the large veins near the heart. Thus lymph drains out of the tissues into the fine vessels and from these into the main ducts, and thence is returned to the blood circulation. Numerous valves (rather like those in veins) ensure that lymph flows in the right direction in the lymph vessels.

At the branching points in the lymphatic system there are numerous oval or bean-shaped bodies called lymph nodes, through which lymph must pass as it enters the larger ducts. The nodes contain cells similar to the leucocytes of the blood which have the function of destroying any bacteria that may be present in the lymph. In this way they guard against the possibility that bacteria infecting any part of the body might be carried via the lymphatic system into the blood and so be distributed to the whole body.

The lymph nodes also produce some of the white blood corpuscles and play a part in the production of antibodies (p. 203).

Food and digestion

The method by which animals obtain raw materials contrasts with that of plants. Plants acquire a limited number of very simple substances from the environment and build them up into all sorts of complex compounds. Animals, on the other hand, take in a wide variety of mostly complex substances in the form of food; they then partly break these down in digestion, and (i) some of the material is used as fuel, (ii) some is used to build new living matter and (iii) some is passed out as waste.

Exhaustive study of the great variety of things that man uses as food has shown that, apart from water, the substances that are actually useful to the body may be classified under five main headings: carbohydrates, fats, proteins, salts and vitamins. The first three are taken in large quantities and make up the bulk of the useful food; the last two are needed in much smaller amounts. The chemical structure and composition of these substances is explained in the following chapter. Here they will be introduced in turn, with only a brief indication of their chemical natures, and their functions described in broad outline.

Carbohydrates, as the name indicates, are compounds of carbon, hydrogen and oxygen. The chemically simplest carbohydrates (in foods) are sugars. Ordinary table sugar is known as sucrose to the chemist. More important in the body is glucose, which most people know as a form of sugar provided for babies and invalids. It is the chief fuel of the body, as such providing energy for all bodily activities. This, indeed, is the main function of all carbohydrates in the diet: they are the great energy-givers.

There are many less familiar sugars than glucose and sucrose, and, in addition, several carbohydrates which are not sugars, although chemically related to them. One example is starch, which was mentioned as the form in which food is often stored in plants, and a very similar storage carbohydrate found in animals, including man, is glycogen. Another carbohydrate of plants is cellulose, which composes the cell wall of all plant cells. All these can be broken down into sugars by chemical action, and this is what happens to starch and glycogen, but *not* to cellulose, in the human digestive system.

Fats are, of course, widespread in foods of animal origin, and vegetable oils, such as olive oil and palm oil, are included in the same chemical class. Like carbohydrates, they contain the elements carbon, hydrogen and oxygen only. Fat is the main reserve food of the body and is stored around the internal organs and under the skin. Like carbohydrates, it is used to produce energy. A second important function is performed by the layer beneath the skin, which acts as an insulating layer, helping to prevent loss of heat and so keeping the body warm.

The third class of foods, proteins, are chemically much the most complex and although, like carbohydrates and fats, they are composed very largely of carbon, hydrogen and oxygen, they always contain nitrogen in addition and usually various other elements (e.g. sulphur, phosphorus, metals).

As we shall see, proteins are essential for life and are therefore present in all living organisms, including those that provide us with food. However, certain kinds of food contain much greater quantities than others, as indicated in Table 2.1.

Food	Carbohydrate	Fat	Protein	Water and salts
lean beef	—	12	20	68
eggs	—	11	13	76
butter	—	85	1	14
cheese	—	38	30	32
milk	5	4	3	88
sugar	100	—	—	—
potatoes	18	—	2	80
apples	11	0·5	0·4	88
lettuce	3	—	1	96
bread	53		9	36

Table 2.1 Percentage of carbohydrate, fat and protein in various foods

Proteins form an important part of the structure of the human body. As in plants, the organism is built up of cells, and the protoplasm of these is composed largely of water and protein. The tissues of the skeleton consist of fibrous material made of protein—in the case of bone hardened by the presence of calcium salts. The skin, the nails and hair are also composed mostly of protein, and the muscles consist of a special variety of protein that has the property of contractility. These various proteins are all derived from protein in the food and we can understand, therefore, that the most important function of this class of foods is to provide the raw material for building the structure of the body. This is especially important in growing children, but even in adults the skin, hair and nails are constantly growing, and material may be needed for the repair of injuries and the replacement of losses. However, more protein is normally consumed than is required, and the surplus is broken down and used to produce energy in respiration.

Most people are familiar with the salty taste of blood, which is due to the presence of about 1% of sodium chloride in the plasma. Small quantities are continually passed out of the body in the sweat and urine, and these losses have to be made good from the food. Other salts are also required in small amounts. For example, calcium salts enter into the composition of bone, as already mentioned. Very minute amounts of iodine (absorbed as iodides) form part of the hormone thyroglobulin (p. 87).

Vitamins form another class of foods required in minute quantities, but, in contrast with salts, these are chemically complex. Historically, they were discovered through the investigation of the deficiency diseases that result from the lack of vitamins in the diet. Thus it was long ago discovered that scurvy can be prevented by the inclusion of fruit (especially citrus fruits) and fresh vegetables in the diet, although it was not until modern times that the cause of this disease was traced to the presence of a particular chemical compound, ascorbic acid (vitamin C), in these articles of diet. Another vitamin, the effects of the lack of which became all too familiar as rickets during the years of the depression, is vitamin D. This is necessary for the absorption of calcium into the skeleton, and its absence results in softening and distortion of the bones. A peculiarity of vitamin D is that it is formed by the action of sunlight on the skin, so that exposure to the sun can help to prevent its deficiency.

Table 2.2 gives further details of other vitamins. In general we can say that all vitamins are complex chemicals which, although required in minute amounts, cannot be manufactured by the body from other materials in the food. Their presence in the diet is therefore essential.

Vitamin	Food sources	Symptoms produced by lack
A	milk butter carrots, green vegetables liver fish liver oils	reduced growth dryness and thickening of the cornea of the eye defective vision in poor light degeneration of nerves
B_1	whole-meal bread milk potatoes meat eggs yeast	reduced growth defective carbohydrate metabolism paralysis mental depression
B_2	milk eggs meat (especially liver) green vegetables	reduced growth and loss of appetite disorders of the eye
C	tomatoes potatoes turnips green vegetables fruit—especially citrus fruits	scurvy (characterised by internal bleeding due to weakening of capillary walls) poor formation of bones and teeth
D	eggs sea fish fish liver oils	rickets

Table 2.2 Some vitamins, their sources and associated deficiency diseases

It should be clear from the foregoing discussion that foods are used for a variety of purposes in the body.

However, it remains true that the bulk of the material is utilised for the production of energy, and the total requirement of the body can be expressed in terms of its energy needs, ignoring the relatively small amount used for other purposes.

The total energy consumption of the human body can be measured and is normally expressed in calories, a calorie being a unit of heat energy. As one might expect, the number of calories required depends upon the size and degree of activity of the individual. Even when completely at rest, energy is used up in activities such as breathing and the beating of the heart, and is also required to maintain the body temperature. Under these conditions the rate of energy use is known as the basal metabolic rate and is equal to about 1350 calories per day in the average person. A normally active person will use more, of course—perhaps 3000 calories per day—and one who does a great deal of hard physical labour may use as many as 6500 calories in 24 hours.

The energy yield of any food can also be determined, and it is therefore possible to calculate the approximate total amount of food required by a given person, knowing their body weight and their type of occupation. In more affluent societies it is common for people to consume too much, with the result that surplus food is stored as fat. This can give rise to various troubles, such as heart disease, as is well known. In cases where food is insufficient internal reserves start to be used up. First, stores of carbohydrate in the form of glycogen are drawn upon and then fat. When this is all gone the substance of the body structure itself will be utilised. In point of fact, however, it is more common for a person to suffer from lack of a particular element in the diet, even though the total supply of calories may be enough, resulting in the appearance of deficiency diseases. Rickets and scurvy have already been mentioned. Amongst poorer peoples kwashiorkor, resulting from lack of protein, is often prevalent in children and may have fatal effects. Even amongst the relatively well-off, however, a certain amount of ill-health may be caused by shortage of vitamins in the diet.

Digestion is the process by which food is converted into such a state that it can be absorbed and used by the body. It is necessary partly because the useful constituents of the food have to be sorted out from those that are of no value, and partly because the useful substances themselves are often not soluble, i.e. not capable of dissolving in water, and are therefore not in a form in which they can diffuse through the walls of the intestine where food is absorbed. Digestion is achieved partly by mechanical means. Food is crushed and mixed with watery digestive juices which dissolve anything soluble, such as sugar. More important, however, is the chemical action of these juices which leads to the chemical breakdown of nutrients. As a result, those that are insoluble at the beginning become soluble by the time the process is complete.

The nature of digestion in general is well illustrated by that part of it which occurs in the mouth. Chewing achieves the major part of the mechanical breakdown of the food and, at the same time, mixes it with the first digestive juice, saliva. This is produced by salivary glands in the cheeks and in the floor of the mouth. Ducts (tubes) lead their secretions into the mouth. Saliva contains water, mucus—a sticky, slimy substance which helps the food to travel smoothly down the gullet and through the rest of the digestive tract—and small amounts of a protein with rather special properties called amylase (also known as ptyalin). The last constituent acts on any starch present, converting it quite rapidly into a sugar (maltose). This is the result of a reaction between the starch and water present (see p. 114), for which amylase is a catalyst. The conversion of the starch is necessary because it is a substance that neither forms solutions nor diffuses at all readily and cannot be absorbed by the intestine, whereas the reverse is true of sugars.

Amylase is an example of the class of organic catalysts called **enzymes**. In common with other catalysts they are able to increase the rate of chemical reactions and influence their course when present in very small concentrations. A great variety of enzymes is present in all living cells, both of animals and of plants, and they catalyse a correspondingly large variety of chemical reactions. In the digestive system

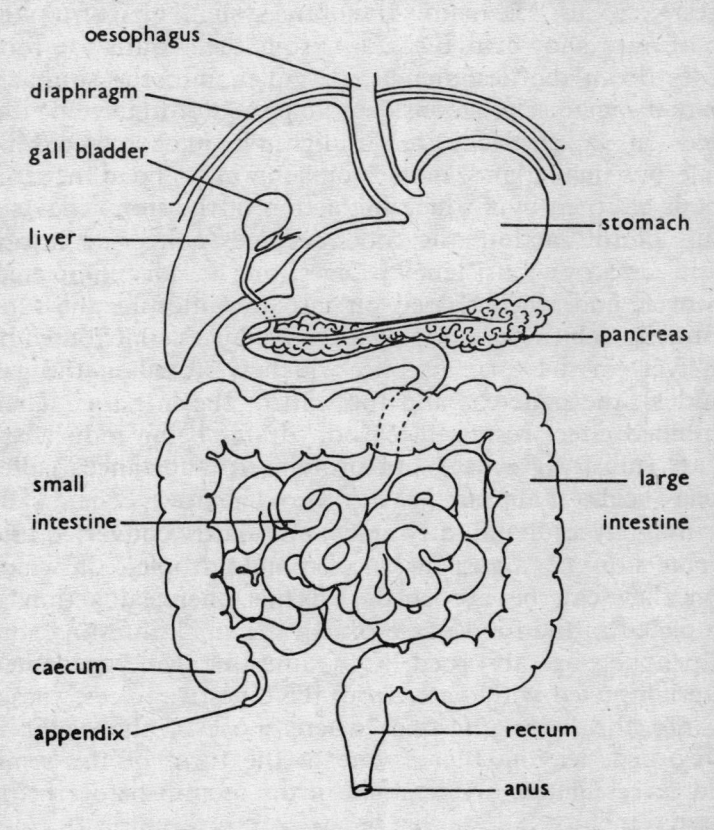

Fig. 2.6 Alimentary canal and associated organs in the abdomen (man)

they have the special task of bringing about the chemical breakdown of the food, and they are found in nearly all the digestive juices.

The remainder of the digestive system consists of a long convoluted tube, the alimentary canal, through which the food is carried as a result of waves of muscular contraction in the walls. To it are attached certain glands which secrete digestive juices. The main parts of the system, apart from the mouth, are shown in Fig. 2.6. From the mouth the food passes down the oesophagus, or gullet, into the stomach, where it remains for a considerable period of time while it is acted on by gastric juice—a digestive juice secreted by numerous small glands in the stomach wall—and at the same time is churned by a squeezing action of the stomach. As a result of this action, the food becomes converted into a liquid creamy consistency. Digestion is not completed, however, and when passed on into the intestine the food continues to be acted upon by digestive juices contributed by the liver (in the form of bile, which is stored in the gall bladder), the pancreas and the wall of the intestine. Their combined effect results in carbohydrates being reduced to sugars (mostly glucose) and proteins to substances called **amino acids**. Fats are partly broken down chemically (forming glycerol and fatty acids) and partly converted into an emulsion, i.e. a suspension of minute droplets, in which form they can be absorbed. All this chemical action is completed as the food passes down the small intestine, and the products are absorbed by the intestine wall. Unwanted material, mixed with water from the digestive juices, passes on into the large intestine, where most of the water is reabsorbed, leaving the residue in the form of the semi-solid **faeces**. These are retained in the rectum before being passed out.

The caecum and appendix (Fig. 2.6) have no known function in man. In some animals they are large and contain bacteria that break down cellulose, a substance that cannot be digested by the human system.

Most of the substances absorbed by the intestine pass into the blood stream flowing through the intestine wall and are carried by it to the liver via the hepatic portal system of veins, which has no direct connection with the heart. The blood is then carried from the liver into the main circulatory system through another set of veins (the hepatic veins). So it is that these substances must pass through the liver before they can reach any other part of the body. (The case of fats forms an exception to this statement, since they are carried into the main circulation via the lymphatic system). The significance of this is that the liver acts as a gatekeeper, regulating the passage of foods into the system.

An example of this regulatory function is afforded by the treatment of glucose. On entering the liver, any of this sugar that is surplus to the body's immediate requirements is converted into glycogen and stored in the liver cells. However, there is always some glucose circulating in the blood, in which the concentration remains constant at about 0.1%. As this is used up to supply the needs of the body, its concentration is prevented from falling, because glycogen in the liver is automatically reconverted to glucose, thus maintaining the level.

Amino acids are the raw materials from which the body builds its proteins. Usually the amounts taken in exceed requirements, but there is no way in which the surplus can be stored—and it is broken down by the liver. In this chemical breakdown the nitrogen of the amino acids is converted into ammonia, leaving a residue which may be utilised for respiration. Ammonia is a poisonous substance and is immediately rendered harmless by being converted into urea through combination with carbon dioxide, a substance present in the liver, as in every other part of the body, as a by-product of respiration. The urea is carried away in the blood stream and excreted by the kidneys.

The functions of the liver outlined above are summarised below.

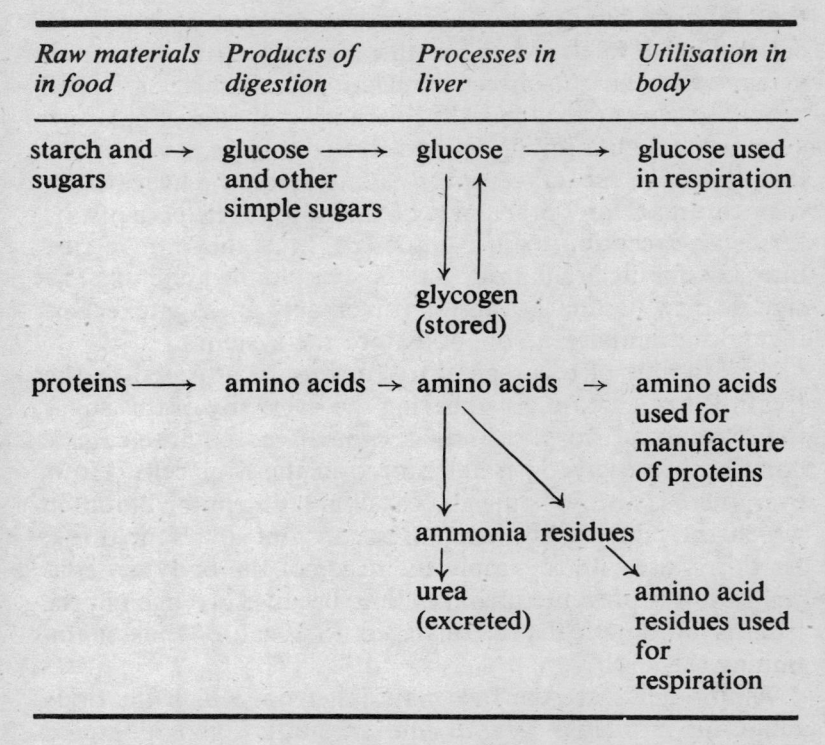

Raw materials in food	Products of digestion	Processes in liver	Utilisation in body
starch and sugars →	glucose and other simple sugars ⟶	glucose ⟶ ⇅ glycogen (stored)	glucose used in respiration
proteins ⟶	amino acids →	amino acids ↘ ↓ ammonia residues ↓ urea (excreted)	amino acids used for manufacture of proteins ↘ amino acid residues used for respiration

Absorption and assimilation of glucose and amino acids

Release of energy

As in plants, the energy needed for the activities of an animal is released in the process of respiration. This term was originally used to mean simply breathing, the means by which the animal obtains oxygen. As biologists came to understand that oxygen was needed essentially to produce energy, respiration came to refer to the whole process, not only of obtaining oxygen but also of using it to provide energy inside the body. Many simpler animals do not actually breathe at all—they do not suck in air and blow it out again—although they do absorb oxygen, and in them respiration may be practically confined to the business of internal utilisation of oxygen. Now it is the latter that the biologist generally has in mind when he talks about respiration, or *internal respiration* as it may be called to make things quite clear.

Internal respiration is a chemical process occurring in every living cell of the body and is identical with the process in flowering plants (p. 23), so that, as in that case, its net effect may be represented as

sugar + oxygen⟶water + carbon dioxide + energy

The rate at which energy is used, and therefore the rate at which respiration takes place, depends upon the type of cell and what it is doing. No cell can exist indefinitely without oxygen, however, and some, such as brain cells, die in a few minutes if the supply is cut off. This is the cause of death in cases of suffocation, although if the supply of oxygen can be restored before irreversible brain damage occurs there may be recovery from apparent death.

The biggest users of energy are the muscles, and, since these are in action all the time in higher animals, such organisms require oxygen in large quantities and have had to develop special means of obtaining it and distributing it in the body, whilst at the same time getting rid of the waste carbon dioxide. Since the same organs usually perform both functions, they are often referred to as organs of respiratory exchange—they exchange carbon dioxide for oxygen. In mammals these organs are the lungs, distribution being cared for by the circulatory system.

The structure of the human chest and lungs is illustrated

diagrammatically in Fig. 2.7. The lungs are thin-walled sacs containing a spongy tissue. The latter consists of a mass of numerous tiny air sacs which open out of minute branching air tubes, or broncheoles. These branch from larger tubes,

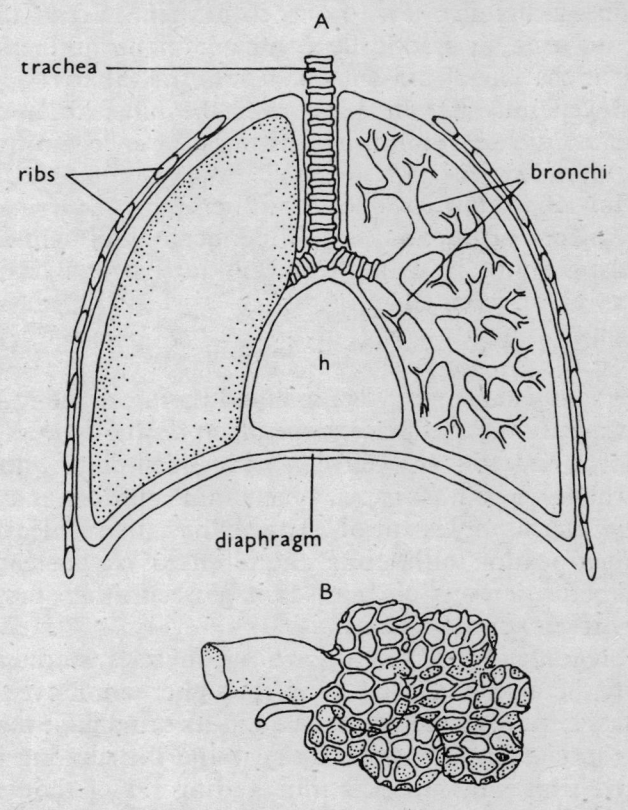

Fig. 2.7 (A) Organs of the thorax (diagrammatic); h= space occupied by the heart. (B) Air sac highly magnified, showing capillary network

the bronchi, which originate from the lower end of the windpipe, or trachea, as shown in the diagram. When we

The Mammal 79

breathe air in it passes down this system of tubes and into the air sacs. Surrounding the sacs is a network of capillaries carrying the pulmonary circulation, which is separated from the air by the very thin, moist membrane forming the lining of the air sacs. So it is that oxygen from the air can dissolve in the moisture and diffuse very rapidly into the blood flowing in the capillaries. There it is absorbed by the red corpuscles, combining with their haemoglobin. At the same time carbon dioxide diffuses in the opposite direction from the blood into the air sacs and is eventually exhaled.

The flow of air into and out of the lungs is caused by movements of the chest wall and a sheet of muscle below the lungs, the diaphragm (Fig. 2.7). The diaphragm is domed upwards, being attached to the body wall at the sides, so that when the muscles in it contract (i.e. become shorter) the effect is to draw the diaphragm downwards. Since the diaphragm forms a partition completely closing off the chest cavity, the result is that the volume of the cavity is increased, its pressure lowered and air flows into the lungs, making them swell out to fill the space. When the diaphragm muscles relax, owing to the elasticity of the lungs, they shrink up again, pressure of the organs in the abdomen pushes the diaphragm upwards and so air is expelled. This is the way we breathe when at rest,* but when more oxygen is needed the chest wall comes into action. Muscles lying between the ribs, when they contract, cause the ribs to rise and move outwards, so increasing the volume of the chest and causing air to enter the lungs. On relaxation of the muscles the ribs return to their original positions and the lungs contract, expelling air.

As blood flows through the lung capillaries it becomes saturated with oxygen, the haemoglobin being converted to

* However, during sleep, breathing is brought about by the ribs only.

oxyhaemoglobin. When the blood reaches respiring tissues (i.e. tissues containing cells that are using oxygen) the reverse action occurs, the oxyhaemoglobin breaking down with liberation of oxygen. This happens because the oxygen/haemoglobin reaction is a chemical equilibrium, the balance of which is controlled by the concentration of oxygen:

$$\text{haemoglobin} + \text{oxygen} \rightleftarrows \text{oxyhaemoglobin}$$

In the presence of a high concentration of oxygen, the balance of this reaction is altered in such a way that more haemoglobin is changed into oxyhaemoglobin:

$$\text{haemoglobin} + \text{oxygen} \longrightarrow \text{oxyhaemoglobin}$$

Where oxygen concentration is low, on the other hand, the reverse is true and oxyhaemoglobin is converted into haemoglobin and oxygen:

$$\text{haemoglobin} + \text{oxygen} \longleftarrow \text{oxyhaemoglobin}$$

It is obvious that the two contrasting conditions exist in the the lungs and respiring tissues respectively. Oxygen concentration is high in the one case because of the continual inhalation of fresh air and low in the other case because of the continual consumption of oxygen by respiring cells.

The mechanism of the transfer of waste carbon dioxide from the tissues to expired air is in many ways similar to the transfer of oxygen in the opposite direction. Respiring cells give off carbon dioxide, which diffuses into the blood. Unlike oxygen, carbon dioxide does not combine with haemoglobin. It is carried in solution in the plasma. In fact, much of the carbon dioxide is in the form of bicarbonate ions. In the lungs it passes out of solution into the air of the air sacs. There is an equilibrium between carbon dioxide not in the blood and carbon dioxide in solution,

$$\text{plasma} + \text{carbon dioxide} \rightleftarrows \text{solution of carbon dioxide in plasma}$$

which is controlled by the concentration of carbon dioxide. Respiration leads to a relatively high concentration of carbon dioxide in the tissues and it enters the blood; but in the lungs its concentration is kept low by the continual exhalation of air and so the reverse action occurs.

Regulation and control

Machines need to be controlled: for example, a car must have a driver. What is, perhaps, not quite so obvious is that many machines have automatic controls. Some cars, we know, have automatic transmission, a complex mechanism that automatically changes gear for the driver without his having to think about it. But even the cheapest and oldest cars have automatic control of the flow of fuel into the engine. This is a pleasingly simple device in the carburetter, consisting of a small reservoir of fuel in which there is a float. As more fuel flows into the reservoir, the float rises until it closes the opening through which the fuel enters. On the other hand, as fuel is sucked into the engine from the reservoir, the level falls until the opening is uncovered and more fuel can enter. In this way the level of petrol in the reservoir is kept steady, so that the rate at which it is supplied to the carburetter jets is constant.

It is hardly surprising that so complex a piece of machinery as the human body has automatic controls—and many of them. Here we shall consider some of the main regulatory systems, with examples of their modes of operation. One system of controls is concerned with the composition of the blood. This fluid permeates the whole body and all cells are in more or less close contact with it, so that in a sense it forms their environment. Even slight changes in this environment can have serious consequences. We have already seen how the sugar content of the blood is kept constant by the regulatory activity of the liver and how the gaseous exchange system maintains its oxygen content. That system is under automatic control too: we do not have to think about breathing, consciously to regulate its depth and frequency to match the demands of the body for oxygen. One organ that plays a very important part in regulating the composition of the blood is the kidney.

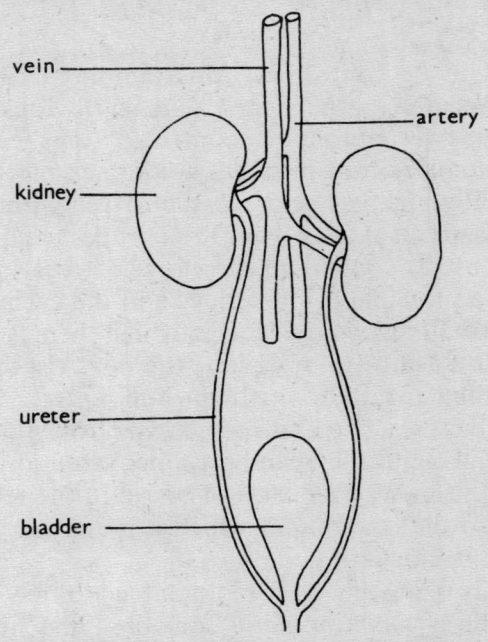

Fig. 2.8 Arrangement of kidneys and associated organs

The kidneys lie on either side of the midline, just in front of the spine and at the level of the small of the back (Fig. 2.8). Each one is connected to the circulatory system by an artery and vein, and has a duct (the ureter) leading from it to the urinary bladder. The kidney tissue consists of a mass of miscroscopic tubes (kidney tubules) tightly packed together (Fig. 2.9). Each starts from a separate Malpighian body in the outer region of the kidney. A Malpighian body consists of the cup-shaped beginning of the tubule into which a little knot of capillaries projects. From the cup-shaped beginning the tubule follows a tortuous course through the kidney, eventually joining with others and opening into a central space at the inner side of the organ. Here the fluid secreted by the tubules—urine—collects, before passing down the ureter to the bladder.

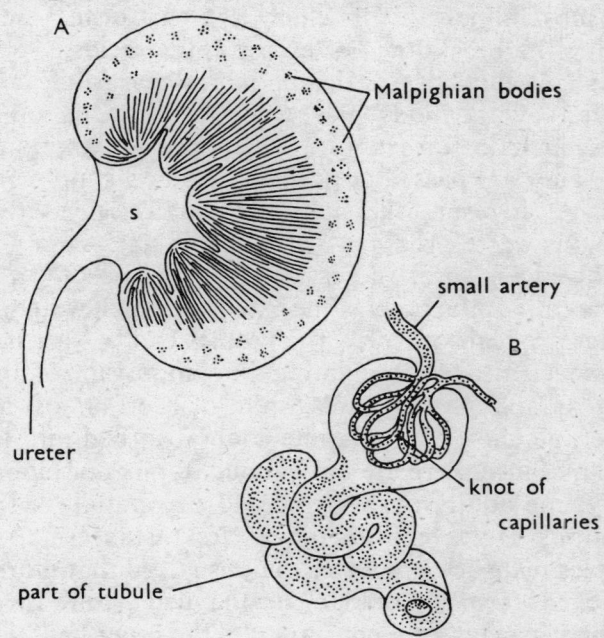

Fig. 2.9 (A) kidney in section: kidney tubules starting from the Malpighian bodies converge towards the space S, where urine collects before passing down the ureter; (B) a Malpighian body much enlarged

The process of urine secretion begins in the Malpighian body. Blood enters the knot of capillaries directly from the arterial system and is under sufficient pressure to cause some of the plasma to pass through the thin capillary walls into the tubule. The capillary membrane, however, does not allow the larger molecules in the plasma (this means, in practice, protein molecules) to pass. Consequently, the fluid in the tubule is, in effect, plasma less protein. It consists largely of water with, dissolved in it, salt, derivatives of the food—such as glucose and amino acids—and waste products, the most important of which is urea, formed in the liver during the breakdown of excess amino acids.

As this fluid passes down the kidney tubule, the things needed by the body are reabsorbed by the tubule wall. These include, for example, water, glucose, amino acids and salt. They are passed back into the blood supply of the tubules. As a result, the fluid that finally leaves the kidney contains waste products—principally urea—and a little salt dissolved in water (necessary as a means of carrying the wastes out of the body). The extent to which water and other things are reabsorbed by the tubules can be varied, and this provides a means of regulating the composition of the plasma. For example, if you drink a pint of beer, almost all of it—water, alcohol, etc.—is quite soon absorbed into the blood stream. Since there are only about 10 pints of blood in your body, the additional water could cause quite a significant dilution. However, in these circumstances, the kidney tubules reabsorb less water than usual, so that more water is removed from the blood to the urine and the amount in the plasma is kept constant. On the other hand, alcohol is not reabsorbed at all, so that eventually all of it is removed from the circulation and its effects on the nervous system cease to be experienced.

Another example of the kidney's regulatory function is seen in people suffering from diabetes. This disease is caused by a malfunction of the mechanisms regulating the storage of glucose as glycogen (see p. 75), which results in the release of too much glucose into the blood. The kidney reacts by allowing excess sugar to pass out without being reabsorbed in the tubules, and in less serious cases this compensates for the extra release of sugar, although it causes a continual wastage. In more severe cases of diabetes, however, the reserve of glycogen is so rapidly lost that serious consequences ensue.

In general, the kidney helps to keep the composition of the blood constant by removing excess substances. These include waste products, such as urea, formed within the body, and drugs, poisons and other foreign substances absorbed from outside. This function of the kidney of getting rid of unwanted substances is known as excretion. The other principal excretory organs are the lungs, which excrete carbon dioxide. The sweat glands are minor organs of excretion, since sweat contains small quantities of urea, but their main purpose has to do with another control function—temperature regulation.

The so-called 'warm-blooded' animals—mammals and birds—maintain a more or less constant body temperature, whereas the temperature of 'cold-blooded' animals fluctuates with the external temperature, rarely varying much from it. The advantage of constant temperature would appear to be that it permits a much finer adjustment of various bodily functions, all of which are affected by changes in temperature. At all events, quite small deviations from the normal level upset the whole system (and especially mental functions) and result in death.

Temperature regulation depends upon maintaining a balance between heat input and heat losses from the body. This is achieved by having a body temperature that is normally higher than that of the surroundings, so that heat energy is always being lost from the body (heat always flows from regions of higher temperature to regions of lower temperature), and by having arrangements that permit

86 *Biology*

adjustment of (i) the rate of loss and (ii) the rate of heat production.

Much of the heat lost from the body passes through the skin, although some is lost in the breath, urine and faeces. The layer of fat below the skin and the fur (or clothing in man) slows heat loss and so helps to maintain the relatively high body temperature. Heat is brought to the skin in the blood, which plays an important part in keeping the temperature of all parts of the body about the same by distributing heat, and the rate of supply to the skin can be adjusted by directing blood to or from the surface by the constriction or dilation (opening) of the supplying blood vessels, with consequent effect upon the rate of heat loss. Heat leaving the skin is carried away by air currents and is also lost through the evaporation of sweat, since heat (latent heat of vaporisation) is absorbed by any liquid as it evaporates. This is how the sweat glands come to have a regulatory function, since the rate of sweat production effects the rate of heat loss in this way. In furry animals the hairs forming the fur can be erected (made to stand up) through the action of minute muscles attached to their roots, so thickening the fur. The hairs trap a layer of stationary air, thus impeding loss of heat, since air is a poor conductor. In man this mechanism exists but has little effect because of the sparsity of hairs on most parts of the body.

Heat is produced in the body by respiration, since much of the energy released appears as heat. The rate of heat production depends mostly upon the degree of activity of the body, but where there is danger of the temperature falling unduly low it may be increased by shivering, in which the increased muscular activity leads to faster respiration, and by increased tension (tone) of the muscles without actual movement, which has the same effect.

The regulatory mechanism works as follows. If there is a tendency for the temperature to rise, either because of increased bodily activity (e.g. when digging ditches) or because of high external temperature (e.g. on a hot day), more blood is diverted to the skin, more sweat is secreted and the body hair is depressed, allowing as free access of air to the skin as possible. As a result, more heat is lost, which prevents a rise in temperature. When body temperature tends to fall, because of low external temperatures, blood supply to the skin is reduced, sweating stops and the body hairs are erected; muscle tone is increased and, in extreme cases, shivering commences. So heat loss is reduced and its production increased, thus preventing the fall in temperature.

Many regulatory systems depend upon substances called hormones which are secreted in one part of the body and affect the functioning of other parts. An example is thyroglobulin. This is produced by the thyroid gland, situated at the front and base of the neck. It has no duct to carry its secretion away, but instead the hormone passes into the blood stream and so is carried to other parts of the body. This is characteristic of the hormone-producing organs. The importance of thyroglobulin was discovered as a result of the study of the disease caused by failure of the thyroid to secrete its hormone. This is observed in certain cases of children who fail to develop into normal adults. Such sufferers are known as cretins. They have an abnormally low level of internal respiration and, unless treated, become dwarfs, retaining infantile bodily proportions with a relatively large head and poorly developed limbs, do not attain sexual maturity and, saddest of all, never lose their childish mentality. It seems that, in some way which is not understood, thyroglobulin plays a vital part in the normal development of the child. Provided that the condition is diagnosed early enough, however, it can be cured completely by the administration of an extract prepared from animal thyroid.

The male sex hormone, testosterone, has a rather similar

function. Its effects have been known since time immemorial, since the results of castration depend upon the fact that the hormone is secreted by the testis. Although it has less far-reaching effects than thyroglobulin, it also controls some aspects of development. In the normal male it promotes development of the sex organs and the secondary sexual characteristics, such as the deeper voice and the growth of the beard.

Not all hormones have such long-term effects. For example, the normal control of the amount of glucose in the blood depends upon the hormone insulin. This is secreted by special cells in the pancreas and passes into the blood flowing through that organ. When it reaches other parts of the body it promotes the conversion of glucose into glycogen (in the liver, for example) and the oxidation of glucose in respiration. Thus it tends to reduce the concentration of the sugar. However, the secretion of insulin is itself controlled by that concentration: reduced concentration of glucose causes less insulin to be produced, whereas increased glucose concentration has the opposite effect. The system may be represented thus:

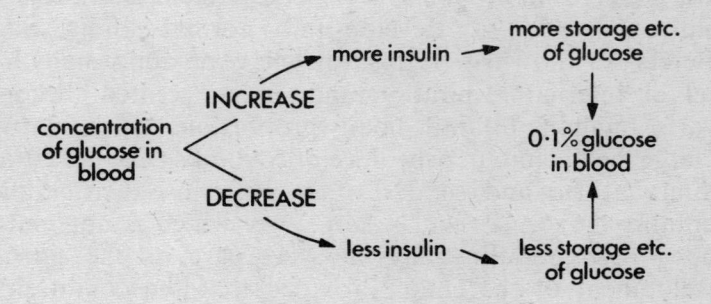

```
                           more insulin ──▶  more storage etc.
                       ↗                         of glucose
               INCREASE                             │
                                                    ▼
concentration  ⟨                             0·1% glucose
of glucose in                                   in blood
   blood                                            ▲
               DECREASE                             │
                       ↘
                           less insulin ──▶  less storage etc.
                                                of glucose
```

The Mammal 89

and it will be apparent that its effect is to keep the concentration of glucose constant. Other systems maintaining a steady state (the kidney and the temperature control system, for example) conform to a similar pattern.

The most highly developed and elaborate control system is the nervous system, which is the subject of the next section.

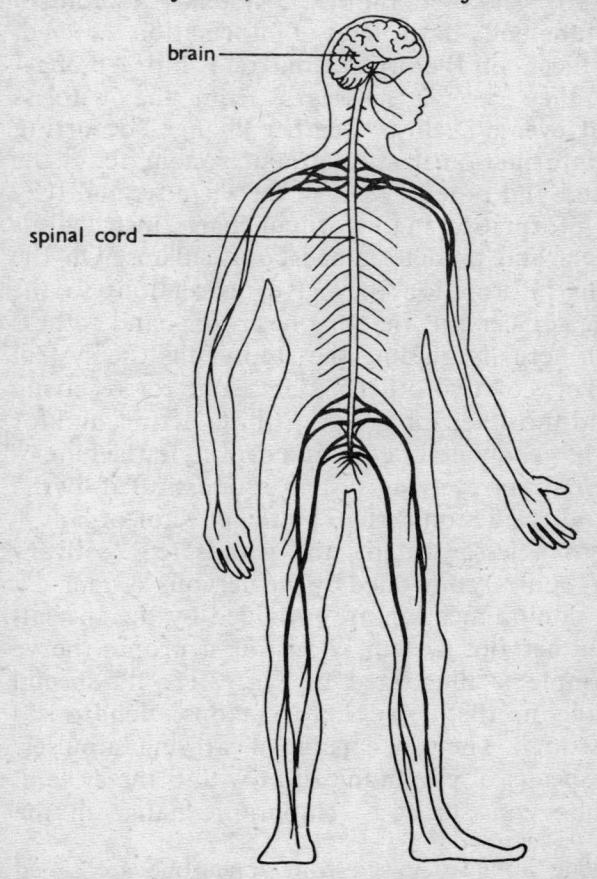

Fig. 2.10 The nervous system. Peripheral nerves radiate from the brain and spinal cord

The nervous system

The nervous system is made up of a central part (the central nervous system, or CNS), consisting of the brain and spinal cord, and, radiating from this, nerves which serve all parts of the body and constitute the peripheral nervous system (Fig. 2.10). The function of the system is to control the activities of the body in the light of information received, rather as the officers on the bridge control a ship. Amongst other things, they receive messages from the wireless operator about events such as weather changes occurring at a distance, information from the radar system about the positions of land and other vessels in the vicinity, and they consult stored information in the form of charts, instructions from the owners and predetermined course plans. On the basis of all this information they give instructions to the helmsman, the officer in the engine room and others concerned with actually guiding the ship. Thus the system acts as a link between two other systems, one for receiving information and the other for bringing about action, and for this purpose it has channels of communication. In the human body the information-receiving system is constituted by the sense organs and the action system by the effector organs—muscles and, to a lesser extent, the glands (e.g. salivary glands, adrenal bodies) controlled by the nervous system.

Channels of communication are provided by the specialised cells of the nervous system known as neurones (nerve cells). An example is illustrated in Fig. 2.11. Its special properties reside in the nerve fibres (axons, dendrons*) which radiate from it. They are capable of carrying impulses, which are the means of communication within the system. A nerve impulse consists of a temporary change in the

* Fibres carrying impulses away from a neurone are called axons. Those carrying impulses towards the cell are dendrons. Dendrites are short, branching dendrons.

surface membrane of the fibre which is accompanied by a minute electrical charge. This disturbance normally starts at one end of a fibre and travels rapidly to the other, its speed varying according to the nature of the neurone but generally being about 30 metres per second. The associated electrical change makes it possible to detect the passage of an impulse using electronic amplifying apparatus. Under natural conditions nerve impulses originate in sense organs or from within the CNS, but they can be produced by electrical stimulation of nerves and this much facilitates experimental study. They can pass from one neurone to others with which it is connected and may eventually reach organs such as muscles, which they stimulate into activity.

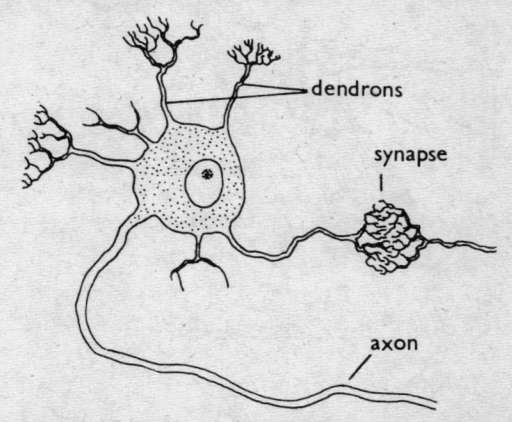

Fig. 2.11 A neurone. A connection (synapse) with another neurone is shown on the right

The vast majority of nerve cell bodies lie within the CNS (an exception being the eye, which develops in the embryo from a portion of the brain), but their fibres may pass out of it and the peripheral nerves are, indeed, composed of bundles of such fibres. A nerve appears as a white thread and may be 3 mm or more in diameter, containing thousands of

92 Biology

fibres. Some, receptor nerves, are connected with sense organs and others, motor nerves, with effector organs. Others contain a mixture of both kinds of fibre. The nerve cell bodies within the CNS are connected to each other by shorter fibres, the whole forming a vastly complicated network. All the time impulses are travelling from the various sense organs along the receptor nerves to the CNS and others out along the motor organs to the effectors.

Fig. 2.12 illustrates the arrangement of two of the muscles that bring about movement of the forearm. A muscle consists of a large number of thin fibres composed mostly of a protein, myosin, which has the power of contractility; that is,

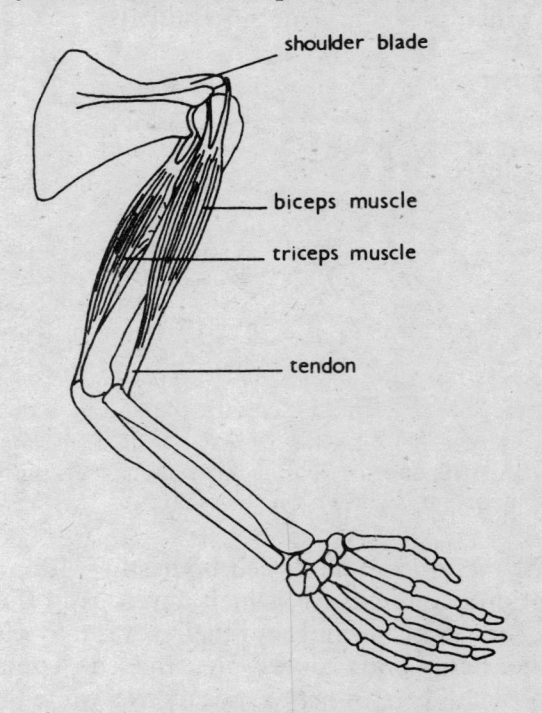

Fig. 2.12 The biceps and triceps muscles

in suitable circumstances, the fibres are capable of becoming shorter. When this happens to all (or most of) the fibres in a muscle, the whole organ contracts, at the same time becoming thicker (an effect familiar to everyone in the biceps). As the diagram shows, the muscles are connected to the bones of the skeleton. In particular, they are joined to the bones of the forearm by tough, strap-like tendons, so that contraction of either muscle causes it to exert a pull, resulting in the bending of the elbow in the case of the biceps and in the straightening of it in the case of the triceps. This arrangement of two muscles in opposition is typical, and is necessary because a single muscle can bring about movement in one direction only.

Movement requires energy, which is released by respiration, and every time a muscle fibre contracts a small amount of glucose is broken down and, ultimately, a small amount of oxygen used up and carbon dioxide released. In fact, muscles can obtain energy by breaking down glucose to form lactic acid in the absence of oxygen, but in the end the lactic acid is always further broken down with liberation of carbon dioxide, while oxygen is taken up. Another requirement is stimulation by the nervous system. Each muscle receives a nerve which branches out within it, the individual axons ending on individual muscle fibres, and the arrival of nerve impulses serves to trigger off the process leading to the conversion of the energy of glucose into the energy of contraction. Muscles cannot otherwise contract, and destruction of motor nerves leads to paralysis of the muscles. This may result from the cutting of the nerves or from the destruction of the motor neurones which are situated in the spinal cord (as in poliomyelitis).

Specialised sense organs are associated with each of the traditional five senses—sight, sound, taste, smell and touch. The simplest are specialised nerve endings in the skin, some sensitive to pressure ('touch') and others to changes of

94 *Biology*

temperature. Other apparently unspecialised endings give rise to the sensation of pain. Special sensory cells, connected to receptor nerves in the tongue, nasal cavities and ear, are responsible for our sensations of taste, smell and hearing. There are other sense organs that do not correspond to the traditional five. Thus in the ear, besides sound-sensitive cells, there are others that respond to the movements and changes of attitude of the head, so giving us our sense of balance, and in all the muscles there are stretch receptors which tell us about the dispositions of the parts of the body.

Perhaps the most complex sense organ is the eye (Fig. 2.13). This is essentially like a camera. The curved transparent cornea at the front and the lens behind it act like the camera lens and focus light onto the surface at the back of

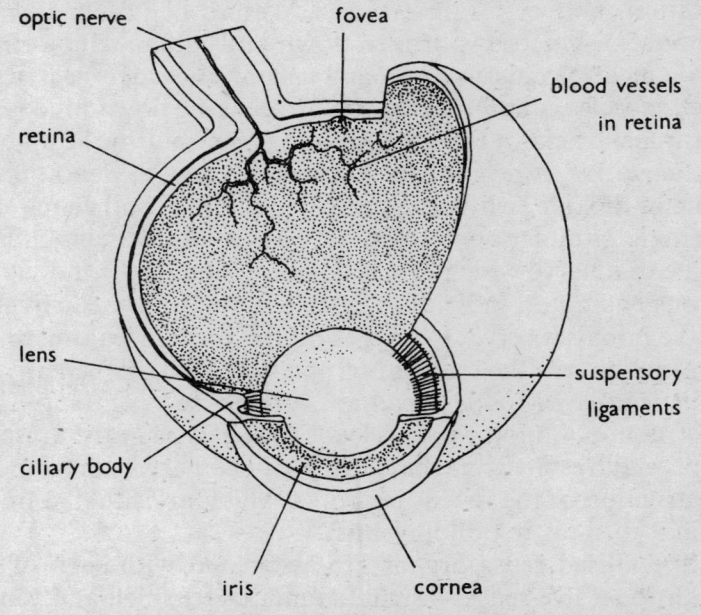

Fig. 2.13 The eye, with about one third of the wall removed and the optic nerve sectioned

the eye, forming an image of whatever is in front of the eye. However, instead of sensitive film, there is a layer containing light-sensitive cells, the retina. Fig. 2.14 shows a few of the cells in this layer. The sensory cells are next to the rear surface of the retina. When light falls upon them, each one emits a series of nerve impulses one after the other. These follow one another more or less rapidly according to whether more or less light falls on the cell. The impulses are transmitted to the neurones with which they are connected and then down the long axons that form the front surface of the retina. These axons converge from all over the retina to one point. Here they pass backwards through the retina and the outer layers of the eye to emerge as the optic nerve, which meets its fellow from the other eye and enters the brain at its base. The nerve fibres continue through the brain and the impulses from the eye finally reach part of the surface of the brain (the visual cortex) at the back of the head, which is the main receiving station for visual signals.

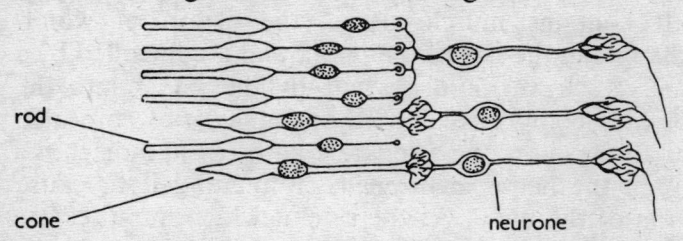

Fig. 2.14 Cells of the retina. The inner surface of the retina is to the right, and light reaches the sensory rod and cone cells from that direction

As shown in the diagram, there are two kinds of sensory cell in the eye known as rods and cones. The cones distinguish between colours whereas the rods do not. On the other hand, the cones do not function at low light intensities, which may be sufficient for the rods. This is why we cannot see colours at night. The sensory cells are much more closely packed in a small central region of the retina (the fovea) than elsewhere, their density becoming gradually less as distance from this point increases. In consequence, we can perceive fine detail of a thing only when its image is focused on the fovea. In fact, when we look at an object directly, we automatically bring this about. The cones are more numerous in the more central parts of the retina and the fovea itself contains them only. A result of this is that we cannot see details in poor lighting conditions. We may think that the full moon is bright enough for us to read a newspaper, but we find in practice that we cannot: we look at the print and the image is focused on the fovea, where the cone cells are insufficiently sensitive to respond.

The efficient working of the retina depends very much upon the amount of light entering the eye being just right—neither too small nor too great—and the function of the iris (the coloured part of the eye) is to bring this state of affairs about. The iris is a thin disc with a hole, the pupil, at its centre. It contains muscle tissue, the action of which causes changes in the size of the pupil, and is controlled by a special nerve. Nerve impulses sent by the retina into the brain, besides being passed to the visual cortex, are also sent back to the eye along a separate pathway and reach the iris through the nerve mentioned, stimulating it to cause contraction of the pupil. As the rate at which impulses are sent out by the retina increases with the intensity of light falling on it and the degree of contraction of the pupil depends upon the rate at which impulses reach the iris, it follows that the size of the pupil is automatically controlled by the amount of light falling on the eye. Thus it contracts when light intensity increases and expands when it decreases, so keeping the amount actually reaching the retina more or less constant.

The above is an example of reflex action, the simplest means of control in the nervous system. It depends upon the existence of a reflex arc, i.e. a series of nervous connections which might be represented schematically as

receptor → CNS → effector

In the example given the receptor is the retina, the effector the iris, and the connection between them consists of a chain of neurones in the eye and brain. Even a simple control system such as this can be thought of in terms of information received and transmitted. The retina receives information about the amount of light entering the eye and converts this into a code 'message' of nerve impulses (more or less frequent, according to light intensity) which is passed on to the iris. Another example of reflex action is the withdrawal reflex, which brings about withdrawal of a limb on receipt of a sufficiently painful stimulus, as when one's hand comes in contact with a hot object. Here the receptors are nerve endings in the skin. If we could follow nerve impulses originating in one of these endings, we should find them travelling in a dendron forming part of a nerve in the arm. The nerve would originate from the spinal cord at the level of the shoulder and the cell body of our dendron would be situated in the root of the nerve close to its point of connection with the spinal cord. The impulses would be sent on through an axon into the spinal cord and there be carried via at least one connector neurone to a motor neurone, still within the cord. A long axon of the last neurone would carry the impulses through a motor nerve leaving the spinal cord and passing down the arm to one of the muscles, causing withdrawal (Fig. 2.15). The passage of a large number of impulses through many similar chains brings about the reflex.

The second example given above has an obvious protective function, but reflexes more commonly have regulatory functions, as in the first case. All sorts of internal functions are regulated in this way, maintaining blood pressure, body temperature (through control of the system already described) and muscle tension, to give but a few examples. We are quite unaware of most of these processes and have no voluntary control of them, and it is characteristic of reflexes that they are unconscious and involuntary.

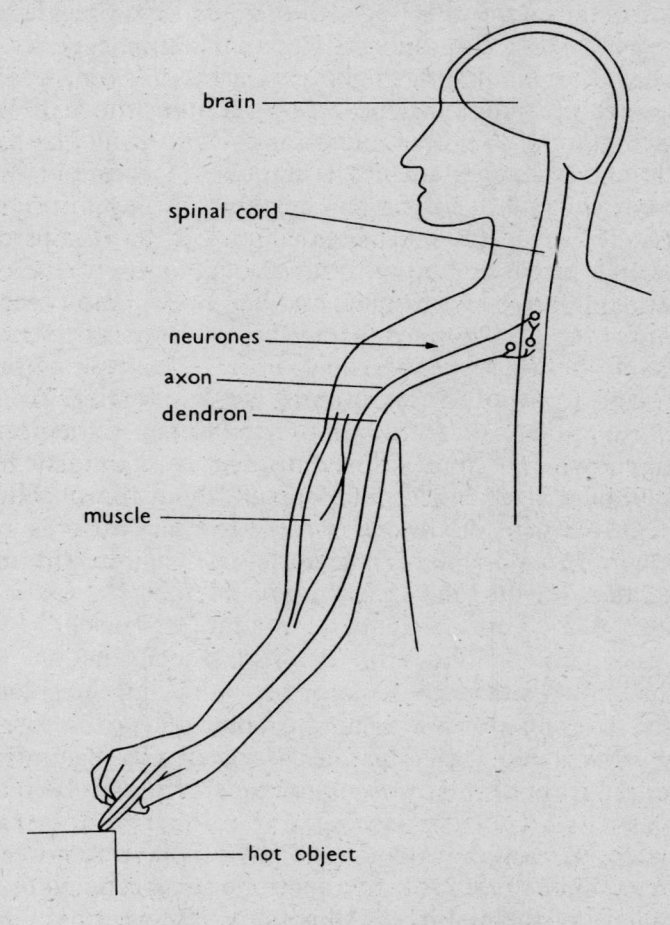

Fig. 2.15   A reflex arc

The voluntary functions of the nervous system are centred in the brain and are related to the capacity of that organ for storing information as memory. This obviously vastly increases the scope of the whole control system, since it frees it from having to respond only to immediately given information, as in reflex action. Thus, if we decide to go to buy a loaf from the shop round the corner, this action has a regulatory function. It serves to replenish the body's store of carbohydrate and to maintain the level of glucose in the blood. It depends upon the reception of information (one's wife says that there is no bread in the bin, or one may just feel hungry) leading to an appropriate response. However, the connection between the receipt of information and the initiation of action is not simple, since it depends upon comparing incoming information with stored information (knowledge that lack of food can lead to unpleasant consequences, knowledge of the location of the shop and so forth); and the response itself is very far from simple, consisting of a complicated sequence of actions (walking down the road etc.) controlled continuously by information gathered by the sense organs (about approaching obstacles, for example) and based on learned patterns of behaviour (such as walking) which are somehow 'stored' in the CNS.

Cells, tissues and organs

Animals, like plants, are generally composed of a large number of cells. Fig. 2.16 illustrates two liver cells. Basically, the liver cell is very similar to a plant cell. It is a small blob of protoplasm with a nucleus. However, there are two important differences: (i) there is no vacuole and (ii) there is no cell wall. In a plant cell most of its volume is often occupied by a water-filled vacuole, but in animal cells vacuoles are rare and usually small if present. The outer boundary of the animal cell is formed by the cell membrane, a structure very similar to that in the plant cell.

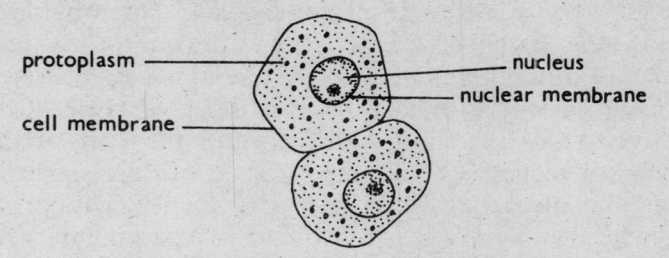

Fig. 2.16 Liver cells

Just as in plants, a variety of cell types are present in animals, each performing special functions. Blood cells (corpuscles) and nerve cells (neurones) have already been described. Other kinds form the skin (many layers of flattened cells), the linings of internal organs, the various

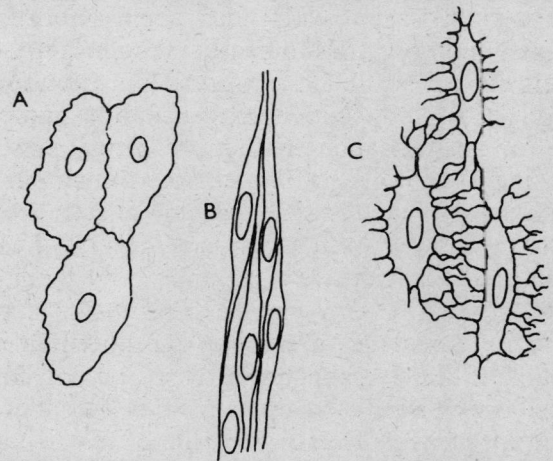

Fig. 2.17 Three types of cell found in animals: (A) cells from the inner lining of a blood vessel; (B) muscle cells from the intestine wall; (C) bone cells (the space between the cells is filled with a hard matrix)

glands, muscle fibres, blood vessels and so on. Examples are illustrated in Fig. 2.17.

The mechanical strength of plant organs depends partly upon the pressure of sap in the cell vacuoles and partly upon the strength of the cell walls, which may be much thickened (p. 41). This system cannot work in animals because of the lack of cell walls and vacuoles. Instead, we find that bone, the tough deeper layers of the skin, cartilage (gristle), tendons and other parts needing to be particularly strong are strengthened by a network of protein fibres lying between the cells and produced by them. This forms a matrix in which the cells are embedded, which in the case of bone is hardened by the presence of calcium salts (Fig. 2.17 (C)).

In the ways indicated above the different kinds of cell co-operate to produce the various tissues of the body, such as skin, bone or cartilage. Each tissue is a substance containing characteristic cell types (one or more) and sometimes a non-cellular matrix. It has one or more special functions. A number of tissues go to make up each organ or distinct part of the body, such as a bone, a muscle, the heart, a hand, each of which has its own functions. Again, organs co-operate in systems such as the circulatory system, the skeleton (Fig. 2.18), the CNS or the digestive system.

These terms—tissue, organ, system—merely represent convenient ways of separating out certain parts of the body in the imagination so that we can think about them clearly. Each tissue, organ or system can be thought of as having its special functions, but they are all linked together functionally so that, ultimately, no one part can be considered in isolation from the rest.

Reproduction

In the account of reproduction by seed in the flowering plant (p. 50) it was explained that the essential feature of

102 *Biology*

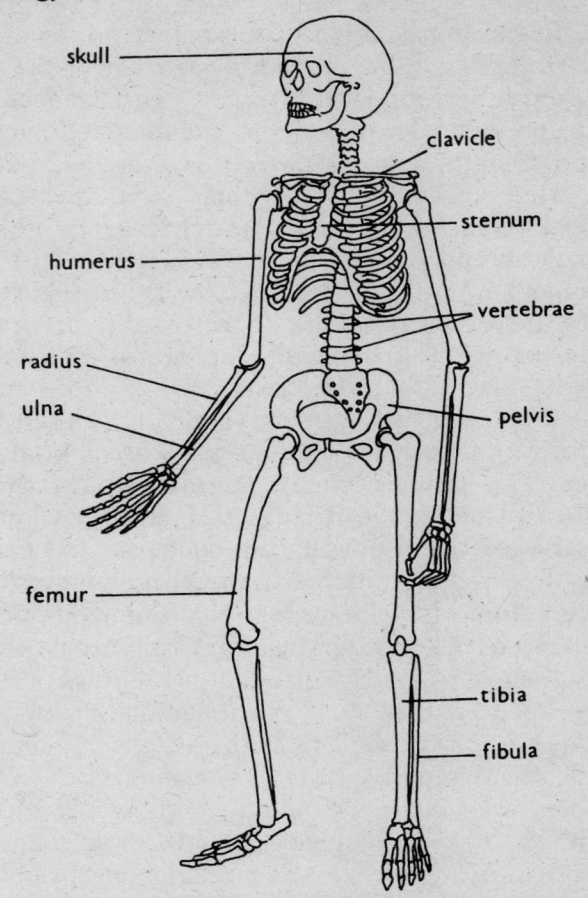

Fig. 2.18 The skeleton

sexual reproduction was the union of two gametes to form a zygote, the cell that forms the starting point for the new individual. The same is true of sexual reproduction in man, as in other animals. The female gametes are commonly called eggs and the male gametes sperms. Fertilisation is the uniting of an egg and a sperm to form a fertilised egg—the

The Mammal

zygote. In the simplest forms of sexual reproduction, as in many fish, eggs and sperms are passed out of the parents' bodies and fertilisation takes place externally in the water. The zygotes then start to develop into young animals in that situation. In many higher forms fertilisation and development of the young are internal, as is the case in mammals.

Asexual forms of reproduction are relatively uncommon in animals and unknown in vertebrates. However, in some of the simpler forms of animal life, types of asexual reproduction, some of which are similar to the vegetative reproduction of flowering plants, do exist. Examples are described later in this book.

Figs. 2.19 and 2.20 show the human male and female reproductive organs. The gonads are the organs that produce gametes. This is achieved by cell division (similar to the process in plants—p.46), resulting in the formation of new cells, some of which become the gametes. Thus the male gonad (the testis) consists of a mass of minute coiled tubes and the cells forming their walls constantly undergo cell division, so producing sperms, which then pass down the

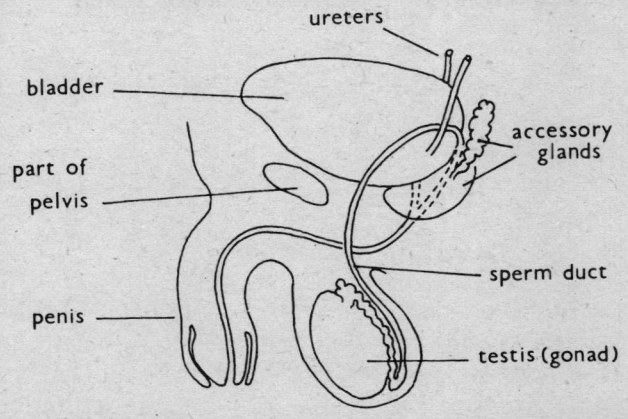

Fig. 2.19 Human male reproductive organs from the left side. Testis and sperm duct of left side only shown

tubes to be stored in the coiled part of the duct leading to the penis (see illustration). The sperm is a very specialised cell, consisting mostly of a head, which contains the cell nucleus, and a long tail, which propels the sperm by an undulating movement (Fig. 2.21). During intercourse the sperms are passed out of the penis, together with secretions of the various accessory glands, in the form of semen. The latter is deposited in the upper part of the vagina, and the sperms swim upwards into the uterus and oviducts.

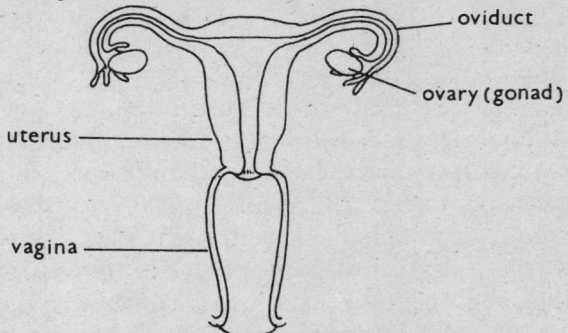

Fig. 2.20 Human female reproductive system

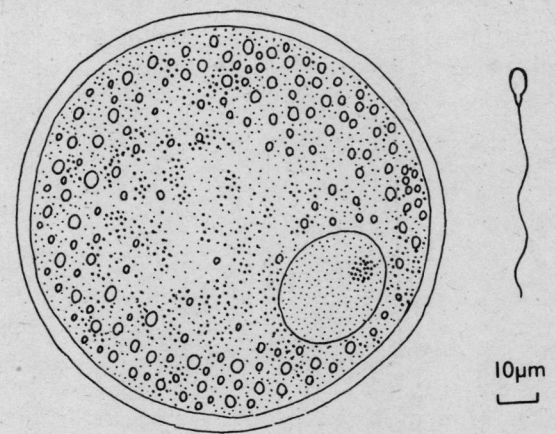

Fig. 2.21 Human egg and sperm

The Mammal

The female gonad (the ovary) is not constructed in the same way as the testis and the eggs are released from its surface when they mature. Usually only a single egg is released each month from one of the ovaries. The egg (Fig. 2.21) is much larger than a sperm and has no means of movement. However, the oviduct and its open end, which partly surrounds the ovary, contain many microscopic hairs, which, by a beating action, produce currents in the fluid that fills them and so carry the released eggs down towards the uterus.

If an egg encounters sperms on its voyage in the oviduct, it may be fertilised. Thus conception is achieved. The resulting zygote immediately begins to undergo repeated cell division, the first stage of development. The single cell first divides into two, these into four, these into eight—and so by repetition a little ball of many cells is produced in place of the original zygote. This soon arrives in the uterus and becomes embedded in its wall. Now a series of very complicated developments takes place, with the result that the embryo after quite a short time (about eight weeks) takes on a recognisably human form. All this time the embryo has been growing and requiring nourishment, and this is supplied by the uterine wall, which becomes richly supplied with blood vessels carrying not only food but also oxygen in the mother's blood stream. The embryo itself grows a

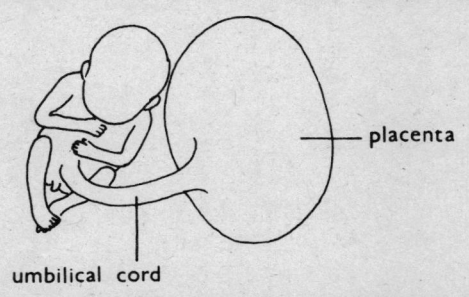

Fig. 2.22 Human foetus with placenta attached

special organ, the placenta (Fig. 2.22), which attaches it to the uterus and has the function of obtaining food and oxygen, and also of getting rid of waste products, such as carbon dioxide and urea, which are removed in the mother's blood. At the same time, membranes produced by the embryo form a protective bag of fluid surrounding it.

When birth occurs, nine months after conception, the muscular walls of the uterus begin a series of contractions, which, becoming stronger and stronger, gradually force the baby through the vaginal opening. In the later stages the mother's stomach muscles assist in this. Normally the baby lies in the uterus with the head downwards, so that this is the first part to pass to the exterior. The membranes surrounding the baby break quite early in the process, releasing the contained fluid, but, together with the placenta, remain within the uterus for a short time after the birth of the child, being expelled later as the 'after-birth'. The cry of the baby on emerging into the world marks its first breath and the establishment of its independence as far as the supply of oxygen is concerned, whilst the cutting of the umbilical cord finally severs the connection with its mother.

3 Biochemistry and the Cell

In studying the flowering plant and the mammal, certain basic patterns have emerged. There are, it is true, many striking differences between the two kinds of organism, some of them perceived only on closer study. Thus we have noted the difference in the types of raw material utilised, and seen how this is linked with the presence of photosynthesis in plants and its absence in animals, and the differences in cell structure. However, it is at the latter point that we also notice one of the striking similarities. At first glance, the structures of a buttercup and a man, for example, seem to show almost nothing in common and it is only at the fundamental level of the cell that we begin to discover the basic unity. That this is no superficial similarity will be shown in the present chapter, where it will also become apparent that this is dependent upon the underlying processes of life.

If we are to appreciate the essential nature of life, it will be through a consideration of the changes that go to make it up. Living organisms are constantly changing. The zygote changes into the embryo, the embryo into the young animal or plant and the latter into the adult, and during all this development there is a constant flow of matter through the organism. It has been stated that almost all the actual material of which the human body is composed is renewed within a period of seven years.

The underlying similarity of flowering plants and mammals is seen most clearly in the processes that they carry out. Thus both types take in and process raw materials, respire, excrete, respond to influences from the environment, and grow and reproduce in ways that depend upon the same process of cell division and exhibit the same basic pattern of sexual reproduction. Fundamentally, these are all chemical processes, that is they all involve the transformation of substances. For example, in respiration, glucose and oxygen are transformed into carbon dioxide and water; in growth, raw materials are transformed into living protoplasm. It follows that it is the study of the chemistry of life (biochemistry) that gives us the key to understanding.

What organisms are made of

A mere list of the elements found in living organisms does not tell us very much. It is the way these elements are combined and organised that is significant. Let us imagine that we could take an organism to pieces systematically, gradually separating out smaller and smaller components. What should we find? We have already seen that the plant or animal is made up of a number of complex organ systems and that these are composed of tissues, which are in turn made up of cells. Having broken down the organism to cells, we have already reached quite a small unit, since, although large cells may be a millimetre in diameter and some may be even larger, the majority are much smaller and often only about a hundredth of that size. A microscope is necessary in order to reveal details of their structure, and even the highest magnifications of an ordinary instrument (perhaps as much as 100 X) do not show the finer details. The enormous magnifications obtainable with the electron microscope (of the order of several 100 000 X) are required to give the full picture.

Fig. 3.1 shows the major structures of a typical cell. In the middle is the **nucleus** and, surrounding this, the **cytoplasm.** The cytoplasm is bounded by the **cell membrane** and may

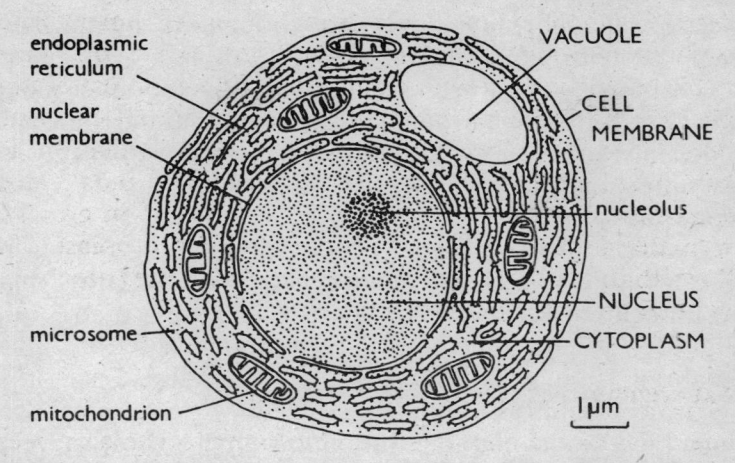

Fig. 3.1 Section of a cell as seen under the electron microscope (centrioles and Golgi apparatus not shown)

(especially in plants) contain a vacuole, or vacuoles, which are separated from the cytoplasm by another membrane. The cytoplasm also contains oval or sausage-shaped **mitochondria** and, although these are not shown in the diagram, there may be **chloroplasts**, grains of stored food, such as glycogen or starch, and various other bodies. The nucleus is surrounded by its own membrane and within it there are often one or more **nucleoli**. In plants the whole is surrounded by the cell wall.

It used to be thought that cytoplasm was a more or less jelly-like solution without any structure, but it is now known that a large part, or nearly all, of it is occupied by a series of folded membranes forming the **endoplasmic reticulum**. In a section (as represented in Fig. 3.1) the membranes appear as thin lines. They enclose a series of narrow spaces. Between the folds are numerous minute granules, or **microsomes** (appearing as dots in the diagram), many of which are attached to the membranes of the endoplasmic reticulum. They are thought to be the sites where protein is manufactured.

The mitochondria are each bounded by a double membrane. The inner membrane, as shown in the illustration, is folded inwards to form a series of transverse partitions across the mitochondrion. Respiration takes place in the mitochondria.

In plant cells carrying out photosynthesis, the cytoplasm contains chloroplasts, which are generally a little larger than the mitochondria; they have quite a complicated structure (Fig. 3.2). The whole chloroplast is bounded by a double membrane similar to that of the mitochondria. Inside this is a watery solution in which there are a number of disc-shaped bodies containing the chlorophyll. These have a sandwich-like structure, with up to 100 alternating layers of chlorophyll and other substances. Each is therefore rather like a stack of coins. Neighbouring stacks are connected by thin membranes continuous with some of the layers in the stacks.

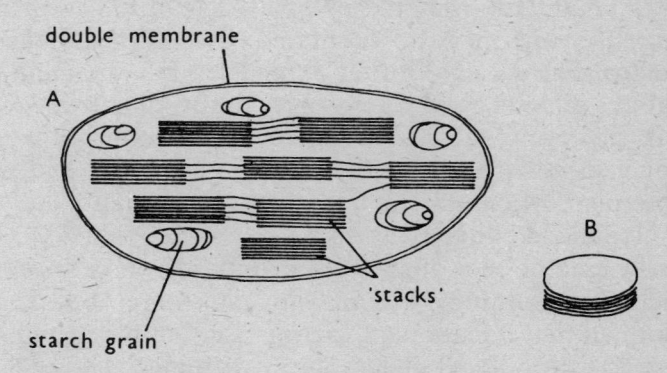

Fig. 3.2 (A) Chloroplast in section as seen under the electron microscope. Its diameter is approximately 5 μm. The 'stacks' consist of layers of chlorophyll and other substances sandwiched together. (B) A 'stack' as it might appear in three dimensions

The chloroplast may contain many grains of starch, a product of photosynthesis.

Not a great deal of structure is visible in the cell nucleus, even when it is examined by means of the electron microscope. However, it is known that it contains a substance, nucleic acid, which is present, in combination with protein, in the form of long fibres or threads. These become much thickened, and therefore easily visible, when the cell is dividing. They are known as chromosomes. The nucleic acid has an essential part to play in the process by which the characteristics of an organism are passed on to offspring, as will be explained. The whole nucleus is surrounded by a double membrane, the outer layer of which is joined at various points to the cytoplasmic reticulum. The nuclear membrane has a number of holes, or pores, in it, some of which are shown in Fig. 3.1.

The above description indicates the important place of various membranes in cell structure. Not only do they form the boundaries of the cell and bodies inside it, such as the nucleus and mitochondria, but they are also the basis of internal structure—of the chloroplasts, mitochondria and, above all, the cytoplasmic reticulum. These membranes are all thought to have a similar structure, consisting basically of a sandwich with a layer of a fatty substance (lipid) between two layers of protein.

At this point in taking the cell to pieces we have reached very small dimensions. Cells are usually measured in terms of micrometres (μm), a micrometre being a thousandth of a millimetre, and a small cell may be about 10 μm across. (A red blood cell is 7–8 μm in diameter, for example.) In the case of cell membranes the nanometre (nm) is more appropriate. One nanometre is equal to one thousandth of a micrometre. The cell membrane is 7.5–10 nm in thickness (i.e. $\frac{1}{100}$ μm at its thickest), while the individual layers in the sandwich are only 2–4 nm. This is the same sort of size as a large molecule—indeed, some of the very largest molecules in the cell are probably much more than 10 nm in length. The building bricks of molecules are, of course, atoms, and especially important in living organisms is the carbon atom. A carbon atom is about 0.15 nm in diameter.

We shall now consider the structure of some of the kinds of molecule that play a vital part in the living machinery.

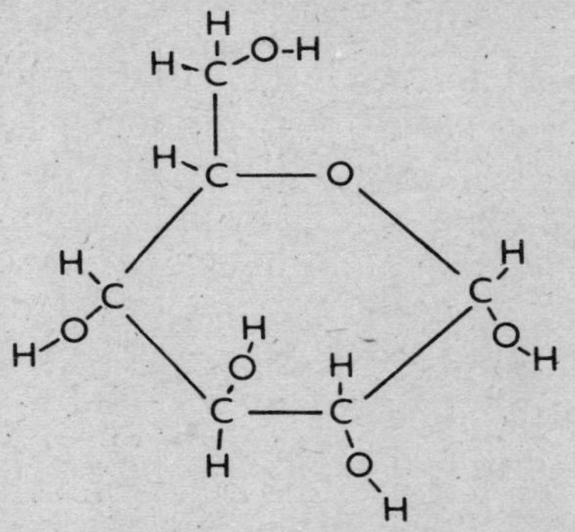

Fig. 3.3 Diagram showing the way the atoms are linked together in a glucose molecule (C = a carbon, H a hydrogen and O an oxygen atom)

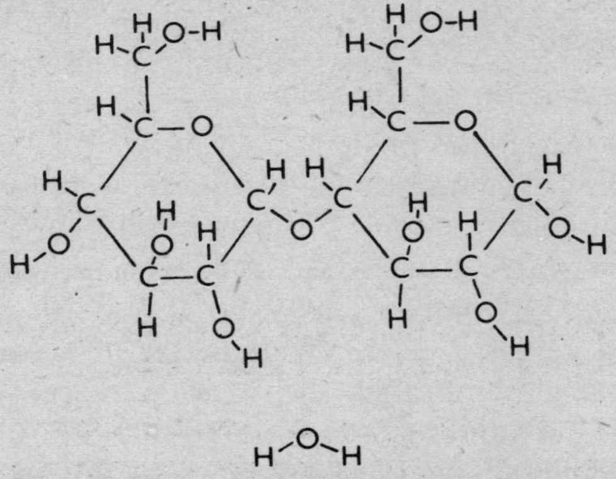

Fig. 3.4 The arrangement of atoms in a maltose molecule and a water molecule—which are formed by the linking together of two glucose molecules (see text and Fig. 3.3)

Carbohydrates

Fig. 3.3 shows the structure of a glucose molecule. It is built around a ring of six atoms: five carbon and one oxygen. Attached to this central core are another carbon atom and a number of hydrogen and oxygen atoms. (The total numbers are: six carbon, twelve hydrogen and six oxygen, represented by the chemical formula $C_6H_{12}O_6$.)

Two of these molecules may become joined together, as shown in Fig. 3.4. In effect, two hydrogen atoms and one oxygen atom become removed at certain points on the molecules, which then become joined to one another. The result is the formation of a new larger molecule containing two six-atom rings. This is the molecule of a new sugar known as maltose (since it is present in malt). The hydrogen and oxygen atoms removed in the process join up with each other to make a molecule of water (H_2O). Thus when this process is repeated millions of times over the result is the conversion of a certain amount of glucose into maltose and water. (Such a change is not easily accomplished by the chemist in the laboratory, but it happens regularly in living organisms with no difficulty at all, in consequence of the peculiar properties of enzymes.)

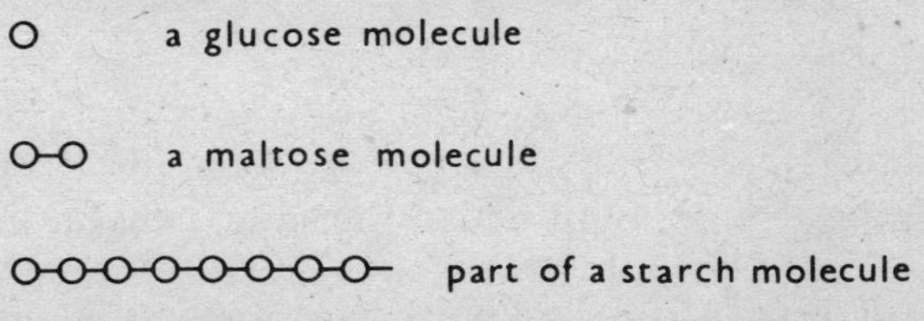

```
O           a glucose molecule

O-O         a maltose molecule

O-O-O-O-O-O-O-O-    part of a starch molecule
```

Fig. 3.5 Diagrammatic representation of a glucose molecule, a maltose molecule and a starch molecule

The linking process may be repeated over and over again, producing chains of hundreds, or even thousands, of glucose units (Fig. 3.5). The resulting large molecule is a molecule of starch. Now we can understand the relationship between this carbohydrate and sugars. When starch is broken down in digestion the linking process is put into reverse. Thus the amylase present in saliva breaks up the starch chain into two-unit pieces—molecules of maltose. Further digestion takes place in the intestine, where more amylase completes the work of the amylase of the mouth and another enzyme splits each of the resulting maltose molecules into two glucose molecules. In this way the original large starch molecules are broken down in two stages into relatively small glucose molecules. It will be remembered that, after absorption, surplus glucose is converted into glycogen. This is accomplished by the building-up process, since glycogen is chemically very similar to starch and is built up in the same way.

Most of the varied carbohydrates of the organism may be compared with those just described. They are either 'single-unit' sugars with one ring structure in the molecule, like glucose, but with variations in the exact number and arrangement of the carbon, hydrogen and oxygen atoms; 'two-unit' sugars, like maltose; or 'multi-unit' carbohydrates, such as starch or glycogen. An important example of the last kind is cellulose, of which the cell walls of plants are largely composed.

Proteins

Protein molecules are built up on the same general principle as the multi-unit carbohydrates. In this case the basic units are molecules of amino acids. A molecule of the simplest kind of amino acid (glycine) is illustrated in Fig. 3.6 (A). Other amino acids have more complicated arrangements of atoms at the point marked 'x' but are otherwise the same. The presence of a nitrogen atom will be noticed. This accounts for the importance of that element in proteins and, therefore, in living organisms.

Biochemistry and the Cell 115

Two amino acid molecules may be linked together in much the same way as two glucose molecules, as illustrated in Fig. 3.6 (B). Repetition leads to the formation of a multi-unit chain, which is a molecule of protein.

Protein molecules are generally much more complex than carbohydrates. This arises from two facts: first, whereas multi-unit carbohydrates are built up from one kind of unit only (e.g. glucose), or at most two, protein molecules always contain a variety of amino acids. There are about twenty

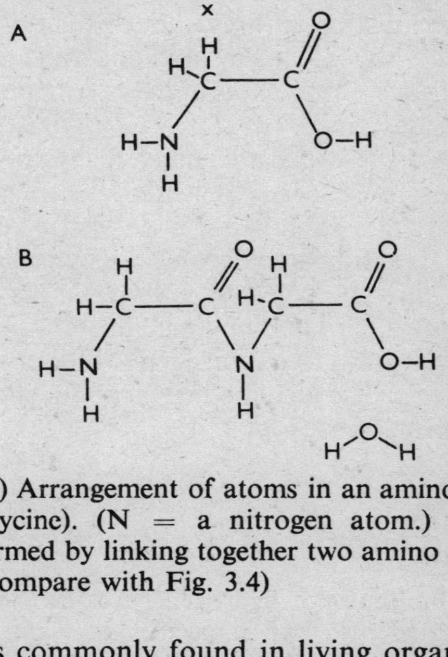

Fig. 3.6 (A) Arrangement of atoms in an amino acid molecule (glycine). (N = a nitrogen atom.) (B) Molecules formed by linking together two amino acid molecules. (Compare with Fig. 3.4)

amino acids commonly found in living organisms. Protein molecules vary in the type and arrangement of the amino acid units of which they are composed. Secondly, the long chains of amino acids may be joined by numerous side-links to produce complex structures. Plate 3 shows a molecule of myoglobin, a protein similar to the haemoglobin of red blood corpuscles. Not only do proteins form a very important part of the structure of the cell—they enter into the composition of the various membranes, as explained above—but they also perform a vital function in the chemical machinery. This arises from the fact that certain proteins, the enzymes, act as catalysts, controlling the chemical reactions going on in the organism.

Enzymes

Enzymes have already been encountered in connection with digestion, but it must be realised that this is only one of the many processes with which they are concerned. To illustrate their characteristics some experiments with one particular example will be described.

The one chosen is especially convenient for experiment because its effect is so easily detected and measured. It is called catalase and is found in a wide variety of plant and animal tissues. Its action is to decompose hydrogen peroxide, breaking it down to oxygen and water. This is a simple reaction, hydrogen peroxide being a substance in which the molecules each contain two hydrogen atoms combined with two oxygen atoms. The enzyme brings about the removal of one of the oxygen atoms (Fig. 3.7).

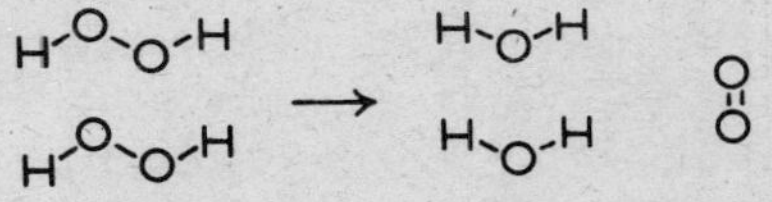

Fig. 3.7 Two molecules of hydrogen peroxide (on the left) are converted into two molecules of water and one of oxygen

A convenient source of catalase is yeast, and its effect can be seen if a pinch of yeast is mixed with a little hydrogen peroxide, such as may be bought at any chemist. The hydrogen peroxide immediately begins to fizz and bubble, owing to the formation of oxygen gas. The gas may be collected and measured, using the apparatus shown in Fig. 3.8. Thus it is easy to discover what volume of oxygen is given off in a given time, which tells us how fast the enzyme is acting. For some purposes it is sufficient simply to count the number of bubbles coming out of the delivery tube.

The effect of heat on the enzyme is interesting. This may be studied by heating the water bath (Fig. 3.8) and measuring the temperature with a thermometer. At first the reaction rate increases as the temperature rises. This sort of effect is familiar to anyone who has studied chemistry. Warming chemicals always makes them react faster. However, in this case something unexpected happens. At about 40°C the rate suddenly starts to fall and soon no bubbles of oxygen appear at all. The effect is shown by the graph in Fig. 3.9. The explanation of this is simple. If some of the yeast is heated to about 50°C for a time, and then cooled and mixed

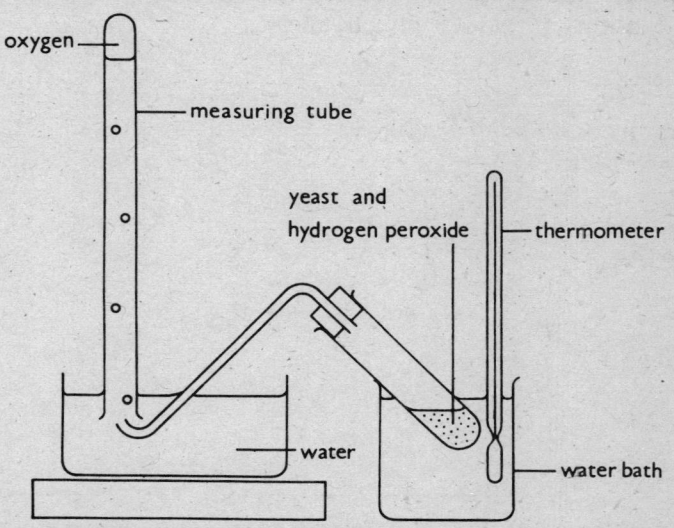

Fig. 3.8 Apparatus used to study the rate of reaction of catalase

with hydrogen peroxide, nothing happens. The catalase in it

has no effect. In fact, too high a temperature destroys the enzyme. This is probably because heat disrupts the complex structure of the protein of which the enzyme is made and this structure is essential for its activity.

Other things may prevent the enzyme from working properly. Thus, if a little acid is added to the yeast and hydrogen peroxide mixture, the production of oxygen may slow down or cease altogether. In this case the effect is not permanent, and if the acid is neutralised by adding an equivalent amount of alkali the enzyme activity is restored. However, if too much alkali is added, again the reaction is slowed down, only to be restored if the excess alkali is neutralised by the right amount of acid. In fact, there is a certain level of acidity—only just on the acid side of neutrality—at which the enzyme works best, and departures from this in the direction of either more acidity or more alkalinity impair its effectiveness.

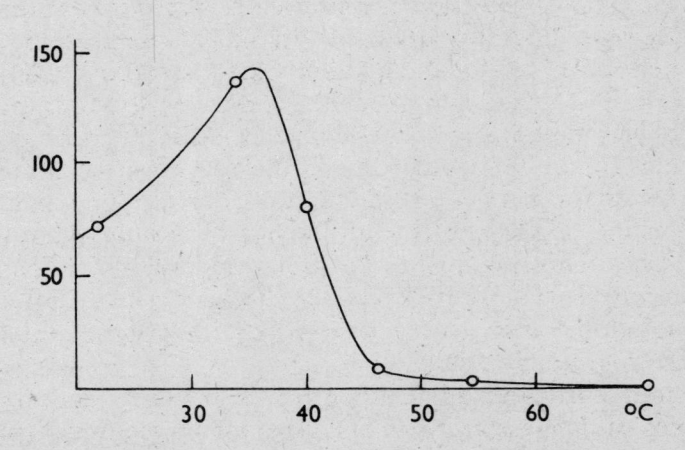

Fig. 3.9 Graph showing effect of varying temperature on rate of action of catalase

All enzymes are affected in the ways described, although the exact temperature or level of acidity at which the effects are shown varies according to the particular enzyme involved. These effects help us to understand some of the properties of living things. For example, the influence of temperature on organisms is well known. All gardeners know that warmth speeds up plant growth. They may also be aware that too high a temperature may kill a plant. Different plants have different temperature requirements, so that tropical plants will usually not grow successfully in temperate regions and, equally, temperate plants may not succeed in the tropics. These effects are generally traceable to the fact that the metabolism of plants depends upon the combined activity of many enzymes and, just as temperature has a twofold effect on the individual enzyme, so it does on the whole organism.

Similar effects can be seen in animals: bees become inactive as the temperature falls in the evening and tortoises as colder days come in the autumn. In the case of warm-blooded animals the effect is obscured by the fact that they are able to maintain a constant internal temperature.

The effects of acidity and alkalinity are also often evident. For example, although saliva is more or less neutral, gastric juice contains hydrochloric acid, so that the stomach contents are quite strongly acid. Bile, however, contains alkaline salts which neutralise the acid when the food enters the intestine, so the acidity of different parts of the digestive tract varies. This is related to the preferred level of acidity of the various enzymes: those in the stomach work best in acid solution, whereas the others require approximately neutral conditions.

Certain particular substances are capable of rendering enzymes completely inactive. Such substances are frequently powerful poisons. For example, cyanide destroys the activity of one of the enzymes concerned with internal respiration.

120 Biology

Very small quantities of the substance block respiration and so cause the death of the organism—a dramatic illustration of the fundamental importance of enzymes to life.

All the enzymes that have been mentioned so far have been concerned with breaking down molecules, but it should be realised that enzymes are equally concerned with building-up processes. Thus enzymes catalyse reactions by means of which glucose molecules are linked together to form starch molecules, and others play a vital part in photosynthesis and the manufacture of proteins.

How do enzymes work? It is thought that they probably bring about their effects by combining temporarily with the substances whose reactions they control. This is illustrated diagrammatically in Fig. 3.10. A molecule of enzyme locks onto a molecule of a substance X. As a result, a strain is set up within X so that it breaks into two parts, Y and Z, which then separate from the enzyme molecule. So the effect is to convert X into Y and Z, while the enzyme remains unaltered

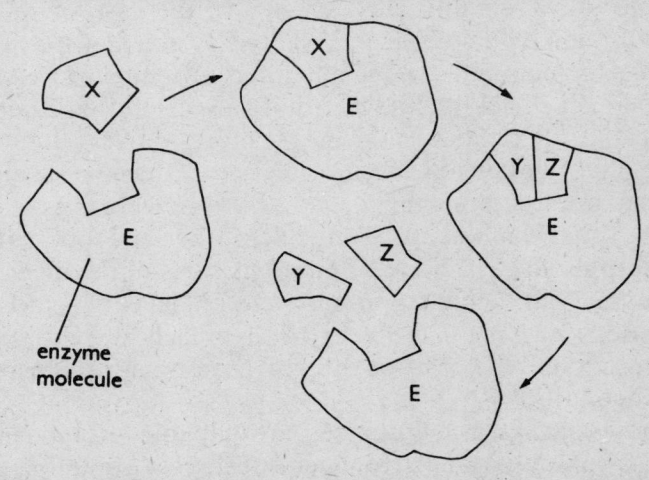

Fig. 3.10 Possible mode of action of an enzyme. See text for explanation

Biochemistry and the Cell 121

and capable of repeating the process with an indefinite number of other X molecules. Because of this, small quantities of an enzyme are able to bring about a large amount of chemical change without being used up.

This picture of the enzyme mechanism also accounts for another characteristic of enzymes: the fact that each kind of enzyme generally affects only one reaction. For example, amylase will convert starch into maltose but not maltose into glucose; the enzymes that break down proteins into amino acids have no effect on starch. This is easily explained if we assume (very reasonably) that the enzyme molecule must be shaped in such a way that it fits onto the kind of molecule that it affects, as suggested in Fig. 3.10. If it fits one kind of molecule it is unlikely to fit another.

This also helps us to understand how heat inactivates enzymes. We know from other evidence that heat must be capable of altering the structure of protein molecules, and it is obvious that such an alteration would have a disastrous effect on an enzyme.

Biochemical systems

The enzyme mechanism explained above may be represented as

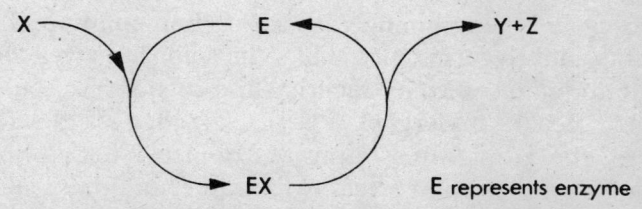

$$X \longrightarrow E \longleftarrow Y+Z$$
$$\searrow \qquad \nearrow$$
$$EX \qquad \text{E represents enzyme}$$

which serves to emphasise the cyclic nature of the conversion of enzyme into enzyme-combined-with-X and back to enzyme, such that the enzyme is not used up in the process. Such an arrangement seems to be characteristic of biochemical systems. An example we have encountered already is afforded by haemoglobin. This combines with oxygen in the lungs and gives it up in the respiring tissues, so that it is ready to take up more oxygen on its return to the lungs:

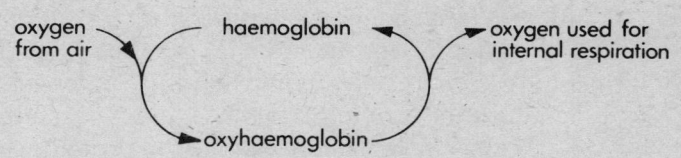

oxygen from air → haemoglobin ← oxygen used for internal respiration
→ oxyhaemoglobin →

An important part of internal respiration itself is made up of a whole chain of chemical reactions forming a cycle, the citric acid cycle. This is rather complicated, but a simplified account may serve to convey the essence of what happens and to indicate the complexity of respiration. The cycle is shown in Fig. 3.11, where the various molecules involved are represented by figures (6, 5 etc.) showing the number of carbon atoms present in each. Oxygen and hydrogen atoms are linked with the carbon atoms in every case.

In the first stage of respiration, the molecule of glucose (containing six carbon atoms) is broken down in several stages to yield two molecules of carbon dioxide (CO_2) and two of a 2-carbon compound. The latter enters the citric acid cycle by combining with a 4-carbon compound (oxaloacetic acid) to form citric acid—the acid that gives the sharp taste to lemon juice—which has a 6-carbon molecule. Now this molecule undergoes a series of changes. In some of these, the atoms are simply rearranged, so that the total number of each kind remains the same; in others, hydrogen atoms are removed, as indicated in the diagram; and in yet others, carbon and oxygen are removed in the form of carbon dioxide. After six of these changes a new molecule of oxaloacetic acid is produced, ready to start the cycle of changes all over again. The net effect of the system is to

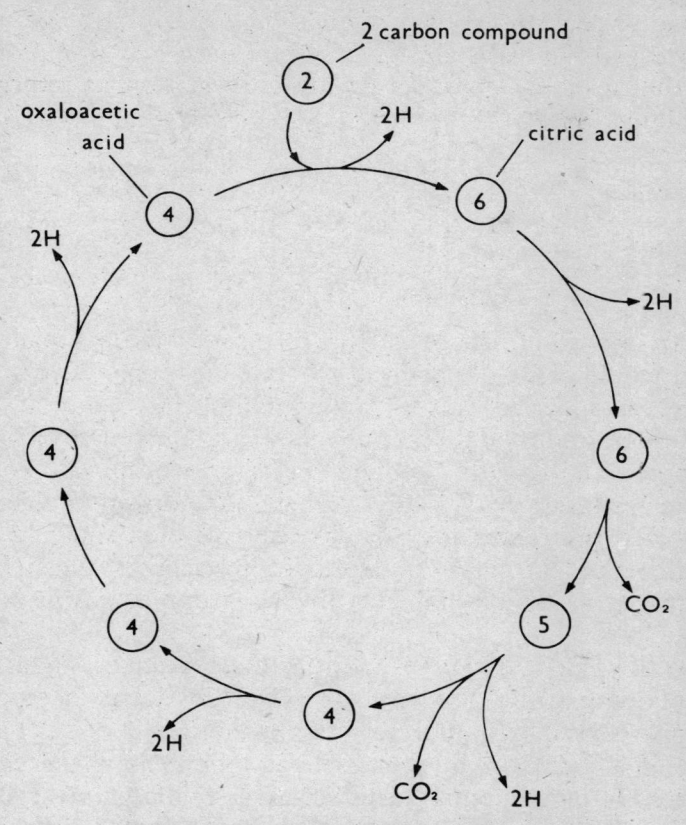

Fig. 3.11 The citric acid cycle

convert the original 2-carbon molecule into two carbon dioxide molecules and ten hydrogen atoms.

The hydrogen atoms are not actually released in the cell. Instead, they are caused to combine temporarily with certain complex molecules present, being passed from one to another through a chain of chemical reactions until eventually they combine with the oxygen absorbed in external respiration and so form molecules of water (H_2O).

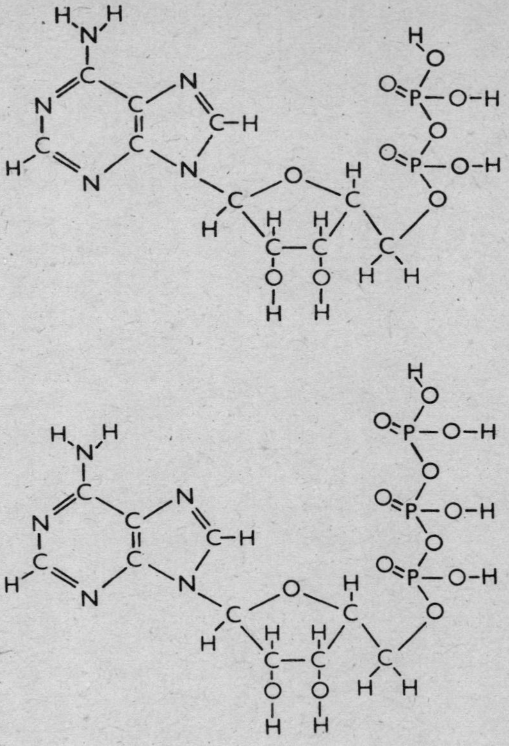

Fig. 3.12 Structures of the molecules of (1) ADP and (2) ATP. The letters represent atoms, as in Figs. 3.3 and 3.6. P = a phosphorus atom

The whole object of respiration is, of course, to release energy from the substance respired (e.g. glucose). The transfer of this energy from respiration to other processes is brought about through yet another cyclic process.

Several of the respiration reactions involve a substance called adenosine phosphate. This can exist as adenosine diphosphate (ADP) or as adenosine triphosphate (ATP).

The molecules of these two forms are illustrated in Fig. 3.12. They look rather complicated, but the thing to notice is that they differ principally in the number of phosphorus and oxygen atoms. In particular, one has two phosphorus atoms and the other three. So the two kinds of molucule might be represented as

A —(P)—(P)   A —(P)—(P)—(P)
ADP   ATP

where P represents a phosphorus atom combined with some oxygen atoms. Adding the extra phosphorus atom requires energy and, equally, if the extra atom is lost energy is given out. Thus ATP can be regarded as containing stored energy. The source of this is respiration. This comes about because, in the chain of reactions which make up respiration, phosphorus atoms are taken up from simple phosphates present in the cell and transferred to ADP. The energy to do this comes from the breakdown of glucose. Thus the mitochondria, where respiration takes place, are like power stations, producing ATP instead of electricity. It passes out into the cytoplasm from the mitochondria and drives practically all the processes requiring energy, such as the contraction of muscle and the building up of large molecules.

The function of the nucleus and nucleic acid

It should be clear by now that proteins are at the very heart of what we call life. Indeed, these substances do not exist apart from living organisms. A few have been analysed completely, and chemists can, by laborious techniques, join one amino acid to another and so begin the process that could lead to the creation of a protein molecule; however, to complete the task using known methods seems almost hopeless, so huge and so complex are these chemical structures. Proteins are essential to life, not merely because

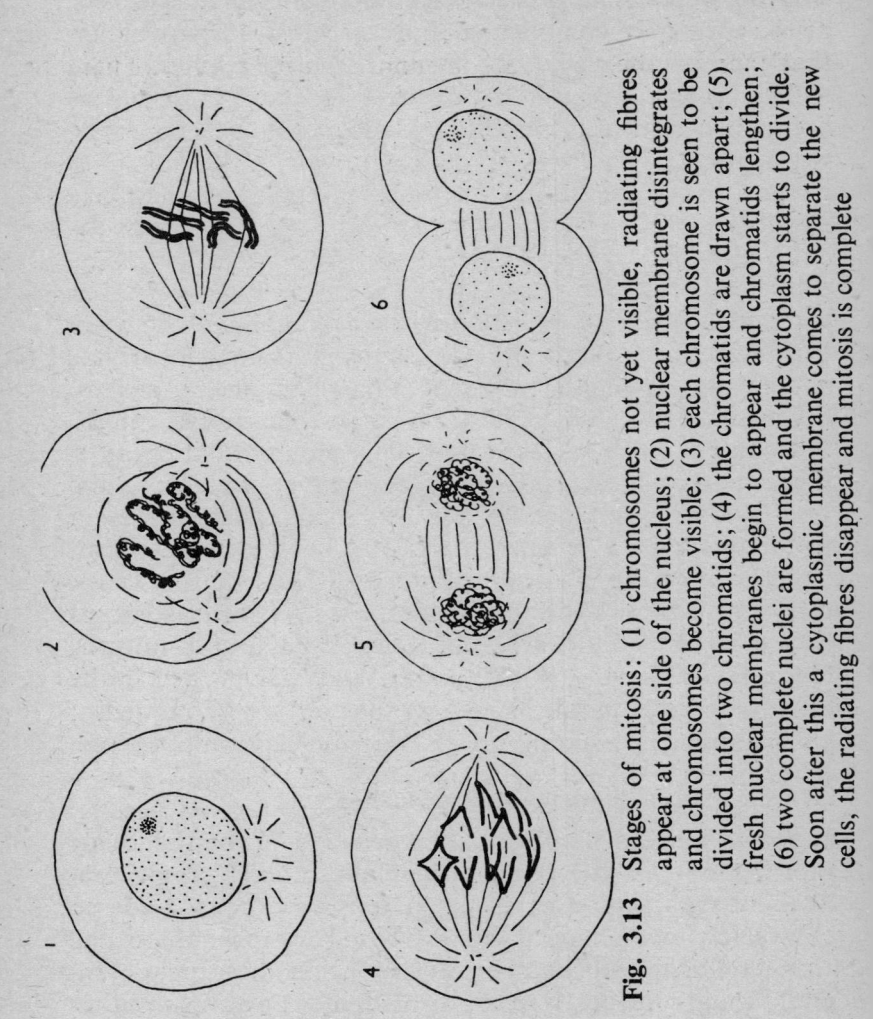

Fig. 3.13 Stages of mitosis: (1) chromosomes not yet visible, radiating fibres appear at one side of the nucleus; (2) nuclear membrane disintegrates and chromosomes become visible; (3) each chromosome is seen to be divided into two chromatids; (4) the chromatids are drawn apart; (5) fresh nuclear membranes begin to appear and chromatids lengthen; (6) two complete nuclei are formed and the cytoplasm starts to divide. Soon after this a cytoplasmic membrane comes to separate the new cells, the radiating fibres disappear and mitosis is complete

they form the major part of living matter but also because, in the form of enzymes, they control all those happenings that, far more than any material, constitute the essence of life.

One might wonder what it is that produces and controls the enzymes themselves. When a zygote has been formed, what sets the whole process of development in motion, with its growing complex of chemical reactions? At first one might think that it was just a matter of a small part of the enzyme system—the part that makes up the zygote—being passed on from the parents and then reproducing itself as the zygote divided and gave rise to the cells of the embryo. But further consideration suggests that it is not the enzyme system, i.e. the cytoplasm, that is concerned, but the nucleus. Some gametes, for instance sperms, consist of not very much more than a nucleus. At fertilisation it seems clear that it is the joining of the nuclei of the gametes that is essential, and when cell division occurs this is started by certain very complex events in the nucleus.

Fig. 3.13 shows what happens when a cell divides in the process called **mitosis**. The sausage-shaped chromosomes (Fig. 3.13 (2) and (3)) are not visible at the start of mitosis, but it seems that this is only because they are present in the form of very long, thin threads, too narrow to be distinguished under the microscope. When cell division begins the chromosomes gradually become shorter and thicker as a result of a coiling process, so that in time they become visible, at first as long, tangled threads and finally as comparatively short, thick objects which collect in the middle of the cell. At this stage it can be seen that each chromosome is made up of two halves, known as chromatids, lying parallel to one another. Meanwhile, a number of fine fibres appear in the cytoplasm, radiating from opposite ends of the cell on either side of the cluster of chromosomes. These are attached to certain points on the chromatids in such a way that contraction of the fibres draws each pair of chromatids apart. The effect is that each chromosome is split in half and the halves move to opposite ends of the cell (Fig. 3.13 (4) and (5)). Next a nuclear membrane appears around each group of chromatids, which meanwhile become uncoiled and finally indistinguishable. Thus two new nuclei are produced by division of the old one. Following this the cytoplasm also divides, being separated into two halves by a new portion of cell membrane (and a cell wall in plants), and so two new cells are formed. Before these divide again, the chromatids in their nuclei evidently produce replicas of themselves, since at the start of the next mitosis they are seen to be double structures—i.e. chromosomes each consisting of two chromatids—as in the previous mitosis.

The most significant feature of mitosis is the fact that it results in the formation of daughter nuclei that have exactly the same chromosome make-up as the parent nucleus. Not only does each species of animal or plant have a characteristic number of chromosomes in each nucleus (e.g. forty-six in man, fourteen in a buttercup), but also the individual chromosomes have their own characteristics (for example, they differ from each other in details of shape). Mitosis ensures that every cell descended from a particular zygote has the same kinds and number of chromosomes.

It is now known that this is necessary because the chromosomes control the formation of protein (and hence the whole structure and activity of the cell) in such a way that every chromosome is needed. The absence of a chromosome may be lethal, or at least cause serious abnormality, as does the presence of extra chromosomes. For example, it has been shown that mongolism in humans is due to the presence of an extra chromosome acquired at conception.

The chromosomes are composed of protein and a substance that has come to be known universally as DNA (deoxyribose nucleic acid). It is the latter that is particularly important. It is a substance with molecules every bit as

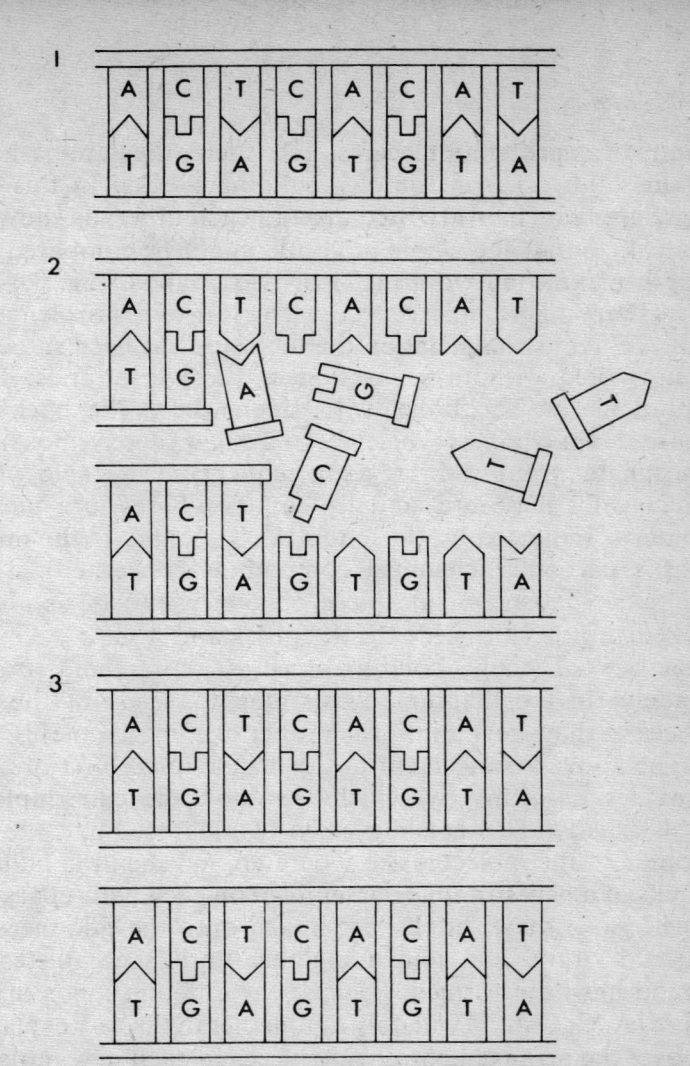

Fig. 3.14 Diagrammatic representation of part of a DNA molecule and its duplication: (1) the complete molecule consists of two strands, each of which is made up of a backbone with side-pieces of four kinds (labelled A, C, G and T) which join the two strands together; in (2) the strands have become separated and new building bricks are being added to each, so that finally (3) two complete molecules are produced, each identical with the original

complex as protein molecules. Like them, they are based on chains built up from simpler building blocks. In this case there are two chains twisted around each other, as shown in Plate 4, so that the whole molecule might be compared to a length of knitting wool made of two strands. Fig. 3.14 (1) shows very diagrammatically the structure of a short length of this. To avoid complication the molecule has been shown as if untwisted without separation of the two strands. Each strand has a 'backbone' with side pieces. The backbone consists of a chain of molecules of a sugar (deoxyribose) and phosphate groups* in regular sequence. The side pieces (chemically these are actually complex bases) are of four kinds, as indicated by the letters A, C, G and T (the initials of the particular chemical compounds concerned). These are such that an A side piece on one backbone is always linked to a T side piece on the other and a C to a G. The necessity of these combinations is represented (rather crudely) in the diagram by shaping the ends of the side pieces so that they fit into each other like jig-saw pieces.

The above arrangement has two functions. First of all, it provides a means by which the molecule can duplicate itself exactly. This is achieved in two stages. First, the two strands of the molecule are separated and then the building bricks of a new strand are assembled on each half separately. One by one these 'bricks' are linked onto the side pieces of the old strand and joined together until a complete new strand has been formed. Because the different kinds of side piece (A, C, G or T) will only fit together in the way explained above, the arrangement of side pieces in each new molecule must be just the same as it was in the old. Figures 3.14 (2) and (3) show how this comes about.

It is this process of duplication (or *replication* as it is usually called) that lies behind the replication of chromatids

* A phosphate group consists of a phosphorus atom with oxygen atoms linked to it, as in ATP (Fig. 3.12 (2)).

mentioned above. Between one mitosis and the next, the DNA molecules are replicated, and this leads to replication of the chromatids in which the DNA is found.

The second function of the DNA structure has to do with the control of protein synthesis. The amino acids that go to make up a particular kind of protein are arranged in a particular sequence in the protein molecule, the sequence being unique for each kind of protein. Thus it would seem that the properties of the protein (for example, whether it is an enzyme and, if so, what reactions it catalyses) are largely determined by this sequence. Similarly, each kind of DNA molecule has a unique sequence of side pieces. It has been shown that the two kinds of sequence are closely related. In fact, the sequence in each kind of protein molecule is decided by the sequence in a corresponding DNA molecule. The A, C, G, T units are like the letters of a code that spells out the right order of amino acids. The 'words' of the code have three letters, i.e. a group of three paired units $\left(\text{e.g. } \begin{matrix} G\,T\,C \\ C\,A\,G \end{matrix}\right)$ is needed to specify one amino acid molecule.

The manufacture of proteins occurs in the microsomes (Fig. 3.1, p. 109), which are in the cytoplasmic reticulum, whereas the DNA of the chromosomes, which controls protein synthesis, is in the nucleus. The exact way in which the two things are connected is complex and not fully understood. It involves a second type of nucleic acid, RNA (ribose nucleic acid), which is built up on the DNA molecules in much the same way as new DNA strands (Fig. 3.14), so that they preserve the code. The RNA then migrates into the cytoplasm and enters into protein synthesis. Here again, it seems probable that the amino acid building bricks are assembled on the RNA molecules, so that the right sequence is achieved. ATP also enters into the process and is the source of the necessary energy.

Chromosome number

When two gametes unite to form a zygote, the nuclei fuse together and so the two sets of chromosomes are added together to form one set. If each gamete has twelve chromosomes, the zygote has twenty-four. As development proceeds, mitosis ensures that each cell in the resulting organism also has twenty-four chromosomes. One might think that, when the new organism reproduced, its gametes would also have the same number and therefore give rise to offspring with as many as forty-eight chromosomes. However, it is clear that this sort of thing cannot happen in practice, since it would mean that in every generation the chromosome number would double and very soon become astronomically large. In real life this does not happen, because there is always a

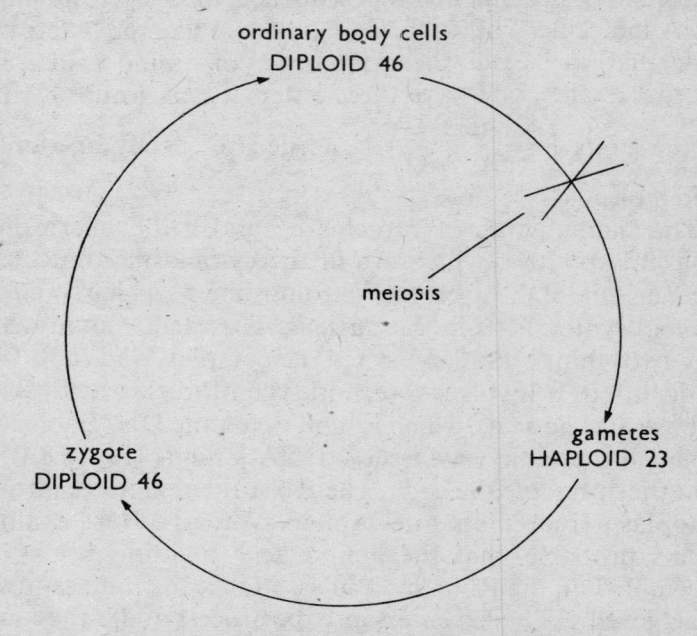

Fig. 3.15 The human life cycle

stage in the life cycle where the chromosome number is halved to compensate for the doubling caused by the union of gametes. The halving is achieved by a special form of cell division, **meiosis**, in which the chromosomes from a parent nucleus are divided into two groups, each containing half the original number of chromosomes. Each group gives rise to future nuclei descended from that division, all of which have half the chromosome number. (Further details are given in Chapter 6.)

In flowering plants and higher animals meiosis takes place at or just before gamete formation and, consequently, gametes have half the chromosome number of the ordinary cells of the organism. The former are said to be *haploid*, whereas the latter are *diploid*. Thus the human life cycle can be represented as in Fig. 3.15.

4 The Variety of Organisms

Although all life appears to have the same biochemical basis, the variety of organisms to which this has given rise is astonishing. It is the aim of this chapter to attempt to portray some of this variety and to suggest some of the reasons for it.

Even casual observation tells us that living things fall naturally into a number of groupings, such as the vertebrates, insects, flowering plants and fungi. Each group represents one general way of organising living matter, although we may recognise that there is still wide variation within the group. (Amongst mammals we find some that eat almost nothing but grass, others that eat nothing but flesh, some that fly and others that can exist only in water, for example.) It follows that in attempting to survey varieties of organisation we are bound to become acquainted with the way in which living organisms are classified.

It has long been customary to divide all life into two kingdoms, the Animal Kingdom and the Plant Kingdom. The first includes not only animals in the popular sense (and the word is often, mistakenly, taken to mean only four-legged animals and their close relatives) but also birds, fish, insects, spiders, snails, earthworms, sea anemones, corals, jelly fish, sponges, sea urchins and many others. They are, typically, organisms that take in food by means of a mouth, or some such organ, and are capable of locomotion. Those exceptions that do not conform to this description are, nevertheless, more or less obviously related to those that do.

The Plant Kingdom includes, as well as green plants and their allies, the fungi and other micro-organisms, such as bacteria. Typically, they absorb food in solution (as flowering plants, with some exceptions, do through their roots) and are not capable of locomotion. It can be argued that it would better reflect the true relationships of some of the major groups if more than two major divisions of the living world were recognised.

Each kingdom is subdivided into a number of divisions, or phyla, each of these into a number of classes and these again into a succession of smaller subdivisions, as in the following scheme:

kingdom

divisions or phyla*

classes

orders

families

genera*

species*

A species is made up of a number of individuals that are all alike, except for minor variations, and, potentially at least, can mate or breed with each other under normal conditions and produce fertile offspring. The meadow buttercup is an example. Other kinds of buttercup (e.g. the creeping buttercup, the bulbous buttercup), although in many ways similar, exhibit distinct differences. The creeping

* The singular form of these words are, respectively, phylum, genus, species.

buttercup has leaves that differ in shape from those of the meadow buttercup and stems that grow horizontally along the ground, for example. On the other hand, the three species have so many likenesses that it seems that they must all be descended from the same ancestral species which existed long, long ago. They are so closely related that they are included in the genus called *Ranunculus*, along with a number of other species. When giving the biological name of an organism, the generic name is always given first, followed by a name that distinguishes the species. Thus the three mentioned above are *Ranunculus acris*, *Ranunculus repens* and *Ranunculus bulbosus*. (It is customary to shorten the name of the genus to the initial letter after the full name has been given once, thus *R. bulbosus*.)

Accounts of representative examples of some of the main phyla will now be given. In a short book it is not possible in most cases to do more than describe one example in some detail and mention others briefly. Some phyla are not mentioned at all, and no attempt is made to go into finer divisions of the classification.

Phylum Protozoa (Animal Kingdom)

The members of this phylum are all microscopic and each consists of but one cell, i.e. a small mass of protoplasm, usually with one nucleus, although there are forms in which several may be present.

Euglena viridis (Fig. 4.1)

The most interesting thing about this organism is that it has both animal-like and plant-like features. Thus it has chlorophyll in chloroplasts and carries out photosynthesis. The cell is bounded by an elastic covering on the outside, similar to a cell wall but not composed of cellulose. On the other hand, there is no large central vacuole, as in the typical plant cell, and, most striking, the organism is capable of locomotion—in fact, it spends most of its time swimming about in the pond water where it lives. The organ of locomotion is the flagellum, a thread of protoplasm that, by means of rapid lashing movements, propels the euglena along a spiral course with the flagellum end foremost. It reacts to light in such a way that it swims towards the source of illumination. This serves to bring it into well-lit regions most favourable for photosynthesis. It has been shown that the reaction depends upon the presence of a spot of pigment and a sensory organ at the base of the flagellum. *Euglena* can also move when in contact with a solid substratum by a wriggling action.

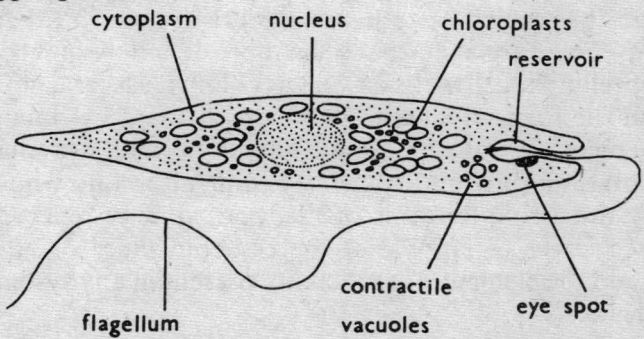

Fig. 4.1 *Euglena viridis* (actual length about 50 μm)

Besides photosynthesising, *Euglena* is able to absorb organic compounds, such as amino acids, from solution.

The purpose of the contractile vacuoles is to remove water absorbed into the cytoplasm by osmosis. The small satellite vacuoles slowly swell through accummulation of water absorbed from the cytoplasm and then suddenly contract, discharging the water into the central vacuole. The latter in turn discharges into the reservoir and the water passes through a canal leading to the exterior.

Reproduction in *Euglena*, as in all these simpler forms of life, is brought about by a form of cell division. The nucleus divides and lengthwise division of the rest of the cell then follows.

No form of sexual reproduction has been observed in *Euglena*, although it does occur in some other members of the phylum.

The Protozoa include a great variety of forms. The majority are definitely animals, lacking chlorophyll and having some form of mouth or gullet through which minute food particles (often bacteria) are taken into the cytoplasm and there digested. Some of these have flagella and appear to be related to *Euglena*. Others swim by means of numerous hair-like cilia which act like minute oars, rowing the creature through the water. Yet others have bristles which function like legs. There are a few that seem more definitely plant-like, having cellulose cell walls as well as chloroplasts and storing food in the form of starch. These are claimed by botanists to be members of the Plant Kingdom and are placed in the division (phylum) Algae. It is difficult to know how to classify these simple forms of life, and we may reflect that this fact serves to emphasise the essential unity of all life forms and the element of artificiality present in any system of classification.

Amoeba proteus (Fig. 4.2)

This is a protozoan that almost everyone has heard of. It used to be held up as representing the simplest form of life. Now, however, we realise that 'simple' is hardly the word to apply to the organisation of even the most ordinary cell, and that bacteria and viruses actually have a less elaborate type of organisation than any of the Protozoa.

This amoeba is another pond dweller. It lives on the bottom, crawling over the mud with a peculiar flowing motion. Except near the surface, the cytoplasm is quite liquid, and during locomotion a rounded projection of the protoplasm (a pseudopodium) develops at one point and, as

The Variety of Organisms 139

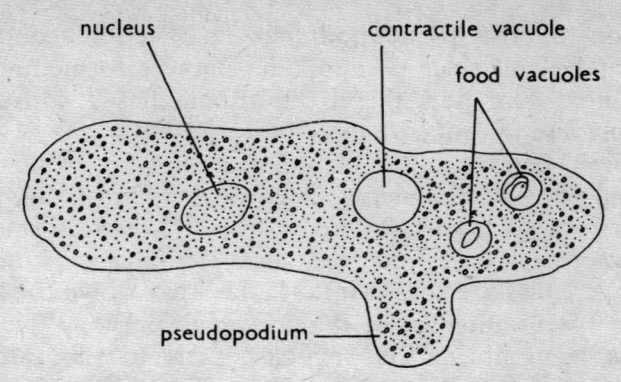

Fig. 4.2 *Amoeba proteus*. This animal may be only about ⅓ mm in length

it swells and elongates, so the cytoplasm flows into it (Fig. 4.3). At the same time, the surface cytoplasm shrinks at other points, so propelling the inner protoplasm in the

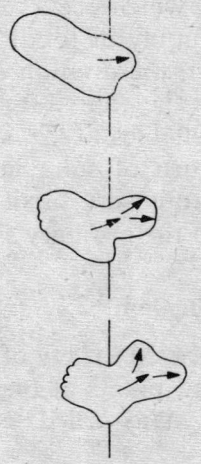

Fig. 4.3 Movement in *Amoeba*. The outline of the animal has been drawn at short intervals. Arrows show the direction of flow of the protoplasm

direction of the pseudopodium. This action continues indefinitely, and since pseudopodia may be formed at any point, now here now there, the animal has a constantly changing and irregular shape.

Amoeba feeds on even smaller organisms, which are engulfed by the cytoplasm as it flows all round them. Each food particle is taken in with a drop of water, forming a food vacuole. This functions as a temporary stomach. Digestive juices are passed into it and break down the food, so that the useful part of it may be absorbed. When the process is complete the vacuole opens to the exterior, expelling the water and any undigested residue.

As in *Euglena*, there is a contractile vacuole, but in this case it is single. It swells gradually as it absorbs water from the cytoplasm and periodically contracts suddenly as the water in it passes to the outside through a temporary opening.

The most usual form of reproduction is by binary fission, i.e. simple cell division, which occurs about every two days when there is a good supply of food. A less common type involves multiple fission, the division of the cell into many parts. This occurs when the animal forms a tough cell wall, called a cyst, which enables it to survive unfavourable conditions. On the return of suitable conditions the cyst breaks open and numerous very small amoebas emerge. In due course they grow to the ordinary size.

Phylum Algae (Plant Kingdom)

This phylum contains a wide variety of forms, ranging from very simple, single-celled plants at one end of the scale to the relatively complex, many-celled seaweeds at the other.

Pleurococcus (Fig. 4.4)

This is familiar to everyone as a thin, green encrustation to be found on tree trunks, old fence posts and palings.

Microscopic examination shows that it consists of nothing but a number of round cells crowded together on the surface. Each cell has a cellulose cell wall, a nucleus, cytoplasm and a single large chloroplast. Reproduction is again by cell division, the resulting cells being attached to each other by their walls. There seems to be no way in which one depends upon another and each is quite capable of surviving on its own, absorbing its requirements, which must be basically the same as those of a flowering plant, from its immediate surroundings.

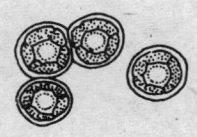

Fig. 4.4 Four cells of *Pleurococcus*. Each cell contains a single chloroplast surrounding the central nucleus

Spirogyra (Fig. 4.5)

This alga is quite common in ponds and slowly flowing streams, and appears as darkish green masses floating just below the surface. When picked up these feel rather slippery —a characteristic which distinguishes *Spirogyra* from other algae of a similar kind. If examined closely it is seen to be made up of a number of hair-like filaments, and use of the microscope shows that these are actually chains of cylindrical cells, as shown in Fig. 4.5 (A). The most prominent feature of the cell is a spiral chloroplast (sometimes more than one is present), which gives the plant its name. The middle of the cell is occupied by a large vacuole and most of the cytoplasm forms a layer lining the cell wall. (The chloroplast, which is flat and ribbon-like, lies in this layer.) However, the nucleus is frequently suspended in the very centre by thin threads of cytoplasm. The filaments are covered by a thin layer of slimy mucilage.

Division of the cells always results in the formation of new transverse walls, so that the number of cells in the filament is increased and growth of the new cells leads to an increase in its length. If the filament is accidentally broken,

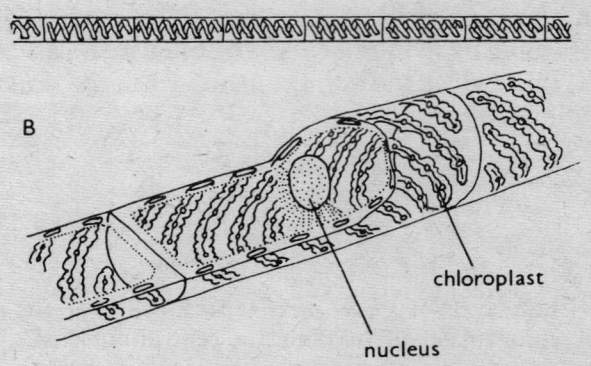

Fig. 4.5 *Spirogyra:* (A) chain of cells forming a small portion of a filament; (B) a cell much enlarged, shown with part cut away to reveal the nucleus suspended in the vacuole

the fragments go on growing independently and the consequence is reproduction of filaments.

There is a form of sexual reproduction in *Spirogyra*, the stages of which are shown in Fig. 4.6. This takes place when a number of filaments come to lie close together. Swellings develop in the cell walls and become joined in the way shown. Following this, the cell walls at the point of junction break down so that a series of tubes are formed, joining the cells of one filament to those of another. The protoplasmic contents of the cells in one filament flow into those of the other and fuse together, i.e. each pair of cells joins to form a single new cell containing one nucleus resulting from fusion of the old. It will be seen that this is a process equivalent to fertilisation in higher organisms. The cells of the filaments taking part function as gametes, and the cells resulting from their fusion are zygotes.

Soon after their formation the zygotes round off and form tough new cell walls, which protect them in the resting stage that follows. They are now called zygospores. Decay of the remains of the filaments releases them, so that they sink into the mud of the pond bottom. Eventually they

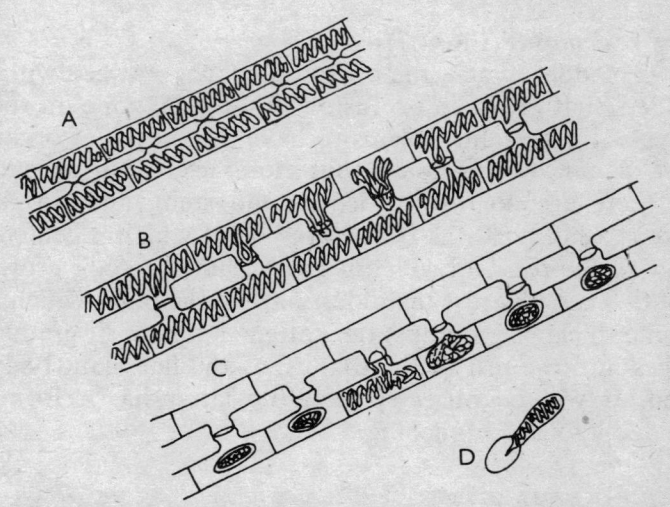

Fig. 4.6 *Spirogyra*—sexual reproduction: (A) early stage; (B) connecting tubes formed and cell contents beginning to migrate from cells of upper filament; (C) zygotes formed in lower filament; (D) zygote germinating

germinate, each growing a new filament. Meiosis (see p. 133) occurs before new cells are produced, so that, although the zygotes are at first diploid, filaments are always haploid.

In *Spirogyra* we see the beginnings of co-operation between cells. In many ways the filament is just a colony of individual cells, reproducing by binary fission, which happen to be joined together end to end. Each cell is a more or less independent unit that would be capable of living on its own. However, one imagines that being joined to other cells may have the advantage of making them less easily washed away by water currents, since the filaments tend to become entangled with larger plants, and the particular mechanism of sexual reproduction depends upon the existence of filaments.

Fucus vesiculosus (Fig. 4.7)

This is bladder wrack, the common brown seaweed with air bladders that grows in profusion in the tidal zone on rocky shores. At first sight it seems to have the degree of organisation of a flowering plant, but closer examination shows that there are no distinct leaves and stem, and no root. There is a holdfast, the base of the plant which is cemented firmly to the rock on which it grows, but the stalk growing from this is really just the oldest part of the plant which has become thickened and lost the flattened flanges. It gradually merges into the rest of the thallus, as the flat plant body is called. It will be observed that the latter has a form of repeatedly forked branching.

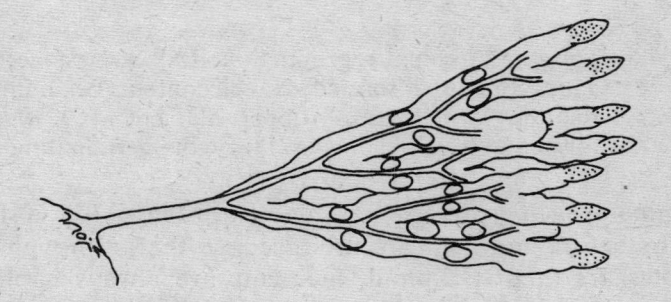

Fig. 4.7 *Fucus vesiculosus* (a small specimen). The dots on the terminal parts of the thallus on the right are the openings of conceptacles

The Variety of Organisms 145

Microscopic examination shows that there are several different types of cell which form at least two distinct tissues (Fig. 4.8 (A) and (B)). There is an outer layer, the cortex, composed of closely packed, rather thick-walled cells forming the tough skin of the plant. Towards the centre the cells are rather elongated and form an open network with a jelly-like substance in the spaces between them. This is the medulla. In the centre itself there are large cells joined end to end and forming what may be a system for conducting substances from one part to another.

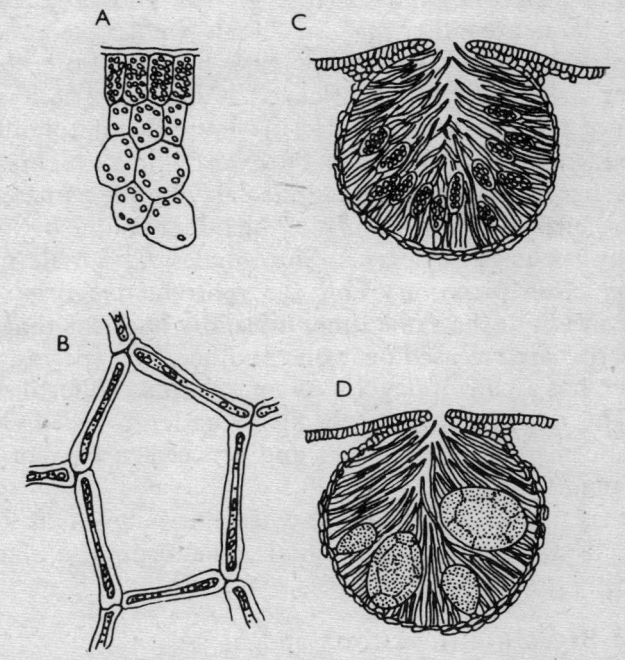

Fig. 4.8 *Fucus vesiculosus:* (A) cells of the cortex (outer layer); (B) cells of the inner tissue; (C) male conceptacle in section (oval organs within it contain sperms); (D) female conceptacle, in which each egg-bearing organ contains eight large egg cells when mature

The brown colour of *Fucus* is due to the presence of a pigment called fucoxanthin. It is contained in small chloroplasts which also hold chlorophyll, and the plant photosynthesises as do ordinary green plants. Raw materials are absorbed from the sea water.

The reproductive organs occur on the swollen ends of the thallus. These are covered with pimples, each one of which marks the site of a tiny flask-shaped cavity, the conceptacle, just below the surface. A number of hair-like cells grow from the sides of the cavities, and amongst these are the organs bearing the gametes (Fig. 4.7 (C) and (D)). In this species plants are either male or female and so the conceptacles produce either sperms or eggs but not both. When gametes are ready to be released a quantity of a slimy substance fills the conceptacles. At low tide the plants are exposed to the air, so that they lose moisture and the thallus shrinks, squeezing the slime carrying the gametes out onto the surface. On the return of the tide the slime dissolves, releasing the eggs or sperms. Since male and female plants grow in close proximity and the reproductive organs all mature at about the same time, it usually happens that eggs and sperms are released near one another. The sperms, each of which has a pair of flagella, swim towards and fertilise the eggs. The resulting zygotes begin to undergo cell division, become cemented to the rocks and proceed to develop into young plants forthwith.

Meiosis in *Fucus* takes place when the gametes are being produced, so that, as in animals, the ordinary plant is diploid.

Phylum Bryophyta (liverworts and mosses)
Pellia (Fig. 4.9)
Many people are unfamiliar with liverworts (although, in fact, they are common enough), probably because they are inconspicuous and easily confused with mosses, lichens and

The Variety of Organisms 147

other lowly plants. *Pellia* is one of the simpler kinds. It grows in damp situations, for example in shady places low down on the steep banks of country lanes or on the rocks beside waterfalls where the spray keeps it perpetually moist. It has a green thallus, in general shape rather similar to *Fucus* because it branches in the same way. However, there is no holdfast and stalk, and the plant is anchored to the soil by numerous hair-like rhizoids growing downwards

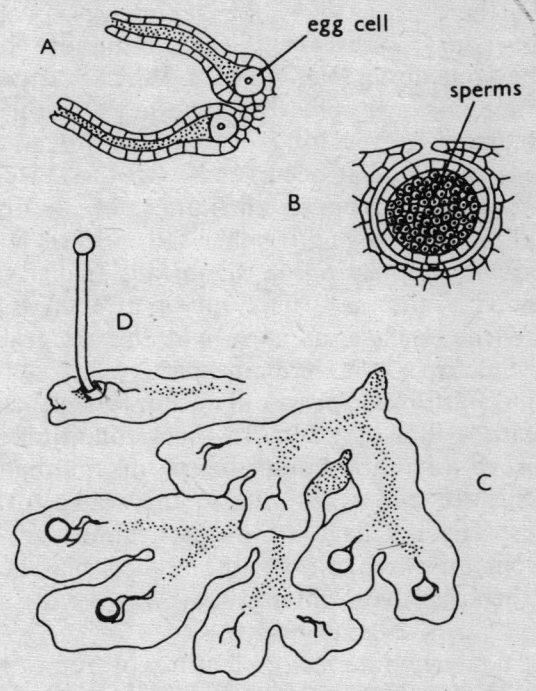

Fig. 4.9 *Pellia epiphylla:* (A) two archegonia ready for fertilisation; (B) antheridium; (C) whole plant with capsules of sporophytes visible near ends of some branches of the thallus; (D) sporophyte capsule being raised on end of stalk. (A and B are shown in section and much magnified; C and D are approximately natural size)

from the midrib of the thallus. Rhizoids are very similar to the root hairs of flowering plants and have similar functions. In microscopic structure the thallus is simpler than that of *Fucus*, since the cells, with the exception of the rhizoids, are all of the same type, very similar to the parenchyma of higher plants.

Perhaps the most interesting thing about *Pellia* is its method of reproduction. Near the ends of the branches of the thallus there are pocket-like depressions protected by overarching outgrowths. In these are minute bottle-like organs, the archegonia (Fig. 4.9(A)). When mature, each of these contains an egg cell, while the neck of the bottle is filled with mucilage resulting from the disintegration of a row of cells that at first occupies it. On the surface of the thallus further away from its ends are the male organs, the antheridia. These are small, spherical capsules with short stalks occupying depressions in the surface. Each is completely surrounded by the thallus, except where there is a narrow opening to the surface, as shown in the illustration. The capsules, when ripe, contain many sperms, each of which has two flagella. Fertilisation can only occur when the thallus is covered with a film of water. In these conditions the male organs absorb water and burst, the sperms finding their way onto the surface and swimming in the water towards the archegonia. The mucilage in the archegonia also absorbs water, swells and breaks open the archegonial necks. The mucilage then dissolves, leaving a pathway for the sperms to swim to and fertilise the egg cells.

The particularly interesting feature of reproduction in liverworts is that, after fertilisation, the zygote remains where it is, proceeds to undergo cell division and gives rise to a new plant which is unlike the parent and remains attached to the thallus. This is called the sporophyte. It is rather simple, consisting of a foot joining it to the parent, a short stalk and a round capsule (Fig. 4.9 (D)). When mature, the latter contains spores. At that stage (which is usually reached in March) the stalk begins to elongate rapidly, raising the capsule 6 or 7 cm into the air. Drying of the capsule wall causes it to split open, exposing the spores. Amongst the spores are a number of long, thin cells with spiral thickenings in their walls. As they dry out and shrink they twist about, so scattering the spores. The latter, on reaching moist soil, grow directly into new thalli.

The liverwort life cycle may be represented as follows (the thallus stage is known as the gametophyte, since it produces gametes, in contrast to the sporophyte, which produces spores):

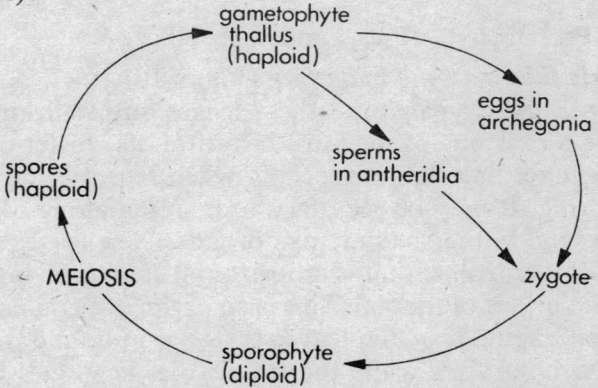

```
                    gametophyte
                      thallus
                     (haploid)
                                        eggs in
                                       archegonia
      spores              sperms
     (haploid)         in antheridia

                                        zygote
       MEIOSIS

                    sporophyte
                    (diploid)
```

In *Spirogyra* we have an example of a plant in which the ordinary cells are haploid, the diploid stage being confined to the zygote. In *Fucus* almost the opposite is true—the ordinary plant cells are diploid and the haploid stage is confined to the gametes. Here there are diploid and haploid stages which are both represented by multicellular organisms, although the former is only short-lived, dying after the spores have been released. This alternation of sporophyte and gametophyte generations is universal (although often much modified) in all higher plants.

Two other forms of reproduction in *Pellia* are asexual.

Spores called gemmae, originating as minute outgrowths of the thallus, are produced in cup-shaped organs on the upper surface. They germinate to form new thalli. Lastly, vegetative reproduction is brought about by the decay of older parts of the thallus, resulting in separation of the branches.

Apart from liverworts, the only other bryophytes are the mosses, of which there are many species. Although minute, they have a slightly higher type of organisation, generally being upright and having a stem with tiny leaves. They often have a remarkable capacity to survive in dry conditions, although requiring water for active growth. The method of reproduction is closely similar to that of liverworts.

Phylum Pteridophyta (Ferns and their allies)

***Dryopteris filix-mas**, the male fern* (Fig. 4.10)
Ferns, with their typically feathery leaves, are well known. The male fern is one of the most beautiful, its cluster of tall fronds being a fine sight, especially when recently unfurled in the spring. It may be seen in woods, often alongside the bluebells, and in the shady banks of lanes. The leaves grow from a short rhizome, that is a horizontal stem growing just below the surface of the soil. This is an organ of perennation. Food manufactured by the leaves is stored in it, and during the winter it survives while the fronds die, new ones being produced from its apex in the following spring.

The life cycle is basically similar to that of liverworts, but in this case it is the sporophyte—the fern plant that we all know—that is long-lived, whereas the gametophyte is small, lasts only a short time and is unknown to most people. The sporophyte produces spores in organs that occur on the undersides of the leaves. Here there are many round flaps, each covering a cluster of sporangia (Fig. 4.10 (B), (C) and (D)). When they are ripe, evaporation of water from a row of large cells in the sporangium wall causes them to shrink and break the sporangium open, releasing the spores. The

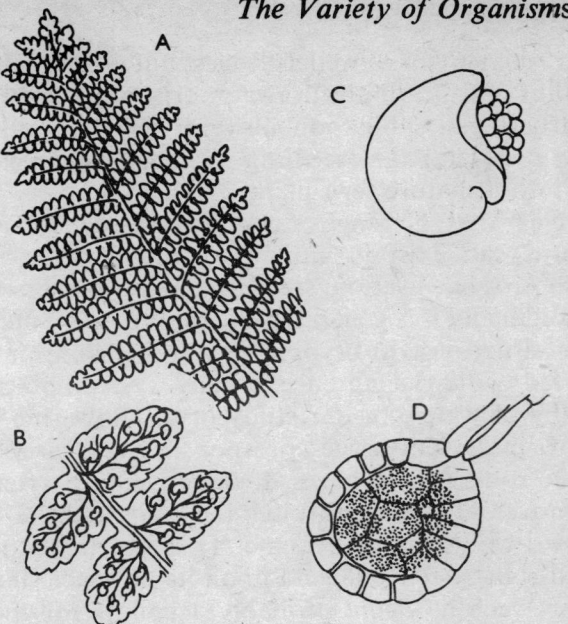

Fig. 4.10 *Dryopteris filix-mas:* (A) portion of a frond; (B) groups of sporangia covered by protective flaps on undersides of leaflets; (C) one such group much enlarged, flap deflected to show sporangia; (D) one sporangium as seen under the microscope, spores visible as dark objects inside it

covering flap has at the same time withered, and so the spores, which are very minute, are easily blown away by the wind and may be carried very considerable distances.

In suitably moist conditions a spore germinates to produce a little plant, the gametophyte, known as a prothallus. It is like a very small (about 1 cm across), heart-shaped liverwort, complete with rhizoids and, eventually, antheridia and archegonia, which are very similar to those of *Pellia* but produced on the underside of the thallus. After fertilisation the zygote remains in the archegonium, just as in *Pellia*, and develops into a new sporophyte. This is like a seedling with its own root system as well as leaves, but it is attached to the prothallus and no doubt draws nourishment from it in the very early stages. Quite soon, however, the prothallus withers up and dies, and the 'seedling' becomes independent and grows into a mature fern plant.

It is clear that the range of conditions in which bryophytes and ferns can exist is limited by the fact that water is necessary for fertilisation, since the sperms must swim to the archegonia, and it is generally true that these plants frequent damper situations. In bryophytes another limiting factor is connected with the absence of any system of transport, especially of water. In our study of the flowering plant we saw how the xylem tissue is responsible for carrying water from the roots to the leaves. If there were no xylem, water could move only slowly through the plant and the supply to the leaves would be inadequate. Thus the highly developed leaf and root systems depend upon its presence. Its absence in plants such as *Pellia* probably accounts for their small size, simple organisation and the fact that they survive only in very moist conditions.

Ferns have transport systems comparable with those of flowering plants, and so they occupy an intermediate position. Provided that a location is damp enough for sufficiently long to enable a prothallus to grow and fertilisation to be achieved, the sporophyte can gain a foothold and survive quite dry conditions, its roots being able to draw on reserves of water at some depth in the soil. Bracken is a fern with long, rapidly growing rhizomes which is able to colonise comparatively dry areas by this means. It remains true, however, that ferns as a group are not completely adapted to conditions on dry land. (Similar incomplete adaptation is seen in various animals, e.g. earthworms and amphibians.) Flowering plants, on the other hand, have a form of reproduction that does not require an external supply of water for fertilisation, and consequently they are less constrained by the absence of water in the environment.

The Pteridophyta include, besides the ferns, the club mosses and horsetails. The former look like rather large mosses and, in Britain, are found only high in the mountains. The latter are quite common in ditches and on waste ground, and have peculiar tassel-like shoots with numerous coarse, hair-like leaves and spore-bearing organs which resemble little pine cones at the stem apices. Both kinds of plant have reproductive processes and life cycles similar to those of ferns.

Phylum Spermatophyta

This phylum contains all the plants that reproduce by seed. A detailed account of the flowering plant (class Angiospermae) is given in Chapter 1. There are also non-flowering seed-bearing plants (class Gymospermae), including conifers and related forms.

From the above very brief survey of some representatives of the Plant Kingdom, it is evident that increasing complexity and size are related to the presence of many cells in the organism. Although in the simpler examples the cells may be all alike, this is rare and commonly there are different kinds performing different functions, as was seen in the account of the flowering plant. Increasing complexity seems to have some connection with the greater success of plant forms, in the sense that more complex types can exist in a bigger variety of conditions. It is true, of course, that simple plants survive in a perfectly efficient way. The same types must have been in existence for millions of years, and an organism such as *Spirogyra*, given suitable conditions, will grow and multiply as effectively as any higher plant. However, the range of conditions in which it is capable of active life are very limited, whereas, by contrast, the flowering plant, as a type, occupies an enormous variety of environments.

Similar differences between higher and lower forms are seen in the Animal Kingdom.

Phylum Coelenterata

Hydra (Fig. 4.11)

Most people are familiar with sea anemones, which are common enough in rock pools on the seashore. As the name suggests, they are somewhat flower-like in shape and, being fixed to the rocks on which they live and capable only of slow movement, might possibly be mistaken for plants. However, they do not have chlorophyll (one of the commoner species is deep red in colour), the 'petals' are really tentacles surrounding a central mouth and the organism feeds on small fish caught by the tentacles. There is no doubt, therefore, that this is a perfectly good animal in the biological sense. Most coelenterates, like the anemones, live in the sea, but here we shall consider one of the few freshwater forms, the hydra, because it well illustrates both the essential features of coelentrates and a rather simple level of organisation.

Although hydras, which live in ponds, are not uncommon, they are not easy to find because of their small size and the fact that they cannot be relied upon always to appear in the same places. However, they can be obtained cheaply from school biological suppliers and are fascinating objects of study. They may be kept for quite a long time in a jam jar if the precautions described in the note at the end of this section are observed.

As Fig. 4.11 shows, *Hydra* is basically like a sea anemone, although much smaller. The long, thin tentacles growing from one end of the narrow body surround a minute mouth. The basal disc at the other end is sticky and attached to the

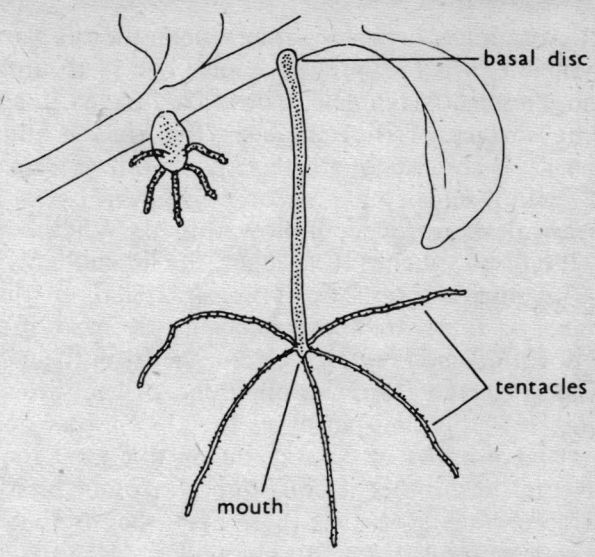

Fig. 4.11 *Hydra*—two specimens attached to water weed, one contracted, the other extended. When extended the body is 5–11 mm in length, excluding the tentacles

water weeds on which the animal is usually found. As it hangs down in the water, the tentacles spread out to form a trap, rather like a spider's web. In this case the prey are the various small shrimp-like creatures swimming in the pond water. If one of these accidently touches a tentacle, it immediately becomes stuck to it. At first it may be attached to only one tentacle, but as it tries to escape it soon blunders into others and so becomes more and more securely caught. At the same time, the tentacles sting the prey, which eventually becomes paralysed as a result. Next they draw it towards the mouth, which slowly opens and engulfs the prey. The hydra's body being hollow, the prey is accommodated inside, there to be digested. When this process has been completed, the indigestible remains are expelled through the mouth and the hydra starts to fish again.

156 *Biology*

Microscopic organs called nematocysts are largely responsible for the prey's demise when it unfortunately brushes against a tentacle. These are formed in special cells on the surface of the tentacle. One kind is illustrated in Fig. 4.12. It consists of a little capsule full of fluid, closed by a lid, with a sensory bristle, or 'trigger', at one side. Within the capsule is a coiled, hollow thread. When some object (e.g. the prey) touches the trigger, the lid suddenly flies open and the thread shoots out (Fig. 4.12 (B)). In this kind of nematocyst there are sharp barbs at the base of the thread which wound the prey as they emerge from the capsule, and poison is ejected from the open end of the thread into the wound. It is this that paralyses the prey. Other nematocysts do not have barbs or poison, but in one kind the thread is sticky and in another it coils tightly around bristles on the prey, so capturing it. It is these nematocysts that cause the prey to become stuck to the tentacles.

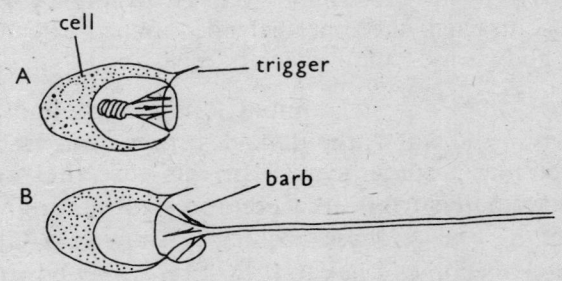

Fig. 4.12 Nematocysts: (A) undischarged; (B) discharged

Feeding is the most spectacular form of behaviour exhibited by *Hydra*, otherwise its actions are simple. When touched, the tentacles contract and, if the stimulus is strong enough, the whole animal shrinks up, only to expand again and slowly spread its tentacles if undisturbed. It can move about slowly by grasping the thing it is sitting on with its tentacles, pulling the basal disc free and then attaching it in a new position, the process being repeated to bring about movement over greater distances.

If the animal has a plentiful supply of food, it reproduces by budding, a process very similar to vegetative propagation in plants. Buds appear as rounded swellings near the base of the body. They grow and elongate, developing into miniature hydras, at first attached to the parent but eventually becoming separated so that they live independently. Sometimes two or three buds may appear on the same animal at the same time.

Sexual reproduction occurs in the autumn. Any individual hydra develops both male and female organs, but not at the same time, the former appearing earlier. The testes, as they are called, are temporary organs in the form of swellings on the surface of the upper part of the body (i.e. that part nearer the tentacles). When mature, they are full of sperms, which are released through an opening at the tip of the testes and swim away in the water.

The female organs, or ovaries, develop later and nearer the basal disc, and at first are very like the testes. However, when mature, each contains a single large cell, an egg cell. This becomes exposed due to the rupture of the thin ovary wall, but remains attached to the parent. After fertilisation by a sperm it begins to develop by cell division and becomes enclosed in a tough horny case. The latter is secreted by the embryo itself. Eventually the embryo drops off the parent hydra and lies in the mud at the pond bottom. In the following spring it hatches out of its case as a very mintue hydra, which proceeds to feed and develop into a fully grown adult.

What kind of organisation lies behind the relatively simple kind of activity exhibited by *Hydra*? The answer is that this is a multicellular organism at roughly the same level of organisation as a plant such as *Fucus*. There are different cell types, the beginnings of tissue differentiation

158 Biology

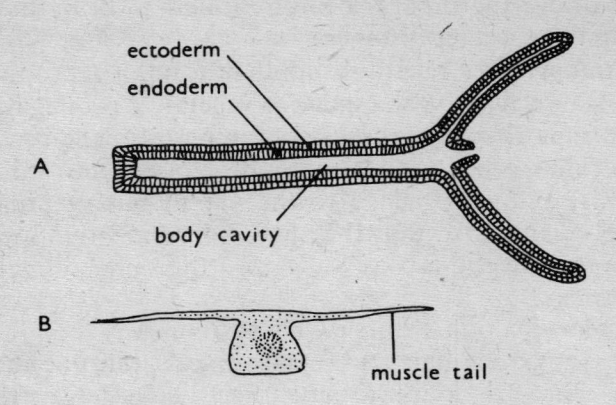

Fig. 4.13 *Hydra:* (A) diagram of longitudinal section; (B) a cell from the ectoderm with muscle tails

and the beginnings of organ systems (for example, the tentacles). Fig. 4.13 (A) illustrates how the cells are arranged in two layers, the outer ectoderm and the inner endoderm. Between them is a thin layer of jelly. We have already encountered one special type of cell in the ectoderm, that which produces the nematocysts. Most of the others have the dual function of forming, as it were, the skin of the animal and, at the same time, part of the muscle system. This is possible because the inner end of each cell is drawn out to form muscle tails (Fig. 4.13 (B)), which extend up and down the body. Their contraction causes the animal to shorten. The endoderm consists mostly of cells that carry out digestion of food in the body cavity and also have muscle tails extending around the body at right angles to its axis. Contraction of these causes the body to become narrower. At the same time, however, it causes it to become longer, since the water in the central cavity cannot escape (the mouth normally being closed) and, when squeezed in sideways, pushes out lengthways to compensate, just as a ball of plasticine when rolled out becomes longer as well as narrower.

Other types of cell include those that secrete the sticky substance on the basal disc, unspecialised cells that can develop into any of the other kinds and fill spaces between them, and sensory and nerve cells similar to those in higher organisms. The nerve cells have short axons which connect up with one another to form a network lying between the endoderm and ectoderm. The nerve net also has connections with the sensory cells and the muscle tails. It is interesting as the most primitive type of nervous system known. There is nothing corresponding to the CNS of higher animals and the sensory cells are quite unspecialised, being all alike and, presumably, sensitive to a variety of stimuli.

An interesting reflection of the low level of organisation of *Hydra* is found in the fact that it can survive almost any degree of mutilation. If the body is severed in the middle, the half with tentacles will grow a basal disc and the other half tentacles and a mouth, so that each becomes a complete new animal. Hydras have been turned inside out or cut up into small fragments, which have been able to reconstitute complete animals.

Hydra is the simplest coelenterate type. Sea anemones, although having basically the same kind of organisation, are a little more complex. For example, the internal cavity is divided by a number of radial partitions, which has the effect of increasing the surface for digestion and absorption of food, and the nerve net, instead of being evenly spread over the body, is concentrated in certain regions to form tracts, which function like rudimentary nerves. Other relatives of *Hydra* are the corals. These include a great variety of forms that produce skeletons, usually composed of hard calcium carbonate. Most are colonial, consisting of a large number of individuals, all of which have originated by the process of budding, starting from one animal. Instead of separating shortly after they are formed, as in *Hydra*, the individuals all remain joined. As their number increases, they lay down more and more calcium carbonate and the whole colony becomes larger. The substance usually referred to as coral is only the dead skeleton. In life the coral organisms grow all over it, occupying minute holes or cup-shaped depressions in the surface.

This phylum also includes jelly fish and other floating forms, commoner in the tropics, such as the 'Portuguese man-o-war', which are colonies in which there are several types of individual specialised for different functions, such as the capture of prey, feeding and reproduction.

Keeping hydras

The main conditions of success are (i) ensuring that the water used is suitable and remains uncontaminated, and (ii) providing a regular supply of food. Hydras are extremely sensitive to traces of various chemicals in the water, including acids, and tap water is frequently unsuitable. The best plan is to collect pond or river water from a variety of sources and, having obtained some of the animals, to place one or two in a small sample of water from each source. The hydras should soon expand and spread their tentacles when left undisturbed. If they remain contracted, this is a sign that the water is unsuitable. The hydras may be kept in a jam jar. All containers should be thoroughly cleaned before use.

The easiest way of feeding the animals is to provide them with live water fleas (*Daphnia*). Aquarium suppliers frequently keep these in stock, or they may occasionally be found in ponds in large numbers. It is important to avoid giving too many water fleas at one time, because there is a danger of the water becoming fouled by their dead remains. (Remember that each hydra can catch and eat only one flea at a time.)

Plate 1 The result of a water culture experiment using barley seedlings. The plant on the left of the top row has been grown in a solution containing all necessary elements. The others lack respectively (above, in order from the left) sodium, sulphur molybdenum, (below, left to right) phosphorus, iron, copper, potassium and nitrogen

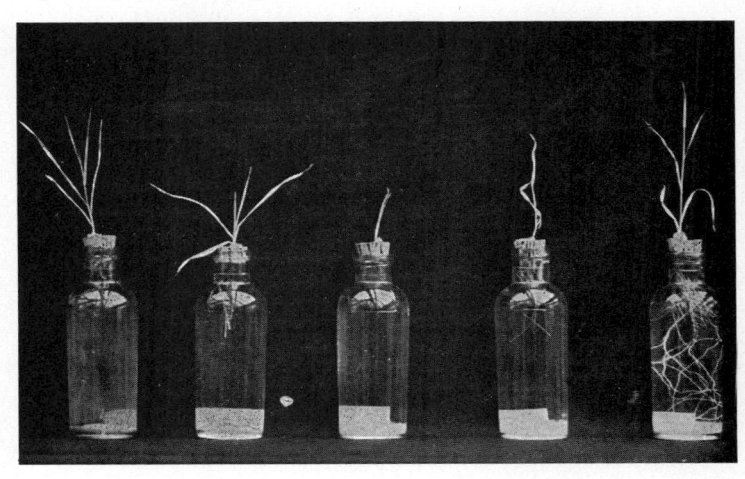

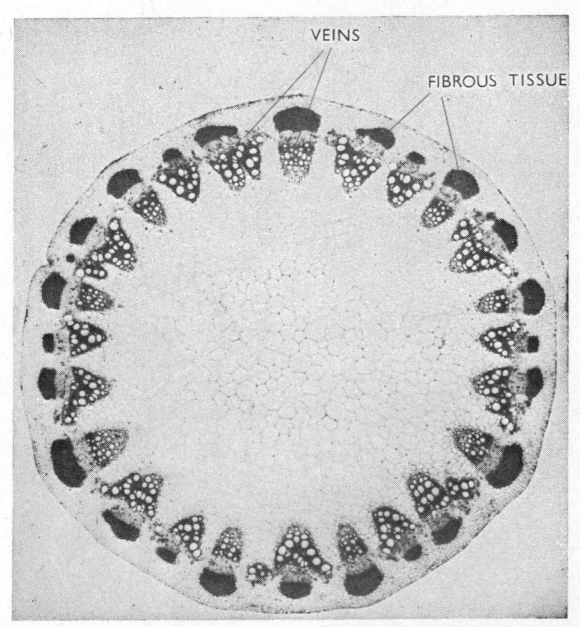

Plate 2 Transverse sections of (above) a sunflower stem and (below) a buttercup root, as seen under the microscope. The cells may be distinguished as rounded or polygonal objects of varying sizes. The small cells in the centre of the root are those concerned with the conduction of food and water (xylem and phloem), whereas in the stem these tissues are found in the veins at the periphery

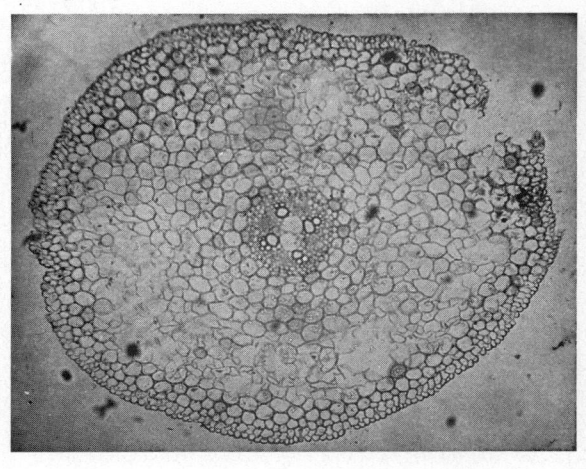

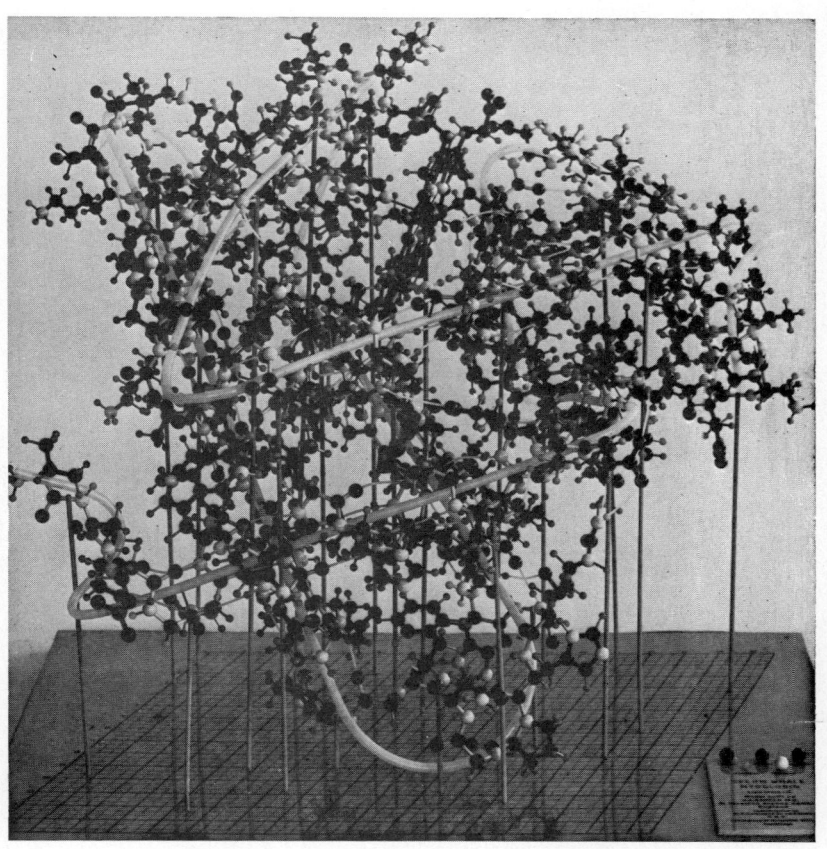

Plate 3 Model of a molecule of protein (myoglobin, a substance found in muscle and similar to haemoglobin). The small spheres represent atoms, of which there are about 2600. 150 amino acid units go to make up this particular molecule

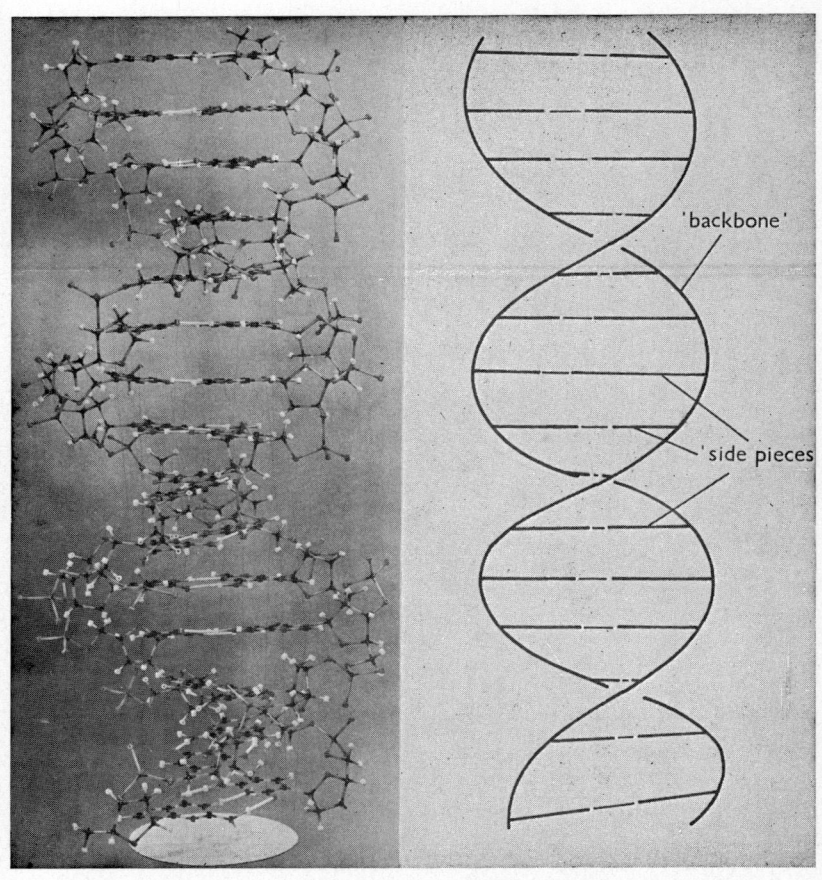

Plate 4 Model of part of a DNA molecule. The objects looking like matchsticks are the links between atoms, which are represented by the match heads. The simplified diagram on the right shows how the molecule consists of two 'backbones' twisted around each other and linked by 'side pieces'

In any case, it is necessary to change the water once every week or two.

Another slightly more difficult method of feeding uses brine shrimp (*Artemia*) larvae as the food. The eggs are obtainable from aquarists and are hatched by placing them in salt water. (Detailed instructions are usually provided with the eggs.) The tiny shrimps which hatch in two or three days *must* be freed from traces of salt before they are given to the hydras. This can be done by tying a piece of fine silk or nylon material over one end of a length of glass or plastic tubing to form a miniature colander. (Tubing measuring about 5 cm × 1 cm would be right, e.g. a plastic vial for pills with the bottom cut off.) Using a dropper (bulb pipette), some of the shrimps are transferred to the colander, and the salt water is drained out and replaced by two or three lots of clean water in succession to wash away all trace of salt. The shrimps may then be given to the hydras.

The feeding behaviour of the hydras may be observed with a magnifying glass. If they are fed regularly they will soon begin to form buds and the number in the culture will increase rapidly.

Phylum Platyhelminthes

Dugesia subtentaculata, a flatworm (Fig. 4.14)
Flatworms are common in ponds or slow-moving streams but are frequently overlooked because of their habit of hiding under stones, dead leaves, etc. and shrinking up when disturbed so that they look like little lumps of jelly. If placed in a dish of water and left alone for a short time, they will extend themselves and proceed to glide about the dish in a rather mysterious fashion. *Dugesia*, the example illustrated, is about 2 cm long and black or dark brown in colour. The body is flattened, like a piece of ribbon. A pair of black

eyes, each surrounded by a whitish area, may be seen at the anterior (front) end. The animal can execute various wriggling movements, but swimming is brought about by

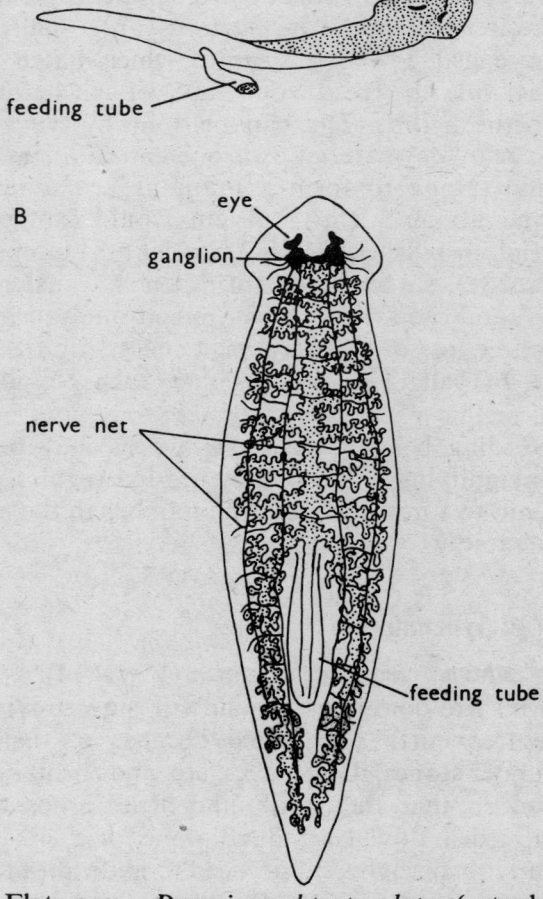

Fig. 4.14 Flatworm, *Dugesia subtentaculata* (actual length about 2 cm): (A) natural appearance; (B) nervous and digestive systems (the latter stippled)

the action of numerous microscopic hairs, or cilia, which cover the surface of the body. They beat like minute oars and produce the gliding motion mentioned above.

Feeding may be observed if a little meat is put in the water with the worms. On their approaching the food, a small tube, attached to the middle of the ventral (underside) of the body, is applied to the surface of the meat and fragments are sucked off it. It is more normal, however, for the flatworm to feed on insects and crustaceans that are small enough to be taken in whole. When not in use the feeding tube is withdrawn into a pouch inside the body.

Flatworms have a level of organisation a little higher than that of coelenterates, with a number of fairly well-developed organ systems. For example, the neurones of the nervous system are concentrated in two masses, or ganglia, near the ventral surface of the head (Figure 4.14 (B)). They are connected to a nerve net similar to that of *Hydra*, except that it contains a number of definite longitudinal strands or nerves. There are also a variety of sensory cells, concentrated near the anterior end especially, some sensitive to movements in the water and others to chemicals, as well as the light-sensitive cells of the eyes. The structure of the eye is interesting, since it is like that of the human eye reduced to its essentials, i.e. sensory cells and black pigment arranged in such a way that the former are stimulated only by light coming from a particular direction (Figure 4.15 (A)). There is no lens. The sensory organs are connected to the ganglia, which function as a pair of relay stations between the receptors and the muscles.

There is an excretory system consisting of two canals running down either side of the body and opening to the exterior near the tail. These have short branches ending in 'flame cells' (Figure 4.15 (B)) which extract waste products from the tissues and pass them, in solution, to the lateral canals and so out.

164 Biology

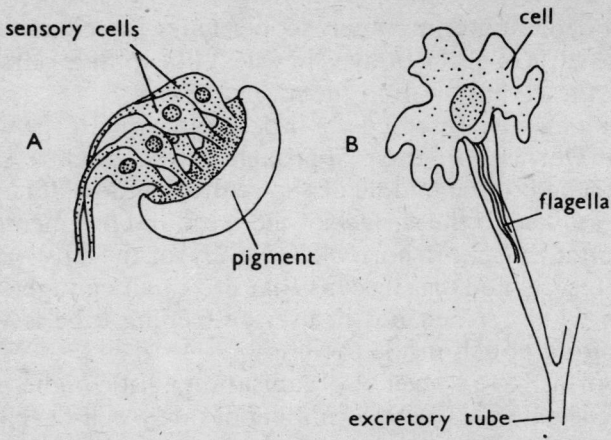

Fig. 4.15 (A) Eye of flatworm. (B) Flame cell: the flagella undulate, propelling fluid down the excretory tube

As in *Hydra*, the digestive system has only one opening, the mouth, through which waste is ejected. However, the system is a little more complicated because it has three main branches with a large number of side branches (Figure 4.14 (B)). This increases the surface area for absorption of food and also means that no part of the body is very far from the source of digested food.

The reproductive system is fairly complex and details will not be given. Each individual contains both male and female organs (i.e. it is hermaphrodite), but there is an arrangement to insure that eggs are fertilised (within the body of the animal) by sperms obtained from another individual. Eggs are laid in a protective cocoon and the young which hatch from them are like miniature adults. The reproductive organs develop only during the reproductive season, degenerating afterwards.

One major system not present in flatworms is a circulatory system. This, no doubt, accounts for the flattened shape. As in other organisms without means of internal transport (e.g. liverworts, seaweeds), this insures that gases (oxygen, carbon dioxide) have only a little way to diffuse between the surface and any cell, since no cell is far from the former.

If we consider the types of symmetry present in *Hydra* and *Dugesia*, we notice an interesting contrast. *Hydra*, in common with other coelenterates, is a radially symmetrical animal, that is the parts of the body are disposed symmetrically about a line forming its axis. No doubt this is related to the fact that it spends most of its time fixed to one spot. The part of the body (the basal disc) that attaches the animal to that spot must be specially modified for this purpose, and it is also clear that it is advantageous for the mouth and tentacles to be as far away from this point (and therefore capable of reaching as much of the space containing the prey) as possible. Consequently, the body has two differentiated ends. Apart from this, however, there is no reason why the tentacles, for example, should be on one side rather than on another—prey and other influences reach the animal equally from all directions—and so the parts are arranged radially.

Dugesia has bilateral (two-sided) symmetry. This means that it can be divided into equal left and right halves. The parts are arranged symmetrically on either side of a central plane, rather than about an axis. So, if we imagine a flat sheet of paper passing through the midline and cutting the body in half, we realise that every part on one side of the paper is balanced by a corresponding part on the other side. This type of symmetry is related to the fact that the animal spends a lot of time moving about with one end forward. Since this end comes into contact with new parts of the environment first, it is hardly surprising that sensory organs come to be concentrated in this region and that, associated with them, there are the two nervous ganglia mentioned on p. 163. The elongation of the body forward and aft, giving rise to a streamlined shape, is also obviously related to the same habit. So an anterior (forward) end is differentiated from a posterior (hind) end. Similarly, a ventral (lower) surface is differentiated from a dorsal (upper) surface. At the same time, there is no reason why the left side should be differentiated from the right, hence the bilateral symmetry.

This type of symmetry is characteristic of all actively moving animals. In higher forms the distinctions between anterior and posterior, and between ventral and dorsal become even more marked. Characteristically, an anterior part becomes specialised to carry a variety of highly developed special sense organs (eyes, ears, antennae, etc.) and to contain a mass of nervous tissue, the brain.

As in the case of *Hydra*, flatworms can withstand quite severe mutilation. So that if, for example, one is cut in half, the halves each regenerate missing organs to form complete individuals.

Many of the Platyhelminthes are parasitic. An example is the liver fluke of sheep and cattle. This is a leaf-like parasite that lives in the bile ducts and may cause severe disease. Another, more like a worm in shape, exists in the abdominal blood vessels of man, causing the disease bilharzia which is very widespread in Africa. Then there are the tapeworms, which are intestinal parasites, and a variety of other forms parasitising a variety of animals as well as man.

Phylum Mollusca

***Helix aspersa**, the garden snail* (Fig. 4.16)
With the snails and their allies we reach a level of organisation that, in essentials, may be compared with that of vertebrates. We find well-differentiated tissues and highly developed organ systems, perhaps the most important new feature being the presence of a circulatory system. This is, no

doubt, an important factor permitting the development of a higher level of organisation, since it is one of the means by which organs devoted to various special functions may be linked together to form an organised whole. An example of this was encountered in Chapter 2, where it was explained that amino acids absorbed by the intestine are carried to the liver in the hepatic portal vein and that some of them are broken down, with the formation of urea, which is then carried in the blood stream to the kidney to be excreted. This is an example of the linkage by the circulatory system of three specialised organs, the intestine, liver and kidney. A circulatory system also makes possible a great increase in size, since it is no longer necessary that every cell should be very near the surface and the digestive system.

The general organisation of the snail is represented in Fig. 4.16. The upper diagram shows principally the digestive and nervous systems, the lower the circulatory and respiratory systems and the kidney. The rather complicated reproductive system is not shown at all: its organs lie in the body cavity above and on either side of the crop and open on the right-hand side of the head, as indicated in the figure.

As the illustration shows, some of the digestive and other organs are contained in a mass (the visceral hump) enclosed by the shell. The covering of this hump is known as the mantle. It has a thickened edge, coinciding with the margin of the shell, which secretes the hard calcium carbonate of which the shell is composed.

The breathing organ is a cavity, the lung, lying within the mantle and having an opening on the right-hand side just under its edge. Air is pumped in and out by up and down movements of the muscular floor of the lung. Its roof looks rather like the underside of a cabbage leaf, there being a network of veins containing blood which absorbs oxygen and releases carbon dioxide. This blood passes into a central vessel leading to the two-chambered heart (on the left

168 *Biology*

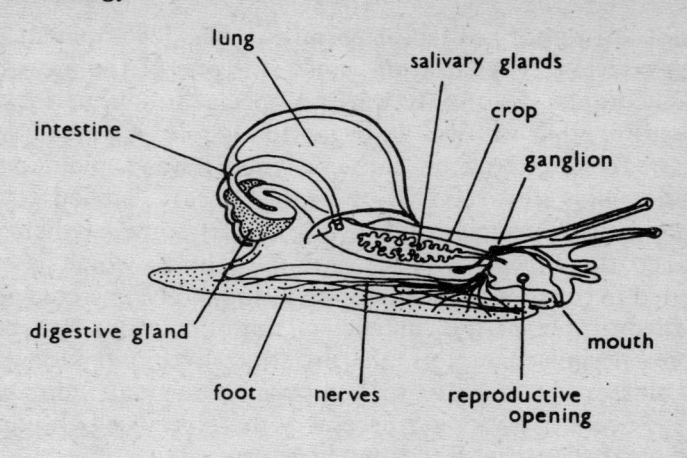

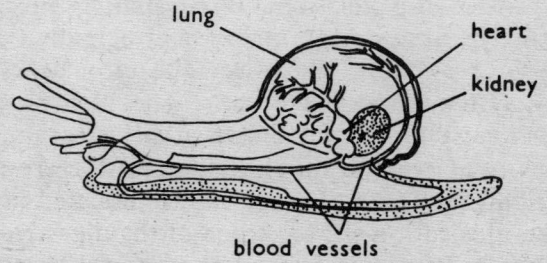

Fig. 4.16 A snail *Helix*, showing some of the principal organ systems. Upper diagram: digestive and nervous systems, lung. Lower diagram: circulatory system and kidney. (Reproductive system not shown in either diagram)

side), which pumps it through a series of branching arteries into the body. These arteries open into the body cavity, which is therefore full of blood, bathing the various organs. There is no system of capillaries, as in vertebrates. Blood eventually passes into a vessel at the lower margin of the lung and from this into the network of veins. The snail's blood is of a pale bluish green colour due to the presence of a copper-containing pigment, haemocyanin, which has a function similar to that of haemoglobin in vertebrates.

Gardeners are familiar with the devastating effects of snails and their kin, the slugs, on plant life. This is traceable to their possession of a very effective eating organ, the radula, which is like a horny tongue covered with hooked teeth and lies in a pocket within the mouth. It acts like a rasp, working against a hard pad in the roof of the mouth, and is capable of shredding plant tissues at a considerable rate. Digestion begins in the crop and is completed in the digestive gland, which contains a system of branched tubes leading out of the intestine. Particles of food are carried into this system by cilia and are taken up and digested by the cells of the gland. Faeces pass out through the rectum, which ends at the opening of the lung. A duct leading from the kidney also opens at this point.

There is a well-defined central nervous system consisting of several pairs of ganglia above and below the oesophagus. Nerves radiate to various parts of the body, including the special sensory organs in the tentacles. The upper longer tentacles have eyes at their tips, the lower ones organs probably of taste and smell.

The foot is the organ of locomotion. Its action may be seen if a snail is made to crawl on a sheet of glass and is observed from below. Waves of contraction will be seen passing from the anterior to the posterior end of the foot. A slime gland secretes mucus, which, passing out onto the anterior end, spreads backwards over the foot, so lubricating it and, at the same time, producing the familiar slime trail. The muscles of the foot are co-ordinated by a nerve net situated in it.

Snails, like flatworms and hydras, are hermaphrodite, but self-fertilisation does not normally occur. A curious feature is that each individual is equipped with its own Cupid's arrow in the form of a sharp dart composed of calcium carbonate in a container that functions like a little gun. (This latter is situated at the reproductive opening.) Prior to mating, two snails approach and fire the darts at each other with such force that they actually penetrate to the internal organs of the opposite partner. This rather violent stimulation leads on to pairing, when both animals pass out and receive sperms, which are then stored temporarily in special receptacles. Internal fertilisation of eggs takes place later, after which the eggs are laid in holes in the soil. (This occurs in the late summer.) They contain considerable quantities of stored food and are protected by hard shells, being rather like miniature hens' eggs. They hatch after about a month.

The garden snail hibernates during the winter. At this time the body is completely retracted into the shell, which is closed by a specially secreted disc of horny material, except for a small hole to permit slow respiration.

The phylum Mollusca contains a very wide variety of forms, ranging from giant squids to delicate little floating 'sea butterflies'. Most are aquatic. The main features they have in common (although sometimes highly modified) are the foot, head and mantle, the last generally enclosing a mantle cavity containing breathing organs and secreting a shell. The majority of the snail-like forms are marine. They are very similar to land snails, but the mantle cavity contains a pair of leaf-like gills which absorb oxygen dissolved in the water that fills the cavity. Another familiar group of molluscs is composed of the bivalves, such as the oyster and the mussel. In these animals the mantle encloses the entire body, including the foot, as do the two halves of the shell which cover it. The mantle cavity and the gills within it are correspondingly enlarged. This is because the gills have been converted into a food-collecting apparatus. They are covered with cilia, which create water currents flowing in and out of the cavity. These carry minute food particles from the surrounding water, and there is a remarkable mechanism for sorting them and conveying them to the mouth. The foot is usually a tongue-like organ which can be protruded from between the edges of the shell and pushes the animal slowly through the sand or mud in which it lives. As becomes such inactive animals, the head is virtually absent, except for a rudiment.

The squids and octopuses are amongst the most highly modified molluscs and also the most highly developed. They are active, predatory animals, capable of rapid locomotion as a result of modifications of the mantle cavity. This contains gills, which are used for respiratory exchange, and is also provided with a very muscular wall and an outlet funnel. This makes it possible for water to be squirted out of the cavity with such force that it causes the animal to shoot through the water by a form of jet propulsion. As one would expect in an active animal, there is a well-developed nervous system and organs of special sense. In particular, the eyes are large, complex and very similar to the vertebrate eye. The shell in these molluscs is either absent (in octopuses) or represented by an internal stiffener. Cuttle bone (derived from a small squid, the cuttlefish) is a well-known example of the latter.

Phylum Echinodermata

Asterias rubens, *the common starfish* (Fig. 4.17)

The echinoderms are a rather curious group of animals related to starfish and all found living in the sea. The name *echinoderm* means 'spiny skin' and refers to a typical feature. *Asterias rubens* is the commonest British starfish. It has five arms, as a general rule, and is usually reddish in colour, although there is quite a large range of variation from yellowish to violet. Specimens are commonly 7 or 10 cm across but may be up to 50 cm in diameter. The creature has a peculiar tough, leathery consistency owing to the presence of bony plates embedded below the surface of the skin. The blunt spines are composed of the same bony substance. Between the spines are microscopic pincer-like organs (the pedicellariae), which are constantly opening and shutting and probably serve to keep the surface free from various organisms that might otherwise find it a convenient place on which to grow. On the underside are numerous legs, the tube feet, of which there are four rows on each arm. They are in the form of flexible tubes ending in suckers. Their movements are co-ordinated so that they are all acting in the same direction, and in this way the animal can move equally well in any direction. The tube feet also play an important part in feeding. The starfish feeds on a variety of animal food but specialises in bivalve molluscs. These it clasps with its arms, attaching the tube feet to the shell and exerting a steady pull until the prey relaxes and opens. The starfish then turns its stomach inside out through its mouth, so that it is applied to the soft body of the mollusc and commences digestion externally.

Internally, there is a body cavity extending into the arms and bounded by the leathery body wall (Fig. 4.17). It is occupied chiefly by the digestive and reproductive organs. The sack-like stomach occupies most of the central cavity, having a mouth opening in the centre of the underside and an anus on the upper surface. Much branched caecae, which are extensions of the stomach, fill up most of the space in the arms. There is a pair of gonads in each arm (the animals being either male or female). These are sacks which become enlarged and full of eggs or sperm in the breeding season and which have ducts opening in the angles between the arms. The gametes are released into the sea, where fertilisation takes place. The microscopic swimming larvae which hatch from the eggs undergo metamorphosis into young starfish.

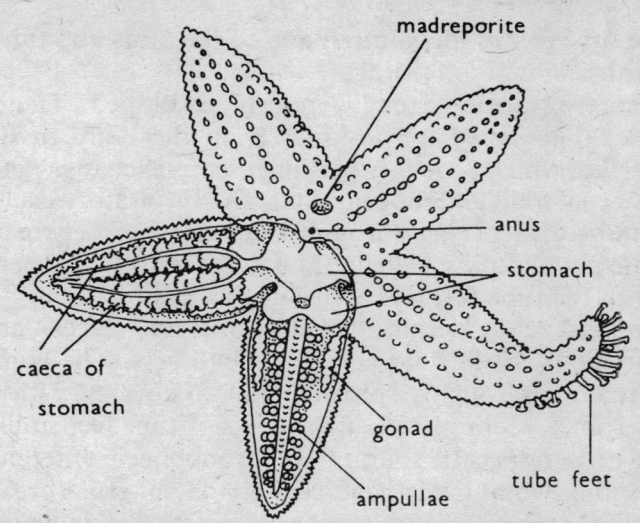

Fig. 4.17 Starfish, *Asterias*. Internal organs exposed in two arms and caecae removed in one

Below the caecae and the gonads on the floor of the body cavity are numerous round capsules (ampullae), each connected directly to a tube foot. The tube feet are also connected to radial water canals, one in the centre of the floor of each arm, which are in turn connected to a circular canal in the central body. The circular canal, finally, has a short tube connecting it to a sieve-like plate, the madreporite, on the upper surface. Through this the whole system, which is full of water, is in connection with the sea.

The nervous system consists of nerve nets below the surface of the skin, the lining of the body cavity and the digestive organs, and of more concentrated tracts, or nerve cords, running radially between the rows of tube feet and connected to circular tracts about the mouth. The only recognisable sense organs are rudimentary eyes at the tips of the arms. This system is able to exercise a simple co-ordinating function. Thus it evidently controls the movement of the tube feet in locomotion and of the arms and tube feet when the animal is feeding.

The respiratory system is poorly developed. There are minute, thin-walled outpushings from the body cavity on the surface which probably permit gaseous exchange between the internal fluid and the sea water, and respiratory exchange no doubt also occurs through the tube feet. There is no definite circulatory system, although there are movements of water in the tube feet and associated canals.

Amongst echinoderms other than ordinary starfish are the sea urchins, brittle stars and sea cucumbers. The common sea urchin is a roughly spherical animal covered with long, sharp spines, amongst which are rows of tube feet similar to those of *Asterias*. In spite of the pronounced difference in shape, the two animals have very similar internal organisation, so that a sea urchin is rather like a starfish in which the arms have disappeared and the upper surface has shrunk up to almost nothing, leaving the lower side, with its tube feet, to form the surface of the sphere. In sea urchins the bony plates become joined together edge to edge to form a delicate mosaic-like shell. The empty shells are well known on beaches where the animals are common. After death the soft parts decay rapidly and the spines fall off, leaving the intriguingly geometrical structure of little plates.

Brittle stars are starfish with thin, rather snaky arms radiating from a small body. Sea cucumbers are soft-bodied echinoderms without arms and elongated in the direction of the central axis. They burrow in mud, feeding on the organic matter contained in it.

In view of the fact that echinoderms move quite actively, albeit slowly, their radial symmetry is a little puzzling. It is probably accounted for by their descent from forms that (like most coelenterates) were attached more or less permanently to the bottom of the sea. Such forms, the 'sea lilies', are well known as fossils, although represented by only a few uncommon species today. They were rather like brittle stars, with a stalk attaching the body to the substratum. Interestingly, some echinoderms have developed bilateral symmetry. An example is the heart urchin, a sea urchin that burrows in sand and in which the whole shape of the body has been altered as a result of the anus moving to the posterior whilst the mouth has become situated near the anterior end. Further examples are the sea cucumbers, which are also burrowing animals.

Phylum Annelida

Lumbricus terrestris, an earthworm (Fig. 4.18)

In some ways earthworms are not very typical representatives of their phylum because, unlike most of their relatives, they do not live in the sea. However, they illustrate the main characteristics of the group especially clearly since they lack the complications of some other annelids.

An earthworm is rather like the tyre of a bicycle—one tube inside another. The inner tube is the alimentary canal, leading straight from the mouth at the anterior end to the anus at the posterior end. The outer tube is a muscular body wall covered with a thin skin. Between the two tubes is a space occupied by fluid. This space, known as the coelom, is divided by thin partitions into about 150 compartments, corresponding to the ring-shaped segments that make up the earthworm's body. Within the coelom are various organs, the most important of which are the main blood vessels, the ventral nerve cord, the reproductive organs and excretory organs called nephridia. Most of these features are illustrated diagrammatically in Fig. 4.18.

Earthworms feed on soil and vegetable matter, extracting nutrients from the organic material contained in the former. The mouth is a small opening, not quite at the tip of the anterior end. Above and in front of it is a small fleshy lobe

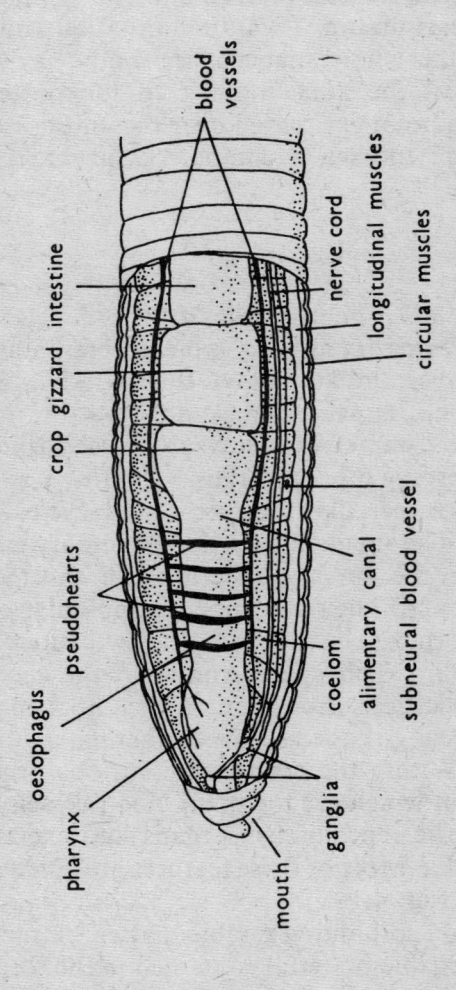

Fig. 4.18 Earthworm, *Lumbricus*: diagram showing organs in anterior part of the body (simplified, reproductive organs omitted)

(the prostomium), which forms the very tip of the body. The pharynx (Fig. 4.18) is a muscular organ that sucks food in by a pumping action and passes it backwards to the oesophagus and so to the crop, where it may be retained temporarily before being subjected to the grinding action of the gizzard, which has thick muscular walls and a hard lining. The rest of the alimentary system consists of a straight intestine, where both digestion and absorption of food takes place. Faeces are passed out through the opening of the intestine at the hind end of the body.

The circulatory system has no heart in the ordinary sense, but waves of contraction continually travel along the dorsal blood vessel, moving the blood in an anterior direction, so that this vessel has the same function as a heart. Having arrived at the anterior end, most of the blood flows through the five pairs of pseudohearts into the ventral vessel and then travels in the posterior direction. The pseudohearts contain flap valves preventing backflow. Some of the blood in both ventral and dorsal vessels flows through their anterior extensions to the pharynx and other parts in that region. The ventral vessel has branches in every segment which supply blood to the tissues, in which there are capillary networks similar to those in vertebrates. Blood is collected from these by other vessels leading to the dorsal vessel. Blood is also collected by the subneural vessel and flows to the dorsal vessel through connecting vessels. Thus, as in vertebrates, the circulatory system of the earthworm is a closed one and may be contrasted with that of the snail, which is open, in the sense that the blood flows out of the arteries into the main body cavity, instead of being enclosed in vessels throughout its journey round the body. For this reason, the body cavity of the snail is termed a haemocoel (from the Greek *haima* = blood and *koilo* = hollow) and is not exactly analogous with the coelom of the worm.

The blood is red, owing to the presence of haemoglobin

dissolved in the plasma instead of being contained in corpuscles. Oxygen is absorbed through the surface of the body, which is covered by a very thin skin. It is kept moist by mucus-secreting glands, so that oxygen can readily dissolve and diffuse into the skin, and loops of the capillary system come extremely close to the surface.

There is a pair of nephridia (excretory organs) in nearly every segment. They consist of folded tubes lying just behind the segmental partitions. Each tube at one end opens to the exterior, while the other passes through the partition, on the other side of which is an opening into the coelom. The coelom is full of a watery fluid, and cilia, covering the opening of the nephridium and part of the inside of the tube, propel the fluid down it and so, eventually, to the exterior. It is uncertain exactly how the nephridia work, but the coelomic fluid contains waste products, such as urea, which are present in fluid leaving the nephridia, and it is also likely that the nephridia absorb some useful substances from this fluid before it passes out.

The central nervous system consists of a ventral nerve cord running the length of the worm and connected to ganglia at the anterior end. (The latter are not as well developed as in some marine annelids which have tentacles with quite complex sense organs.) Peripheral nerves radiate from the nerve cord in every segment and serve the gut, muscles and skin. Neurones are present throughout the nerve cord, as well as in the ganglia, and also in nerve nets just below the skin and in the gut wall. Only two kinds of special sense organ are known: simple light receptor cells and receptors similar to the taste buds of higher animals, which probably are sensitive to chemical stimuli and may also be sensitive to touch. Both kinds are present in the skin and are most numerous at the anterior end. Light receptors are also present in the last segment.

If an earthworm is studied carefully as it crawls over the

surface of the ground, it will be seen that the action consists of the passage of a series of waves of contraction down the length of the body. First, the anterior end may be seen to stretch forwards, becoming narrower as it does so. At the same time, however, the region immediately behind this undergoes the opposite action, becoming shorter and thicker, and careful observation shows that this contraction travels towards the tail. Soon the anterior end stops moving and its segments in their turn begin to shorten and thicken, drawing those behind forwards, while the stretching and narrowing action has meanwhile passed backwards to more posterior parts.

This motion is brought about by the action of the muscles that make up the body wall. There is an outer layer of circular muscle fibres and an inner layer of longitudinal ones (Fig. 4.18). When the circular muscles of a segment contract, that segment, naturally, becomes narrower (smaller in diameter). At the same time, however, it becomes longer, because the contracting muscles press on the fluid in the coelom which is squeezed out lengthways, rather as toothpaste comes out of a tube when it is squeezed. The longitudinal muscles have precisely the opposite action: they make the segment shorter but larger in diameter.

There is one more factor in locomotion. This is the presence of small bristles (chaetae), of which there are four pairs in nearly every segment. The earthworm is adapted to locomotion in a burrow, and in this situation the chaetae can effectively anchor the animal if they are extended and pressed into the walls of the burrow.

Now consider a small portion of the worm during locomotion (Fig. 4.19). At A, longitudinal muscles are contracted and chaetae extended. At B and C, circular muscles are contracted and chaetae withdrawn. At X circular muscles are in the process of contracting, so causing the segments there to lengthen and push B forwards (i.e. to

B   X   A   Y   C

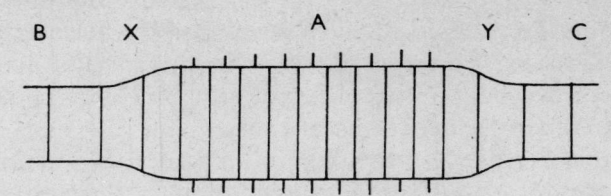

Fig. 4.19 Diagram illustrating the mechanism of locomotion in the earthworm. For explanation see text

the left), A being anchored by the chaetae. At Y, longitudinal muscles are contracting and pulling C forwards. A further effect of the action at X and Y is to cause the region of thickening (now at A) to move backwards. In this way the motion described above is brought about. It is controlled by the neurones of the nerve cord. The contraction of one segment brings about contraction of the next, partly as a result of the presence of reflex arcs connecting neighbouring segments and partly through direct mechanical stimulation of one segment by contraction of another.

In essence, reproduction is similar to that of the snail, earthworms being hermaphrodite. Internal fertilisation is preceded by copulation (which takes place at night on the surface of the ground), during which there is exchange of sperms, and eggs are laid in the soil. The thickened region of the body, which is present in mature earthworms about a third of the length of the body from the anterior end, secretes a sticky sleeve surrounding that part of the worm when eggs are about to be laid. The worm then wriggles out of this backwards, laying the eggs in it as it does so. (The reproductive openings are in the anterior part of the body.) Finally, the ends of the sleeve close up and it hardens to form a protective cocoon around the eggs.

If you enjoy holidays at the seaside, and especially if you fish there, you may know some of the varied kinds of marine annelid, although only those who take the trouble to make a close study are likely to be aware of their great variety and beauty of form. Most people know the worm casts made by the lugworm on sandy and muddy shores, and fishermen use the animal itself as bait. These worms live in a burrow lined with mucus. Other kinds form a more substantial tube, composed of sand or mud stuck together with a parchment-like substance, which forms the animal's permanent home. Some have developed various interesting ways of filtering out food particles from the sea water. Examples are the little worms that make hard, white, calcareous tubes attached to stones or seaweed. One species, the sort found on seaweed, forms little spiral tubes only 3 mm or so across. Another common species has twisted tubes 25 mm or so long which look like the hieroglyphics of some strange alphabet on pebbles or shells. The tube is triangular in section and tapered from one end to the other. If it is placed in sea water, a set of tentacles will be seen to emerge from the broad end after an interval. These are covered with cilia, which create currents of water from which food particles are sifted.

The worms in another group of annelids do not live in burrows at all but swim actively, generally have sensory tentacles and eyes, and frequently jaws. The ragworms, which may be as long as 91 cm, are well-known examples.

Finally, this phylum includes the leeches—worms that have a sucker at either end of the body. They are active, predatory animals, often armed with teeth and capable of piercing the skin and sucking blood from their victims. They are common in ponds and streams. (None found in Britain is harmful to man.) Some live in the sea, others—in the tropics—on dry land.

Phylum Arthropoda
Locusta migratoria, *the migratory locust* (Fig. 4.20)
Arthropods are all those animals with hard, jointed shells or other tough coverings for their bodies: crabs and crayfish,

182 Biology

spiders and scorpions, lobsters and ladybirds, wasps and woodlice, and many others. This phylum is by far the largest in the Animal Kingdom, in terms of the number of species, and its main divisions being correspondingly large and important, are usually referred to as sub-phyla. Of these the sub-phylum Insecta is the biggest. Indeed, the species of insect are more numerous than all the other animal species put together. We shall take an insect as our example of an arthropod.

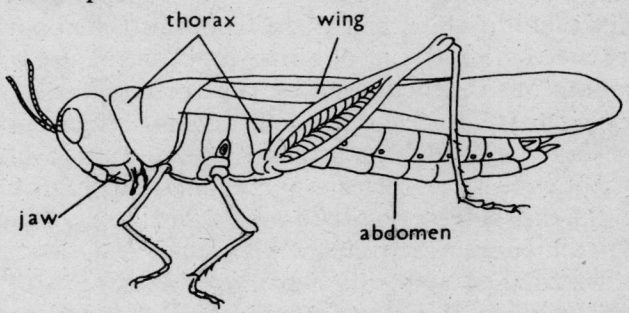

Fig. 4.20 *Locusta*, external features. One spiracle is clearly visible in the thorax, above the second leg, and six in the abdomen

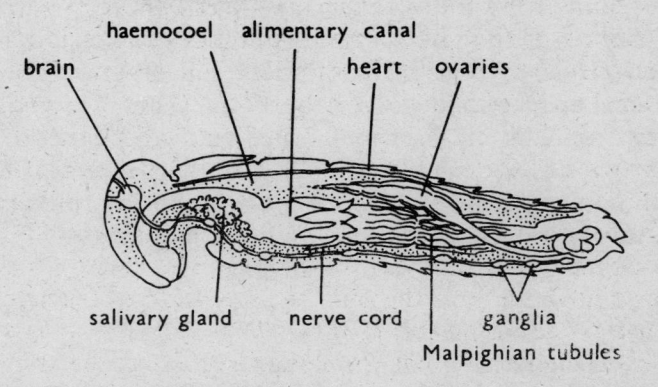

Fig. 4.21 *Locusta*, (female) internal organs (muscles and tracheal system not shown)

Locusts are large grasshoppers, closely related to the common little green grasshopper of our countryside. The only thing that makes them locusts is the fact that, under certain conditions, they form vast and destructive swarms which migrate over great distances, eating every leaf and blade of grass they encounter. The home territory of the migratory locust is near Lake Tanganyika in central Africa. When at home, although a giant compared with the British species, it is normally peaceful enough. However, if, as a result of plentiful food and rapid breeding, the number in a locality increases above a certain level, in the course of a few generations the insect undergoes a change that affects both its appearance (colour and markings) and its behaviour. The effect of the latter change is to give it the urge to leave its home ground in company with many thousands of its fellows, so giving rise to the migratory swarms. These may persist for months and give rise to subsidiary swarms as a result of reproduction. Eventually, however, they die out.

A similar insect is the desert locust (*Schistocerca gregaria*), which is found over a wide area covering parts of Asia, northern Africa and Spain. It is yellow with dark markings, whereas *L. migratoria* is reddish brown in colour.

One of the interesting things about arthropods is that, although they are at about the same level of organisation as vertebrates, they contrast with them in so many ways. If they possibly can, they seem to prefer to do things in a different way. For example, we are used to the idea of the skeleton being made up of bones inside the body, in vertebrates, with muscles attached to them on the outside. This is termed an endoskeleton. Arthropods have a skeleton made up of a jointed shell on the outside: this is an exoskeleton. The muscles are inside this (Fig. 4.22).

The exoskeleton also has the same function as the skin of the vertebrate, but whereas the latter consists of a layer of many cells constantly multiplying in order to replace those

184 *Biology*

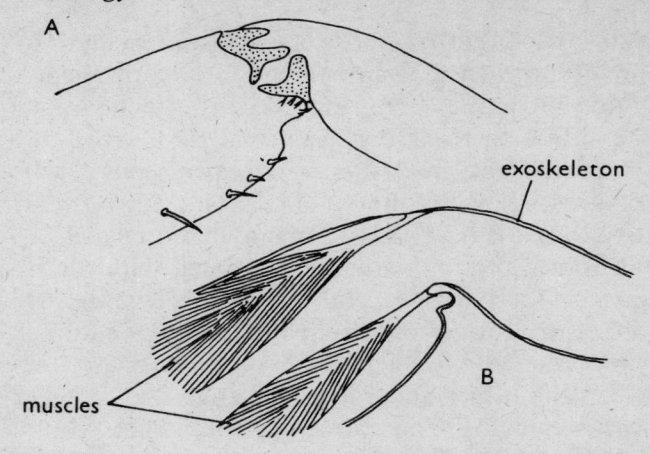

Fig. 4.22 (A) A leg joint of an insect. Stippling indicates areas of thin, flexible exoskeleton which allow the joint to bend. (B) Diagram showing arrangement of muscles in same joint

lost from the surface and potentially able to grow at all times, the arthropod 'skin' is a non-living layer. It is secreted by an underlying layer of cells. It is not able to grow, and this gives rise to a universal feature of arthropods: the fact that, when they are growing, they shed the skin at intervals and replace it with a new one. The skin is soft at first and stretches, so that by the time it has hardened it is larger than the old one. In this way an increase in size of the whole animal is made possible.

The insect exoskeleton is not so much a hard shell—as in a crab, for example—as a supple covering which may be relatively thin. It is called a cuticle.

Like annelids, all arthropods are segmented, i.e. the body is made up of a number of divisions, or segments, one behind the other. This is obvious in the somewhat worm-like millipedes, in which there are a large number of ring-shaped segments all very much alike, or in woodlice, in which there are fewer segments. Some examples (crabs, for instance) do not seem to have segments at first sight, because these are fused together. The only obviously segmented part of the crab is the 'tail', which is permanently bent forward under the body and out of sight. In the locust (and most other insects) the 'tail', or abdomen, is clearly segmented (Fig. 4.20), but segments in the thorax are not quite so clear. There are, in fact, three. The divisions may be seen if the underside of this part of the body is examined, when it will be seen that each segment bears one pair of legs, of which there are six in all. The two pairs of wings are attached to the second and third segments. The head shows no sign of segmentation, but study of some insect embryos shows that there are six segments which have become fused together.

Fig. 4.21 shows the layout of some of the main systems in the locust. The CNS is made up of a ventral nerve cord and ganglia. (Here is another contrast with vertebrates, in which the nerve cord is dorsal.) The nerve is double, i.e. it consists of two nerves—left and right—side by side. They join up a

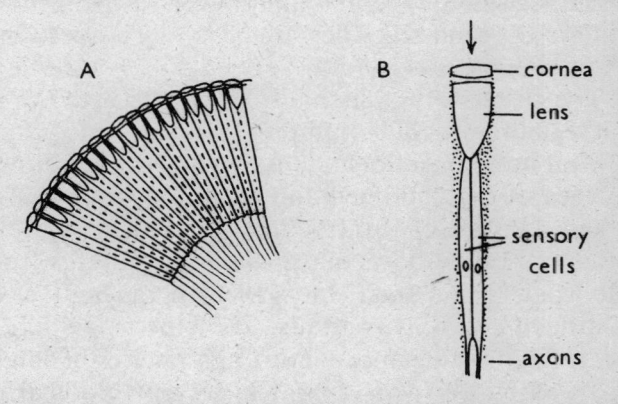

Fig. 4.23 The compound eye: (A) diagram of a section through part of an eye; (B) single unit much enlarged. The arrow shows the direction along which light enters it

row of ganglia, those in the head (forming the brain) and the thorax being especially large.

Insects have a variety of sense organs, the most obvious being the antennae and the eyes. The latter are interesting because they are based on a quite different principle from that of the vertebrate eye. The organ, known as a compound eye, is composed of a huge number of small units (Fig. 4.23). Each unit is represented by a minute window, or cornea, on the surface of the eye. Below this is a lens, which focuses a pencil of light onto sensory cells beneath. These relay nerve impulses through axons to the brain. Thus, instead of an image being formed on a sensory retina, each eye unit responds to light coming from a small part of the field of view, and, if an insect can be said to see an image, as we do, this must be like a mosaic composed of the impressions received from each unit. There are also three much smaller simple eyes with single lenses, one just in front of each compound eye and one between the antennae.

The ears are in the form of a drum-like membrane, one on either side of the first abdominal segment just above the base of the hind leg. They are generally covered by the wings when the insect is at rest.

The circulatory system also contrasts with the type found in vertebrates. The pumping organ, instead of being a ventral heart, is a dorsal vessel situated just below the upper surface of the abdomen and extending from one end to the other. Waves of contraction pass along it towards the head and blood flows out through the aorta, which opens in the head. Blood then enters the general body cavity, which is a haemocoel, as in snails. The blood re-enters the dorsal heart from the haemocoel through a series of small openings guarded by flap valves, which prevent blood from flowing out of the heart at these points. One of the most important functions of the blood in vertebrates is to carry oxygen, but in insects the blood has only a minor role in respiratory exchange. In connection with this fact, the blood is colourless, there being no haemoglobin or other respiratory pigment.

Oxygen enters the insect's body through a series of holes or spiracles, a pair of which exists in most segments (Fig. 4.20). There is a system of air tubes (tracheae) leading from the spiracles and branching out inside the body (Fig. 4.24). The finest branches, which have very thin walls, are found in the various organs, so that oxygen is brought close to the places where it is needed and has to diffuse only short distances. When the insect is active, contractions of the abdomen coupled with the opening and closing of spiracles cause a flow of air through the system, so bringing in fresh oxygen and getting rid of carbon dioxide.

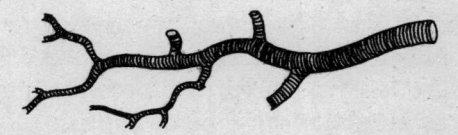

Fig. 4.24 Some of the tracheae from an insect

As in snails, the success of the locust depends partly upon its possession of efficient eating organs. In this case they are a pair of strong jaws. These are hinged at either side of the head (Fig. 4.20) and so move sideways instead of up and down. The alimentary canal, or gut, is an uncoiled tube leading from the mouth to the anus. A number of digestive sacs are attached near its mid-point, and salivary glands in the thorax have a duct leading forwards and opening in the mouth. In the abdomen there are a large number of threadlike Malpighian tubules, which open into the hinder part of the alimentary canal. They absorb excretory products from the haemocoel and pass them out into the gut.

Reproductive organs occupy part of the space in the abdomen and have their openings at the posterior end. Individuals are either male or female and mating occurs prior to egg-laying. The female's abdomen is furnished with horny projections at the tail end and can be forced down into the soil, so making a vertical burrow in which the eggs are deposited, afterwards being covered with loose soil. They generally hatch all at the same time and the young hoppers emerge from the burrow one after another in quick succession. They are like adults on hatching, but lack wings and have proportionately rather large heads. They proceed to eat voraciously and from time to time moult, or undergo ecdysis, as it is called. At ecdysis, the cuticle splits down the back and the animal slowly withdraws itself from the old skin, clad in a new one. The latter is at first white and very soft. It stretches rapidly and then hardens on contact with the air, at the same time darkening and assuming its characteristic colour. Thus at each ecdysis there is a sudden increase in size, until, after five of them, the adult stage is reached. There is then no further growth or development. Wings appear after the third moult but do not reach their full size or become functional until the insect is fully adult.

Insects are the only arthropods with wings. Other arthropod groups occurring commonly on land that may be confused with them are as follows:

(1) Arachnids—spiders and their allies. These have four pairs of legs and only two main divisions of the body, a cephalothorax—like head and thorax combined—and an abdomen. This group includes scorpions, ticks and mites.
(2) Millipedes. These have a large number of similar segments each with two pairs of legs, the body usually being approximately circular in section.
(3) Centipedes. Superficially similar to millipedes, with their large number of segments and legs, they have only one pair of legs per segment and a flattened body.
(4) Woodlice. These animals are amongst the very few

representatives of the arthropod group Crustacea found living on land.

The vast majority of crustaceans, including a tremendous variety of forms such as crabs, lobsters and shrimps, live in water, especially the sea. Many insects also spend part or the whole of their lives in water, as anyone who has studied pond life, even a little, will know.

Phylum Chordata

Salmo trutta, the brown trout (Fig. 4.25)
The sub-phylum Vertebrata forms the most important division of the phylum Chordata. Other chordates (including for example, sea squirts and the lancelet, *Amphioxus*) are not familiar to most people. They do not have backbones and therefore cannot be called vertebrates, although they have other features that show their close relationship. The vertebrates comprise fishes, amphibians (frogs, toads, newts), reptiles (crocodiles, lizards, snakes, tortoises), birds and mammals. The organisation of the last group has been described in detail in Chapter 2, but it may be useful to give an account of a simpler vertebrate for comparison with the arthropods and molluscs at about the same level of organisation.

Fig. 4.25 shows the arrangement of the main organ systems in a trout. The vertebral column forms the central axis of the body. Above and on either side of this is the mass of muscle that constitutes the edible flesh of the fish. Its function is to produce swimming movements. Below the backbone is a body cavity containing the digestive, excretory and reproductive systems, which are essentially similar to those in mammals. (The body cavity is a coelom, as in the earthworm, not a haemocoel.) The head contains the brain, which is connected with the dorsal nerve cord. Just behind the mouth on either side are the gills. Here there are openings

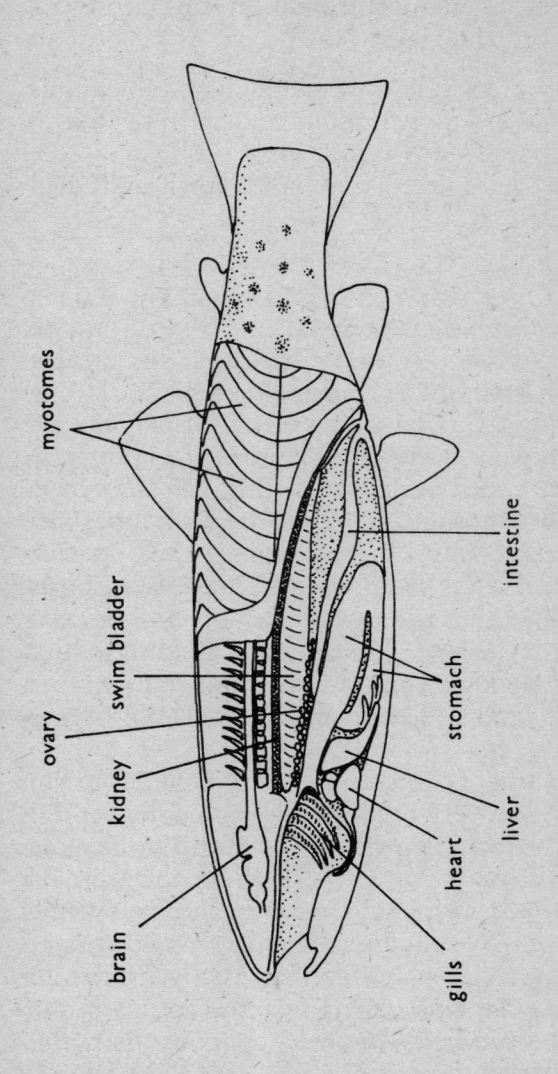

Fig. 4.25 The brown trout, *Salmo trutta*, showing principal organs. The anterior (front) part of the body has been sectioned in the midline; just behind this the skin only has been removed over an area to show the swimming muscles and their division into myotomes

leading from the throat (pharynx) to the outside, closed by the hinged gill covers. Within these covers are four bony gill arches, bridging the openings. Attached to the gill arches are a number of gill filaments richly supplied with blood. They serve to extract oxygen from solution in the water that constantly flows into the mouth and out of the gills as a result of the rhythmical opening and closing of those organs.

The heart is situated ventrally below the pharynx. It is similar to that of a mammal, except that it has but a single ventricle and a single auricle, although there is an additional small chamber, the sinus venosus, just behind the auricle, where the chief veins meet. Thus blood flows from the veins into the sinus venosus, then into the auricle and finally the ventricle. Contraction of the ventricle forces blood forward through a short aorta, which gives off branches to each of the gill arches. Further branching gives rise to a capillary network in the gill filaments, from which the blood is collected by another series of arteries into a dorsal aorta, which lies just below the vertebral column and extends into the tail. Smaller arteries branch from it, leading the blood into capillaries in the various organs, from which it is collected by veins leading back to the sinus venosus. Thus there is no double circulation in the fish.

If you have ever eaten fish you will be familiar with the fact that the flesh is divided up into a number of zig-zag sections following one another along the length of the fish. These sections are called myotomes (Fig. 4.25). Corresponding to the gaps between each pair of myotomes is a vertebra, the small bones attached to the latter, a pair of nerves coming from the nerve cord and arteries that branch off from the dorsal aorta. So the body of the fish is made up of a series of units, one behind the other, in each of which the same structures are repeated. In other words, the animal is segmented, like the annelids and arthropods. This segmentation, however, is not apparent in the organs of the body cavity or in the structure of the head.

In an earthworm the wave-like movement that brings about locomotion involves successive contractions of the segments one after another. Locomotion in a fish is associated with the presence of segments in a somewhat similar way. When a fish such as an eel is swimming, S-shaped waves will be seen travelling rapidly from head to tail. These waves push on the water and so cause forward motion of the fish. Similar waves occur in short-bodied fish such as trout but are not as obvious. They are brought about by the action of the myotomes. The muscle fibres in the myotomes are parallel to the length of the fish, and if a myotome on one side contracts, whilst its opposite number on the other side relaxes, the effect is to cause that part of the body to bend about the bony axis formed by the backbone. The myotomes contract like this in rapid succession one after the other and so a wave of bending travels down the body. Combined with bending in the opposite direction brought about by myotomes of the other side, this results in the formation of the S-shaped waves mentioned above.

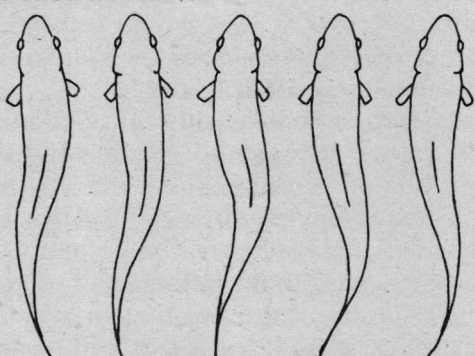

Fig. 4.26 Swimming movements in a fish. The drawings represent successive positions at intervals of a fraction of a second

The tail fin assists in the process just described: the wave motion causes the fin to move from side to side, whilst at the same time it is bent obliquely and so pushes backwards on the water (Fig. 4.26). The reaction of the water produces forward thrust. Other fins are not chiefly concerned with producing forward motion, however. Their main function is to stablise and control the fish's movements.

To control the level at which the fish floats there is an organ called the swim bladder, an air-filled membranous sack just below the vertebral column (Fig. 4.25). One part of the membrane is richly supplied with blood vessels and is able to secrete oxygen, whilst another similar organ absorbs it. It is thus possible for the fish to control the amount of gas in the bladder. This in turn affects its buoyancy: if the amount of gas is increased, the fish floats upwards; if it is decreased, it sinks; and if it is just right, it remains at the same level.

Trout breed in November and December. When the females are ready to spawn (i.e. lay their eggs) they pair up with males. The female then digs a hollow in the gravelly bottom of the stream with her tail and lays her eggs in it. The male swimming nearby sheds 'milt' (sperms) over them so that they are fertilised. Fertile eggs may be purchased from trout hatcheries, and it is easy to keep them and observe their development. They should be placed in a shallow dish through which a steady flow of water from a tap is allowed to flow. Any opaque-looking eggs should be removed, since these will be diseased. On hatching, it will be seen that each baby trout has an orange yolk sack attached to its belly. The little fish is transparent, and when observed with a good lens or a microscope details of the blood vessels and the beating of the heart may be seen. At first the yolk supplies all the food needed by the little trout, but after a time it is used up and the fish has to start feeding. The babies are difficult to keep after this and it is probably best to release them into a suitable stream or lake.

MICRO-ORGANISMS

In order to survive an organism must have access to (i) a source of energy and (ii) a source of raw materials. Green plants and animals represent two major types of organisation, each adapted to take advantage of certain kinds of resource. Green plants have developed a means of utilising solar radiation as their energy source and very simple inorganic compounds as their raw materials. Animals use the chemical energy of complex organic compounds as their source of energy and the same compounds as their raw materials. (Of course, such is the adaptability of living things that these statements are true only as broad generalisations. There are flowering plants, such as the common sundew, that can capture insects and utilise the complex compounds of their bodies as food.) One can imagine that, if the world were a different place, organisms based on quite different principles might have evolved. In fact, there are examples of this kind of thing amongst micro-organisms, which are distinguished not so much by variety and elaboration of structure of the sort seen in ordinary plants and animals as by variations in chemistry.

Fungi

Fungi are sometimes grouped with bacteria and algae to form a major division, or phylum, of the Plant Kingdom, the Thallophyta; alternatively, they may be treated as a phylum in their own right. They are simple plants which never have chlorophyll and reproduce by means of spores. Toadstools are the most familiar examples. These, however, convey a rather misleading picture of the group, because the toadstool is actually an unusually large and elaborate spore-producing organ, formed only for purposes of reproduction. The permanent body of the fungus consists of a network of filaments growing in the soil or in decaying plant material. More typical of fungi in general are the various moulds that appear on decaying food, and one example of these will be described.

Penicillium

This mould appears as green patches on decaying food, the colour being that of the spores produced when the mould reaches the reproductive stage. Within the food the mould is present as microscopic branching filaments called hyphae, the whole network being known as a mycelium. A hypha is a tube with a wall composed of cellulose and containing protoplasm, nuclei and vacuoles. Although there are no regular cells (as in *Spirogyra*, for example), there are partitions, or septa, at irregular intervals. The spores (conidia) are formed at the end of much branched hyphae (Fig. 4.27), where the mycelium is growing on the surface of the food. A spore is a very small cell containing one nucleus. It is so small that it is readily carried long distances by air currents. On reaching suitable food or other dead organic matter, it germinates and gives rise to a new mycelium. There is a form of sexual reproduction that occurs when mycelia of

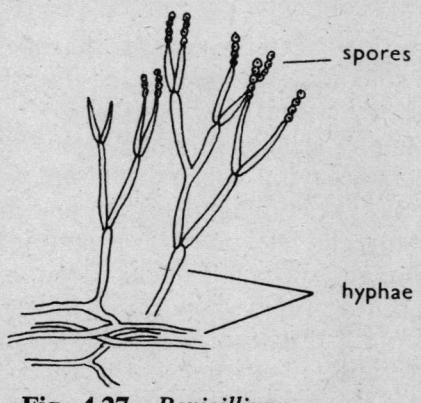

Fig. 4.27 *Penicillium*

differing strains (roughly equivalent to sexes) come into contact. Hyphae from the two mycelia fuse, giving rise to cells containing nuclei from both parents. Later, when spores are formed, the two kinds of nuclei become separated again, and each spore contains but a single nucleus.

The mycelium of *Penicillium* obtains its food by passing out enzymes into the material on which it is growing and by digesting the food present, which is then absorbed. Thus the fungus obtains its raw materials and energy in basically the same way as an animal, although there is no internal digestive system. In spite of the green colour (*not* due to chlorophyll), there is no photosynthesis.

One (uncommon) species of *Penicillium*, *P. notatum*, is famous as the original source of penicillin. The discovery was due to the keen observation of Sir Alexander Flemming, who noticed that, in cultures of bacteria that had become accidentally contaminated with a growth of this mould, the bacteria were being killed in the neighbourhood of the fungus. Research following this observation showed that this was caused by a chemical—later christened penicillin—manufactured by the *Penicillium* and passing out into the culture. The value of this discovery lay in the fact that, although penicillin was found to have a lethal effect on many disease-causing bacteria, it was harmless to the human body and so could even be injected into the blood stream to attack bacteria within the body.

Of the many species of fungi, some are like *Penicillium* and live on decaying organic matter. They are known as saprophytes. The edible mushroom and many toadstools, in which the mycelia feed on organic matter in the soil, and the dry rot fungus, which attacks dead wood, are further examples. Other fungi grow on or in living organisms and are therefore parasites. The mildews that attack garden plants are familiar examples; the rusts and smuts, which cause great losses to farmers, are fungi that parasitise cereals and produce masses of brown or black spores, so giving rise to the popular name; aquarium enthusiasts are familiar with the fungus which can so easily cause the death of their fish. There are a few fungi that parasitise man, one causing athlete's foot, for example.

Saccharomyces, yeast

Yeast is of interest chiefly because of its biochemistry and its practical importance in the preparation of bread and alcoholic drinks. Unlike most fungi, it exists in the form of single cells (Fig. 4.28 (A)), each having a cell wall and containing cytoplasm, a nucleus and a vacuole. The cells reproduce by a process known as budding, in which a new cell appears as an outgrowth from the parent cell, gradually becoming larger and larger, and finally forming a complete new cell. It may remain attached to the parent cell for a time —and sometimes chains of cells are formed in this way—or it may become separated almost immediately. In unfavourable conditions the contents of a cell may undergo division to form two, four or eight spores, which are at first enclosed within the old cell wall (Figure 4.28 (B)). When set free by the rupture of the cell wall, the spores, on encountering suitable conditions, will grow and start to reproduce by budding, so giving rise to ordinary yeast cells. Forms of sexual reproduction do occur and consist simply of the union of two cells to form a zygote, after which spores are formed in the way just described.

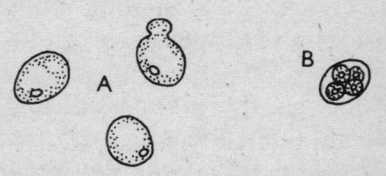

Fig. 4.28 Yeast, *Saccharomyces:* (A) three cells, one with a bud developing; (B) a cell containing four spores

Yeasts favour an environment containing a good supply of sugar and are found naturally in, for example, fermenting fruit. The peculiar feature of their biochemistry is connected with the fact that they are able to obtain energy from sugars in the absence of oxygen. They do this by a process, closely similar to the first stage of respiration in higher organisms, in which the sugar is broken down to form alcohol and carbon dioxide:

$$C_6H_{12}O_6 \rightarrow 2C_2H_5OH + 2CO_2 + \text{energy}$$
$$\text{glucose} \qquad\quad \text{alcohol}$$

This is alcoholic fermentation. Since it is a type of respiration that does not involve oxygen, it is also a form of anaerobic respiration. Yeast can carry out ordinary respiration, in addition, if oxygen is present.

The economic importance of yeast depends upon both products of fermentation. In baking bread, yeast acts on a small amount of sugar in the dough to produce large volumes of carbon dioxide, which cause the dough to rise. In making alcoholic beverages, fermentation of sugar gives rise to the desired alcohol and the carbon dioxide may be retained under slight pressure in the liquor to make it fizzy. Alternatively, it may be removed and made commercially available for various other purposes, including making fizzy soft drinks.

Yeast requires sugar as the raw material for fermentation and alcoholic drinks are prepared from a wide range of naturally occurring substances containing sugar. In the case of beer the basic raw material is grain (barley), which contains carbohydrate in the form of starch. In order to convert this into sugar the grain is allowed to commence germinating. When this happens an enzyme produced in the grain converts the starch into sugar. Germination is halted by drying the grain, which is now known as malt. Then, in the first stage of brewing, the malt is sprayed with warm water, which extracts the sugar to form a solution (the wort) which can then be fermented.

Bacteria

Bacteria have a much simpler structure than any organism encountered so far. They are single-celled but considerably smaller than any of the Protozoa or ordinary plant and animal cells. Thus a small bacterium might be only 1 μm across. (Compare this with a red blood corpuscle—small as animal cells go—which is 7 or 8 μm in diameter.) Figure 4.29 shows the organisation of a typical example. A cellulose capsule surrounds the whole cell, while in the centre is a region containing nucleic acid, which corresponds to the nucleus of higher cells. It is not separated from the outer region, composed mainly of protein, by any definite membrane. Bacteria are variously shaped: they may be spherical, rod-shaped or spiral. Some species have flagella, with which they can swim in a limited way.

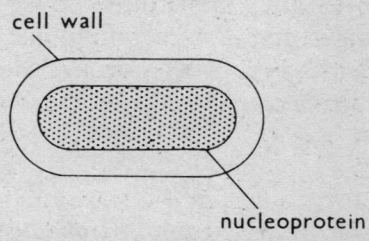

Fig. 4.29 A bacterial cell

Reproduction of bacteria is brought about by cell division, or fission. In favourable circumstances the cells may divide as often as once every half hour, so that they are capable of increasing in numbers at an enormous rate. (Calculate how many cells will result from one bacterium after half an hour, one hour, one and a half hours, up to twenty-four hours, assuming that all offspring go on dividing with the same frequency.) A process similar to sexual reproduction in *Spirogyra* may take place between pairs of cells, so that sex occurs even in bacteria.

The majority of bacteria are saprophytic (like *Penicillium*), that is they obtain both energy and raw materials by the breakdown of non-living organic matter. Decay of organic matter is, in fact, due to this kind of activity of bacteria and fungi. Some are parasitic and cause disease. The discovery of this cause of disease was made by Pasteur, who observed bacteria in the blood of sheep suffering from anthrax. Examples of disease in man caused by bacteria are pneumonia, typhoid, leprosy and boils.

The metabolism of these organisms is not fundamentally different from that of saprophytes, in so far as they utilise complex organic materials derived from the host organism. However, there are some bacteria that have interesting 'unorthodox' ways of obtaining what they need. Some of these are common in soil and, indeed, play a vital part in maintaining its fertility. When the remains of dead organisms get into the soil they are broken down by saprophytes and the amino acids give rise to ammonia. The latter does not survive long, however, because a bacterium called *Nitrosomanas* soon causes it to combine with oxygen to form nitrous acid:

$$2NH_3 + 3O_2 \rightarrow 2HNO_2 + 2H_2O + \text{energy}$$

Another kind of bacterium, *Nitrobacter*, then brings about further oxidation, forming nitric acid:

$$2HNO_2 + O_2 \rightarrow 2HNO_3 + \text{energy}$$

These chemical changes are particularly important, because ordinary plants cannot utilise either ammonia or nitrous acid but can use nitric acid (or, rather, the nitrates that are produced by the reaction of nitric acid with alkaline substances in the soil), which is their only source of nitrogen.

As indicated in the equations, both reactions produce energy. This is used by *Nitrosomonas* and *Nitrobacter* to build up complex organic compounds from carbon dioxide present in the soil air. So the reactions can be regarded as unusual forms of respiration, and these organisms are obtaining energy by oxidising simple inorganic compounds and also using simple compounds as basic raw materials.

Other bacteria contribute to the supply of nitrogen in the soil because they are able to make the nitrogen of the air combine with other elements to form organic nitrogen compounds, which they use in building up their protoplasm. (They are said to 'fix' atmospheric nitrogen.) To do this they need energy, which is obtained in the 'orthodox' way, either (in *Azotobacter*) by breakdown and oxidation of carbohydrates or (in *Clostridium*) by anaerobic breakdown of carbohydrates (i.e. fermentation). A third kind of bacterium (*Rhizobium*) does a similar thing, but only when living in the roots of clover, beans, lucerne and other flowering plants of the pea family.

The relationship between *Rhizobium* and the plant is interesting. At first sight it looks like a case of parasitism. When the bacteria infect the roots they cause the appearance of swellings or nodules, and in the centre of each nodule are cells full of the bacteria. The latter obtain carbohydrate from the plant cells and nitrogen from the air in the air spaces of the root. However, at the same time, the plant obtains nitrogen compounds from the bacteria and needs no outside source of the element. There seems, therefore, to be a balanced relationship in which both partners benefit: it is, in other words, a case of *symbiosis* rather than parasitism.

The nitrogen-fixing bacteria represent yet another variation in the biochemistry of organisms: their source of energy is the chemical energy of complex organic compounds, and their sources of raw materials are the same compounds and nitrogen from the air. The following table is a simple classification of some organisms according to the nature of their biochemistry.

	Sources of raw materials	
Sources of energy	Complex organic compounds	Simple inorganic substances
Light		Green plants
Breakdown of organic compounds	Animals, saprophytic fungi and bacteria	*Azotobacter, Clostridium, Rhizobium*
Oxidation of inorganic compounds		*Nitrosomonas Nitrobacter*

Viruses

Viruses are disease organisms rather like very small bacteria. A large virus would be only 1/3 μm long—one tenth of the size of many bacteria. Not only are they much smaller, but they also differ from bacteria in other important ways. No virus can live independently, like the saprophytic bacteria, and they can only be active and reproduce within the living cells of a host organism and in close association with the cellular machinery, as will be explained below.

Many human diseases are caused by viruses. The list

includes the common cold, influenza, chickenpox, mumps, measles, smallpox, poliomyelitis and rabies. Because the disease organism is inactive and, indeed, cannot survive long outside the host, these illnesses are generally transmitted directly from one person to another. We acquire the disease by contact with somebody else who already has it, either by actually touching them or by coming into contact with the minute droplets thrown out when coughing, for example, which may contain virus particles. When the virus enters the body there is a period of initial multiplication, the incubation period, when it attacks the host cells and increases in number, spreading from one cell to another, until the infection is general and symptoms become apparent. The body defends itself by producing substances known as antibodies. These are proteins that circulate in the blood, attach themselves to the virus particles and so render them inactive. The result is that the virus is destroyed and the patient recovers. The antibody remains, however, and protects the person from any further attacks, so that he is now immune to that particular disease. The antibody protein has in some way to 'match' the virus protein, so that there must be a specific type of antibody to combat each kind of virus. That is why it is never possible for people to become immune to virus diseases in general. In the case of some diseases (notably the common cold and influenza) it seems that the viruses are continually changing and giving rise to new strains that are not affected by antibodies produced in response to the old strains. For this reason, immunity does not last long in these cases.

Bacterial infection can generally be treated by administering antibiotics (e.g. penicillin) or drugs such as the sulphonamides, which attack the bacteria in the patient's body without harming him. This does not work with viruses, which are not affected by drugs and antibiotics. The only available means of defence (apart from avoiding contact between sufferers and healthy people) depends upon use of the antibody mechanism. This possibility was discovered long before the mechanism was understood, when the eighteenth-century physician, Jenner, invented vaccination against smallpox. He had observed that (a) cowhands often contracted a mild disease known as cowpox from infected cows handled by them, and (b) such people were apparently immune to smallpox, a disease that is often fatal and was rampant in England at the time. He reasoned that if people could be given cowpox deliberately they would be protected from smallpox. In order to achieve this he obtained fluid (vaccine—from the Latin *vacca* = a cow) from the pustules on an infected animal and transferred it to a scratch on the skin of the patient to be treated. This is, in essence, still the method used today, although now we take more precautions to avoid extraneous infection. Vaccination in this way results in the formation of a single sore at the site of infection. It soon heals up, leaving a scar, but is sufficient to produce immunity. We now know that the reason for this is that the cowpox and smallpox viruses are so closely related that the antibody produced in response to one is effective against the other. In more recent times, vaccines effective against other diseases (e.g. poliomyelitis) have been produced, the general method consisting of culturing the responsible virus and treating it in such a way that it is no longer capable of causing disease but will result in antibody production when introduced into the body.

Another, less used, method of protection against virus disease involves taking blood given by donors and separating that part of the serum which contains the antibodies. When injected, this provides a patient with some measure of immunity against certain diseases, for example measles.

The way in which viruses act has been closely studied in the case of certain kinds that infect bacteria. These are known as bacteriophages. Fig. 4.30 shows one that attacks a

Fig. 4.30 A virus

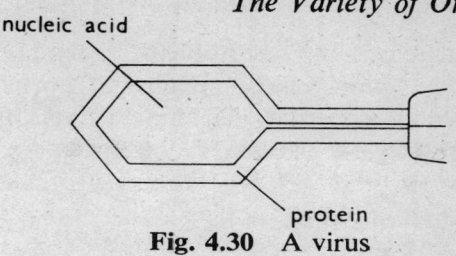

species of bacterium (*Escherichia coli*) found in the human colon. The virus is about 200 nm (= 0.2 μm = 0.0002 mm) in length. The head part of it consists of a core of nucleic acid surrounded by a protein coat. The 'tail' is a tube, also made of protein, with little prong-like structures at its free end. These enable the virus to attach itself to the surface of a bacterial cell. When this happens an enzyme in the tail dissolves the bacterial cell wall, making a hole in it, and then the nucleic acid passes down the tail and into the bacterium. As was explained in Chapter 3, nucleic acid has two fundamentally important properties: (i) it can control processes leading to its own replication, and (ii) it can control the formation of the proteins characteristic of the organism to which it belongs. On entering the bacterial cell, the virus nucleic acid makes a successful takeover bid for control of the cell and proceeds to use the cell mechanism for its own purposes. First, it breaks down the bacterial nucleic acid and uses the resulting fragments (with other materials drawn from outside the cell) to build up more virus nucleic acid. Then it takes over the protein synthesising machinery and makes virus protein. Finally, the nucleic acid and protein are put together to constitute a large number of new virus particles. At this stage the bacterial cell has been almost completely destroyed. It bursts and liberates the virus particles, which may go on to attack further cells.

It is clear now why viruses cannot be other than parasitic.

Their ability to carry out metabolism depends upon their ability to use the biochemical systems of host cells. They have no complete biochemical machine of their own, and so when outside a cell are necessarily inert.

CONCLUSION

In this brief survey of the living world two opposing themes are apparent. On the one hand, we see increasing elaboration leading to increasing adaptability. The most highly complex types of organisation seem capable of existing in the most diverse circumstances. This tendency culminates in man, who can maintain himself from the poles to the equator, or even on the moon. At the same time, there is a tendency towards specialisation, towards various forms of organisation devoted to taking advantage of only certain resources and surviving in limited circumstances, exemplied in the most extreme form by the viruses. The patterns produced by the interaction of these tendencies are explored in the next chapter.

5 Ecology

Most people must know that in recent years there has been a growing awareness of the urgent need for mankind to care for his environment. We hear a great deal about pollution and conservation, and, linked with these, about the science of ecology. Ecology is a branch of biology that makes its chief concern the study of organisms in their natural surroundings. It may be regarded as the more scientific successor to the older study of natural history. As soon as we begin to look at animals and plants in an ecological way, because we are looking not so much into them as at them, regarding them as whole units, and because we are seeing them in their natural settings, we become aware of the many ways in which they interact. We see that the entire interacting community of organisms is a complex system, of which man forms a part, such that disturbance of one part affects all other parts to some extent. It is because of this that ecology and conservation are so closely linked.

Even those with the most casual acquaintance with natural history must be aware that particular species are to be found in particular places. Buttercups grow in meadows, bluebells in woodland; moorhens are most likely to be seen near ponds and rivers, larks in open grassland. Each organism, we say, has its particular habitat, the place in which it lives. More than this, it follows that any habitat is inhabited by a particular set of organisms and that the presence of each species is determined partly by the presence of other species. We might guess (correctly) that the fact that bluebells grow in woods has something to do with the existence of trees there. In a similar way, the people in a town are not just a collection of individuals who happen, quite regardless of the other inhabitants, to have decided to live in one place. On the contrary, most of them are there because they can find work in the town, and opportunities for work are very largely provided by the other town dwellers. Shopkeepers would not be able to sell anything in the absence of customers and garage mechanics would have nothing to repair if there were no owners of vehicles in the neighbourhood. This is what gives rise to the sense of *community*, and this word is used to refer to the organisms in a habitat. We speak of the natural community of a wood, a piece of grassland or a pond.

Natural communities

Let us start by considering a familiar natural community, an oak wood. Enter the wood in the spring or early summer and one is bound to be impressed by the profusion of plants of all kinds, from the largest tree to the smallest moss. Stand back a little, as it were, to see the broad outlines of the vegetation and one will be aware that the foliage forms a number of quite distinct layers. The uppermost layer is formed by the canopies of the trees themselves. If the wood is at all dense, these will be high above the ground, since the lower branches tend to die off through lack of light. Much nearer the ground is the foliage of shrubs, mostly hazel as a rule. Below this again is the field layer containing the various herbaceous plants, such as bluebells, anemones, primroses, celandines, certain ferns, wood sorrel and many others. Finally, growing close to the soil are mosses and, in damper situations, liverworts, forming the ground layer (Fig. 5.1).

Conditions in these layers change gradually from top to bottom, the principal differences being in light intensity, which diminishes progressively, and humidity, which increases, because of the sheltering effect of the plants.

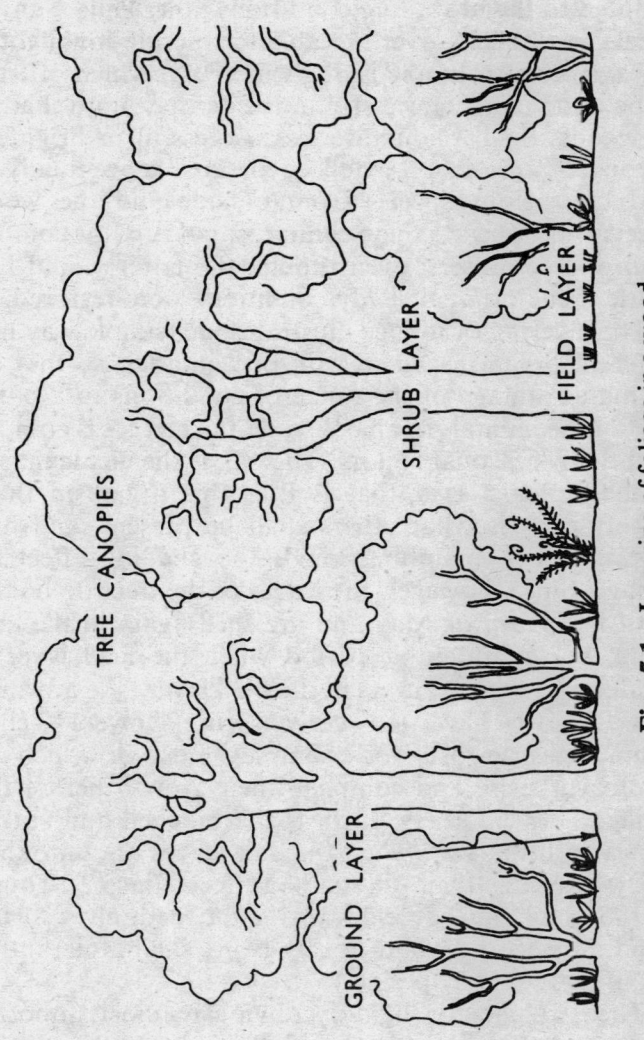

Fig. 5.1 Layering of foliage in a wood

Generally speaking, the species occupying each layer are adapted to the prevailing conditions in it. Thus many of the plants in the field layer are able to tolerate low light intensities. A good example is dog's mercury, which often seems to be particularly successful in the denser, more shady parts of woods. Such plants are less successful in brighter conditions. So, if a wood is felled, the area is eventually colonised by various species from outside and the woodland species disappear: they cannot stand up to competition from the colonisers, even though the latter would lose the battle if the original shady conditions were restored.

The layering of foliage illustrates in a simple way how the different organisms fit in with one another, so that each is taking advantage of the range of conditions in a particular part of the habitat. In an oakwood the picture is complicated slightly by seasonal factors. The oak is the **dominant** species, as the ecologist says, that is it is this organism that very largely decides what others shall be present, and it exerts this influence mainly through the shading effect of the foliage. Since, however, the leaves of the trees do not appear until late April or May and are shed again in the autumn, there is a considerable period when the field layer is not shaded and many flowers in the field layer take advantage of this. So we have the early spring flowers—celandine, anemone, primrose, for example—most of which flower, photosynthesise and complete their growth before the tree foliage is out. Others, such as the bluebell and stitchwort, appear a little later, when the oak leaves are unfolding but not yet exerting their full shading effect (Fig. 5.2). Thus many of the plants in the field layer adapt themselves to lighting conditions in the wood not by being shade tolerant but by avoiding the shady period.

The struggle for light is obviously most important to organisms that rely on photosynthesis, and it is interesting to consider some of the means plants have adopted to obtain

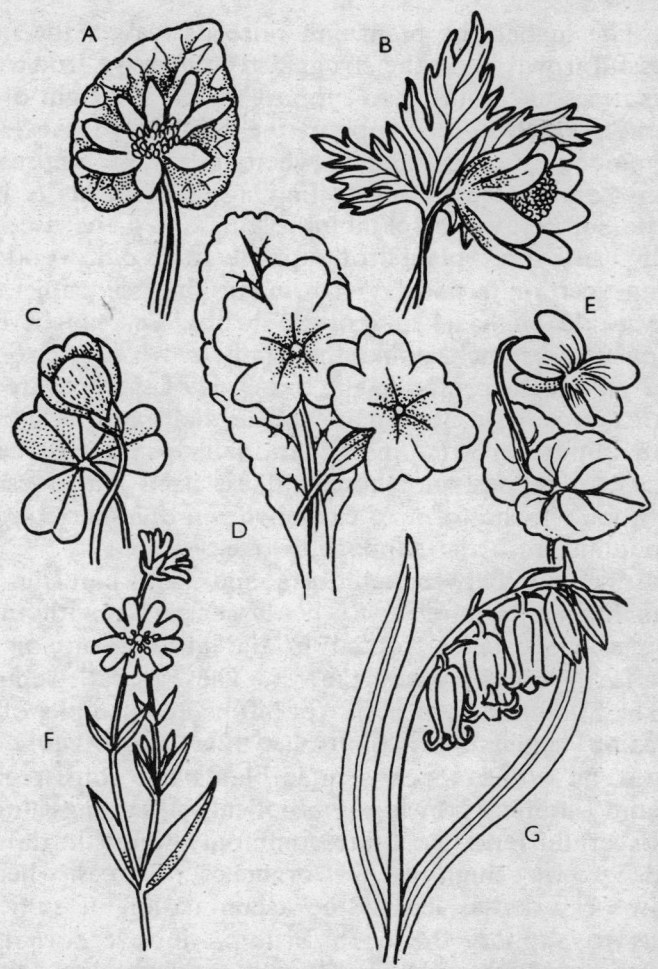

Fig. 5.2 Some common woodland flowers. The time of flowering is given after the name of each: (A) lesser celandine (March–May); (B) wood anemone (March–April); (C) wood sorrel (April–May); (D) primrose (February–May); (E) violet (April–June); (F) stitchwort (April–June); (G) bluebell (May)

light. The higher the plant can raise its leaves, the more successful it will be in the struggle. The massive trunk of a tree is necessary in order to support the great weight of the branches, which in turn support the twigs and leaves. One is reminded of a cathedral, where all those impressive columns and the beautiful vaulting are there merely to keep the roof up. However, climbing plants avoid the need for this by using other plants for support. In an oak wood one is almost certain to find ivy growing up the tree trunks, and honeysuckle on hazel and other shrubs. One might even find mistletoe, which, unlike the climbers, which are rooted in the ground, is rooted in the branches of the host tree. It is an example of a hemi-parasite (i.e. half-parasite), since, although it draws water and mineral salts from the tissues of the host, it carries out photosynthesis itself and does not draw foods in the form of carbohydrate or other complex compounds from the supporting tree.

Intermediate between climbers and hemi-parasites are plants that grow on trees (or other larger plants) without, on the one hand, being rooted in the ground or, on the other, taking anything from the tree. These are called epiphytes. The humble *Pleurococcus* (p. 140) is an example, others are various lichens. (Lichens are also interesting because they are not, as would appear, single plants but consist of an alga and a fungus growing symbiotically.) Amongst higher plants certain ferns are quite commonly found in damper woods growing high on the branches of trees where a hollow or fork has led to the accumulation of sufficient humus to support them. In Britain, however, we have none of the highly specialised epiphytes such as are found in the tropics. There various species of fern and orchid have developed means of supporting themselves on quite bare branches with little or no soil.

So far we have not considered the animals that might inhabit our oak wood. Close examination of the litter of decaying leaves, twigs, etc. on the ground will reveal the presence of all sorts of invertebrates, including beetles, millipedes, small earthworms, spiders, centipedes and woodlice. Others will be found on the leaves of the field layer and on the foliage of the shrubs and trees. Various moths and their caterpillars (feeding on the leaves) may especially be noted. Amongst well-known birds likely to be present are robins, blackbirds, song thrushes, great tits, wrens, woodpeckers, jays and owls (most likely the tawny owl). Mammals commonly found in woodland are the bank vole, wood mouse (long-tailed field mouse), squirrel, common shrew, stoat, weasel, fox, badger and deer (in some parts of the country the little roe deer is much more common and widely distributed than is generally realised).

Food chains

The animals introduce another important type of ecological relationship existing in the system, concerned with the flow of food (i.e. complex organic materials) through it. Green plants, as we have learnt, are producer organisms. By means of photosynthesis they elaborate complex organic substances from simple raw materials. These organic substances serve as raw materials for animals, which are termed consumer organisms. As a result of the tendency for all organisms to specialise, some animals concentrate more or less exclusively on vegetable food and others on animal food. Thus the food of the bank vole is stated 'to consist of green plants, fruits, roots, nuts and fungi and a small quantity of animal material', and the wood mouse feeds chiefly on seeds, 'although, besides fruit and plant material, much animal matter is eaten between April and July, including the larvae of butterflies and moths.'* On the

* Nixon, M., and Whiteley, D., *The Oxford Book of Vertebrates*. O.U.P., 1972, pp. 130, 132.

other hand, these small rodents form a major part of the diet of the tawny owl. So the three kinds of organism are linked in what is called a food chain: plants→rodents→owls. This indicates the fact that food produced in the first place by plants finds its way eventually to owls through mice and voles.

The situation in a natural community is more complex than the picture of a simple food chain might suggest. In reality, the food pathways branch as a result of the fact that few, if any, animals feed exclusively on one kind of food. So the same plants that provide food for mice, and hence owls, might also serve as food for caterpillars, those as food for birds such as robins and those for stoats, or possibly, again, owls. In this way there is a network of pathways constituting the food web (Fig. 5.3). Even so, the final picture adds up to something like that suggested by the simple food chain. Food flows from the producers through various *first-order* consumers to the *higher-order* consumers.

We must not imagine that the quantity of food does not diminish as it flows through the system. Of course it must do, since every organism that takes in food uses a large part of it for respiration, so that it is broken down to form carbon dioxide, water, and nitrogenous and other wastes which are excreted. Only a small part of the food is added to the organism's body and thus is available as raw material for the next animal in the chain. In consequence, the total amount of living matter (biomass, as it is called) becomes progressively less at each stage. There will be a relatively large mass in the form of caterpillars feeding on oak leaves, a much smaller mass in the form of great tits eating them and even less biomass represented by sparrow hawks or owls feeding on them. So the food web may be thought of as forming a pyramid, the base consisting of a great mass of primary consumers and the apex of the relatively few ultimate consumers.

Ecology 215

An effect of the food web that concerns conservationists is the tendency of contaminants to become concentrated in organisms near its apex. This is illustrated in the case of DDT and related substances. These insecticides have the

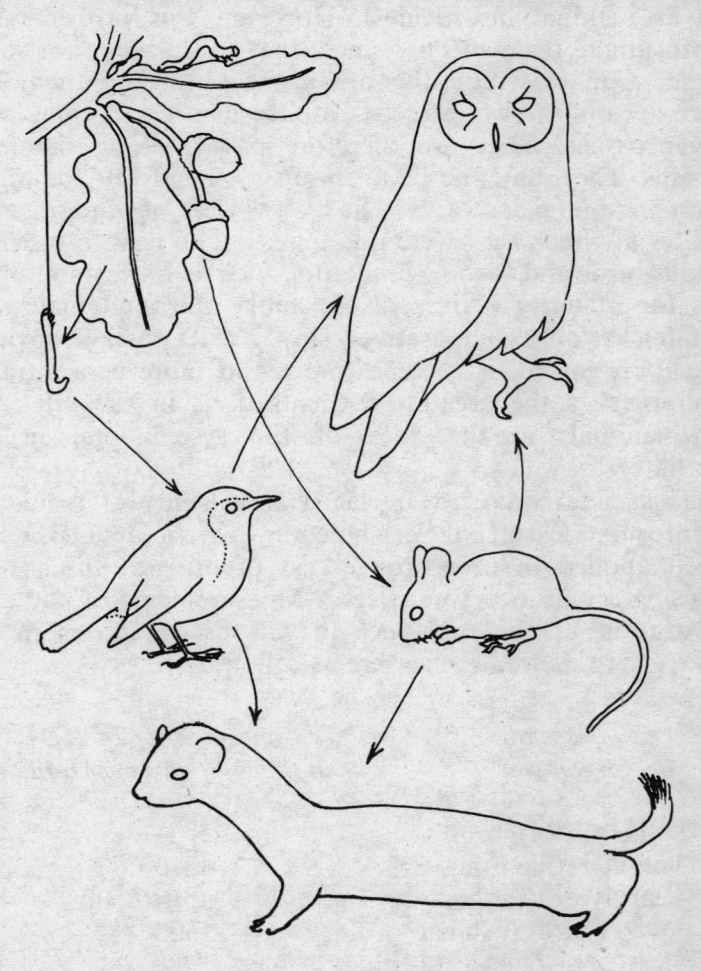

Fig. 5.3 A food web

great advantage that they are only very slowly destroyed under natural conditions. When sprayed on a crop, for example, they leave a residue that remains effective against insects for a very long time (for this reason, they are referred to as residual insecticides). However, this property has unfortunate side-effects, since the substances not only remain intact within the organisms absorbing them but also are only slowly excreted, and so tend to accumulate in their tissues. They are therefore passed along the food chains. They may first be taken up by the insects for which they were intended (as well as by a variety of other invertebrates at which they were not aimed), then pass to insectivorous birds and then to predators, such as hawks and owls. As the quantity of insecticide, unlike the food materials, diminishes only comparatively slowly in its passage through the food chains, it becomes more and more concentrated and reaches the greatest concentrations in the relatively few animals at the apex of the system, i.e. in the predators.

This effect was shown clearly in a study of a lake in California (Clear Lake), where the insecticide DDD had been applied in order to get rid of midges which were causing a nuisance to anglers.* Measurements of the concentration of the substance in various organisms in the lake after this treatment were as follows:

Class of organisms	Concentration of DDD in tissues—parts per million
water invertebrates	5
plant-eating fishes	40–300
carnivorous fishes	up to 2500
water birds (fish-eating)	1600

*Rachael Carson, *Silent Spring*.

Unfortunately, although DDT, DDD and related compounds are *relatively* harmless to vertebrates (whilst, at the same time, lethal to insects in very low concentrations), they are far from harmless if present in sufficiently large quantities. In the case of Clear Lake, almost certainly as a result of the DDD treatment, the population of one species of water bird, the western grebe, was reduced from over 1000 pairs to about 30, which were apparently infertile and incapable of reproduction.

Predatory birds appear to have been particularly vulnerable to this form of chemical poisoning. The recent catastrophic decline of the peregrine falcon in Britain is thought to have been caused at least partly by this, and there is evidence that the golden eagle, which had been increasing in numbers since the 1930s, has also been affected. Man, as the greatest predator of all, is also at risk and may yet receive an unwelcome reward for his carelessness. As it is, the concentration of DDT in the tissues of many Americans exceeds the legally permitted limit in meat sold for human consumption.

The circulation of material in nature

A description of the food web might give the impression that the natural community is a system in which complex organic substances are manufactured and then gradually used up, finally disappearing. There might seem to be a one-way flow from the producers to the higher-order consumers. In fact, this is not true, because in being used up the complex substances are broken down into simpler substances, which eventually return to the producers, so that there is a circulation of material. This is illustrated in broad outline in Fig. 5.4. At the bottom of the diagram are shown the basic raw materials, mineral salts, carbon dioxide and water, which are converted by the photosynthetic organisms (plants) into the complex substances of their own tissues. The word *producers* in the diagram represents the fact that, at this stage, the matter in the system is in the form of the tissues of the producers themselves. If a plant is eaten by an animal (first-order consumer), then the matter is converted into first-order consumer tissues and possibly later into

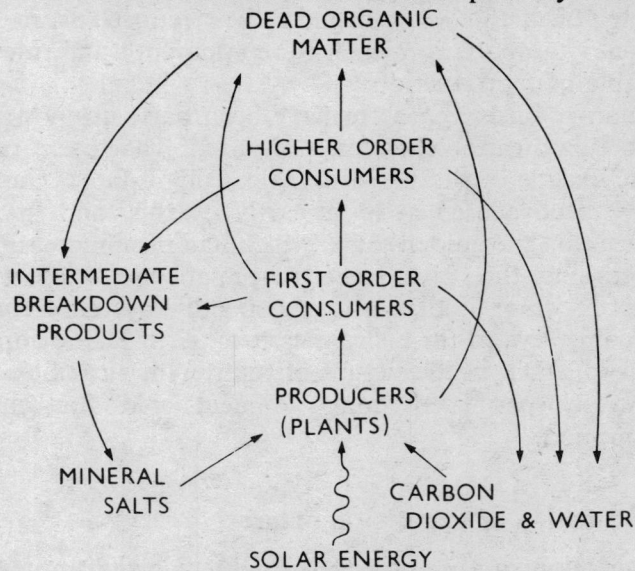

Fig. 5.4 Circulation of material in nature

higher-order consumer tissues. At the same time, all organisms eventually die and so give rise to the dead organic matter shown at the top of the diagram.

Both plants and animals respire constantly, thus converting complex organic compounds into carbon dioxide and water, which enter the system again if they are used by plants in photosynthesis. Hence there is a circulation of these substances, that part of it which involves carbon compounds being referred to as the carbon cycle. It is represented by the clockwise arrows on the right-hand side of the figure.

Ecology 219

There is also a circulation of nitrogen compounds in the nitrogen cycle (Fig. 5.5), part of which was described in the section on bacteria (p. 200). The basic raw material is in the form of nitrates, which are taken up by green plants and largely used for synthesis of proteins. These may be utilised, in turn, by consumer organisms for manufacture of their proteins. However, at the same time, a large part of the nitrogen is excreted in the form of nitrogenous wastes such as urea. This is decomposed by bacteria, giving rise to nitrates. A similar decomposition of nitrogen compounds in dead organic matter yields the same end-product. Thus there is a complete cycle. Nitrogen is fed into the cycle as a result of the activities of nitrogen-fixing bacteria, which convert nitrogen gas from the air into nitrogen compounds, thus making this nitrogen available to the whole living system. (Nitrogen fixation is also brought about by lightning, which causes the combination of atmospheric nitrogen and oxygen to form oxides of nitrogen, which combine with water to form nitric acid, and hence nitrates, in the soil.)

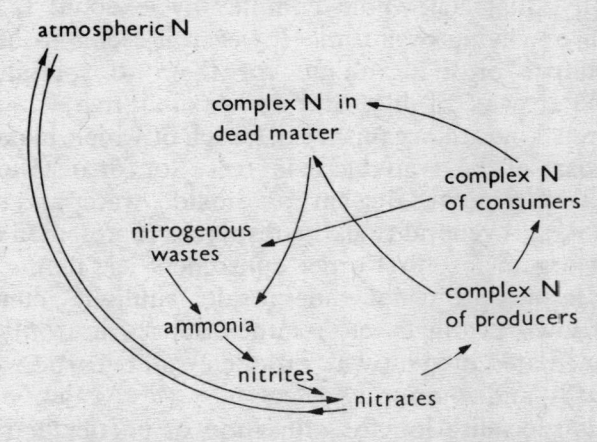

Fig. 5.5 The nitrogen cycle. ('Complex N' = complex nitrogen compounds)

Other, denitrifying, bacteria carry out the reverse process, breaking down nitrates with the liberation of nitrogen gas, leading to loss of nitrogen from the system.

There is a similar circulation of the other elements present in living matter (phosphorus, sulphur, potassium, etc.) and this is represented by the anti-clockwise arrows on the left-hand side of Fig. 5.4. *Intermediate breakdown products* stands for substances such as amino acids or urea which result from the decomposition of proteins or other complex substances and which are themselves further decomposed to yield mineral salts.

Utilisation of natural resources

Figure 5.4 shows that the matter in the community is present in a number of different forms, for example mineral salts, living matter in consumers and so on. Each form of matter represents a different kind of resource which may be used by the organisms present, i.e. it is a potential source of raw material and, possibly, energy. One can visualise, theoretically, that the whole complex cycle could take place within one living organism. However, it seems to be part of the nature of living things for them to specialise in a particular way of life, and so we find that, in practice, different kinds of organism exist, each of which makes use of only part of the available resources. So, for instance, green plants use mineral salts, carbon dioxide, water and sunlight, but not, as a general rule, the resources represented by other living organisms; first-order consumers use plants as their main resource, but not mineral salts, sunlight, intermediate breakdown products, etc.; some bacteria use only certain intermediate breakdown products and carbon dioxide (p. 201)—and so on.

This specialisation for utilisation of particular resources may be more or less narrow. Possibly the most extreme examples are the various parasites, most of which can exist in only one species of host organism. The exact reasons for an organism being adapted to a particular range of resources are rarely known completely, but it seems clear that, when its physiology is adjusted to work most efficiently in one set of circumstances, it is bound to become less efficient for another set. A simple example may help to make this clear. Rodents are adapted for a diet consisting largely of vegetable food. Plant matter is difficult to digest because of its high cellulose content, which is not only mechanically tough but also resistant to digestion. These animals therefore have teeth that are particularly efficient at breaking such food down into small particles. Fig. 5.6 (B) shows the teeth of a mouse. At the front of the mouth are the sharp, chizel-like incisors, which are used to bite off pieces of food, and behind them is a gap (the diastema) and then the molars.

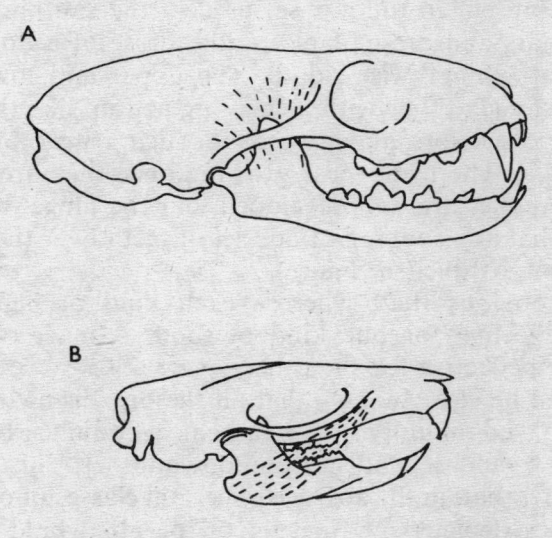

Fig. 5.6   Skulls of (A) stoat and (B) mouse. The broken lines indicate the position of one of the major jaw muscles in each case

The latter have strongly ridged surfaces formed by the alternation of hard enamel and relatively soft dentine. The upper and lower teeth are rubbed over one another so that the food between them is thoroughly ground up. The positions of the muscles producing this action are indicated in the figure. These muscles are strongly developed, while the biting muscles are relatively weak. The teeth are subject to a great deal of wear, and to compensate for this they grow continuously throughout life. The diastema allows the cheeks to be brought together behind the incisors, so shutting them off from the rest of the mouth. This enables the mouse to chew inedible material (e.g. wood, the shells of nuts) without the chips entering the mouth, possibly to be swallowed.

The stoat's dentition (Fig. 5.6 (A)) contrasts with that of the mouse since it is a carnivore. We note the well-developed canines (absent in the mouse) used in the capture of prey. The molars and pre-molars are like those of a dog or cat, with sharp, lengthwise ridges. The upper and lower teeth slide past each other with a shearing action, like the blades of a pair of scissors, and are used for slicing meat rather than grinding it. The teeth cease growing once they are formed. Biting muscles are well developed, but the hinge of the jaw is such that any rubbing of one set of teeth over the other is almost impossible (see figure).

It is obvious that, whereas each kind of dentition is highly effective for one kind of food, it must be almost entirely ineffective for the other.

It must be clear by now that all the organisms that go to make up a community such as an oak wood must be closely adapted to and dependent upon one another. This is shown by the fact that, in the absence of certain classes of organism, the cycles depicted in Fig. 5.4 on p. 218 would cease to function. For example, if there were no green plants, the supply of complex organic material to the system would be cut off and all other organisms would eventually die out; or if there were no bacteria, the supply of mineral salts would not be replenished. One might think that the system could function without the higher-order consumers, but, as will be shown, they often have a controlling function without which the system would get out of balance.

The above considerations are very general and apply to the whole natural system broadly considered. However, it seems that within one particular community there may be a very close adjustment of one organism to another. This is shown by the fact that the range of species within it is quite specific, characteristic of that community and different from that found in other communities. Consider but one group of animals, the rodents: in woodland one might find the wood mouse, the dormouse, the bank vole and the squirrel (red or grey), but in grassland one would be more likely to find the harvest mouse and the short-tailed vole, although the two voles may occur to some extent in either habitat. Thus many species are so well adapted to one particular community that, even if they can survive in another, they are evidently not sufficiently successful to become permanently established.

Effect of physical and biological factors on the environment

So far we have been stressing the influences exerted by organisms on each other. It is obvious, however, that physical factors in the environment must also have a profound influence. For example, oak forest is the main community in the vegetation type that geographers call temperate deciduous forest. A glance at the vegetation map of Europe shows that this occupies an area in the west of the continent extending from southern Scandinavia to the borders of the Mediterranean, a region in which the principal features of the climate are plentiful rain falling in every month of the year and moderate seasonal variations in illumination and temperature. There seems little doubt that it is these factors that determine the characteristics of deciduous forest. We have already seen how flowers in the oak community are adapted to seasonal changes, and the shedding of leaves by the trees in winter must in some way adapt them to conditions in the cold season. However, there is no simple explanation of why this is insufficient in northern Europe, for example, where deciduous forest gives way to evergreen coniferous forest.

There are two kinds of oak forest in Britain, one dominated by the sessile oak (*Quercus petraea*) and the other by the pedunculate oak (*Q. robur*) (Fig. 5.7). The former has a poorer ground flora (i.e. there are fewer species) and is most frequent on the sandy, rocky soils of the north and west, whereas the latter prefers the heavier soils of the midlands, south and east. Here we have another

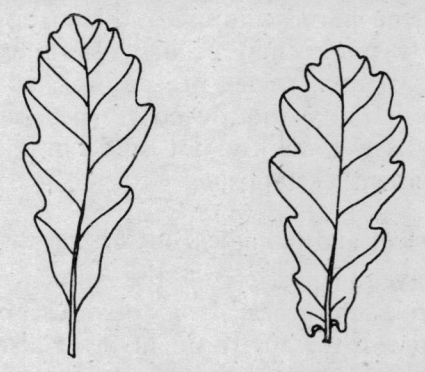

Fig. 5.7 Leaves of *Quercus petraea* (left) and *Q. robur* (right). These show perhaps the most easily noticed difference between the species

example of the controlling effect of physical factors in the environment, in this case *edaphic* (having to do with the soil) rather than climatic.

The biological community also has an effect on the physical environment and, in fact, the two things constantly

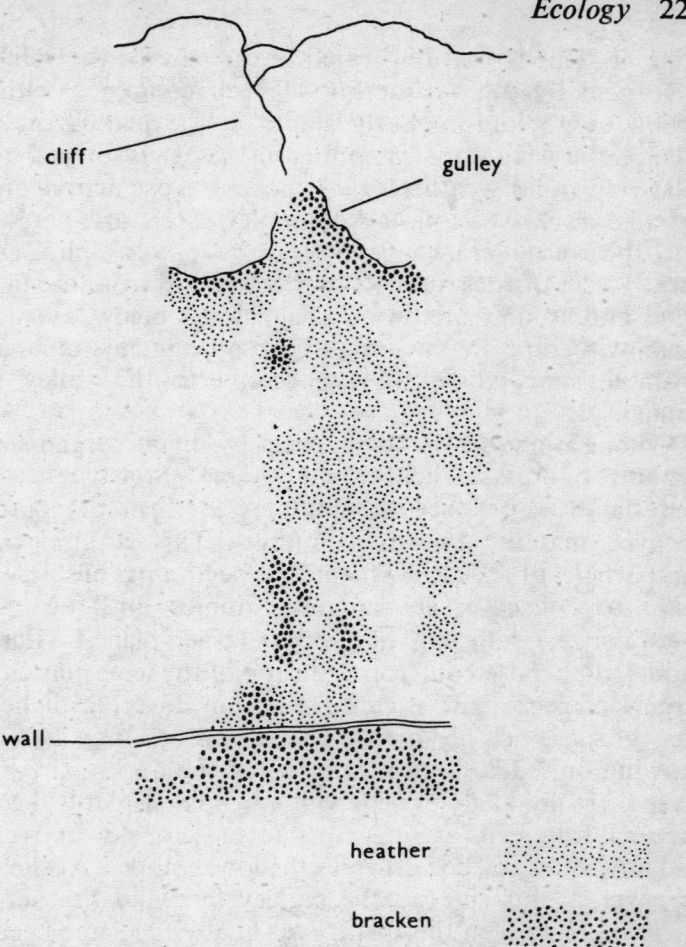

Fig. 5.8 Vegetation on scree (Cader Idris, Merioneth). The areas covered by heather and bracken also contain various other species. Mosses and lichens only are found in the unshaded areas. The scree is most extensively colonised in the region below the gulley, possibly because the latter channels water and soil from the summit into that area. The wall has probably had the effect of stabilising the scree below it, so that here there is a well-developed cover of turf and bracken

interact. This is well illustrated in the case of the soil. Soil is formed by the weathering of rock combined with the action of vegetation. Early stages in the process may be seen on the scree slopes of mountains. Scree is formed by the relatively rapid weathering of rock by frost action on the exposed rock of mountain summits. Moisture percolates into the rock and, when it freezes, expands, splitting the rock. Pieces of rock split off in this way fall from the face of crags and accumulate on the steep slopes below, eventually forming a complete covering of loose fragments in a rather unstable state which slowly descend to the valley floor (Fig. 5.8).

Colonisation of the bare rock by living organisms is begun by mosses, lichens and algae. Slowly the dead material they produce accumulates to form the partially decayed material known as humus. This combines with fine particles of rock to form the first beginnings of soil, which tends to collect in cracks and crannies until eventually there may be sufficient to support larger plants. Thus, although the exposed outcrop at the top of the scree may consist largely of rock, bare except for a thin covering of lichens etc., grasses, heather and even small trees may be found growing on ledges and in fissures. In the upper part of the scree there are likely to be few, if any, higher plants, because the rock fragments are in a constant state of slow movement and any soil is washed down to the lower slopes. At the foot, however, plants such as the parsley fern and heather find anchorage between the rocks, and finally the scree becomes obscured by a complete cover of vegetation—either turf or the heather community characteristic of hills and moors.

At this lower end of the scree there is a quite well-developed soil. That is, instead of there being almost nothing but fragments, there is much finer material between the rocks. This is what permits the development of a complete vegetation cover. Thus, descending from the rocky outcrop downwards, we see the stages of soil formation illustrated. The process consists of (i) the gradual fragmentation of parent rock to yield finer and finer particles, and (ii) the slow accumulation of humus. Vegetation plays a part in this not only by contributing humus (which is essential to the fertility of soil) but also through the action of the roots, which may play a part in splitting rocks and which bind the soil particles, preventing their removal by wind and rain water.

On long ridges in mountainous country it is sometimes possible to see a series of screes illustrating the above process not so much from top to bottom of the ridge as along the length of it. Thus in the central, highest and steepest parts of the ridge erosion is still very active and the screes present are not much colonised. Towards the lower more gentle end of the ridge, however, it is often possible to make out the remnants of old screes that have become completely overgrown, presumably because at the lower altitude frost erosion is so much slower that the scree no longer has new material added, or because the parent outcrop has been almost completely eroded.

This is not, of course, the only situation in which soil may be formed. In fact, it can be and is formed, more or less slowly, in any situation, although naturally its formation is more obvious and dramatic where the solid rock is exposed and subject to rapid erosion. Soil is formed on horizontal surfaces by the erosion of the underlying rock, in which case the soil may remain at the site of its formation; eroded material may be carried long distances by rivers and deposited as alluvium, colonisation of which leads to the formation of ferile soil; or, to provide a third example, coastal erosion by the sea leads to the formation of sand, this may be formed into dunes inland by the action of the wind, the dunes colonised and the sand converted into soil. In whatever way it is formed, however, soil has the same general characteristics. By now it will be clear that it is a mixture of rock fragments, varying in size from large rocks to sub-microscopic particles, and humus, produced by the decay of organic matter. There is a good deal of space between the particles which is able to accommodate considerable quantities of water and air. Both are essential to the well-being of the living constituents of the soil, which include the roots of plants, bacteria and fungi, invertebrates (such as earthworms, millipedes, centipedes and microscopic arthropods) and even vertebrates such as moles.

The composition of soil is not, as a rule, uniform from the surface to the deepest level and usually a series of layers can be distinguished (Fig. 5.9). On the surface is a usually thin layer of decaying leaves etc. Below this is the top-soil, which may be about 30 cm thick (although the thickness varies considerably) and which contrasts with the lower sub-soil in colour and texture. The former is a dark chocolate colour when moist, owing to the presence of humus, and generally has a finer texture than the latter, which is an orangey or yellowish brown colour in most ordinary soils. The sub-soil may be several metres in depth and merges into a layer of rock fragments overlying the solid parent rock.

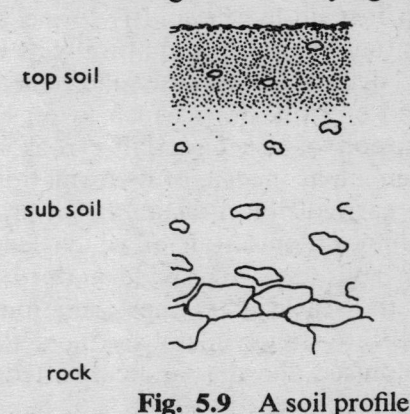

Fig. 5.9 A soil profile

The physical constituents of soil that have the greatest influence on its biological properties are probably those with the smallest particles—the clay and humus, in which the particles are 2 nm or less in diameter. In the first place, they have the property of absorbing water strongly, and the capacity of the soil for retaining water depends very much upon the amount of these two components. On the other hand, they adversely affect porosity, tending to impede drainage and prevent the diffusion of air through the soil. Secondly, clay and humus strongly absorb plant nutrients, especially the metallic ions of the mineral salts. Thirdly, humus, as an intermediate product in the decay of the plant and animal matter that is constantly being added to the soil, is itself a rich source of plant nutrients, which are formed by its decay.

As a result of the above effects, a clay soil, rich in humus, is a fertile soil. (However, clay soils are not necessarily the best agriculturally, since their mechanical properties make them difficult to cultivate and crop growth tends to be slow early in the year because of poor aeration and low soil temperatures resulting from waterlogging.) In contrast, sandy or gravelly soils are well drained and well aerated, and, as a result, humus is rapidly oxidised and broken down through bacterial action. In addition, the deficiency of clay and humus leads to poor retention of plant nutrients, which tend to be washed out of the soil by rain water.

Another soil constituent with important effects is lime (i.e. calcium compounds, especially calcium carbonate). This is slowly removed by the action of carbonic acid in rain water and other acids resulting from the decay of humus. These acids dissolve the calcium compounds in minute quantities and they are carried into the lower horizons by drainage. Lime is alkaline and, as long as it is present, the soil water also is alkaline, or at least neutral. If, however, lime is lacking, the soil may become acidic. Under these conditions and in a well-drained soil (where there is, naturally, likely to be a relatively rapid loss of lime), mineral salts, including plant nutrients, begin to be washed into the lower layers of the soil. This may result in the formation of a type of soil radically different in character from the typical agricultural soil. It is acidic, infertile and supports a characteristic community of the sort found on heaths.

It is clear that both the soil and the living community it supports are subject to slow change, starting from the beginning of soil formation. On the mountainside this may lead from bare rock to a fully developed soil carrying a continuous cover of grass. Often it appears that this represents the natural end-product. However, it seems certain that the process would not stop here but for the presence of grazing sheep and other animals. There is evidence that, before man and his domestic animals occupied the British hills, the latter were mostly covered with deciduous oak forest, except at higher levels. Nearly all this was eventually felled and few, if any, relics of the original forests remain. However, on derelict farmland, old mountain pasture is quite rapidly colonised by scrub and no doubt the oaks would return, given a chance. As it is, in most areas the sheep destroy any tree seedlings and therefore maintain the grasslands.

Forests also covered the major part of what is now agricultural land in lowland Britain, and here again the land would revert to its original state under natural conditions. It is now believed that the vegetation of any area, if it is not interfered with, will slowly undergo a series of changes until it reaches a state of balance, referred to as the **climax**. The series of changes leading up to this is termed a **succession**. For example, speaking broadly, the succession that starts with weathering rock on a hillside may go through the following stages: lichens, mosses and algae; scattered herb and low shrub; continuous grass cover; scrub; woodland. Each stage is a different type of natural community with some degree of permanence, but only the last, woodland, which forms the climax vegetation, is truly stable and permanent. The succession is different if the starting point is different. For example, a visitor to any pond or shallow lake will notice how it is gradually becoming filled in by the washing in of soil and the accumulation of organic matter derived from dead vegetation. This is accompanied by a succession of changes in the vegetation, different stages of which can often be seen in the vicinity of the shore. Deeper water is occupied only by floating plants (e.g. duck-weed), aquatic insects and micro-organisms; less deep water by water lilies and water weed, having roots anchored in the bottom and floating leaves; shallower water by bullrushes (*Typha*); and the water's edge by reeds, aquatic grasses, cresses and others. When the pond or lake becomes completely filled in, trees and shrubs (e.g. pussy willow, ordinary willow, alder) appear, eventually to be replaced by woodland characteristic of drier conditions as the accumulation of soil continues, and the succession finally leads to the climax, which is, again, deciduous woodland.

Although the stages of the succession differ according to the starting point, it is believed that the composition of the climax is dictated almost entirely by the climate and will therefore generally be the same throughout a climatic region. However, the nature of the soil, determined by the underlying rock, may have a considerable influence. On the lime-rich soils of the chalk and limestone regions of southern England, the natural climax is probably beech forest rather than oak, whereas similar soils in the north support communities dominated by the ash tree. Local climatic conditions may also affect the outcome of the succession, so that at higher altitudes it may be that birch and pine woods (also characteristic of the north of Scotland), or even vegetation with alpine or arctic features, are the natural climaxes.

The struggle for life—population control

The changes in a community often have the appearance of a slowly unfolding battle between different species of organism. Where woodland borders on rough pasture, the forest may be invading the grass, first sending in brambles, hawthorn and other scrubland plants which colonise the ground, ousting the grass, and then following these with the advance guard of the trees—birch, ash and sycamore—to be followed by slow-growing oaks or beeches. On the other hand, the presence of a large population of rabbits might turn the tables completely. By destroying any seedlings they might prevent both colonisation by the woodland species and replacement of the older trees as they died off, so that in the end the wood might be colonised by the grassland species.

Such a struggle reflects the tendency of all species to increase in numbers at the expense of their rivals. In the absence of competition, any kind of living organism has a capacity for very rapid increase. Fig. 5.10 shows the increase in size of a laboratory population of water fleas over a period of time. This shows, characteristically, how the rate of increase itself increases as time goes on. This is a natural consequence of the fact that the rate at which new individuals are produced depends upon how many individuals are present in the first place. If an amoeba is capable of reproducing by binary fission once every two days, then after two days one individual will have given rise to two, an increase of one. However, after ten days the population will have increased to $2 \times 2 \times 2 \times 2 \times 2 = 32$ individuals, and after a further two days these will have given rise to 64, an increase of 32.

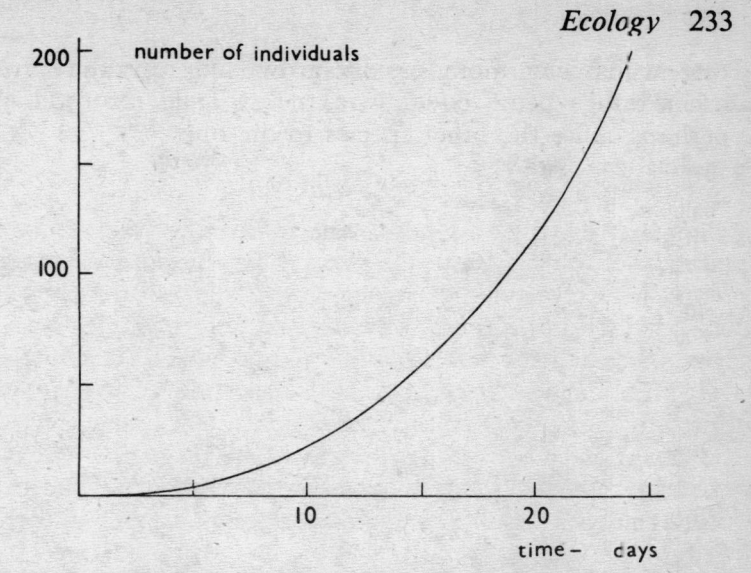

Fig. 5.10 Increase in numbers of water fleas in a laboratory culture, starting from a single female. In the presence of abundant food, the rate of increase itself (represented by the angle of slope of the graph line) increases indefinitely

Under natural conditions such rates of increase cannot be maintained, simply because the supply of food and other resources necessary for growth can never be kept at a sufficient level to support the maximum rate of reproduction. Amoebas will soon use up most of the food they can use and perhaps cause a shortage of oxygen in their environment; water fleas eat up most of the food within reach. In practice, the situation is complicated by the fact that there is generally more than one species present using a particular resource. If two species of flea start to feed on the same mass of food, when the rate of growth and reproduction begins to be limited by shortage of food, the species that can most efficiently convert the food into its own living material, i.e.

that which can most rapidly grow and reproduce, will, other things being equal, win the struggle for food and perhaps cause the other species to die out.

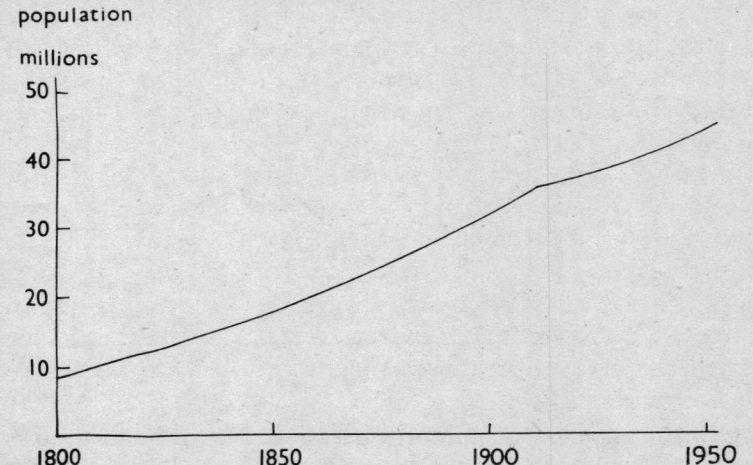

Fig. 5.11 Changes in the population of England and Wales from 1800 to 1950. (It is estimated that the population may have been about $1\frac{1}{2}$ million in the year A.D. 1100, so that in the period represented by the graph the increase (about 35 million) was about five times that in the preceding 700 years)

This is, again, a more simplified picture than any that is likely to be found in nature. The first reason for this is that normally there is not just one source of food, and different species rarely use different food sources to the same extent. The second is that population numbers are limited by the action of parasites and predators (in the case of animals) or herbivores (in the case of plants), as well as by shortage of resources. Normally these various pressures, resulting from the tendency of every population of organisms to increase, are in a state of balance. Alteration of one factor may have a profound effect, leading to the establishment of a quite different state of balance. As explained above, the presence or absence of rabbits may make the difference between the existence of grassland or woodland in the same area. This has been demonstrated experimentally by the enclosure of small areas of grass by rabbit-proof wire netting, resulting in the eventual development of little copses in the enclosures.

The most dramatic example of the effect of the removal of influences controlling population growth is in the case of man. Fig. 5.11 shows changes in the population of England and Wales since 1800. Man has long since ceased to be affected by predation to any significant extent, but until recent times disease has had a profound effect on his rate of increase. Modern advances in medicine have so reduced the death rate that the population has soared. Clearly this cannot continue indefinitely, if for no other reason than that the capacity of the world to produce food is necessarily limited. In fact, in the west we are in a privileged position and can still obtain as much as we need, or more. It is well known that this is certainly not the situation in other parts of the world.

The consequences of the human population explosion are not limited simply to its effect on food supply. There appears to be a real danger that it may throw the ecological system out of balance on a world scale. The signs of this are seen in the form of pollution. In a balanced community there is a continuous recycling of substances, as we have seen, and it is the perpetual circulation of matter that keeps the whole living machine going. Normally the system seems to keep itself in balance. If one part runs too fast, then various processes come into operation to slow it down. For example, studies of elephant populations in Africa show that, if they increase to a level where food supplies are threatened, this situation has an automatic effect on the fecundity of the species, thus tending to reverse the undesirable trend. However, it is possible for a state to be reached where the system seems to lose its capacity to restore itself. Thus, if sufficient sewage is allowed to enter a river, the oxidation of organic matter in it (a normal part of the processes leading to the release of raw materials by decay) leads to such a deficiency of oxygen that practically all organisms, except for bacteria and certain algae, die out. This is usually a comparatively small-scale effect, but in the great lakes of North America it has led to the near sterility of vast tracts of water, and a similar situation is developing in the Baltic. There is no need to point out the potential results of such developments on a worldwide scale.

6 Genetics

Genetics is the study of heredity. It seeks to discover the laws that govern the way in which the peculiarities of parents are passed on to their offspring; why it is that a child may be like his father in some ways, his mother in others and not like either parent in yet others; how we may predict what will be the probable result of cross-breeding two different strains of domestic animal or crop; what is the danger of a child being born with certain hereditary diseases, and so on.

Two fertilised eggs (zygotes) might seem almost identical to all appearances, but one might develop into a mouse and the other into an elephant. What makes this remarkable difference? The answer lies in the nuclei of the zygotes. These contain the DNA that controls the biochemistry of the cells, and hence the ways in which they develop, with the result that one eventually gives rise to an enormous animal with a trunk, tusks, short tail, almost no hair, hoofed feet and so on, while the other produces a little animal with a relatively long tail, fur, clawed feet, etc. The DNA of the elephant zygote is evidently different from that of the mouse zygote.

Clearly the effects produced by the DNA are the result of interaction between it, other substances in the cell and yet others coming from outside the cell, so the final product arises from the combined effect of internal influences (DNA) and external influences. Organisms have a considerable capacity for controlling external influences (p. 81), so that normally the internal influence is the strongest and the final shape of the organism is determined almost entirely by the DNA. However, there are dramatic exceptions. The terrible effects of thalidomide are well known. In this case a chemical substance (the drug), reaching the embryo from the mother's blood stream, in some way interferes with the course of development so that the baby's limbs either do not develop properly or fail to appear at all.

The experimental study of genetics concentrates not so much on the big differences between one species and another as on the minor differences between individuals of the same species. Common observation shows that such individuals vary considerably in all sorts of ways. There are commonly differences in size, differences in exact shape of organs, differences in colouration and other aspects of structure. There may be differences in biochemistry and physiology, and in animals differences in behaviour (e.g. one animal may be more aggressive than another, although both are of the same species). It is clear that some of this variation is the result of differences in environmental conditions. Crop plants grown in poor soil are smaller than those grown in rich soil. In the absence of light, chorophyll fails to develop and plants with yellow leaves result. On the other hand, similar variations exist which have nothing to do with the effect of the environment. For example, the pigmies of the Congo are of small stature, however favourable the conditions in which they live, whereas the Batutsi of neighbouring Ruanda are unusually tall, living alongside the Bahutu, who are of medium height. It seems certain that the height of an individual member of one of these races is very largely decided by the stature of his parents, although diet no doubt has a subsidiary effect. This is another, less dramatic example of the interaction of internal factors, or heredity, and external factors (in this case the supply of food). The fact that tall Batutsi parents have tall children is, of course, an example of an hereditary effect.

The connection between DNA and the well-known effect of heredity may easily be understood if we consider what is the connection between one generation and the next. This connection is, in fact, the act of fertilisation—the union of a male and a female cell, or gamete, to form a zygote. The only significant part of a gamete, as far as heredity is concerned, is the nucleus, the container for DNA. The gamete nuclei join to form the zygote nucleus. So at fertilisation the new organism (represented by the zygote) receives its DNA from the parents and this determines its form, in the same way as it determined the form of the parents.

Mendel's breeding experiments

The practical study of genetics began long before the discovery of DNA and was based on breeding experiments rather than on the examination of gametes, nuclei and zygotes. The pioneer was the Austrian abbot, Gregor Mendel (1822-84), who experimented with ordinary garden peas. An example will show how he set about things.

In one experiment he tried the effect of cross-fertilising a tall strain of peas with a dwarf strain. Garden peas have flowers that are normally self-pollinated because the stamens and style are enclosed near each other in a tubular structure and the anthers shed their pollen before the flower opens, so that it is immediately transferred to the stigma of the same flower. To achieve cross-pollination the flowers must be opened before pollen has been shed and the anthers removed, thus preventing self-pollination. Later pollen is taken from another flower and placed on the stigma of the first. Flowers are enclosed in paper or muslin bags to prevent the entry of insects carrying stray pollen. Using this technique, Mendel pollinated flowers of the dwarf strain with pollen from the tall strain and vice versa. The resulting seeds were eventually germinated, giving rise to hybrid plants (i.e. plants each

240 *Biology*

having one tall and one dwarf parent). All these plants were tall.

In a second stage of the experiment the flowers of the hybrids were allowed to self-pollinate, cross-pollination

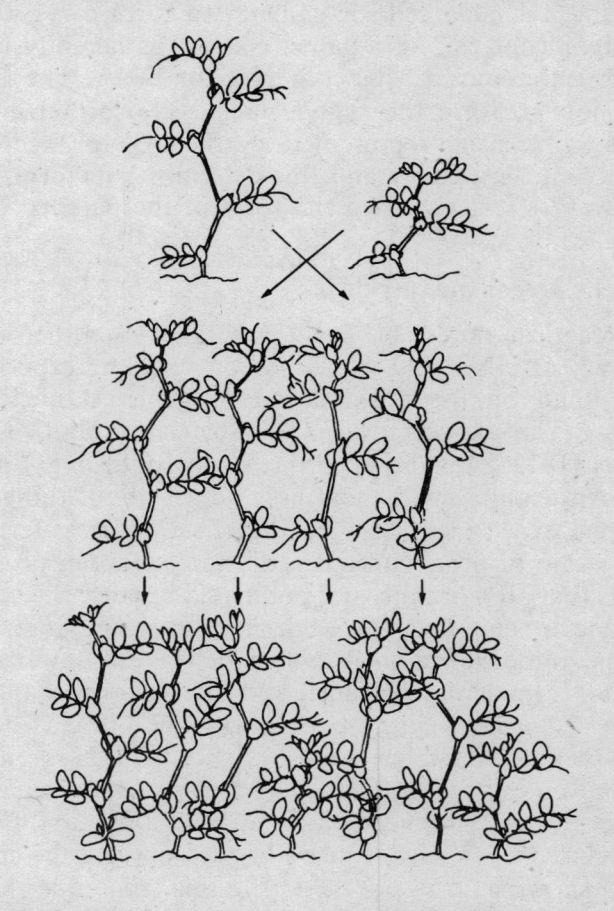

Fig. 6.1 Mendel's experiment with tall and dwarf pea plants. The two plants at the top are the parents of the two succeeding generations represented below

being excluded by enclosing the flowers before they opened. Again, the resulting seeds were germinated. In this case most of the plants were tall, but there were also some dwarfs,

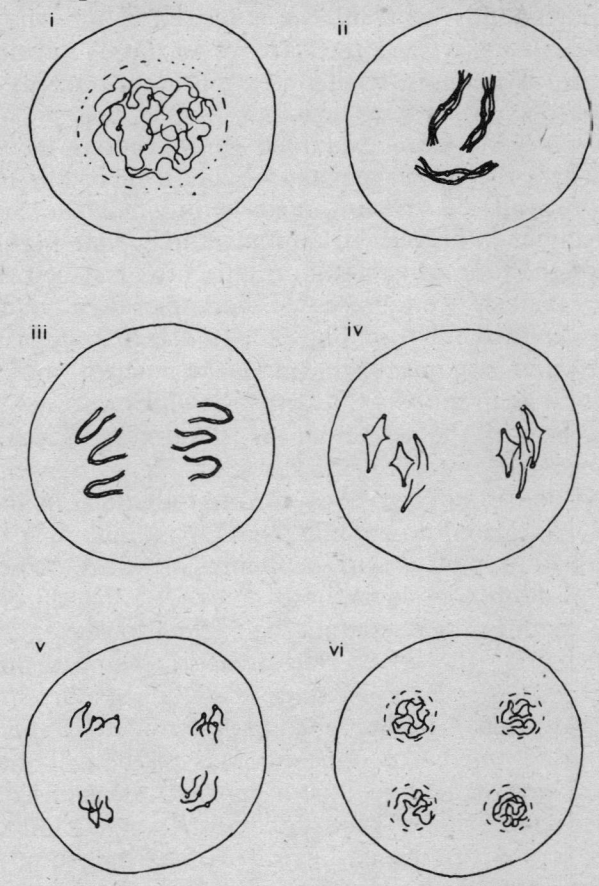

Fig. 6.2 Meiosis (somewhat simplified). At the beginning six chromosomes are present, forming three pairs in (ii). The final result is the formation of four nuclei, each having three chromosomes (vi). Division of the cytoplasm into four parts follows

making up about a quarter of the total in number. The whole experiment in its two stages is represented diagrammatically in Fig. 6.1.

To understand this result we must relate it to the behaviour of chromosomes, the carriers of DNA, during the formation of gametes, fertilisation and development of the zygote into the fully grown plant.

It has already been explained (p. 132) that in all life cycles where there is sexual reproduction there has to be a special form of cell division, meiosis, in which the chromosome number is halved. In animals and higher plants this occurs at the time of gamete formation, or just before. The stages of meiosis are represented diagrammatically and in a rather simplified form in Fig. 6.2. In the first stage (i) the chromosomes become visible and the nuclear membrane disappears, as in mitosis. Next (ii) the chromosomes gather in the centre of the cell, again as in mitosis. The chromosomes become joined together in pairs. It is apparent that each pair consists of two chromosomes identical in size and shape. It is also known that the DNA make-up of the members of a pair is, in the main, identical. (They are known as homologous chromosomes.) In the third stage (iii) the chromosomes separate, half going to one end of the cell and half to the other. Here is a contrast with mitosis, in which, at the corresponding stage, each chromosome becomes divided into two chromatids, and it is the latter that separate and go to opposite ends of the cell. Because of this, in mitosis two groups of chromatids, each equal in number to the original group of chromosomes, is formed, whereas in meiosis the two groups of chromosomes each contain half the original number of chromosomes. In meiosis a further stage (iv) follows, in which the chromosomes are split into pairs of chromatids which separate and move apart, forming four new groups (v), each of which becomes a new nucleus (vi). Division of the cytoplasm follows, resulting in four new cells. The net effect of meiosis is that a single cell containing a double set of chromosomes gives rise to four cells, each containing a single set of chromatids. The chromatids subsequently replicate themselves to form chromosomes. Since meiosis precedes gamete formation, it follows that if, for example, the parents' cells have twenty chromosomes each, the gametes will have ten.

Returning to Mendel's tall and dwarf peas, the difference in height is due to a difference in the DNA of one particular pair of homologous chromosomes. In fact, a small portion of nucleic acid at a certain point along the length of the appropriate chromosomes determines the height of the plant. Such a unit of nucleic acid, controlling one characteristic of the organism, is known as a **gene**. In the tall pea plants with which Mendel started his experiment there would have been only genes for tallness at the given point, whereas in the dwarf plants there would have been only genes for shortness.

Fig. 6.3 shows what happened to the chromosomes during the course of Mendel's experiment. To avoid complication it shows *only one pair* of homologous chromosomes in each parent plant, the pair containing the genes for height. The tallness and shortness genes are represented differently in the diagram, although in fact there is no visible difference and different genes cannot be distinguished under the microscope. We know of their presence almost entirely by deduction from the results of breeding experiments.

When the original parents produced gametes, as a result of meiosis, each gamete contained only one of the homologous chromosomes. (Only two gametes of each kind are represented in the figure.) At fertilisation, the zygote contained two homologous chromosomes bearing one gene of each kind—for tallness and shortness. The zygote gave rise to cells of the new plant by mitosis, so that each would have the same chromosome and gene make-up as the zygote. One

244 *Biology*

original parent cells

gametes

zygote

gametes

three kinds of zygote

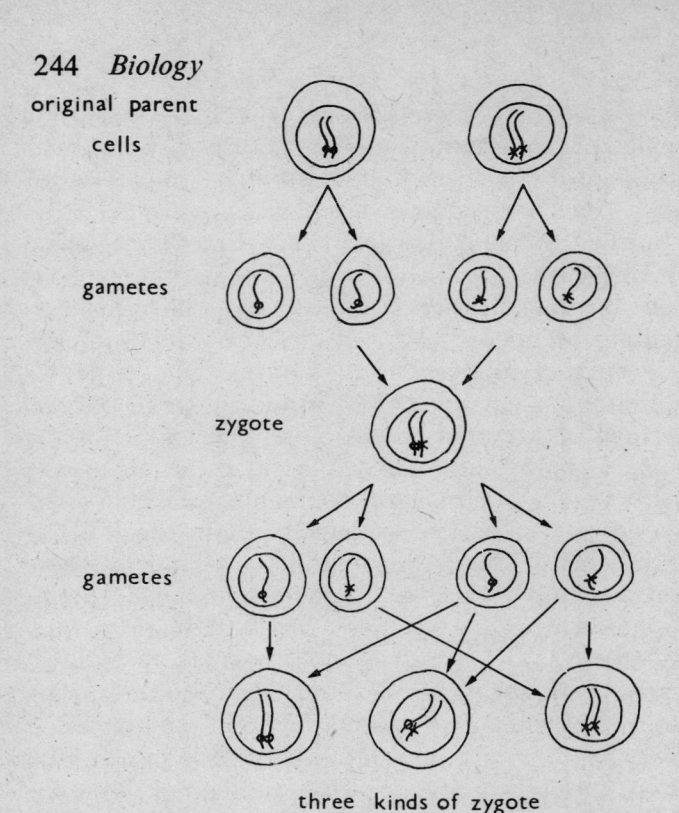

Fig. 6.3 Diagram representing rearrangement of genes accounting for results of Mendel's experiment with tall and short peas. The gene for tallness is represented by 'o' and that for shortness by 'x'

might think that, since both kinds of gene were present, the result might be a compromise—a plant of medium height; but this is not how it works in this case. Nevertheless, the fact that the shortness genes were still there, in spite of the hybrids being tall, was shown by the presence of dwarf plants in the next generation. When the first-generation hybrids reproduced by self-pollination, they produced gametes—egg cells and male gametes—in which, because of meiosis, there were only single chromosomes. Consequently, any egg cell might contain either a tallness gene or a shortness gene but not both, and the same would apply to any male gamete. When fertilisation occurred egg cells with tallness genes might be fertilised by male gametes having either tallness genes or shortness genes, and the same would apply to egg cells having shortness genes. So three kinds of zygote must have resulted, containing either (i) two tallness genes, (ii) a tallness and a shortness gene or (iii) two shortness genes. Both type (i) and (ii) must have given rise to tall plants and only type (iii) to dwarfs.

The above example represents the simplest pattern of inheritance. Many similar examples in a wide variety of organisms are known and genetical experiments have provided information about a correspondingly large number of genes. However, it is only possible to study genes in this way where two or more different genes may exist at the same position on a particular chromosome, as in the case of the tallness and shortness genes. In actual fact, it seems certain that any chromosome consists almost entirely of a string of a large number of genes, each one controlling some process in the organism and having some definite effect on its characteristics.

When two genes with different effects can occupy the same position on a chromosome, it very often happens that one completely masks the effect of the other if both are present, as in the case quoted. The one gene is then said to be **dominant**, whereas the other is **recessive**.

Human heredity

Quite a lot is known about human heredity. There are forty-six chromosomes in ordinary body cells and twenty-three in gametes. Of these a homologous pair is concerned with determining the sex of the individual. In the female they are both alike and known as X chromosomes, but in the male there is one X and a smaller Y chromosome. All the egg cells produced by a woman contain single X chromosomes, whereas the sperms produced by a man may contain either an X or a Y chromosome. A given egg may be fertilised either by an X-bearing sperm in which case the resulting XX zygote develops into a girl, or by a Y-bearing sperm, producing an XY zygote which becomes a boy.

Some diseases of man are of hereditary origin. A well-known example is haemophilia, in which the blood of the sufferer lacks the ordinary capacity to clot as a result of injury. Small injuries can lead to serious, possibly even fatal, bleeding. The disease is due to the presence of a recessive gene which occurs only in the X chromosomes. The dominant gene gives rise to the clotting property present in normal individuals, and this also exists only in X chromosomes. The small Y chromosome lacks any corresponding gene. Because of this, haemophilia occurs in men but not in women. Thus a woman, unknown to herself, may carry the haemophilia gene on one X chromosome without this having any effect on her. 50% of the egg cells she produces will contain the chromosome with the haemophilia gene, and any of these fertilised by sperms bearing Y chromosomes will give rise to haemophiliac males, since the recessive haemophilia gene will not then be matched by any gene on the Y chromosome. None of her daughters by marriage with a normal man will suffer from the disease, because in every case the haemophilia gene, even if present, will be paired with a normal gene on the X chromosome derived from her husband. The 50% of haemophilia-bearing egg cells would, however, give rise to female haemophilia carriers if fertilised by X-bearing sperms. Thus there is a 50% chance that any son would be a haemophiliac and a 50% chance that any daughter would carry the haemophilia gene, but no daughter would actually show

Genetics 247

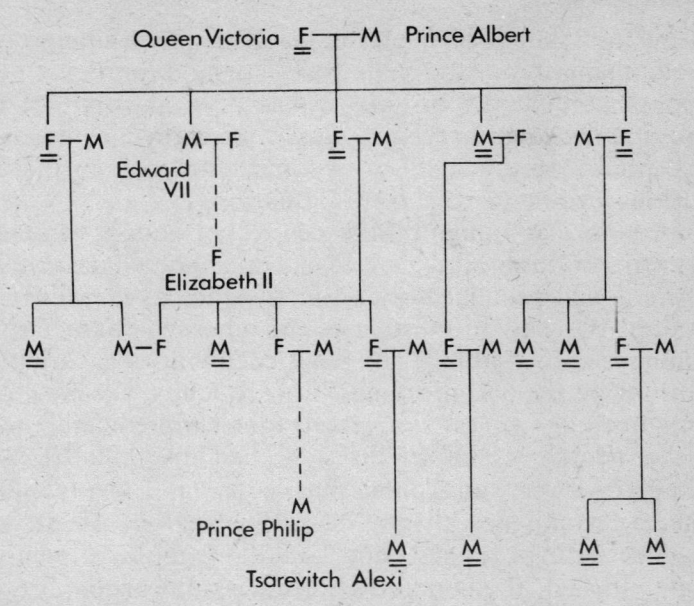

Fig. 6.4 Haemophilia in the descendants of Queen Victoria. M = male, F = female. Underlining indicates the presence of the haemophilia gene (giving rise to symptoms in males only). Members of the present British royal family are not affected

symptoms of the disease. A haemophiliac daughter could arise only from the union of a haemophiliac man and a woman who was a carrier. However, in practice, haemophilia is unknown in women, perhaps because the combination of two haemophilia genes is lethal.

Fig. 6.4 shows the incidence of haemophilia amongst the descendants of Queen Victoria, who evidently carried the gene.

Some abnormal conditions result not from the presence of abnormal genes but from that of extra chromosomes. Mongolism is an example. Mongoloid children have certain facial characteristics reminiscent of the Mongol race and are mentally subnormal, never reaching the adult level of development and at the same time having, typically, a very happy, outgoing disposition. It has been shown that the condition is related to the presence of an extra chromosome. This, presumably, results from some mischance in the cell divisions leading up to gamete formation.

Many normal human differences are, of course, of hereditary origin. Examples are eye, skin and hair colour, stature, facial peculiarities and intelligence as measured by standard IQ tests. In most cases the inherited characteristic is influenced by a number of genes occurring at a variety of positions on the chromosomes. Consequently, the results of cross-breeding are less simple and more unpredictable than in the relatively simple cases studied by Mendel. For example, if a very tall woman married a very short man, the offspring would not all be tall, as the analogy of tall and dwarf peas might suggest, nor would they all be of medium height. In fact, the children's stature would probably vary over quite a wide range. The reason for this is that stature is determined by a number of genes, some tending to produce tallness and others shortness. A tall person has a preponderance of tallness genes but also some shortness genes, whereas in a short person the situation is reversed. The exact proportion of tallness genes handed on by a parent will vary according to the chance way in which the chromosomes carrying the genes separate in meiosis. Accordingly, any one child may receive more or fewer.

Some human characteristics are determined by single gene differences. Thus blue eye colour and red hair are each due to a gene recessive to genes producing the other colours. The effect of this is that if, for example, a red-haired person marries someone without red hair in their ancestry (so that they carry no red-hair gene) none of the children will have red hair, although all will be carriers of the gene. However, if one of the children marries another person who is also a carrier of the gene, some of the grandchildren may have red hair.

It may be asked how different types of gene arise. The answer appears to be that this happens as a result of the alteration of existing genes which modifies their effects. Such changes are called **mutations** and are well known in the organisms used in the study of genetics. Geneticists favour organisms with short life cycles and high reproductive rates, such as fruit flies and certain micro-organisms. Naturally the pedigrees of the organisms used in breeding experiments are recorded minutely so that the genetic history of any individual is known with certainty. Consequently, it has been possible to prove the completely new appearance of characteristics due to the production of new genes by mutation. In fruit flies, for example, numerous mutations affecting eye colour, wing shape, size, colour of body, etc have been recorded. These mutations may arise spontaneously, i.e. without known cause, or as a result of treatment by X-rays, atomic radiations or certain chemicals.

A mutation probably occurs as a result of an alteration of a DNA molecule of such a nature that the protein whose synthesis it controls either ceases to be produced or is synthesised in altered form. In this connection it is of interest that many mutations in micro-organisms result in changes in their biochemistry, which often seem to be due to the lack of single enzymes normally present.

The practical application of genetics

The everyday practical application of genetics is the breeding of improved crops and farm animals. The popular concept of the plant or animal breeder is, perhaps, one who seeks to produce entirely new breeds, and one may think of the numerous strikingly different varieties of domestic dog or the modern breeds of cattle, so enormous by comparison with their forebears. However, apart from the rather uncommon occurrence of mutations having desirable effects, the breeder obtains his results mainly by producing new combinations of genes. Thus it may happen that a high-yielding strain of cereal is susceptible to disease, whereas another strain with poor yield is highly resistant. The plant breeder may cross-breed the strains, so producing a hybrid race containing a variety of individuals with varying combinations of the characteristics of the parent varieties. He will then attempt to discover which hybrids both give high yields and have high disease resistance and use these to breed from, so eventually establishing a new strain with the desired characteristics. Or a dairy farmer who has a non-pedigree herd of mediocre milkers may upgrade it by purchasing a pedigree bull. Over a number of years he will keep careful records of the milk yields of each cow and try to select the good milkers to be mothers of the future herd. In this way the proportion of genes favourable to high milk yield (most of them derived from the bull) is built up, while the unfavourable genes are gradually eliminated.

In both the above examples the process involves (i) cross-breeding two strains, so producing a new mixture of genes, and (ii) selective breeding, leading to the elimination of unwanted genes and the retention of desirable ones. The effect of selection may be clarified by considering how one might produce a pure race of tall garden peas from a number of hybrid tall/dwarf plants. Suppose that these were allowed to reproduce by self-pollination, producing a new generation consisting of both tall and dwarf plants (p. 240). If the latter were discarded, this would eliminate some of the unwanted shortness genes. However, some of the tall plants would contain these genes (p. 245), and when a third generation was produced it would still contain some dwarfs. Again, these would be eliminated, taking more shortness genes with them. Now, at the beginning, the two kinds of gene would have been present in equal numbers and, if reproduction had been allowed to continue without interference, this would have been true of every succeeding generation, because every time reproduction occurred each type of gene would have the same chance of being passed on to the next generation. However, if, as described, some shortness genes are discarded in every generation, this is bound to have the effect of gradually reducing the proportion present, until after a sufficiently long time all have been eliminated.

Processes of selection, leading to genetic changes, are known in nature and are thought to be partly responsible for evolution, as explained in the next chapter.

7 Evolution

The general idea that present-day plants and animals are the products of millions of years of gradual change, or evolution, in which earlier more primitive organisms gave rise progressively to more and more varied and complex forms, is now probably familiar to most people. Little more than a hundred years ago, before the publication of Charles Darwin's *The Origin of Species*, this would not have been so. Evolution is one of those ideas that, like the Copernican theory of the solar system and the discovery of the vast distances separating the stars, has completely revolutionised our perspective of the universe and made modern man, perhaps wrongly, feel cut off from earlier generations. Accordingly, it is of considerable general interest. In biology it was the first comprehensive theory and might still be considered the most important.

The evidence for evolution

We shall begin by considering some of the lines of evidence that show that evolution is a fact and afterwards discuss the theory of how it came to pass. The most direct and easily understood evidence is provided by fossils. These are the traces of former living organisms preserved in rock. They occur only in sedimentary rocks—those formed by the accumulation of enormously thick deposits of sand, mud and other sediments converted into rock by the action of great pressure. Remains of organisms embedded in these sediments may leave impressions on the rock, or sometimes the bones or other hard parts may be preserved and gradually mineralised by slow chemical changes. A very minute fraction of all the plants or animals that existed in the past have left fossils and, naturally, it is those with hard parts that have been generally so preserved. For this reason, there is a more complete fossil record of vertebrates than of any other group.

Fig. 7.1 shows the different geological ages and gives an indication of the kinds of vertebrate that, according to the fossil evidence, existed at different times in the past. The names of most of the geological ages were originally those of different series of rocks laid down at the various times. Some of the early geological research was carried out in Wales, and the names Cambrian, Ordovician and Silurian are derived from those of three Welsh tribes of Roman times that occupied the areas studied. The Carboniferous rocks include those that contain the coal measures. Cretaceous comes from the Latin word for chalk, since the chalk of southern England was formed during this geological period. The ages of the periods in millions of years are chiefly based on studies of the radio-activity of rocks, which decreases at a known rate.

The most significant feature of the fossil record is that, although all the main divisions of the vertebrate subphylum had appeared by about fifty million years ago, as we go back in time their number becomes fewer and fewer, until, in Devonian times, fishes were the only kind of vertebrate in existence. Moving onwards from that point the other main groups appear in the order Amphibia, Reptilia, Aves (birds) and Mammalia. This is an order of increasing complexity—just what one would expect to be the result of an evolutionary process. One can see how a bird might, by a process of elaboration and modification, have evolved from a reptile, but it is much more difficult to believe that a reptile

254 *Biology*

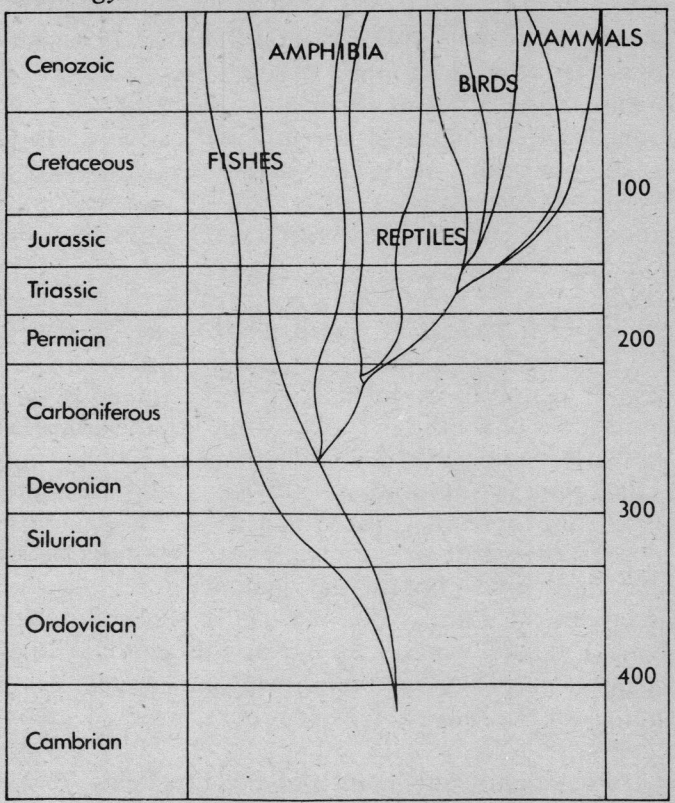

Cenozoic		AMPHIBIA		MAMMALS	
				BIRDS	
Cretaceous		FISHES			100
Jurassic			REPTILES		
Triassic					
Permian					200
Carboniferous					
Devonian					300
Silurian					
Ordovician					
					400
Cambrian					

Fig. 7.1 Evolution of vertebrates. Names of geological epochs are shown on the left and time scale in millions of years on the right

might have evolved from a bird. Apart from this very broad effect, there are examples of fossil series showing what must be the same species undergoing gradual change during a long period of time (Fig. 7.2).

A rather more indirect kind of evidence for evolution arises from the detailed comparison of the anatomy of related animals, i.e. the study of comparative anatomy.

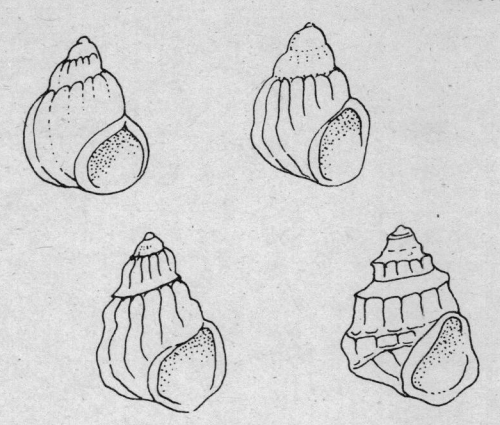

Fig. 7.2 A series of fossils illustrating gradual evolutionary change. The earliest specimen (top left) existed several million years before the most recent (bottom right). A complete series of intermediate forms is known

Fig. 7.3 illustrates a well-known example provided by the fore-limbs of several vertebrates. It will be noticed that all possess the same basic pattern of bones: a single long bone (the humerus) in the upper part, two long bones (radius and ulna) joined to this in the lower part, then a number of small bones (the carpals, metacarpals and phalanges) corresponding to the wrist, palm and fingers in man. The remarkable thing about this is that the pattern remains broadly similar in spite of the fact that the various limbs are used in different ways (e.g. for walking, flying or swimming). One may easily understand that the structure of an organ is quite largely determined by the use to which it is adapted, but similarity of structure in this case calls for a quite different explanation. The only one conceivable is that the animals illustrated are all descended from the same ancestors. Thus we can understand why a whale's paddle contains a complete set of finger bones if we assume that whales evolved

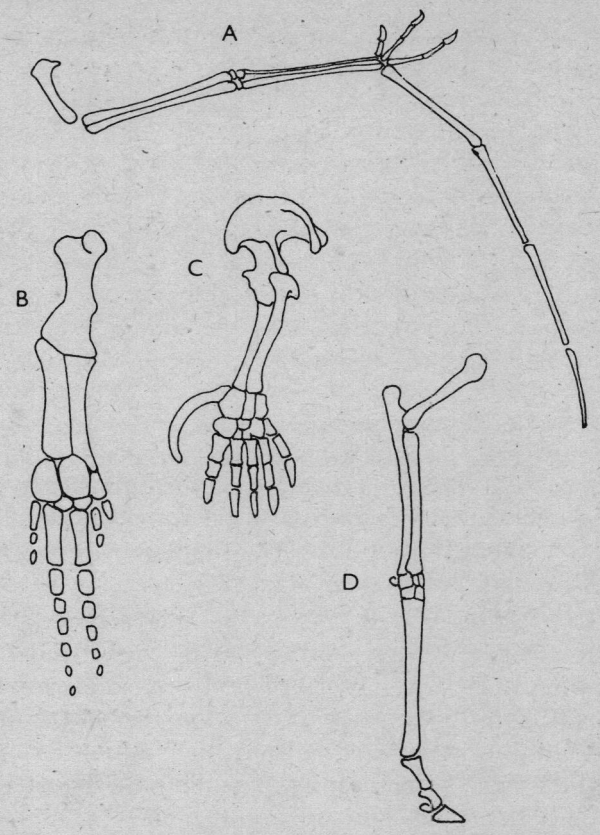

Fig. 7.3 Vertebrate fore-limbs: (A) pterodactyl (extinct flying reptile in which the fore-limb was modified as a wing, rather as in bats); (B) porpoise; (C) mole; (D) horse (in the horse the lower part of the limb consists of a single, very much enlarged 'finger')

from land animals having feet like other walking land vertebrates.

A contrast is provided by the comparison between a vertebrate limb and an insect leg (Figs. 4.20, 4.22, pp. 182, 184).

There are certain broad similarities—the presence of two long elements in the upper limb and a number of short ones at the free end, and of claws at the tip—but the differences are more striking: the exoskeleton in place of an endoskeleton and completely different arrangement of parts, for example. The contrast is easily accounted for by the absence of a close evolutionary relationship between insects and vertebrates.

Extreme examples of retention of structure originally adapted to some function that has been lost are provided by the functionless vestigial organs found in numerous animals. In man there are the coccyx (the remnant of the tail), rudimentary ear muscles (functional only in some individuals), and the caecum and appendix, which have no apparent function, although in herbivorous mammals they are frequently large and play an important part in cellulose digestion.

Yet another kind of evidence comes from the study of comparative embryology. Fig. 7.4 illustrates the embryos of three different vertebrates at approximately the same stage of development. The similarity is striking. At later stages, of course, they become increasingly different; at earlier stages, more and more alike. This effect is just what the idea of evolution might lead one to expect, since, according to it, one would suppose that two related species, such as a bird and a mammal, must be the end-products of two different lines of evolution starting from the same point —some ancestral species (in this case a reptile, probably of the late Carboniferous period). Thus the fossil evidence shows that the very earliest reptiles soon became differentiated into a few groups, which proceeded to evolve independently. One of these groups, after about eighty million years (in the Triassic period), gave rise to mammals. Another produced a diversity of forms, including dinosaurs, pterodactyls, the crocodiles and primitive birds, which also first appeared in the Jurassic period. Since all these animals retained the same fundamental features of anatomy, which

258 *Biology*

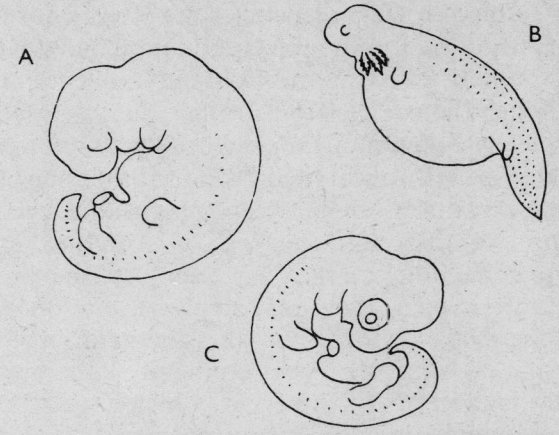

Fig. 7.4 Vertebrate embryos at corresponding stages of development: (A) human; (B) amphibian; (C) bird

are laid down early in embryological development, one would expect that the changes constituting evolution would mostly affect the later stages of development. Consequently, during the 200 million years or more that have elapsed since the late Carboniferous period, one might expect that the early stages of development would have been little changed in all the various forms of animal descended from the primitive reptiles. The similarity of embryos is, therefore, not surprising.

The point may be emphasised, as in comparative anatomy, by contrasting the above examples with a comparison of the embryos of unrelated forms, for example an insect and a vertebrate. Here there is hardly any similarity, except in so far as both embryos start from a single cell which initiates development by undergoing repeated cell division.

Not infrequently the study of comparative embryology throws light on the classification of organisms that might otherwise be difficult to place. Barnacles provide a good example. A species common on the rocks of the seashore looks not unlike a limpet, being completely enclosed by a hard shell. Others look like mussels attached to rocks or timber by thick stalks. When covered by water the shells open and little tentacles can be seen waving about inside. The animals might easily be mistaken for molluscs. However, one look at a barnacle larva (i.e. the free-living embryo) leaves one in no doubt that in reality it is a crustacean, so closely similar is it to other larvae of that group of arthropods (Fig. 7.5).

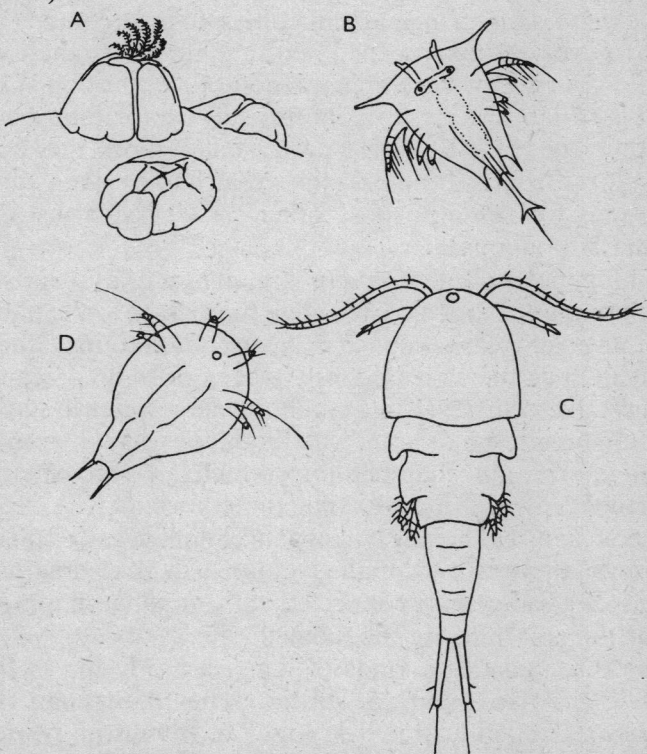

Fig. 7.5 (A) *Balanus*, a common barnacle; (B) microscopic larva of *Balanus;* (C) *Cylops*, a minute crustacean found in ponds; (D) *Cyclops* larva

The fossil evidence summarised in Fig. 7.1 on p. 254 suggests that the land vertebrates evolved from fishes. The study of the origin of the earliest amphibians by evolution from fishes existing in the late Devonian or early Carboniferous periods well illustrates how the three kinds of evidence outlined above may combine to establish the details of evolution.

If one tried to work out how a fish might have evolved into an amphibian, one might start from the fact that it would have two principal difficulties to overcome: (i) the need to evolve a system for breathing air rather than water and (ii) the need to develop a method of locomotion suitable for use on land. Since it could not survive for long on land without having first at least partly solved both these problems, it must have been a species that had evolved suitable structures for some purpose other than survival as a fully fledged land animal.

Taking need (i) first, there are, in fact, a surprisingly large number of kinds of fish alive today that are capable of breathing air. This capacity is an adaptation either to survival when the water the fish lives in dries up, because of drought, or to survival in oxygen-deficient water in swamps. The air-breathing organ sometimes consists of a modification of the gill chamber into which air can be drawn, sometimes of the mouth and sometimes of the rectum. These structures do not correspond anatomically to lungs. However, there is one small group of fish that breathes by means of a sac or sacs connected with the pharynx, in other words lungs. These are the lungfish.

The three surviving kinds of lungfish are found in South America, Africa and Australia. The Australian kind, *Neoceratodus*, is illustrated in Fig. 7.6. Interestingly, details of the anatomy of their circulatory, urinogenital and nervous systems show various similarities to the Amphibia and differences from other kinds of fish. Their embryological development is also like that of amphibians and on hatching the young lungfish is quite similar to a tadpole.

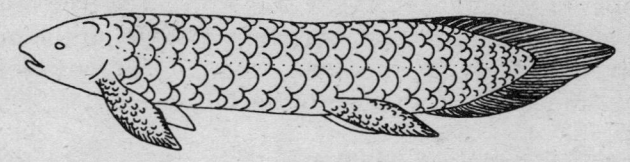

Fig. 7.6 *Neoceratodus*, the Australian lungfish

The second requirement mentioned above is for structures that could be adapted for locomotion on land. Nearly all fish have two pairs of fins (pectoral and pelvic) as well as median fins, and it seems reasonable to suppose that the two pairs of limbs in land vertebrates arose by modification of paired fins. However, the bony structure of the fins in most fish shows little similarity to that of the amphibian limb, consisting of a number of slender bony rays radiating from little bones embedded in the surface of the body. There is but one group of fish that differs in this respect, having fins with a bony axis which might become the bony axis of an arm or leg. This group includes the lungfish. (Other members, besides fossil forms, are the Coelacanths, recently discovered in the Indian Ocean but previously known only as fossils.) The Australian lungfish, although unable to survive out of water, has been observed to use its fins for walking slowly along the bottom when in water.

It begins to look very much as if the first amphibians evolved from lungfish or their near relatives. But what of the fossil evidence? First, it has been possible to trace the ancestry of lungfish backwards. There were forms very similar to *Neoceratodus* in the Triassic period, and before that other lungfish existed as far back as the Devonian. They can be identified as lungfish by certain details of bony structure. They formed part of a large group of fish with the peculiar fin structure described above. Thus we have evidence for a group of fish of the right kind existing at just the right time to give rise to the Amphibia. It has not been possible to trace a series of fossils leading from a fish to a land vertebrate, but the earliest amphibians and the lungfish group show so many anatomical similarities that biologists are certain of their close relationship.

The mechanism of evolution

So far the discussion has indicated some of the evidence for evolution having actually happened. No one seriously doubts this today, but when Darwin first published his theory of evolution it is probably true that it won acceptance as much because it provided an understandable explanation for evolution as because of the weight of evidence he presented. Darwin observed the enormous fecundity of living organisms—the fact that a single plant may produce thousands of seeds or a fish thousands of eggs—deduced that the vast majority of these potential organisms must die before reaching maturity and concluded that there must be an intense struggle for survival not only between one species and another but also between individuals of the same species. He also observed the fact of variation between individuals and, drawing attention to the fact that, because of this, some must be more efficient in the struggle than others—they were more fit for survival—he concluded that only the fittest survived. This would have had no significance unless the survivors were able to pass on their advantages to their offspring. Assuming this was so, Darwin pointed out that it would mean that the individuals having even slight advantages over their fellows would be more likely to survive, reproduce and hand on their special characteristics to future generations, so that such characteristics would become more widespread. Thus any new feature appearing in an individual would quickly spread to the whole species if it were such as to aid the species in the struggle for survival.

(Conversely, any deleterious feature would be eliminated.) Consequently, with repetition of the process, the whole species would be subject to slow change.

An example may help to clarify this explanation. Suppose that there is a species of mammal that feeds on the leaves of trees. Assuming that it is successful, numbers are likely to be limited by the amount of available food, and less vigorous or efficient individuals will be eliminated through inability to obtain enough. Having a slightly longer neck than average would secure a considerable advantage in these circumstances, because more greenery would be within the animal's reach, and the lucky long-necked individual would survive longer and have more offspring than his brothers and sisters. So the number of long-necked animals would slowly increase at the expense of the shorter necked, until finally all would be longer necked. Repetition of this process could lead to a gradual increase in neck length until, after a sufficiently long period of time, the average length might become relatively enormous. It is assumed that something of this sort brought about the evolution of the giraffe.

Darwin called the above process *natural selection*, because he likened it to the selection carried out by animal and plant breeders (p. 250). Instead of breeding stock being selected by some outside agency, it is in effect self-selected, in so far as it is the particular qualities of successful individuals themselves that lead to their survival and 'selection' to be the parents of the next generation. Looking at it from another point of view, however, it might be said that it is the environment that selects, since it eliminates those organisms that are insufficiently well adapted to its demands.

In Darwin's time the modern science of genetics was unknown. (Mendel's work was published only six years after *The Origin of Species*, but it did not become generally known until the beginning of this century.) His theory of evolution, however, rested on certain assumptions about the nature of heredity. It assumed, for example, that the variations we see in living organisms can be passed on from generation to generation and that there is some source of new variation that can lead to indefinite change. Broadly speaking, these assumptions are now known to be in agreement with the facts, although a hundred years ago this could only be a matter for conjecture. Some of the beliefs held by Darwin and his contemporaries—such as that there is a blending of inheritance from male and female parents in the offspring, and that peculiarities acquired during the life-time of the individual might be passed on to later generations—were actually wrong. Nevertheless, Darwin's theory, with elaboration and modification in the light of modern knowledge, is regarded as essentially correct.

In the light of the discoveries of genetics, it is now realised that the genes form the basic material on which natural selection acts. It is not true that all the observed variations in organisms can be inherited, since it is only those due to variations in the genetic composition of individuals that are, and when an individual is eliminated or preserved by natural selection the effect that matters is that certain genes are eliminated or preserved. In this way genes that are harmful or cause the organism to be less efficiently adapted to its environment are discarded, while those that are advantageous spread through the population. This cannot be the whole story, however, because natural selection alone can only lead to changes in the proportions of genes that are already present in the population (just as the animal or plant breeder can only hope to produce new combinations of genes, p. 250) and cannot produce further change beyond the point at which the most favourable selection of genes has been attained. In fact, ultimately, the only thing that can produce the fund of raw material for continuous long-term evolutionary change is mutation. This produces new genes and entirely new characteristics on which selection can act.

An example that well illustrates the roles of both mutation and selection is the case of the peppered moth *Biston betularia*. This moth has white wings speckled with black, which camouflages it very efficiently when it is resting on the lichen grown bark of a tree, as is its habit. Owing to the enthusiasm of collectors, we have a full record of the variation and distribution of this and other butterflies and moths over quite a long period of time. Thus, when a new colour variant with black wings appeared in the latter half of the last century, we can be confident that we know where and when it appeared and how fast it spread. The first known specimen was, in fact, captured in Manchester in 1850. After this it was at first rare but later began to spread through the industrial areas of Britain, until it is now the more common variety throughout the more heavily populated regions and in the eastern parts—those areas that are most affected by atmospheric pollution.

Breeding experiments show that the black colour in the new variety is due to a single dominant gene, which must, therefore, have been produced by a mutation that occurred, most probably, not long before 1850, although it is impossible to be certain how long it might have gone undetected. The record of the progress of the black variety is a record of the spread of this gene through the *Biston betularia* population.

The success of the gene can be accounted for by natural selection. The colouration of the normal variety protects it from birds very effectively in unpolluted areas, but where there is atmospheric pollution its camouflage fails, partly because lichens, which are very sensitive to pollution, are absent and partly because deposits of soot blacken the surfaces of trees and make moths resting on them conspicuous. The black form, on the contrary, is less conspicuous on blackened trees than on those unaffected by pollution. That this does, indeed, have the expected effect on the rate at which the insects fall prey to birds has been confirmed by experiment. When released in a wood near Birmingham almost three times as many of the normal variety as the black were taken by birds; but in a Dorset wood the ratio was more than six black to one normal.

So far it has, perhaps, become clear how evolution can lead to change in a species, but this does not, apparently, bring about a multiplication of species. This is, of course, essential in order to account for the variety of living things. Thus, if the whole of Britain became one vast polluted city, all peppered moths would be black and we should, in a sense, have a new species. However, this would simply replace the old one and there would still be only one species. As it is, there are two *varieties* of the insect, but could these ever become species?

First, the difference between *variety* and *species* must be clarified. Varieties differ from one another in only a few minor characteristics. The two varieties of *Biston betularia* differ only with respect to one character controlled by one gene. Between species there are normally many differences. Another important distinction is that the members of two varieties can normally breed freely with one another, whereas the members of two species cannot: either mating is practically impossible, or more or less unproductive. These two distinctions are closely related, as will appear.

How may a sufficient number of new genes be added to a variety in order to make it so different from any other that it might be regarded as a species? One might imagine that, in the course of time, successive mutations producing favourable effects might occur in black peppered moths and that other mutations also producing favourable, but different, effects might occur in the normal variety. Consequently, the required difference might arise. This, however, neglects the effect of gene flow. In the situation as it is there are very few, if any, areas in which only black peppered moths exist, in spite of the disadvantage suffered by normal moths in the 'black' areas. The reason is that moths near the centre of such areas mate with others a little further out, those with others further out still, and so on—until the country is reached. Every time mating occurs there is a coming together of genes from the parents in the offspring, and this represents transport of genes in both directions. In addition to this, there is the actual movement of individuals migrating from one area to another. Both these effects cause a slow, two-way flow of genes, so that any new genes originating in black areas would in the end find their way to unpolluted areas and vice versa. Thus there is a constant mixing-up process, which tends to prevent groups within a species from differing too much.

The only way in which two such groups can give rise to new species is by their becoming isolated from one another, so that interbreeding cannot take place. Gene flow is in this way stopped and accumulation of different mutations may lead to gradual divergence. One of the effects of this is to make interbreeding gradually more difficult. This may be due to changes in mating behaviour, changes in the anatomy and physiology of the reproductive organs, or in the chromosome make-up of the emergent species, leading to failure of cell division following cross-fertilisation. In the end such changes prevent interbreeding altogether, so that the groups are permanently separated genetically and form distinct species.

An interesting small-scale example of the way in which species may arise is seen amongst the animals, and more especially the birds, of the Galapagos Islands. These were observed by Darwin and evidently exerted a considerable influence on his thinking about evolution.

The Galapagos archipelago is a group of small islands

in the Pacific, lying on the equator about 600 miles from the South American coast. Geologists think they were formed by volcanic action about twenty million years ago, which is very recent on the geological time scale, and it seems certain that all the forms of life on them reached the islands across the ocean. There is, in fact, a very limited range of types, as one might have expected, that being so. There are only twenty-two species of bird, which is a very small number compared with those existing in other tropical areas, including the South American mainland. Of these birds thirteen species, the Galapagos finches—relatives of the British chaffinch—are closely related to one another, all being very similar in appearance. The main differences are in their bills and feeding habits, which are adapted to various kinds of food. Thus, like typical finches, four are seed eaters, finding their food on the ground; two feed on cactuses; and six are like tits in their ways, inhabiting trees and feeding mainly on insects. One of the latter, however, behaves like a woodpecker, prizing insects out of the bark, except that, instead of using its beak for this purpose, it employs a cactus spine held in its bill. Lastly, a thirteenth species is something like a warbler and eats small, soft insects.

The most interesting feature of the Galapagos finches is the way that this group of closely related birds has members adapted to such a diversity of ways of life, which in a more normal situation would be exploited by specialised forms probably belonging to a number of different families. (Thus in the British Isles there are the finches, tits, woodpeckers and warblers.) It is clear that, when the ancestral Galapagos finches (all, no doubt, of one species) reached the islands, in the absence of specialised competitors of this type, a wide range of environmental resources were available to them. In this situation evolution led to the modification of the original species in various ways, so that new species, specialising in various kinds of food resource, soon began to appear.

Because it began so recently, the process has not gone very far and the various finches differ comparatively little.

In the evolution of these birds, the geographical nature of the region—the fact that it consisted of a number of scattered islands—must have played an important part. Although the greatest distance between islands is about 100 miles, in many cases it is much less and movement of birds from one island to another is by no means impossible. Nevertheless, once established on an island, the birds are unlikely to stray. Consequently, the isolation of sub-groups of the population mentioned above is established and provides the necessary condition for evolution of a number of different species. One can imagine that conditions on one island might especially favour, say, ground-feeding seed eaters and conditions on another tree-dwelling insect eaters. The virtual isolation of the two groups and the operation of natural selection on a series of mutations would lead to the evolution of two different forms. Subsequent occasional migrations might lead to these eventually occupying the same terrain, but by then they would be capable neither of interbreeding nor of competing with one another, since they would be utilising different resources.

Evidence for the importance of geographical isolation in evolution is provided by the fact that it is the most scattered outer islands of the Galapagos archipelago that have the highest proportion of species or varieties of the birds peculiar to them. In other words, in any of the more central islands (which are relatively close to one another), few or none of the varieties are not found in other islands, but in some of the outer islands the majority occur only in one island. A familiar example of a similar effect on a large scale is seen in Australasia, where a whole subdivision of the class Mammalia, the pouched mammals, or marsupials, has evolved in isolation.

The diversification of the Galapagos finches as a result of

adaptation to a variety of circumstances is characteristic of the evolution of any group of organisms that has come to occupy, as it were, virgin territory. The effect is known as adaptive radiation: starting from one form, representing the point of origin, the type radiates in all directions to fill all the available 'slots' in the environment, or ecological niches as they are called. Again the marsupials give us another example. Until recently, few ordinary mammals existed in Australasia and marsupials had evolved a whole range of forms corresponding to familiar ordinary mammalian types. Thus, amongst others, there were marsupial 'wolves', 'cats', 'mice' and 'moles'.

Adaptive radiation frequently follows the evolution of some new and successful type of organisation. The classic example is that of the reptiles, which, appearing first in the middle Carboniferous period and, representing a major advance in vertebrate organisation, by the Cretaceous period had given rise to an enormous variety of forms, including carnivores and herbivores, animals capable of flight and others as fully adapted to life in the water as present-day whales. A further advance produced the mammalian type of organisation, which largely replaced that of the reptiles and led to another burst of adaptive radiation.

Human evolution

Darwin's theory produced considerable controversy at the time of its first publication, not least because it appeared to contradict traditional Christian teaching about the creation and especially, perhaps, because of his suggestion that man was as much the product of evolution as animals. At a famous public meeting at Oxford in 1860, an eminent bishop enquired of T. H. Huxley, an ardent supporter of Darwin, whether he traced his descent from apes through his grandmother or his grandfather. This piece of sarcasm received the scornful reply it deserved. Nevertheless, although clearly very plausible, there was little direct evidence to support the idea of man's descent from apes at the time. However, in the century since then, and especially more recently, sufficient fossil evidence has come to light for us to feel fairly certain about the course of human evolution. A widely accepted view is that it started with the appearance of a type of ape that walked and ran upright (unlike modern apes) and inhabited open grassland rather than forest. Instead of feeding largely on vegetable food, these animals hunted the animals of the plains. Connected with these differences were probably also differences in social organisation and intelligence which, developing over a period of perhaps a million years, led to the appearance of man.

It may be asked whether man is still evolving. May we expect the appearance of a superman at some time in the future, as G. B. Shaw once suggested?* The forces that produce evolution are, of course, still acting and affect human beings like other animals. The various races of mankind might be regarded as incipient species, although they are not (by the criteria mentioned on p. 266) actually distinct species now. However, there are some factors that profoundly modify evolutionary influences on man. In the first place, although in the recent past different races were effectively isolated from one another, this is rapidly ceasing to be true. Accordingly, it would seem that adaptive radiation and diversification will not affect *Homo sapiens* in the future. Unless he succeeds in placing a colony on some remote planet and then loses contact with it, he will remain a single species. Secondly, he is learning so effectively to control his environment that he is immune to many of the pressures that bring about natural selection in other animals. Medical science has made it possible for many people with hereditary diseases or weaknesses to survive who

---

* In *Back to Methusela*.

would otherwise have died and been unable to pass on their deleterious genes to succeeding generations.

A more profound reason for thinking that human evolution may be quite different from that of lower organisms is connected with the fact that man has evolved a new way of adapting himself to his environment. Evolutionary change in ordinary animals and plants consists of alterations to the physiological machinery that makes them able to survive in the circumstances in which they live. This machinery is controlled by the genes and, as we have seen, evolution depends upon the fact that they are subject to modification. Man, however, copes with his environment very largely by complex behaviour patterns which he learns from his fellows; by an elaborate social organisation, with its farmers to produce food and shopkeepers to distribute it, builders to make houses and tailors clothes, and so on; by all sorts of ideas, ideals, theories and religions which guide his actions; in short, by all that we call human culture. This is not controlled by genes and so its evolution must occur in a different way.

8 Animal Behaviour

Much of this book has been concered with the various ways in which living organisms are adapted to their environment. We have seen how there is a great variety of structures and physiological and biochemical devices which enable them to utilise the resources of the environment for their own ends. Looking at a plant or animal in the laboratory, we naturally tend to concentrate on the details of its anatomy and the ways in which this exhibits adaptation. Observing animals in the field, however, we are more likely to be struck by the things they do and the way their actions enable them to survive. Indeed, to many people, the behaviour of animals is much the most interesting thing about them.

The behaviour patterns exhibited by animals are as varied and as much characteristic of different species as anatomical structure. They are also in the same way subject to evolution. This is illustrated rather well by the weaver birds of Africa. These are closely related to house sparrows, although the males, at least, are generally brightly coloured, with striking yellow and black or sometimes scarlet plumage. There are about a hundred species, mostly very similar to one another, and it seems certain that they are a group that has quite recently evolved and is undergoing adaptive radiation. It may well be that they have obtained a special advantage through the evolution of the characteristic nest. This is woven from grass, strips of palm leaf, etc. and forms a remarkable light, basket-like structure, which, instead of being supported from below, may be suspended from the slender tip of a twig. The advantage of this is probably that in this position it is very well protected from predators of all kinds. Whatever the truth of this, there is no doubt that the weavers are an extremely successful group of birds which have exploited a wide range of habitats

Broadly, there are three groups of these birds: (i) those that inhabit savanna (grassland with scattered trees), (ii) those that live in forest or scrub and (iii) those that are found in open grassland without trees. These differ far more in details of behaviour than of appearance. The savanna dwellers hang their nests from the branches of trees. They are built by the males and, being generally gregarious, a colony of nests—sometimes a hundred or more in the same tree—is very often formed. The males arrive at the colony site first and, after building his nest, each advertises his presence to any females that may be near by hanging upside down from the nest and flapping his wings, uttering loud cheeping sounds. A whole colony performing in this way is a striking sight. If a male is lucky, a potential mate will arrive and inspect his nest. While this is happening he will hop about anxiously on a nearby branch. When the female emerges he approaches, but at first she usually flies away. However, with more luck, she will return repeatedly and eventually permit the male to approach and mate with her. The male does not try to follow the female far from his nest, probably because other males are only too likely to come and steal nest material from it when his back is turned.

The weavers of forest and scrub differ considerably from this. They are insect eaters, unlike the first group which feed mostly on grass seeds, and do not form flocks or nest colonies. (The two facts are probably connected: grass seeds form a more abundant source of food, supporting a larger population of birds, and it is possible that oraging for it is more efficiently carried out by birds in flocks.) The insectivorous weavers build solitary nests, do not advertise them in the same way and have a form of courtship behaviour that involves quite a lot of chasing of the female by the male.

The grassland weavers differ from this again. They are gregarious seed eaters, but the colony consists of scattered nests built in tufts of grass. Obviously, since the nests have no protection from marauders except for their concealment in the grass, the formation of a dense colony might be disastrous. The males advertise their nests by flying high above them.

Here we have examples of three different behaviour patterns varying with respect to (i) siting of the nest, (ii) advertisement of the nest, (iii) courtship behaviour, (iv) social behaviour (flocking, colony formation) and (v) feeding. The variations seem fairly clearly to be related to the nature of the environment and so provide an example of adaptation, and therefore evolution, primarily affecting behaviour.

The above is an example of rather complex behaviour, and one might well ask how it comes to be acquired by the birds. Is it inherited, like the details of plumage or anatomy, or is it learnt by each bird as it grows up? In fact, both methods of acquiring behaviour are found amongst animals and examples of this will now be discussed.

Automatic behaviour

The reflex action (p. 96) is the simplest kind of behaviour, and it is clear that in many cases this is something inherited or inborn. No one has to learn the control of the pupil of the eye, for example, and newborn babies exhibit various reflexes. The same applies to much more complex pieces of behaviour. The spider's web is the product of quite a complicated series of actions and yet every spider 'knows' how to carry them out almost from the moment of hatching, producing the kind of web characteristic of its species without having to see an example or needing to copy the actions of an older spider.

This type of instinctive behaviour can look very intelligent. For example, honey bees have a remarkable way of communicating to each other the whereabouts of food supplies. When a bee has found a supply of food, she returns to the hive and performs a special dance on the face of the comb. The German biologist Karl von Frisch discovered how this indicates both the distance and the direction of food. If the food is near the hive, the dance consists of a series of rapid turns, first to the right and then to the left, performed over and over again. As she does this, other bees crowd around and follow her movements. They will eventually leave the hive to find the food for themselves. If the food is at a greater distance (more than 50 or 100 yards away), a different dance is performed. In this the bee describes a series of semicircles, first to the right and then to the left, with a straight walk in between each. During the straight part of the manoevre she wags her abdomen vigorously from side to side. Because of this von Frisch called it the 'waggle run' and referred to the dance as the 'waggle dance', the other type being the 'round dance'. He was able to show that the amount of time spent on the waggle run was related to the distance of the food: a slower waggle run, and therefore a smaller number of complete dances per minute, corresponded to more distant food; a faster waggle run and a greater number of dances per minute to nearer food. Thus, for example, six runs per minute indicated food at a distance of about 8 kilometres, eighteen runs food at about 1 km.

The direction of the food is indicated by the orientation of the straight part of the dance. If the bee walks vertically upwards in this part of the performance, the food is in the direction of the sun (as seen from the hive). If it is 30 degrees to the right of the vertical, the food is 30 degrees the right of the sun. Thus the bearing of the food source in relation to the sun is given by the angle between the waggle run and the vertical.

That the behaviour of insects is largely instinctive is shown not only by the fact that it is produced without having first to be learnt but also by its stereotyped nature. This is high-lighted by the effects of interrupting or frustrating activity. For example, the potter wasp builds a nest of mud in which she places food and, after laying an egg in it, closes it up. The egg hatches into a grub, which completes its development inside the nest, emerging as an adult after pupation. It can be seen that the completion of the nest is brought about by a sequence of activities, in some stages of which the same actions are repeated over and over again to achieve the desired result. Thus, after selecting a site, the wasp proceeds to make a number of journeys to collect mud, each lump being added and moulded to the shape of the nest immediately after being fetched. In the next stage caterpillars or spiders are collected, being placed one at a time in the nest, and finally more mud is fetched and the nest sealed. It seems that the completion of each operation leads to the next phase of activity and that the insect, as a general rule, cannot return to an earlier stage once it is completed. Thus, if a hole is made in the bottom of the nest when it is being filled with provisions, so that the food falls out as soon as it is added, the wasp may, nevertheless, go on fetching more and may even lay an egg in mid-air inside the nest before closing it up!

Much of the behaviour of birds appears to be instinctive in a very similar way to that of insects. For example, when herring gulls are feeding their chicks, they present the food to them held at the tip of the bill and the baby then pecks at it and eventually gets hold of it in its own beak. A newly hatched chick will respond in this way to a rough cardboard model of the adult's head. How effective this is depends upon the colouration. The natural pattern is a white head and yellow bill with a red spot near the tip. Naturally the best response is obtained if the model has corresponding colours. However, considerable variations in colour are possible without making very much difference. The chick will still peck at a white bill with a blue spot on a green head. The thing that matters most is that there should be a spot of contrasting colour near the tip of the beak, and the most effective colour for this spot is red. So it looks as if the action of the young bird is set off, or released, by the red spot. It seems to be very much like a reflex action, except that neither the stimulus (the releaser, as it is called) nor the response is simple.

The building of a weaver bird's nest (or any other nest, for that matter) must be largely instinctive. However, one has to recognise that very considerable flexibility of action is involved: no piece of grass fits into the structure in quite the same way as any other, for example. Some sort of modification of an inborn pattern in the light of experience is involved in other activities too. A famous and rather curious example was investigated by Konrad Lorenz. This is the phenomenon of *imprinting*, which he observed in ducklings. (This has even been used as a basis for a Tom and Jerry cartoon.) Ducklings normally follow their mother about wherever she goes, but this depends upon their encountering her soon after birth. If they are being looked after by a human foster parent, then they may fix on him instead and follow him about for evermore! It seems that imprinting happens during a very short period immediately after birth. It will not occur later and cannot be changed once established.

The modification of an instinctive pattern in a less bizarre fashion has been observed in song birds. Each species, as is well known, has its own characteristic song.

However, in the case of robins, it has been shown that this is not invariable. There are slight variations characteristic of different regions of the country, rather as though there were robin dialects. It seems that, although the basic pattern of the song is inborn and will be produced by birds reared in isolation, the modifications are learned by young birds by imitation of the adults, so giving rise to the possibility of local variations.

Learned behaviour

By learned behaviour we mean that which is acquired as a result of experience. Because of this it is not present at birth, always making its appearance some time later. However, it should be distinguished from unlearned behaviour, such as nest building, which also appears some time after birth but is the result of maturation rather than learning from experience. Learned behaviour is characteristically flexible rather than stereotyped, is often open to radical alteration to suit changed circumstances and varies considerably from one individual to another.

The simplest type of learned behaviour is the conditioned reflex. This was first studied by the Russian scientist Pavlov, who conducted his studies with dogs. He noticed that, although the newborn puppy reacts to the taste of food by producing saliva, he does not so react to the smell of it. This reaction only appears later. Pavlov wished to see whether it were possible for the animal to acquire responses to other kinds of stimuli and was able to show that this could indeed be brought about by a modification of the original reflex reaction to taste.

Pavlov's procedure was as follows. He first arranged a method of continuously collecting and measuring the saliva from his experimental animal. This was necessary so that he could follow accurately the rate of flow and detect small changes in it. Secondly, he arranged to sound an electric buzzer and shortly afterwards to blow meat powder into the animal's mouth. The result of this was that at first, as one would expect, the flow of saliva increased when the meat powder came into contact with the dog's tongue. However, when the procedure was repeated a number of times, saliva began to be produced when the buzzer was sounded—before the arrival of the powder. This would continue happening for some time even though the buzzer might be sounded in the absence of meat. (However, in the end the new response would be extinguished, unless it were strengthened by repetition of the original procedure.)

In this way a new reflex action had been established. It was new because it formed a connection between a stimulus and a response which had not previously been connected. Such a reflex is known as a conditioned reflex and the process of establishing it conditioning. Numerous examples have been studied experimentally. They are always based on an already existing reflex, or stimulus response connection. If this is represented as

$$S_1 \longrightarrow R$$

then conditioning may be represented as

$$S_2$$
$$S_1 \longrightarrow R$$

$$S_2 \longrightarrow R$$
$$S_1 \longrightarrow R$$

$$S_2 \longrightarrow R$$

where S_1 represents the stimulus (e.g. the taste of meat powder) that sets off the original reflex, S_2 the new stimulus (e.g. the sound of a buzzer) and R the response (e.g. production of saliva). Note that, to produce conditioning, S_2 must come before, but not too long before, S_1. If it takes place even a small fraction of a second after the latter, conditioning will not occur.

The young puppy's acquisition of the response to the smell of food is an example of naturally occurring conditioning, which arises because, in the natural course of events, the food is smelled immediately before being tasted.

A different kind of conditioning is illustrated by the way in which a dog may be trained to sit up and beg. This is achieved in some such way as the following. The dog's master presents him with, say, a biscuit, held at some distance above his head. When the dog reaches up for it, his master attempts to coax him into roughly the correct begging position and allows him to take the food only when this has been achieved. This is repeated at intervals and quite quickly the animal will adopt an approximately correct position of his own accord when the titbit is offered. Now the trainer will begin to be more strict about the exact position for begging, not giving the food until this has been achieved. In this way the dog will eventually learn to adopt the position perfectly. Moreover, he will do this even though the food is not actually given to him, or, if his master has accompanied the offer of food with a word of command ('beg'), he will do it in the complete absence of food.

Notice that in this case conditioning is not based on an already existing reflex. The essential features of the situation for conditioning to take place seem to be as follows: (i) the required action must be such that it can be built up from actions in the animal's normal repertoire; (ii) the animal must be presented with some stimulus (the word 'beg', for example) or stimulus situation (e.g. the offer of food) which it is capable of recognising; (iii) when the required action is performed the animal must be rewarded; and (iv) the whole process must be repeated a sufficiently large number of times. The result is that eventually the animal produces the required action (response) to the appropriate stimulus even without reward. As in Pavlov's type of conditioning, however, the response may be extinguished in the end if no reward is given when the stimulus is presented repeatedly. This type of conditioning is referred to as 'operant conditioning' to distinguish it from the 'classical conditioning' of Pavlov.

A story is told of how a certain Canadian river was restocked with trout and the fishermen were very disgusted because, when they appeared on the banks, the fish rushed towards them. This was unfortunate, because the essence of the angler's sport is the difficulty presented by the fact that the trout normally swims rapidly in the other direction as soon as he catches sight of the fisherman. The reason for this untoward behaviour of the trout was that they had been reared in ponds where they were fed by hand. There they had learnt that the appearance of a man on the bank meant that feeding time was at hand and they had better be first in the queue if they wanted a good dinner. Putting this more scientifically, the fish had been conditioned to respond to the sight of their keeper by swimming towards him.

This story illustrates the adaptive value of conditioning. It enables the organism to modify its behaviour to take advantage of the exigencies of its particular situation. In the pond it was greatly to the fish's advantage to be able to anticipate the arrival of food. The fact that the response was actually dangerous in the river only serves to emphasise the fact that here we are dealing with the capacity to adapt to very particular circumstances. (Presumably, in fact, their behaviour underwent further modification quite rapidly once the fish arrived in the river if only because the conditioned response would have been extinguished in the absence of continued reinforcement.) The great advantage of learned responses, compared with innate or instinctive ones, is that they are flexible. Instinctive behaviour would enable the organism to respond correctly either in the pond or in the river, but not in both.

A great deal of learned behaviour in animals (and not a little in humans) can be explained in terms of conditioning. Indeed, according to one school of thought, this can be applied to all such behaviour, even that of the most complex kind. As one might expect, monkeys and apes exhibit very advanced forms of learning. One kind, based on operant conditioning, is particularly interesting because it suggests how animals may learn to cope with general rather than particular situations. It has been extensively investigated in monkeys, using a technique that requires the animal to solve a simple kind of problem. A table is placed within reach of the monkey just in front of its cage. There are two holes or wells in this table, one on the right and the other on the left, each big enough to contain a reward of suitable food (e.g. a banana) and such that it can be covered conveniently with various objects. A screen can be placed in front of the cage so that the experimenter can change the food in the wells etc. without the animal seeing. The monkey has to learn to guess correctly which well contains food. Thus the experimenter may decide in the first stage of the experiment that he will always put the food in a well covered by a red cover, whereas the empty one will be covered by a blue cover. Repeatedly food is placed in either of the wells in random order and covered before the monkey is allowed to try to find it. At first the animal removes the covers at random, but after a time he begins to get the hang of it and guesses correctly more often than not. Now the rules are altered, perhaps by using differently shaped covers (e.g. a cup and a plate), and the whole procedure is repeated. Again, the monkey gradually begins to learn which of the two covers is the 'right' one. The rules are changed yet again and a different set of covers is used. And so the experiment goes on, using all sorts of different pairs of objects as covers. The interesting result of all this is that the monkey gradually comes to solve these little problems faster and faster, until eventually, after many repeats, he may reach the stage where he can get the right answer every time after making only one trial, i.e. he only needs to uncover the wells once when he has been presented with a new pair of objects to learn which is 'right'.

The importance of this experiment is that it shows that animals may learn to deal with a general type of situation. Simple operant conditioning enables an animal to respond appropriately to a specific situation. In the case of the monkey this means that it can learn to solve a simple problem, for example 'Is the food more likely to be in the well covered by a blue cover or that covered by a red one?' But conditioning, by itself, will not help the monkey to solve a more general problem of the type 'Is the food more likely to be in the well covered by X than that covered by Y, if the food was under X on the first occasion, and where X and Y are any pair of different objects?' It is just this more general type of problem that the experiment described above shows the monkey learning to solve.

Some investigations of chimpanzee behaviour show how the more general type of response may be learned in nature. A German scientist, Wolfgang Köhler, carried out a classic series of experiments with these apes in which he attempted to test their problem-solving ability. The problems were all of the type in which food was placed beyond the animal's reach but in such a position that it could be reached if the chimpanzee made intelligent use of available materials. For example, the food might be hung from the roof of the cage and could be obtained if boxes were placed one on top of another so that the animal could climb nearer to the roof. Or the food might be placed outside the bars of the cage so that it could only be reached by the use of a stick, or even, in one series of experiments, by joining two sticks together. In a number of cases Köhler reported solutions to these problems that seemed to indicate a high level of intelligence. He interpreted the chimpanzee's behaviour as exhibiting insight.

Insight implies the ability to see into the general nature of a problem. Later investigations have focused attention on the way in which this ability might be acquired. Is the animal born with it, or is it in some way learned? A limitation of Köhler's work was that he had no detailed knowledge of the past history of his chimpanzees and so was in no position to answer such questions. Some later studies used groups of animals that had been observed scientifically since birth, so that much information was available about their earlier experiences. These showed that apes indulged in a great deal of play with objects, which included some of the apparently intelligently directed actions seen by Köhler, such as piling up boxes and manipulating sticks, without any particular end in view. Older animals showed a greater variety of such activity, and there seemed to be some relationship between the individual animal's ability to solve problems involving the use of tools and the amount of play activity they indulged in. In one particular experiment six young chimpanzees were used, of which only one was known to have had previous experience of playing with sticks. First, they were given the problem of obtaining some food by using a T-shaped stick. Four were quite unable to solve it and of the other two, one was the animal that had had previous experience with sticks and the other apparently solved the problem by accident. Next the chimpanzees were provided with sticks during a three-day period. During this time it was noticed that they gradually came to play with the sticks in a greater variety of ways. Finally, the same problem was presented again and, in this case, was solved by all the animals without difficulty.

All these observations suggest that, in their play, apes learn various patterns of action with whatever materials may be at hand and that these action patterns may be employed to solve simple problems—but only after having been learnt, of course. Because the action patterns can apply to a variety of circumstances, they give rise to the ability to respond appropriately to a general type of situation.

Learning in humans

It is a remarkable fact that man takes so much longer than almost any other animal to grow up. And it is not merely that he grows slowly, he is also dependent on parents for such a long time. How this contrasts with what we observe so often in nature, where the young animal is not looked after by its parents at all and is born fully equipped with all the capacities it needs in order to survive. The reason for the prolonged dependence of the human child is undoubtedly the fact that not only does he not possess the necessary behaviour patterns for independent survival at birth but also a long process of learning is necessary in order for him to acquire them. This is, no doubt, linked with another interesting fact: the human brain goes on growing and developing physically for over twenty years. Contrast this with development in the chimpanzee, where the brain reaches the adult state within a year.

This is not the place to go into a detailed consideration of how learning takes place in man and only one aspect of human learning will be discussed briefly. This has to do with the role of language. Experiments similar to those described for monkeys (p. 283) have been carried out with infants. For example, the child may be presented with a pair of paper hats, one large and one small, the small one hiding a sweet. On repeating this he will quite soon learn always to look under the small hat. However, it is found that learning is very much speeded up if the experimenter utters the word 'small' every time the child picks the correct hat. Not only does he learn faster, but he also remembers what he has learnt better and transfers his learning to new situations more easily. Thus, if the experiment is repeated using, say, large and small boxes, the infants who have been assisted by the use of words are found to adapt to the slightly different situation more readily than those who have not.

The children in these experiments are only a year or eighteen months old and thus have not yet learnt to speak, so that the observations seem to point to the idea that language has a very fundamental role in human learning—even more fundamental than is suggested by the obvious fact that, when we are older, we learn almost everything through the mediation of language.

This function of language implies that in man learning is an essentially social process. We have to learn from other people. So, if learned behaviour is the most advanced way in which the organism can adapt itself to its environment, human adaptation must depend upon that complex interaction of habits, language, ideas and customs which we call culture. As has already been suggested, it is this that sets man apart from other animals.

Further Reading

The following is a short personal selection from the very wide range of books available.

Allen, G., and Denslow, J., *Seashore Animals*. Oxford, 1972.
Asimov, I., *The Genetic Code*. Murray, 1964.
Broadhurst, P. L., *The Science of Animal Behaviour*. Penguin Books, 1963.
Buchsbaum, R., *Animals without Backbones*. Penguin Books, 1951.
Darwin, C., *The Origin of Species*. Dent, 1963.
Dobzhansky, T., *Evolution, Genetics and Man*. Wiley, 1963.
Dowdeswell, W. H., *Animal Ecology*. Methuen, 1959.
Dowdeswell, W. H., *The Mechanism of Evolution*. Heinemann, 1955.
Fritsch, F. E, and Salisbury, E. J., *Plant Form and Function*. Bell, 1953.
Jevons, F. R., *The Biochemical Approach to Life*. George Allen & Unwin, 1964.
Kermack, W. O., and Eggleton, P., *The Stuff We're Made Of*. Arnold, 1948.
Leach, W., *Plant Ecology*. Methuen, 1957.
Lorenz, K. Z., *King Solomon's Ring: new light on animal ways*. Methuen, 1955.
Nichols, D., Cooke, J., and Whiteley, D., *The Oxford Book of Invertebrates*. Oxford, 1971.
Ramsay, J. A., *A Physiological Approach to the Lower Animals*. Cambridge, 1952.

Romer, A.S., *Man and the Vertebrates*. Penguin Books, 1954.
Schmidt-Nielsen, K., *Animal Physiology*. Prentice-Hall, 1964.
Tinbergen, N., *Social Behaviour in Animals*. Methuen, 1965.
Wheeler, W. F., *Essentials of Biology*. Heinemann, 1964.
Young, J. Z., *The Life of Vertebrates*. Oxford, 1950.

The following titles, published by Teach Yourself Books, are also available: *Botany, Genetics, Human Biology* and *Human Anatomy and Physiology*.

Glossary

(All nouns are given in the singular and, where it is not formed in the usual way, the plural ending is given in brackets.)

adapt Make able to live efficiently in particular circumstances.
amino acid Type of organic acid containing the amino group—a nitrogen atom with two hydrogen atoms joined to it.
amphibian A member of the Amphibia, the class of vertebrates characterised by the possession of a thin skin without scales, hair or feathers, adaptations to life on land in the adult and a larval stage which takes place in water.
animal Member of the Animal Kingdom, which comprehends organisms that (typically) take in raw materials in the solid and/or liquid state and digest them internally, and that (with exceptions) are capable of locomotion.
anterior Towards the front or head, or that end of the animal which is in front when it is moving normally.
artery Vessel that carries blood away from the heart towards the capillaries.
arthropod Animal belonging to the phylum Arthropoda,

characterised by the possession of a segmented body and a tough, jointed exoskeleton.
axil Angle between a leaf and the stem to which it is attached.
bacterium(-a) Type of extremely small single-celled organism.
capillary Minute blood vessel forming part of a network connecting arteries with veins.
carbohydrate Class of compounds, including sugars, starch and cellulose, composed of carbon, hydrogen and oxygen.
cell Unit of protoplasm generally containing a nucleus and bounded by a cell membrane and, in plants and bacteria, a cell wall.
cellulose Carbohydrate making up the bulk of the cell wall in typical plants.
chlorophyll Green substance in leaves and other plant organs, having the function of absorbing light energy required for photosynthesis.
chloroplast Body containing chlorophyll found within the plant cell.
chromosome Thread-like body seen in the nucleus during cell division. Chromosomes contain the genes or carriers of heredity.
cilium(-a) Microscopic thread-like organ composed of protoplasm attached to the surface of a cell. Where they occur, they are usually found in very large numbers. Their beating action causes movement of fluid over the cell surface.
community The collection of organisms found in a particular habitat.
cotyledon Modified leaf of the embryo containing stored food in the seed of the flowering plant.

cuticle	(i) Waxy layer covering the surface of the epidermis in plants; (ii) tough skin or exoskeleton of insects.
cytoplasm	Protoplasm lying outside the nucleus of a cell.
diffusion	The spontaneous movement of gases or substances in solution from regions of high concentration to those of low concentration due to random movement of their molecules.
DNA	Deoxyribose nucleic acid. See **nucleic acid**.
dorsal	Towards that side of the body which is normally directed upwards; in man, however, it refers to the region of the back.
ecology	Study of organisms in relation to the natural environment.
enzyme	Type of catalyst (a substance that increases the rate of a chemical reaction without being used up in it) which is produced only by living organisms and consists of protein.
evolution	Process by which species become slowly altered during the course of long periods of time and which gives rise to new species.
excretion	Process by which waste products are removed from the organism.
fertilisation	Union of a male gamete with a female gamete or ovum, resulting in the formation of a single cell, the zygote.
fruit	Structure consisting essentially of the enlarged ovary containing mature seeds, which is formed after pollination in flowering plants. Other parts of the flower sometimes form part of the fruit.
fungus(-i)	Member of the group of simple plants (the Fungi) characterised by lack of chlorophyll and a structure generally composed of hyphae rather than cells.

gamete	Cell that unites with another cell to form a single cell or zygote, which gives rise to a new organism in sexual reproduction.
gene	Unit of hereditary material (DNA) giving rise to a particular characteristic of the organism.
genus(-era)	Group of closely related species.
gland	Organ that has the function of manufacturing substances.
gonad	Organ that produces gametes (in animals).
habitat	Place in which an organism lives.
hormone	Chemical secreted by one part of the body and carried by the blood to another part, which is thereby stimulated in some way.
humus	Partly decayed organic matter in the soil.
hypha(-ae)	One of the filaments of which fungi are composed.
immunity	Resistance to a particular disease resulting either from having suffered from the disease (natural immunity) or from various artificial treatments (artificial immunity).
insect	Animal belonging to the class of arthropods (the Insecta) characterised by the possession of three pairs of legs, wings in the adult (in most cases) and three main divisions of the body.
invertebrate	Any animal that is not a vertebrate.
ligament	Band of strong tissue joining two bones together.
locomotion	Movement of a whole organism from place to place.
lymph	Colourless fluid removed from the tissues by the lymphatic system.
mammal	Member of the class Mammalia, characterised by the possession of 'warm blood', fur

	or hair, double circulation and internal development of young (with very few exceptions), which suckle their young.
metabolism	The sum total of chemical changes taking place in the living organism.
micrometre (=micron)	Unit of measurement equal to 1/1000 millimetre represented by the abbreviation μm. (Micron is abbreviated as μ, the Greek letter *mu*.)
mycelium(-a)	Network of hyphae in a fungus.
nanometre	Unit of measurement equal to 1/1 000 000 millimetre represented by the abbreviation nm.
neurone	A nerve cell.
nucleic acid	Complex chemical substance originally discovered in the nuclei of cells but now known to occur in the cytoplasm also. Genes are composed of the kind of nucleic acid known as DNA.
nucleus(-i)	Round body present in nearly all living cells. (The mammalian red blood corpuscle is an exception.) It contains the chromosomes bearing the genes and is normally essential for the life of the cell.
organ	Distinct part of an organism specialised for one or more functions.
osmosis	Process in which solvent passes from a weaker solution into a stronger one through a semipermeable membrane.
ovary	(i) In animals the organ that produces ova (eggs); (ii) in the flowering plant the part of the flower that contains ovules, or the corresponding part of the fruit containing seeds.
ovule	Round object found in the ovary of flowering plants which develops into a seed after

	fertilisation.
ovum(-a)	Female gamete.
photosynthesis	Process by which complex carbon compounds are manufactured in green plants with the help of light energy.
phylum(-a)	Principal division of the Plant or Animal Kingdom.
plant	Member of the Plant Kingdom, which comprehends organisms that (typically) absorb raw materials in solution or in gaseous form without the aid of an internal digestive system and that (with the exception of some microscopic forms) are incapable of locomotion.
pollination	Transfer of pollen from stamens to stigmas.
posterior	Towards the hind end, the end opposite the head or that part of the organism which is at the rear when it is moving normally.
protein	Type of extremely complex chemical substance produced by living organisms, having very large molecules built up from amino acids and always containing the elements carbon, hydrogen, oxygen and nitrogen at least.
protoplasm	The living substance in plant and animal cells and the hyphae of fungi.
reflex action	Rapid automatic response to a stimulus brought about by the nervous system of an animal, the response to a given stimulus always being the same.
reflex arc	Chain of neurones which is responsible for the occurrence of a reflex action.
reproduction	Process by which a new organism is produced by one or a pair of parent organisms of the same kind.

296 *Biology*

Asexual reproduction: non-sexual reproducuction.
Sexual reproduction: any form of reproduction in which two cells (gametes) unite to form a third cell (the zygote), which then gives rise to the new organism.
Vegetative reproduction: form of asexual reproduction in plants in which some part of the plant not specialised solely for reproduction becomes separated and grows into an independent plant.

reptile Member of the vertebrate class Reptilia, characterised by the possession of a scaly skin, adaptations to life on land (including lungs and often, but not always, legs) and reproduction usually by eggs laid on land, although young develop inside the mother in some cases.

respiration (i) (Internal or tissue respiration) process by which the organism obtains energy by chemical reactions usually involving the breakdown of complex organic compounds; (ii) (external respiration) process by which oxygen required for internal respiration is obtained from the environment and carbon dioxide produced is excreted.

saprophyte Plant obtaining its raw materials from decaying matter.

secretion Production of a substance useful to the organism.

segment One of the divisions in cases where the body of an animal is divided along its length into a number of more or less similar divisions.

skeleton Supporting structure that serves for the attachment of muscles. An internal or

Glossary

	endoskeleton lies within the body, an external or *exoskeleton* encloses it.
species	Group of organisms that are all alike, apart from minor variations, and (where sexual reproduction occurs) are capable of interbreeding with one another.
sperm	Male gamete capable of locomotion.
spinal cord	Thick cord of nervous tissue in vertebrates enclosed in the vertebral column and connected to the brain at the anterior end.
spore	Microscopic reproductive body (in plants and bacteria) usually consisting of a single cell.
stimulus(-i)	Any influence from the environment to which the organism responds.
stoma(-ata)	Opening in the epidermis of a plant which has the function of allowing gases to pass in and out.
symbiosis	Association of two organisms of differing species such that neither is harmed and both may benefit.
tendon	Band of strong tissue connecting a muscle to a bone.
testis(-es)	Organ producing male gametes (in animals).
tissue	Distinct mass of cells and any non-living material secreted by them which helps to make up the structure of an organism.
transpiration	Loss of water by evaporation from the aerial parts of a plant.
tropism	Response of a plant organ brought about by uneven growth, in which the direction of the response is related to the direction of the stimulus.
vacuole	Space containing fluid in the cytoplasm of a cell.

vein	(In animals) vessel that carries blood from the system of capillaries towards the heart.
ventral	Towards that side of the animal which is normally directed downwards; in man, however, it refers to the front of the body.
vertebra(-ae)	One of the bones composing the backbone in a vertebrate.
vertebral column	Backbone.
vertebrate	Member of the Vertebrata, a major group of animals characterised by the presence of an internal skeleton including a dorsal vertebral column.
virus	Minute disease organism invisible under the light microscope and unable to reproduce outside the cells of host organisms.
vitamin	Food substance essential to health but required in minute quantities only.
zygote	Cell formed by the union of two gametes.

Index

adaptive radiation 270
adenosine phosphates 124
ADP 124
alcohol 198
Algae 140
alimentary canal 73, 74
amino acids 74, 75, 114
Amoeba proteus 138-40
ampullae 173
amylase 72, 114
Angiospermae 153
Annelida 175, 180, 181
antheridia 148
antibodies 203
aorta 62
appendix 74
arachnids 188
archegonium 148
arteries 58
Arthropoda 181, 182, 188, 189
ascorbic acid 69
Asterias rubens 171-4
athlete's foot 197
ATP 124
atrium 61
auxin 48
axil 27
axon 90
Azotobacter 201

Bacteria 199-202
bacteriophages 204
Balanus 259
barnacles 258
bees (communication by) 276

bile 74
bilharzia 166
biomass 214
Biston betularia 265
bivalves 170
brain 90
brittle stars 174
broncheoles 78
bronchi 78
Bryophyta 146, 150
buttercup 26, 55

calorie 71
caecum 74
capillary 58
carbohydrates 18, 20, 22, 66, 67, 113
carbon
 - atom 112
 - in plant 14, 15, 17, 21
 - cycle 218
carpel 51
catalase 116
cell 28, 29, 30, 38, 100
 - division 46, 127, 242
 - egg 51, 102
cellulose 29, 67, 114
centipedes 188
chaetae 179
chlorophyll 19, 30
chloroplast 30, 110
Chordata 189
chromatids 127
chromosomes 46, 127
circulatory system 58 ff.

citric acid cycle 122
classification 134
climax 230
Clostridium 201
clotting of blood 64, 65
club mosses 153
Coelenterata 154, 159, 160
coelacanths 261
coelom 175
community 208
comparative anatomy 254
– embryology 257
conceptacle 146
conditioning 280–84
conidia 195
conservation 207
coral 159
cornea 94
corpuscles 63, 64
cotyledon 42
cowpox 204
Crustacea 188
culture solutions 16
cuticle 31, 184
Cyclops 259
cytoplasm 108, 109

Darwin, Charles 252, 262
deciduous forest 223
deficiency diseases 71
dendrite 90
dendron 90
denitrifying bacteria 220
dentition (mouse and stoat) 221, 222
diabetes 84
diaphragm 79
diffusion 31–3
digestion 66, 72
digestive system 58, 72 ff.
diploid 133
DNA 128

dominant (genetics) 245
– species 210
double circulation 60
Dryopteris filix-mas 150
Dugesia subtentaculata 161–6

earthworm 175–180
Echinodermata 171, 174, 175
ecology 207
ectoderm 158
edaphic 224
effector organs 90
egg 51, 102, 105
embryo 42, 52, 105
endoderm 158
endoplasmic reticulum 109
endoskeleton 183
energy 22, 23, 25, 71, 76
enzymes 73, 116–21
epidermis 31, 36
epiphytes 212
erythrocytes 64
Escherichia coli 204
Euglena viridis 136–8
evolution 252 ff.
– of man 270–2
excretion 85
exoskeleton 183
eye
– compound 186
– human 186
fats 66, 67
fatty acids 74
fermentation 198
ferns 150
fertilisation 52
fertilisers 17
flagellum 137
flame cell 163
flatworms 161–6
Fleming, Sir Alexander 196
flower 50, 51
foods 66 ff.

food chains 213
— web 214
fossils 252
fovea 96
fruit 50, 52, 53
fucoxanthin 146
Fucus vesiculosus 144–6
Fungi 194–8

Galapagos Islands 267
gall bladder 74
gamete 51, 52, 102
gametophyte 149, 150
ganglia 163, 168, 178, 185
gastric juice 74
gene 243
genetics 237
genus 136
geological ages 253
geotropism 49
germination 42–5
glucose 67, 113
glycerol 74
glycogen 67, 75, 114
gonad 103
growth 13, 45 ff.
Gymnospermae 153

haemocoel 177, 186
haemoglobin 64, 79, 80
haemophilia 246
haploid 133
heart 58, 60 ff.
Helix aspersa 166–70
hemi-parasites 212
hepatic portal system 75
heredity 237
hermaphrodite 164
herring gull 277
hormones 87–9
horsetails 153
humus 228
Hydra 154–161
hyphae 195

immunity 203, 204
imprinting 278
insecticides 216, 217
insight 285
insulin 88
intestine 74
iris 96

jelly fish 160
Jenner 204

kidneys 82 ff.
Köhler, Wolfgang 284

lactic acid 93
language (and learning) 286
leaf 30–6
learning in animals 279 ff.
leeches 181
leucocyte 64
liver 74–6
liver fluke 166
liverworts 146
locust (*Locusta migratoria*) 181–8
Lorenz, Konrad 278
lymph 65
lymphatic system 65, 75
lugworm 181
Lumbricus terrestris 175–80
lungfish 260
lungs 78, 79

madreporite 173
Malpighian body 83
— tubules 187
maltose 113
mammals 57
mantle 167
meiosis 133, 242
membranes 29
— semipermeable 37
— of cell 108, 109, 111

Mendel 239
micrometre 111
micro-organisms 194–206
microsomes 109
mildews 196
millipedes 188
mitochondria 109, 110
mitosis 127
Mollusca 166, 170, 171
mosses 150
mouse (teeth) 221, 222
muscle 92
mutation 248
mycelium 195
myotomes 191

nanometre 111
natural selection 263
nematocyst 156
Neoceratodus 260
nephridia 178
nerves 90, 92
nervous system 90
neurone 90
Nitrobacter 200
nitrogen
 – cycle 219
 – in plant 16, 22
 – in amino acids 114
Nitrosomonas 200
nucleic acid 111, 128–31
nucleoli 109
nucleus 29, 108, 111, 127

oak forest (types) 224
oak wood 208 ff.
octopuses 171
oesophagus 74
optic nerve 95
organs 101
osmosis 36–40
ovary 105

oviduct 104
ovule 51
oxygen
 – in photosynthesis 19, 20, 26, 34
 – in respiration 23, 26, 57

pancreas 74, 88
parenchyma 29
Pasteur 200
Pavlov 279
pedicellariae 172
Pellia epiphylla 146–50
penicillin 196
Penicillium 195, 196
petal 51
petiole 28
phloem 30, 41
photosynthesis 18 ff.
phototropism 49
phylum 135
placenta 105
plant composition 14
plasma 63
platelets (of blood) 65
Platyhelminthes 161, 166
Pleurococcus 140
plumule 42
pollen 51, 52
pollination 52
 – insect and wind 53
pollution 235
population 232–5
Portuguese man-o-war 160
potter wasp 277
proteins 22, 66, 67–69, 114–16
 – synthesis of 131
prothallus 151
protoplasm 29, 38
Protozoa 136, 138
pseudopodium 138
Pteridophyta 150
pulmonary artery 61

Queen Victoria 248
Quercus 224

radicle 42
radula 169
ragworm 181
raw materials 14, 15
rectum 74
recessive 245
reflex 96
 − conditioned 280
reproduction
 − asexual 54
 − by seed 50
 − human 101-6
 − vegetative 54-6
respiration 23, 76 ff., 122-5
 − anaerobic 198
retina 95
Rhizobium 202
rhizome 150
rickets 69
root cap 46
 − hair 39
roots 26, 39
rusts 196

Saccharomyces 197
saliva 72
Salmo trutta 189-93
salts 16, 22, 40, 66, 69
saprophytes 196
scree 226
sea anemone 159
 − cucumber 174
 − lilies 174
 − urchins 174
seed 42, 50, 51
 − dispersal 53
selective breeding 250
sense organs 93
sepal 51
sex determination 246
skeleton 102
smallpox 204
smuts 196
snail 166-70
soil 226-30
species 135, 266
sperm 102, 104
Spermatophyta 153
spiders 188
spinal cord 90
spiracles 187
Spirogyra 141-4
sporangium 150
spores 149, 150, 195
sporophyte 148, 150
squids 171
stamen 51
starch 17, 18, 21, 67, 72, 113
starfish 171-4
stigma 51
stoat (teeth) 222
stomach 74
stomata 18, 31, 34, 35, 41
succession 230
sugar 67, 113
swim bladder 193
symbiosis 202
symmetry (of animals) 165
synapse 90
systems 101

temperature regulation 85-7
testis 103
testosterone 87
tissues 101
Thallophyta 194
thallus 144
thyroglobulin 69, 87
thyroid gland 87
trachea (human) 78
tracheae (of insects) 187
transpiration 40
trout 189-93

urea 75, 84
ureter 83
urine 83
uterus 104

vacuole 29, 109
vaccination 204
valves
 - auriculoventricular 61
 - of veins 59
 - semilunar 62
varieties 266
vein 59
ventricle 61
Vertebrata 198
 - evolution of 253 ff.

viruses 202
vitamins 66, 69, 70
von Frisch, Karl 276

water (in plants) 14, 35, 36, 39, 40
weaver birds 273
woodlice 188

xylem 30, 34, 41, 42

yeast 197, 198

zygospore 143
zygote 52, 102